A NOVEL

NOBODY

A NOVEL

CRESTON MAPES

MULTNOMAH
BOOKS

NOBODY
PUBLISHED BY MULTNOMAH BOOKS
12265 Oracle Boulevard, Suite 200
Colorado Springs, Colorado 80921
A division of Random House Inc.

Scripture quotations are taken from the New American Standard Bible®. © Copyright
The Lockman Foundation 1960, 1962, 1963, 1968, 1971, 1972, 1973, 1975, 1977,
1995. Used by permission. (www.Lockman.org). Scripture also quoted from the King
James Version.

The characters and events in this book are fictional, and any resemblance to actual
persons or events is coincidental.

Grateful acknowledgment is made for the use of the poem "I Stand By the Door"
excerpted from *Stand By the Door: The Life of Sam Shoemaker* copyright © 1967 by
Helen Smith Shoemaker. Used by permission of Nickie Shoemaker Haggart.

ISBN 978-1-59052-624-8

Copyright © 2007 by Creston Mapes, Inc.

Published in association with the literary agency of Mark Sweeney & Associates,
28540 Altessa Way, Bonita Springs, Florida 34135

Library of Congress Cataloging-in-Publication Data
Mapes, Creston, 1961-
  Nobody : a novel / Creston Mapes. 1st ed.
    p. cm.
  ISBN 978-1-59052-624-8
  1. Homeless men—Crimes against—Fiction. 2. Journalists—Fiction. 3. Las Vegas
(Nev.)—Fiction.
  I. Title.
PS3613.A63N63 2007
813'.6—dc22

                                                      2007020643

Printed in the United States of America
2007—First Edition

10 9 8 7 6 5 4 3 2 1

Other Novels by Creston Mapes

———

This story is for Abigail, Hannah, Esther & Creston—
Pursue the dreams God sows deep within your hearts.
And stand by the door.

ACKNOWLEDGMENTS

During the last winter of his beautiful life, my father, Bernie Mapes, nudged me and pointed to a homeless man sitting on a park bench in St. Augustine, Florida. The man tore pieces of bread from a stale loaf he clutched in his arms, eating some and tossing others to the dozens of blackbirds pecking at the ground. "There's an idea for a book, Cres," Dad whispered. Thank you, Dad...for everything.

The experience and insight of my editor and friend Julee Schwarzburg made *Nobody* a much finer book; also, thanks to editors Lisa Ham and Amy Partain for their great eyes and to Mark Ford and Chris Tobias for the fine cover. To each person at WaterBrook-Multnomah who helped get this novel out far and wide—Tiffany Lauer, Joel Kneedler, Liz Johnson, Allison O'Hara, Melissa Sturgis, Alice Crider, Ginia Hairston, Dudley Delffs, Kim Shurley, Jessica Lacy, Chris Crosby, Stuart McGuiggan, Tim Vanderkolk, Ron Garcia, and team—thank you very much.

Agent Mark Sweeney and wife, Janet, you are tops; thanks for guiding us. Steve Vibert, you are a priceless friend.

Patty and kids, your love and generosity overflow and bring me joy.

Thanks to the Shoemaker family for allowing us to print Samuel Shoemaker's poem "I Stand By the Door."

Brian Brooks of the Nevada Health Centers, I am most grateful for the tour you gave me of the Las Vegas homeless areas and the rest of the city, and for your keen insights. Thanks to Dr. Suresh Prabhu, who spent time with us at one of the clinics. To Jud Wilhite and Jayne Post of Central Christian Church in Las Vegas, you really helped me get this story off and running. Blessings! Thanks to security guard Frank Ferrara, at the top of the Stratosphere, for your knowledge.

Friend and attorney Joseph Cheeley III gave me help with the legal aspects of this book, and author/cop/friend Mark Mynheir helped with police details…thanks, brothers.

For their support, thanks to my friends in Sta Akra, ChiLibris, and ACFW. Special gratitude to Dale Cramer, Chris Well, James Scott Bell, Wanda Dyson, Robin Jones Gunn, Chris Sundquist, Rick Stevens, and Rob Glass.

I STAND BY THE DOOR

I stand by the door
I neither go too far in nor stay too far out
The door is the most important door in the world.
It is the door through which men walk when they find God.
There's no use in my going way inside and staying there
When so many are still outside and they, as much as I, crave to
      know where the door is
And all that so many ever find is only the wall where a door
      ought to be.
They creep along the wall like blind men with outstretched, grop-
      ing hands
Feeling for a door, knowing there must be a door, yet they never
      find it.
So I stand by the door.

The most tremendous thing in the world is for men to find that
      door—
The door to God.
The most important thing any man can do
Is to take hold of one of those blind, groping hands and put it on
      the latch—
The latch that only clicks and opens to the man's own touch.
Men die outside that door
As starving beggars die on cold nights in cruel cities in the dead
      of winter
Die for want of what is within their grasp
They live on the other side of it, live because they have found it
Nothing else matters compared to helping them find it
And open it and walk in and find Him.
So I stand by the door.

Go in great saints, go all the way in
Go way down in the cavernous cellars and way into the spacious
        attics
It is a vast roomy house, this house where God is.
Go into the deepest of hidden casements of withdrawal, of
        silence, of sainthood
Some must inhabit those inner rooms,
And know the depths and heights of God
And call outside to the rest of us how wonderful it is
Sometimes I take a deeper look in, sometimes venture in a little
        farther
But my place seems close to the opening
So I stand by the door...

I admire the people who go way in,
But I wish they would not forget how it was before they got in
Then they would be able to help the people who have not yet
        even found the door
Or the people who want to run away from God again
You can go in too deeply and stay in too long and forget the
        people outside the door
As for me, I shall take my old accustomed place
Near enough to God to hear Him and know He is there
But not far from men as to not hear them and remember that
        they are there too.
Where? Outside the door.
Thousands of them, millions of them
But more important for me, one of them, two of them, ten of
        them
Whose hands I am intended to put on the latch
So I shall stand by the door and wait for those who seek it.
I had rather be a doorkeeper, so I stand by the door.

—SAMUEL SHOEMAKER

'd seen stiffs at crime scenes before, one flat on his back in the middle of his garage with a twelve-inch meat cleaver sticking straight up out of his rib cage like a Halloween prank; self-inflicted, to boot.

But this one beat all.

I got there before the cops. Saw the guy from my Mustang GT. It was 5:54 a.m.

He was positioned upright at one of the dozens of covered bus stops along the Strip. Beneath flickering fluorescents, it looked as if he was just sleeping, like a thousand other bums scattered like garbage across the sand-blown outskirts of "fabulous Las Vegas." I rolled down my passenger window and leaned closer. Blood, dark like burgundy wine, but thicker—a pool of it, absorbed into the seat of his pants and ran shiny down the concrete block he was perched on, forming another smaller puddle beneath his black Converse high tops.

I shivered, remembering the call I'd heard on the scanner in the newsroom at the *Review-Journal.* Las Vegas Metro Police got an anonymous call about a potential shooting at the Civic Center North bus stop. I was wrapping up the obits and crime beat from the night shift and had some time to blow, so I headed out.

Leaving my car parked in a vacant lot along Las Vegas Boulevard, I did a three-sixty as I approached the body but saw no one. There was plenty of traffic, because Las Vegas was always pulsating with life, but this was not an obvious crime scene yet.

For more than eight minutes I waited, finally sitting right next to that dead man, with the cops nowhere to be found. That's the way they were in Vegas, slow as sludge, especially if it had anything to do with the homeless. For all I knew, it might have been another hour before they showed.

That's when I thought about searching him. Nothing bad, just find the wound, maybe get an ID, see if he had anything else on him. It was a fleeting thought. But as another minute, two, then three crept by, the vapor of the idea began to crystallize. I pictured how everything would come to a painful standstill once the cops finally arrived. They would boot me, tape off the area, and withhold the bum's identity and cause of death until it was old news.

My heart rate kicked up a notch. I had no gloves. Would I leave prints? On what, clothes? It's not like they're going to go over this nobody with a fine-tooth comb. At first glance I wasn't sure where the wound was. Blood covered the upper quarter of his torso. Ignoring my own sick disregard for the human being next to me, I scoped the area again, saw no one near, and gently leaned his 150-or-so-pound frame forward six inches.

To the touch, his body felt normal, as if he were still alive. There was no exit wound on his back. Dropping to one knee, I examined the bloody mess at the upper left portion of his chest. His coat was torn there, and yes, there was a bloody hole. Whether it was a messy knife wound or a bullet hole, I wasn't sure.

That was as far as I should have gone. In fact, knowing myself—that I would dare to do more if the fuzz didn't show up soon—I passed the time by jotting notes on the pad I always kept in my back pocket.

He had a thatch of red hair, bleached the color of sand by the scorching Nevada sun. The city had felt like Hades lately, going on seven consecutive days of 109 degrees or better. His peaceful, middle-aged face, the side part in his hair, and the back of his hands and neck were a burnt brownish red; not raw sunburn, mind you—he was way beyond sunburn.

The stubble on his face was speckled blond and gray. He wore a gold T-shirt with dirty creases and a black, lightweight overcoat unbuttoned. Funny thing is, he didn't smell bad. In fact, he smelled clean, like laundry soap. The pants were navy Dickies, and each sneaker had a hole just above the big toe. He wore two pair of thick gray socks on each foot. Perhaps most odd were his left ear and wrist. The skin on each looked melted, as if it had been surgically repaired with some sort of skin graft.

I was still within the bounds of the law. I'd taken my time with the notes, describing the scene, the wound, and the slumping corpse next to me—and hoping the LVMPD would hurry up and get here before I did something both stupid and illegal.

A steady flow of cars darted north and south, their drivers oblivious to the dead man twenty feet away. As always in Las Vegas, nightlife rolled seamlessly into morning within the mammoth hotels up and down the Strip.

My time limit had expired. The cops didn't care. Likely, no one cared about this destitute beggar. A few hours ago he'd probably been as nasty and senile as the rest of the riffraff who shake their fists and wag their heads at me when I drive past them on Owens or D Loop.

.Who would know if I searched the guy? My editor didn't know I was here, no one did. My eyes darted about. My heart stormed high in my chest. And then I just did it—reached into his shallow outside coat pockets. Nothing there. Easing back his thin coat, I found an inside pocket—empty. I scanned again for onlookers and saw none. I was doing him and his family a favor by trying to identify him. As I braced him at the shoulder with my left hand, I jammed my right into his pants pocket. Again, nothing.

Convinced the Las Vegans breezing up and down the Strip were both oblivious to the crime scene and in a colossal hurry, I filled my lungs with morning air and took another plunge. Being careful to swing around the puddle of blood in front of him, I changed sides, leaned him forward, and slid my hand beneath his coat and into one back pocket, then the next. No wallet. The guy had nothing. Or so I thought, until I propped him up firmly by the opposite shoulder and stuffed my hand into that last front pocket of his navy Dickies.

Bingo.

He had something. Not much, but something.

Getting my fingers around what felt like some folded papers, I pulled, but my fist caught. My prints were on whatever was in that pocket. The sound of sirens arose far off from the south. My head jumped, and sweat started to bead on my forehead. Seeing no police lights, I braced him again and twisted my wrist back and forth, yanking hard. My heart almost catapulted from my throat as the man's stomach gurgled and his head dropped and swung toward me, as if he'd decided to watch.

Trying awkwardly, desperately, to square the man's hunching

shoulders and swivel his jaw back to where it had been, I panicked, as his entire upper body started to collapse, quite unlike I'd found it.

Blue police lights canvassed the neon skyline.

I rehearsed excuses, lies, the truth—any way out of the developing mess.

Then I realized the only way out was to get out.

But the object I'd ripped from the man was still in my hand. I looked down. It was a tattered bankbook with a worn maroon cover. As the screams from the sirens grew louder, my trembling fingers found the last page and the handwritten balance: $689,800.

The bus stop spun.

I felt my fingers press firmly into my forehead, as if trying to steady the ship.

He was rich.

It didn't compute.

Figure it out later. Get out!

I stood to run, but something fell from the book, splattering into the puddle at the man's feet.

A key, now three-fourths covered in blood.

I froze.

The sirens beckoned me to look up.

A squad car was in view, maybe a mile down the Strip.

Something inside told me to give up, wait for them, explain what happened.

Something else jolted me to the ground where I plucked the blood-drenched key from the crimson puddle and bolted toward my car.

Sprinting faster than I had since I was a boy, my mind wound down to slow motion, and I became disgusted by the cool, thick liquid making my fingers stick grotesquely to the palm of my clenched hand. But I was even more repulsed by the type of man I'd become—stealing from a bum.

After scrubbing hard at my hands and the key in a long, hot shower back at my place—a stucco two-story in a cluster neighborhood west of the Center Strip—I put on some old cutoffs, went downstairs, popped a can of Dr Pepper, and examined the tattered bankbook at my kitchen table. It contained no name and little writing but was stamped with the address of a First Federal Bank of Nevada branch near Arville and Flamingo, not too far from my house.

Periodic deposits had been made in amounts ranging from $155 to $12,650 with no indicator of where the funds had come from. A number of withdrawals had also been made, mostly in the three- and four-digit range; on those occasions, the only word ever written in the memo area was "cash."

One transaction stood out, dated the day before I found the body. The word "cash" was scribbled in the ledger. The amount withdrawn: $425,000.

"Hmm."

I took the flat, gold key that had fallen from the bankbook over to a lamp in the living room and studied it closely. Although it was shaped like an old-fashioned key, it appeared to be brand-new, imprinted with the name of a well-known security company.

Tossing the key on the table, I studied the bankbook once more, this time searching specifically for any information about a safe-deposit box. When I was almost through, I spotted the number "1510" penned neatly in black ink on the bottom corner of the inside back cover.

Did I want money? Was that what this was about? Was I following the footsteps of my old man? At least he had a reason to steal; I had none. My life was okay. I'd done well as a journalist. I was planning to get away, write novels at a cottage on the beach, perhaps marry someday. One way or another, I would show the old man I was somebody, that I could make something out of this life, on my own, with or without him.

Wandering into the garage, I flipped on the overhead light then drilled the black Everlast heavy bag with a firm right. It swayed. I pummeled it with both fists, six or seven quick, hard jabs. The bag's metal chains squeaked as it swung from the ceiling, and I watched it in a daze.

What if there was easy money to be had? Could I get away with it? No, I wouldn't do that. I just wanted to get the scoop on a dead homeless guy with almost three-quarters of a million bucks in the bank. It was a blockbuster story. That's what I was after. At least, that's what I kept telling myself as I went back into the house, threw on a T-shirt, stepped into my army green flip-flops, and headed for the First Federal Bank of Nevada at Arville and Flamingo.

As I devoured a second biscuit from Jack in the Box while waiting in my car for the bank to open at 9 a.m., I was faced with a number of tricky questions. What if the key in my pocket wasn't to a safe-deposit box at all? Or what if it didn't go to a box at this bank? What would I say? If the box was there, would I be required to sign in? What excuse would I give if they requested my name or ID?

Next thing I knew I was standing in the sterile lobby, grasping the key in my fist similar to the way I had only hours ago when it was covered in the bum's blood. Three tellers faced me, and there was no sign of any safe-deposit boxes. Then I spotted a thin black woman on the phone at the customer-service desk to my right.

"May I help you, sir?" one of the tellers called out in a high-pitched voice.

Pretending not to hear her, I headed for the black woman on the phone. She smiled and made eye contact. I waved the key at her between two fingers, lifted both hands, and looked around the room, as if to ask where the boxes were. I didn't want to talk, just wanted her to point.

She spoke into the phone, "Just one moment," then looked up at me. "Do you need help with your box?"

Uh-oh. "No. I'm sorry. I didn't mean to interrupt. Where are they?" I glanced around the room. "This is the first time I've—"

"The self-entry boxes are right through that door," she pointed, "and to your right. You'll see them. There's a room beyond, where you can have some privacy."

Whew.

I sauntered around the corner, relieved to be out of sight. The small room—with its wall of boxes—was actually a walk-in safe, the enormous, foot-thick door of which stood wide open.

No sign-in?

The silver box fronts that covered the wall ranged in size from that of a postcard to that of a large folder. Looking around, I saw a telephone and a security camera. That was it. Clean, simple, secure and—at the moment—vacant.

Unbelievable.

Scanning the numbers—1300s, 1400s, 1500s—I knew I was in luck; my soul soared. The gold key slid in like a gem and turned easily. I couldn't believe where this was going. Swinging the little door open, I bent over, reached in, and pulled out a long, black box, only about three inches top to bottom, but ten inches wide and two feet long. It was fairly light, but several items shifted as I slid it out of its slot.

Gulping back my trepidation, I headed for the tiny adjacent

room, my eyes glued to the hallway, my heart thundering, and my mind convulsing with fantasies of taking the contents of the box and heading for the airport. I could be in Hawaii or even overseas, in Italy or France, by the next day. I had no ties in Vegas or in the States. All bridges had been burned between me and the old man.

Once inside the small room, I pushed the button lock on the doorknob, set the box on the wall-mounted desk, and took a seat in the leather chair. After pressing a release button at one end of the box, I lifted the lid. The cash caught my eye first, prompting me back to my feet. Hundreds, twenties, fifties, tens—scores of bills scattered throughout. I sifted through with both hands, snapping them up in a mad, rushed state of euphoria, stopping every ten seconds or so to look out the narrow window in the door.

My mind reeled. *What next?* I was giddy. No matter what else was in the box, there was cash—lots of it. If I played this thing smart, I could be set for a long time. Somehow, find out his name, withdraw the rest of the money, maybe a little at a time. Before I knew it, I could be writing books at a beach pad on stilts overlooking the Mediterranean.

Take it slow, be smart, breathe. I could easily go to jail for this. My mind rewound to the trail of blood drops I'd left at the bus stop when I took the key. I was whisked back to the last visit I'd made to the penitentiary in Victoria to see the old man. Hotter than Hades. No AC. Putrid, overpowering smell of urine and body odor. Screaming, yelling, betting, and brawls. Wacko ward.

I could never do time.

Perched upright on the edge of the chair like a kid who was just served a double helping of chocolate cake, I put the money down on the desk and sorted through the items remaining in the box. Most intriguing were two rings that had wound up together in the same corner. One featured a humongous solitary diamond on a gold band; the other was a white gold men's wedding ring. Each contained an engraved inscription that I would need steadier hands and a magnifying glass to decipher.

As I placed the rings with the money on the desk, a sudden wave of anguish came over me. The stuff in the box was personal. It dealt with people's lives and history and secrets and loves. *This is none of my business.*

But since when did my curiosity and greed ever succumb to my guilt?

I came to several newspaper and magazine clippings, folded and paper-clipped. I smoothed them out. They were business articles, some dating back twenty years, from the *Atlanta Journal-Constitution, USA Today, Atlanta Magazine,* and *Business Week.*

That's when I recognized the dead homeless man from the bus stop. He was heavier in the pictures, and flashier, but it was him— the common denominator in almost every photograph. He wore expensive suits, a slick hairstyle, and a big, plastic grin. Schmoozing with the big dogs. Looked to have been some kind of business mogul in Atlanta.

Most beautiful of all, I had discovered his name: Chester Holte. Maybe, just maybe, my ticket to paradise.

Voices beyond the door. I slid the stack of money and rings to the side of the box, out of view. Through the window I watched, almost breathlessly, as the black woman escorted a short, elderly man into the vault of safe-deposit boxes, eying me through the glass as she turned the corner. I set the lid on the box and waited, feeling the heat in my face and wiping the perspiration from my brow.

Less than a minute later she was at the doorway again, telling the man to let her know if he needed help but peering in at me once more, eyebrows lifted, before turning to head back toward her desk.

Rattled and running on empty after zero sleep, I needed to get out of there. But when I lifted the lid and looked back at the clippings, I stopped. It was a photograph of the man's wife. Her name was Candice. A tall, shapely, striking brunette, pictured in sequins in one photo and a formal gown in another, with a glowing smile, arm in arm with her husband.

My curiosity was in overdrive. What was all this stuff doing in this box? Was it all he had left of his past life? I was sitting on one powder keg of a story, if I chose to pursue it. How did a rich, big cat from Atlanta—married to a sleek gazelle—end up on the streets of Sin City, apparently of his own choosing, with money to burn?

Movement distracted me. The old man, oblivious to me, was tucking an envelope in his coat pocket and shuffling toward the exit in his beige walking shoes.

Something else in the box piqued my interest, confirming that Chester Holte had some business savvy indeed. Opening up a number of stiff, white stock certificates, I was flabbergasted to learn he had been the proud owner of hundreds of shares of Atlanta-based stocks, including Coca-Cola and Home Depot. There had to have been enough value in those shares alone for him to have retired a wealthy man.

As I gathered everything up to leave, a different clipping fluttered to the floor—this one sickeningly different from the others, especially its large, severe, blocky headline on soft, yellowing newsprint:

HOLTE PLANE DOWN, WIFE LOST

The photograph showed rescue boats and searchlights scouring the rolling Atlantic. A door to my heart opened, ushering in a heavy robe of shame.

The article was six years old. He had tried valiantly to save her, clinging to part of the Cessna's wing, disregarding his own fuel burns and fighting savagely to hold on to the love of his life in the frigid waters. But he could not hold on. And Candice had slipped away.

I found Candice's obituary next. A long one. I put it in my pile of things to take home.

I'd had all I could take for one sitting and didn't want to press my luck.

About to close the box, I stopped and stared at the impressive stack of money, rings, and other articles, letters, and paperwork I'd set aside to take home.

Don't do anything stupid. Think it through.

Hesitantly, I returned the money and stock certificates to the box. *I'll take the rest home, study it, and bring it back.*

Snatching up the rings, letters, and clippings, I closed the box, returned it to its slot, held my breath, and gave the woman in customer service a confident nod as I glided breathlessly out of the building.

It was already sweltering. I would need sleep sometime that day, before the night shift.

As I headed west on Charleston I noticed a young, humpbacked woman walking in the direction I was driving. The sun shone hard on her back, casting a crisp, stark shadow on her path. She wore a black windbreaker and carried a gallon jug of water in each hand. A quarter-mile farther an elderly man and woman sat in old lawn chairs at the side of the road beneath a pink blanket they'd hung to protect themselves from the coming sun. Maybe that had been their daughter back there, bringing water for the day.

I'd never taken the time to think about homeless people as human beings before and wondered about the man I'd found at the bus stop. Where did he live? Where were his clothes and possessions? How had he made all that money?

Something had happened after his wife died.

What?

Why had he chosen to live like a bum? Why Las Vegas? Why would someone want to kill him?

I knew me, and I knew I had to find out.

2

My name, by the way, is Hudson Ambrose, reporter for the Las Vegas *Review-Journal.* I grew up in San Antonio where my old man owned a dark, cool, musty bar on the River Walk called the Cat's Tail.

Some of my fondest memories are of the hot days when I cruised my black banana bike along the stone-paved borders of the curving river, delivering packages back and forth from the colorful delis and gift shops to the hotels and Realtors' offices. Late in the humid afternoons I would box at Gordy's Gym, tucked in a shady alley near the old man's bar, nurturing hopes of becoming an Olympic boxer someday.

Everyone along the River Walk knew me simply as Hud. And I knew the River Walk as well as I knew my worn-out Rangers cap. All the ins and outs, the ramps and steps, the waterfalls, the stone benches, the overpasses, and the best places to stop, catch a Texas breeze, and watch the pretty ladies float by in their sundresses on the crowded riverboats.

Then my mom passed away.

I was just a boy.

That's when my old man began to drink the stock, and my heart grew as dark as the Cat's Tail.

The bum incident had me wired. I couldn't sleep. Although it was the middle of the day, that normally didn't keep me from snoozing on the weekends when I had to go into the paper at night to write the obituaries and police beat. A bunch of us reporters switched off, so I only had to do it once every five or six weekends. And I never minded, because it was quiet. In fact, I enjoyed working in peace with the lights low, the scanner on, and just a few people moseying in and out of the newsroom. I liked quiet.

But that day—the day I found Chester—was different. Even though I had closed my eyes for more than an hour that afternoon, I did nothing but thrash in my messed-up bed, contemplating whether to try to cash in on Chester's fortune, or delve more deeply into his life and write a Pulitzer Prize–winning feature series.

I headed downstairs to the kitchen, grabbed a large bag of pretzels from the pantry, and set up shop at the kitchen table, fingering through all the stuff I'd collected from Holte's safe-deposit box. Lying in bed, I'd created a mental list of things I needed to do. First on the list was to call Reed O'Neil, whose cubicle was next to mine in the newsroom at the *Review-Journal*.

"O'Neil," he answered.

"Hud here. What's going on?"

"No, I can't fill in for you tonight, Ambrose. Try Suzette."

"Dude, chill. I'm coming in tonight."

"What's up then?"

"Nothing. What's goin' on there? Anything hot?"

"Ambrose, I don't have time to sit around and give you a run-down of today's top stories."

"I heard something was going on up north. A gunshot victim or something?"

"Where'd you hear that?"

I paused, knowing Reed's paranoia would get the best of him, and listened as his fingers kicked into action, pecking hard at his keyboard.

"Okay…I got nothin' on any murders," he said. "Today's lineup's right in front of me. Crash survivor improves. Ivana's office tower on hold. Four-year-old drowns in pool. Population increase. No murders. All's right with the world."

"You sure? It would have been at a bus stop…"

"I'm sure! I gotta go, Hud. I'm on deadline." He hung up.

I set the phone down, stared at Chester's belongings, and tried to figure out why Reed hadn't heard about the murder. It had been ten hours since I'd witnessed the murder scene firsthand. The newsroom should have had the story.

The police definitely will.

Flipping open my phone, I searched the address book and hit the speed dial for Nelson Truax, my main contact within the LVMPD, and the next thing "to do" on the list in my head. He loved getting his name in the paper, so I could always count on him to help me when he could.

After making small talk, I zeroed in. "Did you hear about something going on up around the Civic Center North bus stop this morning?"

"Such as?"

"I dunno… I heard there may have been someone hurt pretty bad up that way."

"I would've heard about it. Where'd you get your information?"

"Heard it on the police scanner early this morning."

Truax paused, and I found myself practically holding my breath.

"You must've gotten your signals crossed. It's been slow, especially for a weekend."

"Can you double-check for me, please? This is really important."

"Blazes, Ambrose, you're a pain." There was shuffling and a momentary silence. "Call me back in ten."

Relishing a sense of pride from having built such a thorough network of contacts throughout the city, I closed the phone, snatched a Dr Pepper from the fridge, and approached the bulky PC that sat on a tilted, particle-board computer stand against the wall in the dining room. The place looked like a frat house. I might as well have hung one of those huge black velvet rugs with the dogs playing poker.

A word search on "Chester Holte" brought up several of the articles I'd seen in the man's bank box and another that pictured Chester amid a bunch of dark suits on the board of trustees at a large industrial tool manufacturer. He and Candice had been long-time residents of Atlanta, with one son, Andrew, who would be twenty-five years old, if he was still walking the planet. Chester had probably been in his late fifties.

I hit Redial for Nelson Truax.

"I got nothin'," the officer said. "You must've heard wrong."

His terse words made me wonder if he had checked at all. "Nelson, I...I appreciate it, man," I mumbled. "Listen, while I got you, confirm something for me, will you?"

"Talk fast, Ambrose, I'm popular today."

"If someone's murdered within city limits, the body goes to the county coroner to determine cause of death, right? Autopsy done if necessary?"

"Affirmative."

"Okay…just one more thing."

Dare I go there with a Vegas cop?

"Would the body go to the hospital first?" I almost coughed out the next words. "A dead body, I mean?"

Truax's end of the line grew uncomfortably quiet.

"Are you telling me everything, Ambrose?"

"I heard there was a body, possibly a murder. I don't think I was hearing things. I'm gonna follow up on it, that's all."

"Knock yourself out."

Papers shuffled, and Truax's muffled voice spoke to someone at his end, then he groaned. "Okay. That it, Ambrose?"

"Ah, almost. So…hospital first…"

"Hospital first, then coroner."

"That's what I need. Thanks, sir. I owe you."

"Darn right you do. Call me if you turn up anything I should know about."

"Will do."

I spent the next hour on the phone, slicing through nasty red tape with the information people at three Las Vegas hospitals. In the end, none of them had any record of having admitted Chester or any other deceased, unidentified male.

Realizing a private ambulance company or smaller hospital might have handled Chester's body, I called the Clark County coroner's office, feeling ninety five percent sure they would have seen his body. Of course, I didn't get anyone live, so I left a message. The fact that I was a reporter with the biggest paper in Las Vegas usually got me a call back in pretty good time.

But I wasn't about to wait around drooling over the Holte wedding rings.

I had to drive by the bus stop again, just to see it taped off, to see the activity, to make sure I hadn't completely lost my marbles.

Heading up Dean Martin Boulevard to avoid the gridlock on the Strip, I slid the sunroof closed to block out the glare of the late-afternoon sun and cranked the AC. It blew my hair back as I leaned over and searched the glove compartment for the pack of smokes I'd stashed. Considering all that had happened in the past twelve hours, I was proud this would be only my third smoke since going into work the previous night. I'd almost quit completely—until I found Chester Holte.

Turning down the AC and lighting the Vantage, I vowed not to use finding Chester's body as an excuse to start smoking a pack and a half a day again. This would be my last one.

I smirked at the hundreds of cars crawling like turtles along Las Vegas Boulevard and the main streets of the city. Not many out-of-towners knew about Industrial Road—now, Dean Martin Boulevard—which whisked me north in a hurry.

As I drew closer to the Civic Center North bus stop, I glanced in the rearview mirror, reached up, and fingered the vertical trench in my forehead just above my nose. I was stressing again. *How could his body not have been found?* The cops had been within a mile, two at the max.

Could Reed have known about the dead man when I called him? Maybe Nelson Truax wasn't telling the truth. Maybe they all knew about Chester and that I had tampered with the body. The police could have a warrant out for my arrest, for disturbing a crime scene, or worse!

Calm down.

I again looked in the rearview mirror, trying to relax my muscles to flatten the gully of worry that was becoming a permanent fixture between my small, brown eyes. My beard had grown thick and full. There was a hint of gray in my sideburns, but not in the hair yet; it was still brownish blond, but darkening with each year that passed.

Oakley. *That's my exit.*

I merged off, hopped onto 15 North, and took several deep breaths knowing I was just minutes from the bus top where it had all started a half day ago.

It had happened, hadn't it?

The call on the scanner? The body? The bankbook? The key?

The key.

I'd left blood drops trailing away from the man's corpse toward my car. But the police would have no clue it was me—unless someone saw me. A witness.

Don't be paranoid.

Lake Mead Boulevard came in a flash. I exited, made a left on the Strip, and was quickly in the vicinity.

I'll drive by first.

There it was.

No. It couldn't be.

I scanned for the sign above the vending machines: "Civic Center North."

But nothing's happening!

Nothing.

It should be taped off.

But it wasn't. It was normal. Two people sitting. Waiting. Right where Chester had been murdered.

I checked the sign again. It read the same.

There should be cops all over this place. At least yellow tape.

Gunning the Mustang down to the next light, I hung a U-turn

and headed back. As I parked in the same place I had that morning, the cigarettes called from the glove box, but I was in too much of a hurry. Slamming the door, I hustled over to the covered bus stop.

Ignoring the man and woman seated about twelve feet apart beneath the silver, rainbow-shaped roof, I zeroed in on the concrete block where I thought I'd seen Chester that morning.

Which one?

I couldn't tell.

This is nuts.

I examined each one.

Bloodstains. There should be bloodstains!

There were none.

I started speaking while I was still staring down at the concrete block where I'd seen Chester. "Do you know anything about a crime that happened here this morning?" I finally looked up, first to the man, who wore a yellow, hooded Georgia Tech sweatshirt and a brown beret. His face was filled with crisscrossing lines and cracks from the sun and a hard life. His blue eyes were big and watery, but the whites of them were the color of cotton. His leathery hands were interlocked atop a homemade cane.

"You talkin' ta me?"

"Either of you." I swung around to face the woman, wearing a red T-shirt and denim overalls, and pinching a white foam cooler between her legs. "A crime took place here early this morning. Someone was murdered right here." I pointed to the block where I'd found Chester or, at least, thought I'd found him. "Do you know anything about it? Have you heard anything?"

The woman looked away, stared straight out at Las Vegas Boulevard, and shook her head. The middle-aged man leaned back, set the cane across his lap, and spit off to his side. "You a cop?"

I scowled as my eyes drilled into him. "I'm just someone who needs to know."

"Relative?"

"No! Look, do you know anything, or not?"

"Hmmm, let me think on it." The man flipped the wood walking stick from one hand to the other, then clicked it hard on the pavement. "You couldn't spare a single or two, could ya?"

You two-bit—

My phone rang. I turned my back on him and marched to the far end of the bus stop. "Hello."

"Mr. Ambrose?"

"Yes, who's calling?"

"Gene Umberger, Clark County coroner's office, returning your call."

I covered my free ear. "Thank you for calling back, sir. You got my message?"

"We did. But we've had no one come through our office fitting the description of the man you mentioned."

What?

"You're sure?"

"We take our work very seriously, Mr. Ambrose. I'm sure."

"Could I ask you to save my number and call me back if he, if that man's body turns up?"

"I would like to tell you yes, Mr. Ambrose, but we're extremely busy. You can always call us back and check."

I thanked him and hung up. Ignoring the panhandler, I walked over and sat hard on the block where I'd sat that morning, right next to Chester's body. There was not one trace of blood. The cops must have done their job and arranged for the scene to be cleaned up fast. But I'd never known a crime-scene team to work so quickly.

Well, they did.

Mumbling, with a pointing finger, I recalled picking the key out of the blood right there, that morning.

You're not crazy. You saw the safe-deposit box and what was in it. You have some of his stuff at the house.

As I got up to leave, the smelly city bus came puffing and squealing to a halt right beside me. The woman shot me a glance and hurried on sideways, cooler under her arm. The beggar ambled over, put one foot on the first step of the bus, turned toward me, lifted his wood stick to my chest, and spit off to his side.

"What was that fella's name you was lookin' for?"

Why even bother?

"Holte." I took several steps toward my car and a cigarette. "Chester Holte."

But the man's stillness made me stop and face him. Something had come over him. His mouth opened and he froze, his cane still in midair.

He took in my eyes, my face, my whole being.

The driver yelled, "On or off, fella!"

Staring right through me several seconds longer, the homeless man slowly looked up at the driver, then dropped his head and staggered back from the bus as its doors folded closed, just missing him. A shot of hot air burst forth from the front of the bus, and it roared to life, chugging away from Civic Center North.

"Are you okay?" I buried my nose in my sleeve amid a brown cloud of diesel exhaust.

The man stumbled, then dropped like a dead soldier, his walking stick cracking to the concrete beneath his collapsing frame.

I knelt at his side. "What is it?"

He was flat on the pavement, his face to the stone, his arms crooked above his head.

Heart attack.

"Are you hurt? Should I call an ambulance?"

He was crying.

Hesitantly, I touched the back of his sweatshirt. "Did you know Chester Holte?"

He nodded, and his body retched.

I reached for the brown beret that had fallen from his head.

"It's gonna be okay, man." I rubbed his shoulder. "Come on, let's get you up."

He shook his shoulder from my hand and turned awkwardly to look up at me, his weathered face glistening with tears. "He was my brother," he moaned. "He can't be gone. Tell me it wasn't Chester. Please. Tell me it's a mistake."

3

his reporter, this Hudson Ambrose fella, was a fair enough chap. He waited there with me in the wretched heat while I cried out every last ounce of fluid in me. Then I let him help me up. He was well under six feet, but strong and lean. Said he was from Texas, but sounded more like a Yankee, and I wagered he could hold his own like one too. I guessed him to be thirty-seven. Looked a bit shaggy, if I do say so, but I could tell he wasn't lazy. I can't stand lazy.

After the shocker about Chester, my knees hurt bad and I was frail, like all the blood had been drained clean outta me. Hud bought me crackers and a bottle of Gatorade from the machines and got himself a Dr Pepper. Then he asked a lot a questions. Took a lotta notes. Wanted to know how I could be Chester Holte's brother when my name was Arthur Peabody. So, I had to go back to the beginning, back to that spring night several years earlier.

A bunch of us, including Chester, were campin' out in a dried-out streambed west of the city. A lot of us bedded down in them washes at night, because they was dry, low, and surrounded by brush and rock, which made it next to impossible for Needermire and the other redneck Vegas cops to spot us.

When we hit the sack that night, I didn't know Chester Holte. But I did by mornin'.

I went to sleep hungry, as usual, but after several years on the streets, my stomach was used to the churnin', achin', burnin' for food. I guess I can tell ya I had a little buzz on too, that night I laid my head on my brown beret in the Nevada dust. My friend Jack Rabbit always found a way to score some reefer. He worked day labor. Spent his dough on one or two fingers of pot a day, whatever he could scrounge up. And he always passed his big ol' hand-rolled joints around late at night—to me, Weaver, Jenkins, and Cinderella Man. So, what I'm tryin' to say is, I was 'bout passed out when I closed my eyes that night.

By the way, bums don't watch news. That means we don't watch weather neither. So that day the forecasters said rain may be acomin', but none of us knew about the horrendous storm that was headed our way. Oh, lookin' back, I think I may've caught a whiff of it in the air that afternoon, but I didn't say nothin'. No one would've believed me. Shoot, Las Vegas only got four inches a rain a year; next to nothin'. But when it did rain, sister, it was a big event. Gusher city. The floodgates would open, and water would rush down Black Mountain and Sunrise Mountain (the one that looks like a sleepin' Indian), Mount Charleston and Spring Mountain, in torrents. You'da thunk the Hoover Dam done broke wide open and sent its fury down to bury this modern-day Sodom.

Anyway, we'd done bedded down for the night, and I didn't know anything was wrong till I was under water, tumblin' knees over head in what seemed like a tidal wave. Somethin' hit me hard on the side of the head as I was swept down into the city's drainage system. Even though I knew how to swim from when my mama taught me as a pup, it didn't help in that flood. No sir.

The best I could muster was to just barely get my head above the surface for a quick puff of air each time I thought I was about ready to breathe in a lungful of grainy water and meet my Maker. Then back under the current would pull me. Dark as midnight it was in that black tunnel. And brutal. My body was beat raw by floating boots and tent poles, blankets and fryin' pans—and the bashing bones of other bodies.

When I finally realized I was gonna die, was gonna take in that deep, watery breath that would put the lights out and end my pitiful existence once and for all, that's when his hand snatched the hood of my sweatshirt, practically choking me to death pulling against the power of the current.

Chester held on to me in that dirty, churning cesspool for nearly four hours, clinging all the while to a rickety ladder that remained barely attached to the slimy drainage wall. Using a crutch he'd grabbed as it floated by, he jabbed and banged at a manhole cover above our heads until a stunned utility worker found us early that morning.

When we got out of there, Chester walked me to the nearest corner, somewhere along Decatur Boulevard, where we plunked down like two drowned alley cats. I was coughing to the point of throwing up because of the water I'd swallowed, and the side of my head was burnin' like a you-know-what.

"We gotta get you to a doctor," he said.

"I'll be all right." I gasped, coughing till my insides felt like they was gonna cave in. "Need dry threads."

"What's your name?" he asked.

"Arthur Peabody."

"I'm Chester Holte." His arm rested on my soaked back. "I got some clothes that will fit you. But first, let's walk over to the Rescue Mission. They got an Outreach Clinic. Ever been there?"

"I been there once, for a spider bite."

"They take good care of you?"

"I suppose."

"I got some friends who work there. They'll make sure you're okay. Treat that head wound." He leaned in closer to have a look-see at what felt like an ugly gash above my ear. "They'll bandage you up, give you medicine, if you need it. May even find some dry clothes. If they don't have any, I think I got some at a van where I hang my hat sometimes, up at an abandoned casino, the Lucky Lady."

Well, I stared at the drops of water falling from my chin to the puddle on the pavement between my feet and wondered if I wouldn't have been better off dead. And I examined this Chester Holte character. He was sopping wet too, a course. His eyes were blue and clear. He wore a slight smile, seemed like, all the time, and had nice teeth, for a homeless man. The weather had worn his skin, like everybody else, and beard stubble filled his face, but there was somethin' healthy lookin' about him. Maybe the thing that stood out most was, he wasn't afraid of me.

"Why you doin' this?" I broke the silence.

"'Cause you need help. You could get an infection."

"What do you care?"

"I'd want you to do the same for me."

"Well, I wouldn't."

He laughed and didn't look away. "That's okay. I want to help you. I didn't hold on to you all that time to lose you now to pneumonia." He stood. "Come on. Let's walk over there. It's not far."

I shook my head, wantin' to be alone. The whole thing was weird, like a dream, like this guy was baitin' me. You couldn't trust anybody on them mean streets. Then again, maybe I didn't want to be alone. Maybe "alone" was a habit. There was an opportunity to make a friend. Maybe, a real friend. I couldn't remember anyone treatin' me like he had.

"Let's go, Arthur Peabody"—he nudged me with his black Converse high top—"before the lines get too long."

I groaned and stood. "I don't know why I'm goin' with you, you crazy bum."

His smile grew. Then we walked together, me and Chester Holte. Rising sun on our faces. Water sloshin' in our shoes. Just like brothers.

4

I f nothing else, Arthur Peabody confirmed to me in that sweltering Las Vegas heat that I wasn't going nuts. Chester Holte had lived, and apparently it had been a most unselfish life. The polar opposite of my old man, who'd clung to his pride and possessions until he was left with nothing. Curse him.

Chester and Arthur, it turned out, had been soul mates, sharing "meals" they salvaged from garbage bins, coins they collected in their hats while panhandling, and blankets they found to use for makeshift beds. But Chester had never given Arthur any eye-popping gifts of money or material things. And Arthur swore he didn't know a soul who would want Chester dead. On the contrary, he said whoever killed the lovable Chester Holte was "gonna burn in a special cauldron stirred by God Himself."

I had three hours to kill before my night shift at the *R-J*. Sitting in the cool McDonald's on palm-lined Sahara Avenue across from the Palace Station Casino, I sucked on a large chocolate shake, told myself I had to start eating better, and jotted down some leads to

follow up on, stemming from my talk with Arthur. My list looked
like this:

~ Chester's "friends" at Las Vegas Rescue Mission

~ Cop, Needermire, heads up LVMPD homeless patrol

~ Abandoned van w/ Chester's clothes (north, near abandoned casino: Lucky Lady)

~ Other homeless people who may know Chester: Jack
Rabbit, Weaver, Jenkins, Cinderella Man

I knew of the Rescue Mission. It was near the newspaper, close to
Glitter Gulch and the heart of Old Downtown. I planned to go there
on my way to work that night and address the other leads as soon as
I could.

A yellowish curtain of dust and smog hung over the desert mountains surrounding the ever-changing Las Vegas skyline as I drove back
to my place to shower, dress for work, and find out if anyone besides
me had finally heard about Chester's death.

What was he doing in Las Vegas?
I couldn't shake the question.
What am I doing in Las Vegas?
Couldn't dodge that one either.

This was where I'd landed after doing all I could for my old man
and feeling the need to bust out of the claustrophobia I was experi-
encing in San Antonio. I loved the city and the River Walk; they
would always be home. And the people of that fair city poured their
souls out to me after I lost Mom and watched Dad get hauled off to
prison. But because of those misfortunes, I felt like I was constantly
being watched—and favored. I needed to make something of myself
without any help from the good-old-boy network back home. I guess
I had something to prove to the old man, and I picked Vegas because
I thought maybe it was someplace where I could make a splash.

The instant the traffic light turned green, the guy behind me lay on his horn, going through a series of hand, arm, and body maneuvers reminiscent of someone being stung by a swarm of bees. Swinging his cheap little car into the other lane, he got behind a bus that was chugging along next to me. It featured a huge, horizontal photograph of the nude review at one of the new casinos in town. I couldn't help but drink it in with my eyes. *If Mom were alive, she'd be completely baffled as to why I chose Sin City, of all places, to make my mark in life.*

On the side of every bus, the back of every cab, every outdoor video screen, and every backlit billboard, there were ads for shows, magicians, heavyweight boxing, comedians, and most of all, women: scantily clad in leather and lace, too-good-to-be-true women—with a capital W.

But I'd lived in Las Vegas long enough to know that none of it was real. The neon promises were empty. The town was built on maxing out your senses. It was alluring, no doubt. Especially after the sun went down, when the neon glowed, the music played, and the fountains danced. But in the daylight, it reminded me of waking up with a hangover, as reality struck and everything was way too bright, and you could see the cracks, flaws, and ugliness of it all. A sick feeling.

I'd met plenty of women in Las Vegas, but it seemed every one of them was running from something, hooked on drugs, trying to make it big in the entertainment industry, or all of the above. Many came across as phony as the silicone implants and toxin injections that were the norm rather than the exception along the Strip.

Suzette Graham, a reporter at the *Review-Journal,* was the exception. I'd known her several years. She'd grown up in the suburbs of Las Vegas. Her old man was in the hospitality industry, and her brother was the pastor of some megachurch over in Spring Valley. She and I had been thrown together on a couple of stories—one an intense piece about a local boy from a wealthy family who was kidnapped and held for ransom near L.A. They found him alive. We got close on that piece. Suzette had a vibrant smile and laugh. Knockout shape. Long, blond hair. And she was just a good person, to boot.

I slowed to enter my subdivision, noticing a fifteen-foot stretch of new graffiti, spray-painted in gang code, on the ten-foot-high stone wall that attempted to block the neighborhood from Nevada's whipping dust storms.

Loser gangs are gonna ruin my property value.

I took the winding road back to my house. It really was a cool neighborhood. Mostly two-story stucco places in earthy, southwest colors. The homes had terra-cotta roofs and tiny yards landscaped with pebbles, tropical plants, and shrubbery.

The driveway was only about a car length long, so it looked junky to park out there, even though a lot of neighbors did. I hit the door opener and pulled into the two-car garage, beat on the heavy bag for five minutes, grabbed my stuff, headed in, and cranked the AC.

No messages on the answering machine in the kitchen. No calls from Reed or Truax.

Huh.

I threw my keys on the kitchen table, headed for the stairs, and started to take my T-shirt off on the way.

But something was wrong.

The way the keys slid across the table.

I swung around and raced back to the kitchen.

Everything that had to do with Chester was gone. The clippings, the letters, the rings—all of it.

I froze, listening hard, but sensing no one in the house.

My head automatically went into motion, my eyes panning the downstairs like a virtual three-sixty tour. TV, stereo, DVD player, headphones, computer—all accounted for.

And there was no visible damage. No windows broken.

Realizing they hadn't come through the garage, I dashed for the side door. It was shut, but a beam of light shown bright near the doorknob, and splinters frayed out from there and lay on the foyer floor. I pulled and it swung open. The lock was mangled.

I dashed for the steps, but stopped. My head whipped back toward the kitchen table.

The key.

My heart plummeted, thinking it was gone.

No...

My hand was in my pocket before I could take another breath, and in one clenched fist I brought everything out.

I have it!

The small safe-deposit-box key was there amidst my change and pocketknife.

I checked my watch.

No!

The bank was closed. And tomorrow was Sunday.

My shoulders dropped and I sighed. It would be a full day and a half before I could check the safe-deposit box. Would the cash still be there? The stocks? Did whoever broke in here know about the box at the bank? Did they have another key?

Chester's bankbook had been on the kitchen table.

I bashed the table with a fistful of change and ran for the steps. But, as I suspected, the upstairs was undisturbed.

Someone knows I know about Chester.

I separated the slats on the blinds in my bedroom and peered down at the residential street below.

The only thing moving was an obnoxiously loud, low-riding silver Golf station wagon with tinted windows. Two dark-skinned young men wearing gleaming Nikes, loose black clothes, and sideways baseball caps with flat visors half chased, half skipped after the car.

It screeched to a standstill.

The left rear door bounced open. Laughter and raucous hip-hop spilled out. The two men cursed and shot punk gestures toward the inside of the vehicle. The driver barked something, and reluctantly the men scrunched over and packed themselves into the car. Before the back door was fully closed, the Golf's tires chirped, the car revved, lurched, and zipped away, the back door still banging, but never latching shut.

5

should've gotten the cops involved right then, when my place had been broken into. I could've told them about finding Chester's body that morning, the safe-deposit box, and the break-in at my place. At that point, I might have gotten off with a slap on the wrist.

But no. I kept getting in deeper. That was my nature. I didn't know if it was greed that was driving me or the desire to land this huge story or something else, something beyond myself.

After dodging the mean eyes and rude comments and gestures of several homeless characters on the way into the Las Vegas Rescue Mission that evening, I found out the Downtown Outreach Clinic was closed for the weekend.

Great.

I had well over an hour to blow before I was due into work.

Out of curiosity, and to avoid the bums I'd run into before, I went the long way around the Rescue Mission to check out the clinic, which resembled a tiny, one-story house, about the size of a mobile home. Oddly enough, the place was lit up like a concession stand.

I eased up the wood steps at the back of the building, knocked, and waited. The door, one of those cheap ones with a Styrofoam core, was locked. I heard nothing inside and knocked again. Several seconds later, there was a click at the doorknob, then the door squeaked and pushed open several feet, only to reveal a woman with long black hair in a white nurse's coat and white tennis shoes, walking back into the small clinic.

"Where are you takin' me?" she asked.

Amused, I stepped inside. "How 'bout the buffet at the Rio? I hear they have great sushi."

She spun around like an acrobat, her clipboard clattering to the floor, her brown eyes flashing big and bright.

"Who..." She came at me, arms outstretched. "You are not allowed in here. We're closed. Now get out. We'll be open at seven thirty Monday. You can come back then."

"I'm sorry." I laughed, crossing my hands at my chest and letting her guide me out the door. "You need to be more careful about who you open up to."

She looked up at me. Very cute. Ivory complexion. Black eyebrows. Small mouth with full lips. A lot of animation.

"Thank you very much for the security tip." She reached for the doorknob.

"My name's Hudson Ambrose. I'm with the *Review-Journal.* Do you mind if I ask you a quick question?"

I backed away as she pulled the door within four inches of being closed and peered back out at me. "What are you gonna do, run another bogus story about how great the care is for Las Vegas's homeless? You guys don't have a clue. For the record, there are ten thousand homeless people in this town. Three thousand are teens, and three thousand sleep on the streets each night."

"Whoa, whoa, whoa." I stepped back, raising my hands. "I don't know anything about that. Never covered it. All I want to know is if you or anyone else who works here knows a guy by the name of Chester Holte, that's all. He's homeless. I heard he knew some people here."

"Chester?" The door opened. She looked like she'd just witnessed an eighteen-car pileup.

"Yes, do you know him?"

"I do," she backed into the white clinic, squinting. "Is anything wrong? Is he sick?"

I stepped inside. "Look, what's your name?"

"Never mind my name, Mr. Ambrose." The skinny bones at the base of her neck protruded. "Tell me what this is about! Is he hurt?"

I hadn't expected such an eruption. "I'm not sure. I heard a report that it may be serious. I don't know if that's true or not. I'm trying to find out more." I usually didn't flinch about lying, but this girl seemed so strait-laced, and she was obviously close to Chester. The fib nagged at me. "Was he a friend of yours?"

"He *is* a friend of mine. A dear friend."

"When did you see him last?"

She put her hands on her thin waist, exhaled loudly, dropped her head, and paused. "Just this week. Wednesday or Thursday. He brought doughnuts. Where did you hear this, about him being hurt?"

"Are we talking about the same Chester Holte? The guy I'm talking about is homeless. He wouldn't have money to buy doughnuts—"

"Every penny he finds, Mr. Ambrose, Chester gives away. Okay? He's not your typical displaced person."

Again, her deep-seated emotion and familiarity with Chester both put me on the spot and made me need to know more. But I had to tread carefully. "You sound like you know him well. Can I buy you a cup of coffee? The more I know about him, the better I'll be able to help—"

"Help with what, Mr. Ambrose? Where did this report come from that Chester's been hurt? You haven't even told me that."

This chick was not going to be snowed. I could see her going to the cops faster than a pit bull goes to raw meat. My face grew hot. I wished I'd never knocked on her door.

Footsteps behind me, on the steps.

"Holly?"

A tall, solid dude with a crew cut, brown bomber jacket, and dress pants ducked his way into the clinic, glared at me, then at her. "What goes on?"

She nodded at me. "This is Hudson Ambrose, a reporter with the *R-J*." She looked back at him and swallowed hard. "This is Ken Van Dillon."

I put my hand out to shake, but no such luck.

"What's he doin' here?"

"He heard Chester may be hurt. He's following up on the story." Van Dillon stared at me. "Where'd he hear that?"

"From the police," I lied again, not feeling so bad lying to Mr. Manners. "I'm still puttin' together all the pieces. Everything's really sketchy."

He turned to me. "Ever think you may want to wait and contact her during business hours?"

This was all I needed—a hot-headed, military-brat boyfriend.

"Look," I said to her, "If you prefer, I can call you Monday—"

"You talk to *me*, reporter!"

"No." Holly stepped toward the tall guy, clasped his coat with her left hand, and looked up at him. "I need to help. I'm gonna tell him what he needs to know."

"Not now, you're not!"

"Yes, Kenny, I am." She arose to her tiptoes, getting closer to his face. "You know what he means to me."

The guy's nostrils flared and he stared down at her, his cheeks glowing red and his lips sealed tight. Then he fixed his sights on me. "I don't expect to *ever* see you again, reporter." He brushed her hand from his coat and shoved me hard on his way out the door, but I let it go, wanting only to get the information I needed.

The door slammed and bounced open five inches.

"Sorry about that." She rolled her eyes. "We had a date."

"I'm sorry." I pulled the door shut.

"It's okay." She nodded, taking off the white jacket. "Chester's what's important right now."

Maybe Suzette Graham isn't the only classy lady in Las Vegas, after all.

I picked the clipboard up off the floor and handed it to her. "Your name's Holly?"

She set the clipboard on the counter, hung the jacket on a hook, and turned back toward me, wearing a plain, black tank top and jeans. "Holly Queens."

She stuck her hand out. It was cold and her shake was firm.

"My friends call me Hud."

"I'll take that drink you mentioned if it'll help Chester."

"Great. Do you know Maxine's?"

"Seen it. Never been there."

"They've got good coffee and desserts. I'll drive, if you like."

"Okay."

She grabbed her purse, turned out the lights, and locked up, and we headed down the steps.

"I'm around this way," I walked in the direction of my Mustang with Holly at my side, trying to figure out how I was going to dodge her specific questions about Chester. Should I keep lying? Could I trust her enough to share the truth? If I did, there would be no money in this thing for me. And she'd wonder why I hadn't waited for the cops to show up.

"Tell you what," she stopped suddenly, turning her back toward a dark car she'd been eying as we walked. "I think I'll drive myself, okay?"

I smelled cigarette smoke. Something moved in the dark car. I couldn't see for sure, but I suspected it was Ken Van Dillon. Sitting there. Watching us.

"What's the deal?" I tried to keep my eyes on her. "Is your boyfriend gonna follow us?"

"Look." Her eyes closed, and her head dropped back. "I'm sorry about this. Please, if you can, just ignore him. My truck's right over here." She nodded toward a little Toyota pickup. "I'll meet you at Maxine's; I'll do all I can to help Chester; and we'll be done."

She headed for the red truck, dug in her purse, and keyed her way in.

Turning toward my car, I saw the orange glow of a cigarette in the driver's seat of the suspicious car. Then smoke billowed out the open window. Old Kenny was still sitting, waiting, watching—and he obviously didn't care who knew it.

6

Hudson Ambrose handed me a bottled water and large banana-nut muffin at the sofa I'd found near the fireplace at Maxine's, away from the windows. Kenny had followed us. I'd seen him in my rearview mirror. He wasn't even trying to go unnoticed.

Will he come in? Sit at another table? Humiliate me?

Although I was at my wit's end with him and his jealousy, and afraid I'd pay for my independence later, I had to block that out and focus on helping Chester.

Sitting there with a seven-seed bagel, a Dr Pepper, and a little notepad, Hudson insisted he couldn't divulge any more details about Chester, only that he'd been hurt and might be missing. The whole thing was twisted, but for some reason, I was supposed to trust this guy, Hud. He wanted to know all I knew about Chester, and whether he had any enemies who would want to hurt him. So, I laid it out there for him, starting back at the beginning.

"I didn't realize it back then," I told him, "but each one of us is only a few weeks away from homelessness. I don't care who you are."

Hud's dark brown eyebrows rose, he tilted his head and chewed his bagel but said nothing, so I went on.

"What I mean is, we become so dependent on our jobs and our incomes and those who provide for us, that we don't realize what can happen when the faucet suddenly turns off."

"That's what happened to Chester?"

"To me! My whole world fell apart one Friday three years ago. My husband came home from work and said he was leaving me for a woman in Phoenix he'd met on the Internet."

"No way."

"We didn't have kids and had pretty much fallen out of love within a year after getting married, so there wasn't a whole lot of fallout there. The rub was, I hadn't worked in years. I'd gotten into a rut of meeting my girlfriends for drinks, playing the slots, shopping, and having pretty much whatever I wanted. I'm just trying to explain to you how easy it is to suddenly be homeless."

"Wait a minute, you're not trying to tell me you were homeless…"

"When my husband left, I was alone with no income or responsibilities." I couldn't believe I was telling him all this, but he seemed genuinely intrigued. "I fell into a black hole. I don't know how else to put it. I slept most of the time—just like my mother used to—only getting up to go to the bathroom or grab whatever was left in the fridge. With money from the few hundred dollars my husband left, I paid a neighbor kid to restock some essentials: pita bread, carrots, spring water, cheese, crackers."

"Whoa."

"Yeah. I would just sit there in the glow of the TV with the blinds drawn. A lot of times I didn't know what time it was or what day. I stared at CNN or soap operas, fooling myself into believing I'd get a job when the money ran out."

"So what happened?"

"The unopened bills piled up. I got an eviction notice, then a visit from the police. I packed my clothes and went to my girl-friend's. But she had a new roommate—" The memory of it cut me off in midsentence. The aloneness took my breath away and filled my eyes with tears. But I quickly swiped them away. "I was an unwanted third wheel. She told me I needed to see a doctor, get some meds for depression. I was so numb and despondent, I couldn't bring myself to approach any other friends for shelter; most of them were married anyway."

"I can't believe that," Hud insisted. "What did you do?"

"It's surreal. The next thing I knew it was dark, and I was sitting on the steps of a Catholic church, falling asleep on my suitcase, just wanting to curl up and die. Then it was morning—"

"No way."

"Yeah. I'd slept on the streets of Las Vegas. And the awful thing was, I let it keep happening, because I didn't care about anything any-more. I just wanted to sleep and somehow blank out or fast-forward through that season and wake up on the other side of it."

"So is that when you met Chester?"

"Yes." My head dropped more from thankfulness than anything else, I guess. "The morning I met him, I was just waking up beneath a sheet-metal roof some friends had put up a couple of weeks earlier in a homeless camp along Owens Avenue."

"Wow."

"There must have been a hundred of us living along that chain link fence. We used anything we could get our hands on to build lit-tle, temporary homes; you know, stuff like cardboard boxes, old tables, sheets of plastic, tents, tires, shopping carts…"

"I know we've done stories on that Owens Avenue area—"

"Oh, your paper is the worst when it comes to the homeless. The politicians in this city bribe and lie to cover up the problem, and you reporters buy it."

Hud shook his head and wiped the crumbs off his shirt. "That's news to me."

"Look, forget it, I'm not gonna go there now. You're here to find out about Chester. The deal is, a bunch of us living along Owens Avenue had heard that Drake Needermire and the LVMPD had an abatement notice. Parents and business owners along there had been up in arms about the so-called health and safety risks we presented. Needermire was set to run a sweep of the encampment, and word was that it wasn't due to go down for another week, and word couldn't have been more wrong."

The shrieking whistles woke me. Down the line, things crashed and spilled. Loud banging echoed on metal. I squinted into the bright white dirt and gravel. My homeless neighbors were running, bleeding, holding wounds, and hitching up their clothes amid clouds of gray dust. I could almost feel the ground shaking as the ruckus drew closer, and I swallowed the nausea that rose up in my throat.

I would run. My shoes were already on. I checked my pockets. My change was there. I scanned my blankets and clothes, my bucket of toiletries. I could get more of that stuff. A man howled, not far down the line. Not far.

They're almost here.

On all fours, I stuck my head out and looked right. They were close, three of them in beige police uniforms, dark green stripes down the side of the pants, black boots, and gloves. With helmet shields down, legs stomping, and billy clubs flying, they bashed legs and arms, ripped makeshift roofs, cracked feet and hands, and kicked in columns of junk that had been carefully constructed to separate our "homes." Many of the victims lay lifeless in the dust like heavy mannequins being kicked across a desert.

I pulled back inside and drew a breath. If I ran, they'd tackle me, hurt me. I scrambled for the two-by-four, near where I'd slept. Clutching it in my lap, I gathered my knees up to my chest and wrapped my arms around my shins, careful to bury my hands under my armpits. When they got to me, I'd nestle my head between my knees and brace for the worst. If I had to, I'd use the board that lay across my lap.

It dawned on me to pray. But I didn't. It felt cheap. I'd never given God the time of day.

A scream rang out, something heavy crashed sickeningly close to my right, and my blanket "wall" blew with the wind from the impact.

"These guys are on something." Out of nowhere, a sweating, out-of-breath red-headed man came face to face with me. He'd crawled to my side from between a wall of boxes to my left.

"What do we do?" I squirmed.

With dark, powerful hands, he gripped the piece of wood wedged in my lap.

"Give me this."

I looked into his eyes. They were tropic blue. They said, "Trust me."

I let go. He slid it out, propped himself up on one knee, and rested a hand in the middle of my back.

"You're not going to be hurt."

Right. Dude's probably some mental case. Brace yourself, Holly, just brace yourself.

"Father," his head dropped. He clutched the piece of wood, about the length of a baseball bat, in the crook of his left arm. He kept his right centered on me. "Holly and I ask that You'll keep us safe now."

My name.

How does he know my name?

"Be in our midst. Protect us…"

Just as he raised his head—*bam!*

The ribbed sheet metal above our heads rang out. *Bam, bam, bam!* It began to shimmy.

"…Teach you lazy sons of slobs to camp on my turf."

Bash!

Black leather boots shuffled in the dust beside us.

My protector put a finger to his lips. "Shhh." He nodded and winked. "It's okay."

The roof was caving.

"I'm going to cover you," the man yelled, his body draping over me like a blanket.

The metal roof wobbled one last time and, *gong,* like a cymbal, banged down on my protector's back, the fort lighting up with sunshine.

Dropping the piece of wood, he rose up on his knees and pushed the metal off us, then put his arm around my shoulders.

"What we got here?" Needermire, the ringleader cop, hunched over, panting. "You find yourself a little whore, dirt ball?"

Maybe he's run out of steam.

Needermire stuffed his billy club into my protector's side and drilled. "Get your skinny tail out of my way, dirt ball."

Maybe not.

The man's body contorted, but his arm stayed firm around me. He said nothing.

"I said"—Needermire's knee shot up like a machine on an assembly line, smashing the poor man's jaw—"move away from her!"

My protector's teeth clacked and his head snapped back. Blood ran from the corner of his mouth. But he didn't move an inch from me.

"Stop it, you moron!" I yelled. "Leave us alone."

Thrusting his shoulders back, Needermire lifted his billy club above my head and huffed, his dark eyes shrinking. "Why, you little piece of homeless trash…"

The nicked, black stick was almost in motion. As time slowed to freeze frames, I estimated the club would strike the front left quarter of my skull within milliseconds. I scrunched my eyes shut and covered my head with my hand. My protector's arm never left me.

"Needermire!"

My whole body was locked up, waiting for the blow.

"We got company!" The voice yelled from down the line. "Backups are here."

Silence and anticipation, unbelief and thankfulness buzzed in my brain.

My protector leaned near. "It's okay," he whispered. "God's here."

Hud had moved up to the edge of the couch at Maxine's. His mouth was gaping and he'd stopped writing.

"Some of my homeless friends told me later that Chester had been lurking in my shadow ever since the first week I'd arrived on the streets," I explained to Hud. "Without my knowing it, he'd found out my name and anything anyone could tell him about me. He even slept nearby and steered away a couple of predators. Sometimes he left fresh bread in the dumps where he knew I searched for food."

"Why did he do all that?"

"He was concerned about me. He knew I was new to the streets."

"So you became friends?"

"Yeah. After the sweep, we started hanging out together. It was the oddest thing, because I could tell from his eyes that he wasn't interested in me, you know, physically or in a romantic way. He was more like a father. Soon, we got into this cool groove where I'd bring him broken appliances and electronics I found—radios, phones, small TVs—and he'd repair them, sell them, and we'd split the money. Chester hated to panhandle, but he was the best at it. Before I ended up on the streets I'd heard it said that good panhandlers, those who had the right 'look,' could make more money in a year than someone working behind the desk at a Holiday Inn or Best Western. The way Chester raked in the dough, I became a believer."

"Do you know if he had any other kind of income?" Hud swigged his Dr Pepper and leaned back on the couch.

"You keep talking in past tense. Why is that?"

He laughed and gave a bounce of the shoulders. "I guess it's just…I've never met him, so it's like he's some character in a book."

"He doesn't have any other income," I said. "At least, I think I'd know about it. One of the reasons he earns so much is because he gives it all away. I mean all of it. Not just to me. He constantly inquires about other people, asks where they're from, if they have any income, and what their needs are."

"Does Chester have any enemies? What about this Needermire, and who were the other bad cops?"

"Their names are Loy and Sanchez. They and Needermire are rednecks. They've got it in for all the homeless, not just Chester."

"Why?"

"Homeless people make the city look dirty, like it's full of criminals. I think Needermire, Loy, and Sanchez are some of the Vegas cops who're charged with keeping an eye on the homeless community."

"What about other enemies of Chester's?"

"I don't see how he could have enemies. He makes the most destitute beggar feel important, like he still has value. And he has this uncanny ability to defuse walking time bombs, because he's so meek and honest. I'll never forget this one time I saw him standing outside the municipal pool, faced off against this freak named Giovani, one of the most violent, unpredictable street people in the city."

Speaking of violent, I realized I needed to finish with Hud. Kenny was probably beside himself.

"Anyway, I just held my breath, and in his easy manner, with that warm smile, Chester patted that man's shoulder, gripped his arm, and just listened to him. Pretty soon, they were sitting on the wall, chatting and laughing like old school chums. He has a way with people. A lot of times, he'll be right in the middle of an argument about food or clothes or bedding spots, and out of nowhere, he comes up with a fair solution that just defuses the whole thing."

"This guy sounds too good to be real."

"I'll tell you what, homeless or otherwise, I've never met anyone with a zest for life like Chester's. Not even close."

Once again Hudson turned the page on his small notepad, then checked his watch. "I'm going to be a little late getting into work, but it's okay. Will you excuse me while I call my editor?"

"Look, I've got to go anyway, really." I did my best to hide my anxiety.

"No, listen, let me call my editor and get you something else to eat or drink. How 'bout it?"

I told him I didn't want anything more, although I could have devoured another muffin or three. While he stood to call the paper, I imagined Ken sitting outside in his car, growing hotter by the minute.

Maybe he's left.

But I knew better. The longer I stayed, the more livid he would become. I forced him out of my mind.

Hudson returned to his place. "Everything's cool."

"What more do you need to know?" I asked.

"Well, how did you get where you are today, and what part has Chester played in that?"

So I began to tell him about the day things began to change for me—how it began on a scary note.

As often happened, a group of kids had gathered around Chester as he jested and played his harmonica outside the NASCAR Café at the corner of Sahara and Las Vegas Boulevard.

Sitting on the ground, leaning against the wall next to him, I began to notice the heads of tourists, in our midst and afar, turning east. A scream rang out and people began shouting. Shock disfigured their faces. Some scurried from the area. Others froze with wide-mouthed stares. Others lifted their video cameras.

Before I could see what was happening, Chester's music stopped and the closed circle of kids surrounding us busted apart. I got to my knees, trying to stand, but was slammed to the pavement, screaming, as a man bounced hard on my legs and rolled off. He looked like a beggar and was bleeding from the ear. A destitute-looking black man charged him like an animal, booting him in the ribs with all he had. All the while, three men with professional-looking cameras knelt, ducked, and bobbed, capturing it all on video.

Chester hovered over me, propping my head up. "You okay?"

I groaned for a breath and blinked back the tears, telling myself I'd had the wind knocked out of me, remembering when it had happened as a girl, falling off the swing.

"I know what this is about," he whispered. "Stay here."

In a flash, Chester ripped the camera away from one of the stunned videographers, skipped three steps, and smashed it to smithereens against the brick wall.

That seemed to be the cue for the brawlers to quit fighting, as they collapsed to the sidewalk, side by side.

Dozens of people closed in on the scene.

"What the Sam Hill do you think you're doing?" One of the videographers charged Chester, shoving him four feet. "We're making a movie here!"

"At whose expense?" Chester squared off with the young man, driving his fists into the man's chest. "Huh?" He jerked his head toward the fighters. "They're human beings."

"They're being paid for their parts in this!"

"Paid in what? Used clothes? Booze? Twenty bucks, maybe?" Chester drove his fists into the man's chest again. "While your little company makes millions?"

The man knocked Chester's hands down. "People buy our films, okay? We don't force them on anyone. It's entertainment." He threw up his hands, with a look of disgust. "Why am I explaining this to a piece of garbage? You're lucky I don't have you thrown in jail. Now, get out of my face, bum. Go back to your cardboard box."

Someone booed. Another yelled an obscenity. Then a hushed sense of anticipation came over the crowd, which had enlarged to no less than two hundred people.

Chester's gaze left the man.

He looked down at me, then panned the faces.

The sweating, dark-skinned man with whom Chester had argued cranked his finger, telling his partner to keep his camera rolling.

It was hot. The air was gritty. I thought it might be over. The two brawlers lay flat on their backs near me. I'd caught my breath, but was entranced and motionless.

"Oh, dear God," Chester's head dropped back, and he faced the blue sky with clenched fists at his sides. "Forgive us," he moaned, "we know not what we do. Forgive *me* for losing my patience."

The dark-skinned man crossed his arms hard, sighed, and closed his eyes.

"We know You're standing at the door," Chester cried. "We know You're knocking. Longing to come into each of our lives. Help us. Have mercy on us…"

Several women in the sea of people were moved to tears by the surreal scene that was unfolding.

The dark-skinned man slowly shook his head, stroked his jaw, got his partner's attention, and slashed an index finger across his throat. As his partner lowered the camera, he walked quickly toward the dozens of pieces of broken video equipment strewn on the pavement. As he picked up the largest piece, what was left of the body, Chester approached him from behind.

"I'm sorry about the camera and losing my cool—"

"Yeah," the man spun around, "but sorry doesn't fix it or make up for the time we've lost on this shoot."

Chester stared into the man's solemn face. Without taking his eyes off him, he put his hand in the pocket of his baggy Dickies and slowly pulled out a small wad of bills.

I sat up for the first time, gawking at the roll of green.

"How much for a new one?" Chester asked.

The crowd stirred with sighs of awe, notes of surprise, and scattered laughter. "Don't do it," someone barked. "Keep your money," another yelled.

Staring flabbergasted at the bills, the dark-skinned man backed up a step and scowled, then met Chester's eyes. "It's a professional rig. Digital. Sony. It'll cost me thirty-two hundred. Whatever you can give me toward it."

Chester licked his fingers, thumbed through the bills, and stuck out a wad.

"Whoa!" someone yelled. And a smattering of applause broke out.

"Here's thirty-two," Chester said. "And again, I'm sorry I lost my temper. But what you're doing is wrong. We're all God's children. You know that. Don't ignore it. These men have feelings, just like you and me."

The dark-skinned man reached for the money, shooting Chester a tense glance. "I didn't expect this."

Chester put his remaining money back in his pocket and gently grasped the man's free hand. "Sometimes we get what we least deserve," he said.

As if in a trance, the man looked down at Chester's reddish-brown hand locked in his.

Time seemed to freeze.

Then Chester whispered something I couldn't hear. I don't think anyone could, except the man, who continued staring at Chester's hand in his.

After several moments,' Chester shook hard one time, leaned close, whispered something more in his ear, patted his shoulder, and nodded good-bye. The dark-skinned man watched him all the way over to me, then looked down, turning his palm upward, examining the hand Chester Holte had so tenderly held.

1

After explaining that Chester had known some of the workers at the Downtown Outreach Clinic, and that he'd helped her land her job there, Holly rose suddenly. "I'm sorry." The fingers of both of her hands were intertwined in front of her, and her face was pink. "I've really got to go."

"Okay…"

"I don't mean to be rude."

"No, I'm grateful for your time." I gathered our trash. "Let me walk you out."

She'd started for the door. "You don't have to."

"Wait." I disposed of the trash, made sure I had my pad and phone, and caught up with her. As soon as Holly and I pushed the doors open to leave Maxine's, she clammed up and practically made a beeline for her pickup.

"What's the hurry?" I asked.

A car roared to life thirty yards away.

That was the hurry. It was her boyfriend, that Kenny character, sitting there in the dark, starting to rev his engine.

Great.

As the smell of fuel filled the warm night air, I thought we might have a showdown on our hands.

Holly hurried into the Toyota and yelled an out-of-breath "See you," barely looking back. It surprised me that a smart, strong girl like her would be involved with such a domineering nut case. And it ticked me off that he was there, waiting for her, like she was some teenage schoolgirl.

I huffed toward my car, jaw locked tight, wearing my nastiest Clint Eastwood face, eyes fixed on Kenny boy. As I got in my car, Holly scooted her pickup out to the main road. Sure enough, old hot rod smoked his tires and jumped right on her bumper. I wanted badly to follow but had to get to work. And then they were gone, him squealing behind her into the Las Vegas night.

Shaking my head, I rolled out of Maxine's. The way Holly had described it, Kenny caught her on the rebound from her down-and-out days on the streets, and she felt as if she owed him. She'd told me he was an air force brat, stationed north of the Strip at Nellis Air Force Base. He had some mental issues after having served in Operation Desert Storm, so, in a way, it was like the blind leading the blind.

I couldn't help but wonder if he'd ever hurt her physically. But Holly seemed way too sharp to let that happen.

Back at the *Review-Journal* newsroom, city editor Beth White, wearing jeans and an orange T-shirt, insisted she didn't mind me being late, especially because I'd called in. All she cared was that I got the obits and police beat to her on time; she knew I was good for it.

I knocked the obits out in less than an hour and a half at my cubicle, situated adjacent to a large window overlooking the *Review-Journal*'s courtyard and fountain. Then, before heading to the police station, I stared out at the shimmering water and blue fountain lights, the cash in Chester's safe-deposit box haunting me. The newsroom was dark and still.

You should have taken some while you had the chance.

But this was a murder case. Sooner or later, the cops would find out. Why they didn't know already baffled me. I was coming to the reality that I probably needed to go to them, before they showed up for me.

What was I thinking, searching his pockets?

Idiot.

Although I hadn't treated him like one, Chester had been a human being, a much more honorable man than I am. I was sitting smack-dab on top of his murder case and someone knew it.

Will whoever killed Chester show up for me next?

Seeing no one in the basement reception area at the LVMPD, I rapped on the large window that separated me from the fluorescent glow of police radios, maps, clipboards, telephones, and small, blinking red and orange scanner lights.

I hoped I'd get somebody who was in a good mood. So many cops were puffed up, rednecks with nothing better to do than give reporters—and everyone else—a hard time. Then again, it took a special breed to keep the streets safe. I'd learned if I stroked cops' egos a bit, I could usually get what I needed.

After knocking on the glass again, harder, I paced the waiting area. It was dark, except for a light shining from a glass showcase containing various LVMPD trophies and plaques, which I'd viewed a hundred times while waiting during past visits.

"Whatchya need?"

Didn't know this guy. Heavyset. White coffee mug in fist. Round face. Thick black mustache and a small amount of black hair arced across the top of his wide forehead.

"Hey, I'm Hudson Ambrose with the *R-J*." I held my ID up to the window. "Just need all your reports from the past twenty-four."

He stepped closer, squinted at my press badge, and sipped. "Take me a few minutes."

"That's fine."

As often happened on those weekend night shifts, I seriously doubted I'd been given all the information I should have. The clipboard the officer slid through the silver opening ten minutes later contained about fifteen one- and two-page police reports, filled out by LVMPD officers who'd responded to the scenes of various crimes and accidents since I'd been there the night before.

There was nothing on Chester. Nothing about the Civic Center North bus stop.

Ignoring numerous fender-bender reports, I quickly jotted notes about several messy domestic disputes, a drug bust in the parking deck at the MGM Grand, a public disturbance outside Bally's, a suicide threat down in Green Valley, and two hookers who'd been arrested outside Barbary Coast.

Standing from one of the many shiny, black chairs that bordered the waiting room, I slid the clipboard back through the metal slot and debated whether to press the guy.

"Thanks a lot."

"No problem." The officer was sitting amid a stack of papers, squeezing some kind of exercise ball in his big fist.

I decided to give it a shot. "You haven't heard anything about any kind of attack up at the Civic Center North bus stop, have you?"

He tossed the ball into the opposite hand, leaned back in his squeaky chair, and peered up at me. "What kind of attack?"

"I heard someone may've been hurt up that way this morning, early."

"If a report was filed, you'da had it here." He nodded toward the clipboard, scratched his wide nose, and looked up at me.

"Can I ask, what would happen if officers responded to a call there but found nothing? Would there be a record of it?"

"Our CAD system keeps a record of all calls." He leaned forward and tapped several keys on his keyboard. "Where'd you say it was? Civic North?"

"That's right." I couldn't believe he was helping me. "It would have been about six this morning."

His badge read Murphy, and his face glowed white in the reflection of the computer screen as he pecked at the keyboard.

"Here it is." He lifted an index finger toward the screen, which I tried to see but bumped my head on the glass and couldn't. "It was a false alarm. Let's see, we got an anonymous tip about an injured person. Turned out to be nothing. One of the officers that checked it out reported the scene was secure."

"So there *was* a report filed?"

"No, I didn't say that. There was no paper report. The officer documented the scene using the mobile data terminal in his car. He wrote that everything checked out fine. No formal report was filed."

"Okay." I nodded. "Can you tell me, by any chance, which officers responded?"

Murphy stared at me for what seemed like thirty seconds. "I can't give that out."

"Can you say how many cars responded?

He looked at the screen and back at me. "I've said enough. There was no crime up there, okay?" He wheeled his chair backward and clasped his hands behind his head. "Is that gonna do it for you?"

I didn't want to blow a good contact.

"Yeah, you've been a big help. Thanks."

After hammering out the police beat back at the paper, I saved it along with the obits and began drilling around on the Internet, confident Beth would think I was still working on official *R-J* business.

"Drake Needermire" was the first topic I searched in Yahoo. His name came up on several long lists of LVMPD officers honored with local auxiliary awards. But I wasn't looking for honors; I was digging for dirt.

The only other reference I could find led me to some quotes Needermire made in the middle of a story written by the *R-J* 's own Suzette Graham, entitled "Homeless Get Early-Morning Eviction." The lead described the city's homeless as "wandering the streets" of Las Vegas after the mayor ordered an early-morning crackdown on the Owens Avenue encampment.

"The businesses and families in this area have been furious, almost to the breaking point," said Sergeant Drake Needermire of the LVMPD. "You can't blame them. These encampments are a safety hazard, a health risk, and they're illegal; they do an injustice to local business owners and to the kids trying to catch the school bus down here. It's not a matter of *if* this place is going to be cleaned up, but *when*. This type of filthy habitation shouldn't be accepted here any more than it should in Aliente or Summerlin. There are plenty of shelters and housing vouchers for these people."

Belligerent tough guy, just like Holly described.

But an official with the Nevada Health Centers commented in the story that the local shelters were overcrowded and that the "sweep" did nothing more than disrupt the lives of the homeless and scatter them to other parts of the city.

I made myself a note to get Needermire's contact information from Suzette Graham, then did a search on the other two "bad" cops Holly had mentioned, Loy and Sanchez, but found nothing of consequence.

It was almost 2 a.m. when I got up to stretch. Suppressing the desire for a cigarette, I strolled to the city desk and asked Beth if she wanted a soda, but she held up one of those big gallon drinks from 7-Eleven and a bag of pork rinds. *No thanks.*

In the empty courtyard outside, a warm breeze nudged my hair as I looked up at the gibbous moon. The soothing sound of water splashing in the fountain made me aware of how tense I was. Reaching up, I felt the crease in my forehead, then made myself relax by releasing the tension, starting in my head and shoulders, and working all the way down to my feet. I'd seen the exercise on TV.

Scraping together all my change, I bought a can of Dr Pepper at one of the machines and took a seat at a brown, wrought-iron table next to the fountain, counting the hours—thirty-one—before I could get back into Chester's safe-deposit box.

Why would anyone want such a nice person dead? Maybe whoever killed him knew about his money and was trying to get to it. What was Chester doing, living on the streets? He couldn't have just been spreading good cheer, or "the Gospel"; there had to have been some kind of personal gain.

"The Gospel." That's what my old man had called it the last time I saw him. "The Good News." After my mom died and he drank himself and his business into oblivion, he ended up stealing to feed us. That earned him twelve years in the big house in Victoria, and he got another five for throwing a prison guard off a three-story embankment where he was washing windows. Luckily, the guy lived.

Once behind bars, that's where my old man bought into my mom's religion. Even though she was long gone, he finally accepted her "Jesus" and swore he'd be meeting her in paradise. The last time I saw him, his blue eyes were so clear, his hair was combed neatly; somehow he just looked healthier. He searched my eyes, asked questions, and sat uncharacteristically still. It was almost spooky. After Mom died, when the drinking was at its worst, I was certain demons had ransacked his soul. But on that last visit, on that fall day in Victoria, the peace and light that enveloped him made me wonder if my mother's God really lived.

Whatever.

If he needed a crutch, more power to him for finding one that worked for him.

Just like my old man did with me that last visit, Holly told me Chester had invited her to go to church. But, unlike me, she did go— to Spring Valley Community Church, a megacongregation of nine thousand people on the outskirts of Las Vegas. She described the facility as "more like a theater than a sanctuary." She called it the "clapping church," because there was a band with guitars, drums, and music videos. There was even a divorce-recovery group, where the people "loved her back to reality."

"There's a late service at eleven o'clock," Holly had said at Maxine's, "you should try it sometime." I politely declined. Number one, I didn't want to go to church, and number two, I had planned on going to check out the abandoned van Arthur Peabody had told me about, where Chester's belongings were supposed to be—if they weren't already picked over by then.

On the way back inside to my desk, I wondered about a "bad

experience" Holly said Chester had gone through at his church in Atlanta. She hadn't expounded on it, only saying that he'd found God after Candice died, but following several years of involvement, almost completely turned his back on the church—until he met Suzette Graham's brother, Ellery, in Las Vegas.

Setting the Dr Pepper on my desk, I plunked down and typed "Ellery Graham" into the Yahoo search. Spring Valley Community Church was the first listing to appear, followed by Amazon listings of the pastor's books, seminars where he'd spoken, and various TV and newspaper stories in which he'd been featured.

Popular dude.

One story in the online version of *Time* magazine, in particular, grabbed my attention. I clicked and scrolled and clicked again. But the young man pictured—with a toothy grin, freckles, one dimple, and short, messy blond hair—couldn't possibly be a pastor, especially not the pastor of the so-called megachurch in Spring Valley.

What could a kid like him possibly do, say, or know that could attract so many people? I began reading.

SCANDALOUS GRACE

By Steve Vinton

What do some of Las Vegas's most well-known gamblers, strippers, celebrities, musicians, gangsters, attorneys, crack addicts, comedians, and even lap dancers have in common? They attend Spring Valley Community Church, just west of the Strip, where boyish pastor Ellery Graham insists, "We're here to reach people who are far from God."

In a neon metropolis that's known for its love of underdogs, Ellery Graham's church is beating all odds. But why?

Why is Graham's church—which, as you approach it via
sprawling parking lots, looks more like a pro-football stadium
than a house of God—succeeding in reaching so many Las
Vegans for God?

"Las Vegas is one of the lower educated cities in America,
but our people have remarkable street smarts," says Graham,
from his richly appointed office. "People size me up in two minutes. If I'm real, they'll accept my quirky weirdness. But if I'm
fake, they'll walk in a New York minute."

So what does Graham do?

Quite simply, he and his flock love people.

"You don't have to tell people in Las Vegas they're lost.
People here know about evil and sin; they've lived it, they
already feel guilty about it, and many of them are open to another
way of life," says Graham. "Jesus came to seek and save the
lost, and that's what our church is here to do."

Graham believes many of the six thousand to eight thousand people who move to Las Vegas each month do so to
escape their pasts and to try and make a new start. "The only
problem with a U-Haul is that 'U-Haul' your problems with you.
You want to drown your sorrows, but sorrows swim. The broken
come to Las Vegas, not perceiving their need for God. But
when they find out the promise of Vegas is empty, that it's all a
facade, and they crash and burn, we want to be here for them."

That they are. The church baptizes an average of 250 people
each month, and offers a myriad of Christ-centered support
groups for those struggling from the fallout of divorce, abuse,
addiction, homelessness, bereavement, incarceration, grief,
depression, and on and on. The place is almost always open.

However, there is one thing Graham is clear on—Christians

cannot have a judgmental, "legalistic" spirit if they are going to have an impact for God in Sin City.

"You cannot be on a crusade against gambling and the Strip and at the same time live and witness in this town. Life in Las Vegas is inseparable from the Strip. People say the city has diversified with different industries but at the end of the day, we're kidding ourselves if we think this town is ultimately thriving on much more than what happens on Las Vegas Boulevard."

So, instead of fighting the gambling clubs and strip joints of Las Vegas, the people of Spring Valley Community Church take their faith into the enormous casinos and plush hotels that have essentially made Las Vegas the most visited destination in the world.

"The culture war is over, we lost, and we refuse to fight that battle," says Graham. "What we do want to do is get down in the trenches and love people into God's kingdom."

Graham's church members work as cocktail waitresses, maids, chefs, actresses, parking attendants, and card dealers. "Are we changing the moral climate? No. Are we closing down porn shops? No. But, are people's lives being changed for eternity? Yes. C. S. Lewis once said, 'The greatest political act is a changed life,' and that's what we believe."

After gambling away his family's savings, Jon Tangier, sitting at an empty blackjack table with dealer and Spring Valley Community Church member Jodie Fernandez, says he was ready to end his life—until Fernandez reached out to him.

"She could see the anguish in my countenance," recalls Tangier. "I was at the end of my rope. I was not going home again. But Jodie asked me what was going on. I actually broke down at her table. She shared Christ with me. She shared His

concern. She kept me alive another day. Then we went to her
church and my whole family got baptized. We've never been so
strapped, financially, but we've never been happier either."

Graham admits some Christians may be uncomfortable
attending church with the likes of strippers and notorious gamblers, but he insists every member of his congregation is a
"work in progress."

"In the Bible Belt we may get questioned, but in this town,
we're a force for good. We accept people where they are," he
says. "It can be a slow process. I know of an exotic dancer who
began attending our church and accepted Christ, but found it
very difficult to take a job at Starbucks and say no to the $6,000
a week she was making dancing. But people like her are being
impacted by God's Word, their hearts are being pierced, and
they are transitioning."

At two million people strong, Las Vegas is the fastest
growing city in America. It is visited by forty to fifty million
people each year (more than visit the White House annually),
and projections show its population could double within the
next ten years.

"The city has reinvented itself," says Graham. "It's almost
like a suburb of L.A. So, it's really 'in' right now. They say the
city lights of Vegas are the first sign of life from space, and we
hope our church is the light of the Strip. Our hope is to minister
to the poor, help the helpless, and step up and be Jesus to the
orphans, widows, and homeless of this town."

Humph.

I closed out of Yahoo before finishing the article, drained my Dr
Pepper, tossed the can in the wastebasket, pulled out my notepad, and

stared. The soapy smell of Chester's dead body drifted back, vividly, as did the scratchy, cheap feel of his empty pockets, the weight of his leaning body, and the black overcoat and Converse high tops—stuck in the puddle of his own blood.

I pictured helpless Arthur Peabody being washed away in the night storm, Holly Queens bracing for death beneath the blows of a deranged cop, and Chester—being there in the fire with them. I imagined the startled look on the cameraman's face when Chester handed him thirty-two hundred bucks and clasped his hand like a father.

Okay, cut the drama. You need sleep.

Snapping out of it, I composed a brief e-mail to Beth at the city desk, attached the obits and police beat, and fired it off. Straightening clutter and collecting my things, I built a plan for the hours ahead: get some sleep, check out the vacant van in the morning, and track down Sergeant Drake Needermire after that. On Monday I'd be at the bank when it opened to check the box. Then I'd weigh everything and decide what to do next.

Throwing away some unneeded paperwork, I glanced at my watch, 4:50 a.m., then my desk calendar, August 13. *The day Mom died.* Twenty years ago. How the years had flown.

"One thing I want you to do," my old man had said that last visit with him at the Victoria penitentiary, "please, Hudson, take care of your mother's grave. Maybe do some flowers on special occasions."

Weeds. I envisioned weeds everywhere, sprawling over her gray headstone in that blazing San Antonio cemetery.

"Hud?" Beth squinted down from the city desk, holding her phone in the air. "This lady asked for you. I'm gonna transfer her. She sounds kind of out of it."

Who would be calling this early?

It rang once and I picked up. "Hudson Ambrose."

Maybe it's about Chester.

Nothing.

"This is Ambrose."

There was movement, breathing, then a soft squeal. "Can you help me?"

"Who is this?"

"Holly." She moaned. "Ohh…it's bad this time."

8

olly's was one of several houses on a short cul-de-sac smack dab in the middle of Old Downtown, just minutes from the *Review-Journal*. My headlights swept over her light blue, one-story, cinder-block house on First Street, complete with whitewashed shutters, rocking chairs, American flag, and bars on the windows.

Her pickup was in the driveway, and after hearing no answer, I discovered the front door unlocked.

"Holly?" I stepped into the darkness.

"Here."

Light from another room cast shadows over the couch where she lay. My eyes adjusted to the dimness. Framed paintings hung neatly about. There were rugs and candles and books. It was clean and welcoming. I would have liked to have been arriving for dinner or a date.

"Sorry." Several quick, stuttered breaths came loud. "I couldn't reach anyone else. I knew I could trust you."

"What happened?" I walked toward her, slow and gentle, almost afraid of what I might see.

A clump of bloodied, wet paper towels lay on her neck.

"He's jealous," she whimpered, adjusting a plastic bag of ice on her forehead. "I can't get out of it. I'm sorry I called. I thought I may have a concussion or something. I'll be okay."

She wore the same jeans and black tank.

I knelt and lifted the wad of paper towels. A thin, two-inch sliver of blood still glistened at the base of her neck.

"What did he do?"

"Cut me. It's not the first time."

"With what?"

"He's a knife freak."

"Let me see your head."

She lowered the bag of ice.

My hand shot to my mouth, and my breath left me. I stared at the kitchen light, as if gathering strength, then peered back down at her.

"What on earth happened here?"

The welt at the center of her forehead was the size of a quarter of a baseball. Shadows orbited beneath her eyes, or were they bruises? I pushed the bag of ice back up where it belonged as my shock rapidly transitioned to rage.

She stared at me, as if in a trance. "My arms ache."

I leaned close. Dark spots from his grip seemed to grow even as I examined them, above the crease on each arm. "How long has it been happening?"

"Long."

There was an extended pause as I repeatedly tapped my fist to my mouth. "Did he do this because we met tonight?"

She nodded.

My teeth clenched.

"What did he do, hit you here?" I eyed her forehead.

"Uh-uh." She closed her eyes and shook her head slightly, then motioned toward a grapefruit-size hole in the drywall in the dining area.

My heart bashed against my rib cage.

"He hit your head against the wall?"

One slow nod and I was on my feet.

"Where does he live?"

I was shaking.

"Near the base."

"Specifically!"

"You can't...he's a maniac," she blurted. "He'll kill you."

I huffed and crossed my arms, feeling like the space shuttle at liftoff.

"Count to ten," my mother would say. "Slow to anger, remember?"

Lowering my head into the palm of my hand, I felt the ridge in my forehead and rubbed it softly with my fingers.

One, two, three, four, five...

"I'm gonna get new ice." Making myself cool down, I took the sweating bag into the kitchen. A framed photo on the counter showed Holly and Van Dillon in better days. Or were they better? Pictures sometimes did lie, I decided right then.

Like the living room, the kitchen was clean, simple, and cozy. There was a low, wooden table with benches in an eating nook against a bay window, and old-fashioned wall hangings filled the room, including tapestries and pewter and copper cookware.

Dumping the sloshing cubes into the sink, I got fresh ones out of the freezer and debated how to handle the situation. Between my lack of sleep and the whole Chester ordeal, the last thing I needed was to do something stupid and step into another hornet's nest. I could give her the bag of ice, wish her the best, and go home.

But I liked her, and she needed help. Not to mention the fact that she was cute. I knew, if given the chance, I could make her laugh and help her forget her past. But this was not the time…

"Are you still in danger?" I knelt beside her, placed the bag of ice on her forehead, and held it there. "Or, is this over?"

"He'll lay low." She sighed and turned away. "Then he'll come crawling back, crying, apologizing…"

I looked at the welt again. "Are you gonna be okay? Maybe I should take you to the emergency room."

She felt the lump, sighed, and closed her pretty eyes. "It'll be all right."

"Well, we've got to do something, Holly." I gripped her left shoulder and forced her to look at me. "What do you want me to do? Call the police? Take you to a safe house? Beat the tar out of the guy?"

She blinked slowly at me. "Do you pray?"

At the sound of quick, hard knocks at the front door, I let go of the ice and jumped to my feet. Ready to bash the lights out of Ken Van Dillon, I took one last glimpse at wide-eyed Holly before throwing the door open.

"Whoa!" The fists of the young man I faced jutted up, and the dark-haired woman beside him blew backward three steps.

"Who are you?" My heart thundered.

"Friends of Holly's," the guy yelled. "Who are you?"

Holly said something I couldn't make out. I turned to ask what, and the guy took the frightened woman's hand and barreled through the front door.

"Oh, Holly!" The lady ran and hugged Holly. The man approached and knelt beside her as well, examining her face, neck, and arms, as if he were a social worker who'd seen this kind of abuse before.

"This is my friend, Hudson," Holly eyed me.

"Hey," the young man turned toward me and sighed. "Sorry about that at the door. I guess we surprised each other." He smiled, reached out his hand, and I shook it. "I'm Ellery." He gestured toward his wife, who was still clinging to Holly. "This is my wife, Jenna." He nodded. "Thanks for being here."

"You too," I said, realizing this was the boy-wonder pastor I had just read about—and reporter Suzette Graham's brother.

An awkward silence floated in the darkness.

Ellery nodded to Holly. "What do you think, Jenna?"

Without turning from Holly, his wife spoke. "She's gonna make it. The cut on her neck isn't deep, thank God. I think there are going to be some dark circles under her eyes from where the blood's draining from the bump."

I crossed the room, stood over Holly, and saw what Jenna meant, even in the dark.

"This has gotta be the last time." Jenna flared. "I say we call the police right now. Get a restraining order. I don't care what Van Dillon says. I'll stay here, live here, if I have to; or she can come live with us. This has gotta stop!"

"I don't know if you know," Ellery addressed me, "but Van Dillon has threatened to kill Holly if she ever goes to the police. And he's been…specific about his threats."

"Says he'll kill me, then himself, with his hunting rifle." Holly's head turned away from us. "I know he'd do it."

"Our elders have confronted him," Ellery said.

"He doesn't go to your church!"

"He did. We asked him to leave."

"Because of this?"

"Yeah. The ultimate hope is that he's restored to the church—and saved."

My old man had used that word the last few times I saw him: *saved*. Thing was, I didn't need "saving" because I wasn't enslaved to anyone, and I certainly was no Ken Van Dillon.

The girls squeezed each other and began to whisper as Jenna stroked Holly's silky black hair.

"How do you know Holly?" Ellery turned to face me.

"We just met, actually." Then it dawned on me that it was five thirty in the morning and that answer probably didn't sound too great, especially to a pastor. "I'm doing a story. I'm a reporter for the *R-J*. I know your sister, Suzette." I snickered at my own clumsiness. "Holly and I spent a few hours together last night, because I'm researching a homeless man who's missing; he's a friend of Holly's. In fact, she said you know him: Chester Holte."

Ellery grimaced. "Missing? What do you mean? What happened?"

"Through some police contacts, I heard Chester was hurt. They say he's missing. That's all I know." I didn't like the fact that the lies were rolling off my tongue so effortlessly. "I went to the Outreach Clinic because I knew he had friends there. That's where I met Holly and Van Dillon."

Ellery rested his hands on his waist, glanced down at the girls and back at me. "First of all," he whispered, "Van Dillon's got serious problems. I don't know if he's bipolar or what. We've tried to get him in for psychiatric treatment, and away from Holly, for months." He ran a hand through his messy blond hair, peered down at Holly, and shook his head. "This has got to stop."

I waited to see what he suggested we do.

"Tell me more about Chester. Are you sure he just hasn't been out of sight for a few days? That happens with him sometimes. Where'd you hear he was hurt?"

"One lie always leads to another," Mom would say.

"Through a police contact."

"So the police are on it?"

"Right." I turned my back on him and walked to one of the front windows.

"Are you sure he's not in a local hospital?"

I hesitated, treading carefully. "No, he's not."

"Do you know how bad he's hurt?

"I'm trying to find out more."

He came to me at the window. "Chester's special. He's a dear friend. I'll do anything I can to help."

I looked into his unflinching brown eyes and said, "I'd like to sit down and talk with you, when I'm fresh. I just worked the night shift…"

Ellery pulled out his wallet, fished out a business card, and handed it to me. "My cell phone's on here. Call anytime."

He asked if he could follow up with me on Chester, and I gave him my number.

Ellery walked toward Holly and looked down at her. "I do think it's time for intervention. There are places you can go to get away, Holly."

"I am not leaving this house," she yelled, then withered from the exertion. "Besides, he knows where I work. What am I supposed to do, quit my job? And what about church?"

Ellery shook his head. "It's so tricky."

"He would be booked for this," I said. "Assault and battery. He could go to jail for a long time."

"You do *not* want to do that," Holly said.

"Sooner or later, someone's got to stand up to the guy, Holly," I said. "Whether that means calling the cops or beating him to a pulp. I'd like to go pay him a visit myself right now!"

The room was silent, except for a clock ticking somewhere and slight movement from the plastic bag at Holly's head.

"You guys haven't seen what he's like," Holly whispered. "We cannot call the police. He doesn't care about his life. He'd just as soon die—"

"This is nuts!" I burst. "This guy cannot control you like this."

"All right, all right." Ellery held up a hand. "I really think the right thing to do is to call the police, Holly." She began to object, but he pointed an index finger at her. "I know you don't want to, but we, as outsiders looking in, see the physical damage that's been done, and we can't close our eyes to it."

"He's right." Jenna leaned near Holly's face. "If we let this go, you *will* die."

Holly's eyes closed, she shook her head, and a tear streaked down her face.

"I agree," I said. "This guy needs to be put away."

"That'll be fine, for now." Holly glared at me. "But you and the police won't be here when he gets out. I'll be here, alone, just like this morning—and it won't be pretty."

9

etween hotels and casinos, the rocky desert horizon was just
starting to turn a hazy yellow as I drove Holly to police headquarters. I was exhausted, but wired, feeling like a bodyguard,
scanning every car and bystander for Ken Van Dillon. A friendly, red-
cheeked cop named Tom Fitzgerald offered us coffee, photographed
Holly's wounds, took a full report, and said he'd call Holly or me
when an arrest had been made.

Instead of taking Holly home, I told her she could hang with me
until Van Dillon was arrested, and she agreed.

Back at my house, she returned to the kitchen with the cup of tea
I had made for her minutes earlier. "What happened to your door?"

"Huh?" The heat rose in my face and I swallowed hard. "Oh, I
had a break-in."

"Recent, I guess."

"Yeah." I swigged my Dr Pepper and fought for words. "Within
the past few days."

She chuckled. "Well, sheesh, I'm definitely glad I came *here* instead of my place."

I laughed but felt uncomfortably deceptive.

"Did they take anything?" she asked.

Careful.

"They got away with a few valuables, but everything else was pretty much left untouched. Weird."

"Like, what did they take? Jewelry?"

It really wouldn't be lying, there were the rings.

"Yeah, mostly jewelry."

I wanted desperately to tell her the truth, to give her the whole story about Chester, from start to finish. She was a cool girl. I liked her. I thought there might even be a spark between us. But I knew I had probably already blown it by waiting too long, continuing the lie.

"This place has a lot of potential." She wandered from room to room.

"Yeah, I know." I followed her into the living room, with its bare walls and basic oak furniture package from Rooms To Go. "It's a great house. I just haven't had time to do much to it. Seems like I'm always working."

"It's got some cool angles and nooks and crannies. I could have a field day in here, with the right budget." She turned to me with a smile, but it faded quickly, and I knew she must be aching—physically and mentally—behind the dark purple half circles that underlined her eyes.

"You need sleep. How 'bout we put you to bed in my room upstairs? It gets nice and dark in there." I started for the steps. "I'll throw on some clean sheets."

"You don't have to give up your bed for me."

"I want to." I swung around. "It's really comfortable."

"I won't sleep." The words barely got out before she cupped her mouth, winced, and turned away.

"Oh." I rushed over, touching her back. "It's okay. They're gonna get him. He'll get what he deserves, okay? You're going to be all right. It's gonna be a whole new start for you."

She leaned toward me. "I'm scared."

"Don't be." I drew her close, my head above hers, each of us looking in different directions. "I'll be right here on the couch."

"Where will you be when he gets out?"

"I can be close if you need me to."

"Where's Chester?" she whispered. "Is he dead?"

Like long, crooked fingers, her words probed painfully within the caverns of my soul, and I couldn't answer.

We stood in silence.

"I'm gonna make your bed." I patted her back.

"Do you have a Bible?" She pulled away, rubbed her eyes, and looked up at me.

I knew the answer immediately, but for some reason it took me a few seconds to respond. "Yeah, I do. I was just trying to remember where it is. It was my mom's."

"Was?" She sniffed.

"She died a long time ago. I was fifteen."

"I'm sorry. How did it happen?"

"Pneumonia." I remembered Mom's stuffy hospital room and her last radiant, teary-eyed smile from beneath the light blue blanket.

"That must have been hard for your family."

Talking about it is foreign to me.

"Yeah." Dad had clung to her for ninety minutes after she

closed her beautiful eyes for the last time. "We hit the skids after that."

"Sit down." She guided me to the couch, pulling my arm. "Let's talk."

Is this happening? She's so lovely. Fantastic figure. A face you'd never grow tired of... Don't get carried away, Ambrose, she's a Christian, remember? They're all supposed to be caring like that. Although most aren't, she just so happens to be the real McCoy.

"Tell me about it." She plopped down.

"Why?"

"I want to know more. Do you have brothers and sisters?"

I sat. "Nope, just me."

"Where're you from?"

"San Antonio. The old man had a bar on the River Walk, one of my favorite places in the whole world."

"You don't sound like a Texas boy."

"I know. For some reason I never picked up the accent."

She smiled. "How old are you?"

"Thirty-four."

She nodded, and I wondered if she'd thought I was older or younger than that. I was curious about her age and guessed she was in her mid to late twenties, but knew from my mother's upbringing that it wasn't polite to ask a lady.

"You ever been to San Antonio?" I said.

"Never."

"You need to go. It's special. The river winds right through the city. There are all kinds of romantic cafés and restaurants, right on the water, with candles and music."

"Sounds wonderful."

I nodded, picturing a flatboat packed with tourists, drifting down the San Antonio at dusk; tasting the homemade raspberry chip ice cream from Snyder's; and working out with buddies in the stale air, on the creaky wood floors at Gordy's Gym.

"What happened after your mom died?"

"The old man started drinking—never had before."

"Uh-oh."

"Yeah. We lost the bar. He's in jail now in Victoria."

"For what?"

"Armed robbery. He was stealing food for us."

"Oh my goodness, Hudson, how sad." She leaned close, the bruises beneath her eyes darkening by the second. She looked like damaged goods, and I felt like them. "I'm so sorry for you. Do you stay in touch with him?"

"I did for years, but it got to a point where I couldn't take it anymore. He never showed remorse for anything." I squirmed and scanned the room for cigarettes. "Anyway, all I did was work and drive to Victoria, work and drive to that blasted prison."

"Where'd you work?"

"A newspaper in San Antonio. The *Express-News*. City hall reporter. I was there a long time."

We were totally engaged. I could have sat there all night, all morning, whatever it was. But at the same time, I found myself embarrassed by my past, angry for ever having lied to her in the first place, and afraid she would catch me in it.

"How long will he have to serve?" she asked.

"Originally, eight years. But he hurt somebody pretty bad and got another four. He used to have a wicked temper. Runs in the family."

She shrunk back, and I rewound my last words, figuring out what a dunce I was.

"Oh, he never touched my mom or anything." I reached out to her. "I didn't mean to make it sound like that, like he abused us."

She caught her breath and nodded.

"He's changed a lot anyway."

"So, you do keep in touch?"

"No." I dropped my head, massaging my forehead, feeling that darn ridge. "We had an argument a year or so ago. That's when I left town."

"And you haven't talked to him since?"

"Uh-uh."

"What was it about?"

"You'd make a good reporter."

She blinked slowly and arched her dark eyebrows. "Well?"

"No comment at this time." I smirked.

"Off limits?"

"For now." I shrugged. "It's a long story."

She seemed to explore my mind with her gaze.

"He still writes," I heard myself say.

Her attractive mouth opened, her eyes widened with surprise, and she waited for more.

"I don't read the letters, and I don't write back."

She slapped her thigh. "I'm sorry, Hudson Ambrose, but that is so immature. You owe it to him to read his letters; he's your father!"

"I don't owe him anything," I snarled. "He waited too long to get my mom to the hospital, trying to save money. The idiot! The letters are gone anyway. I pitch 'em the minute they get here."

"Oh, so you blame him for your mother's death?"

"I'm telling you, he waited *days* before getting her to a hospital! What kind of love is that? Business was bad, he was having a hard time making payroll, and my mom's health was one of the places he decided to save some coin."

"I see. So you're bitter and you're going to stay that way the rest of your life."

"I have reason to be bitter! How responsible was it of him to start hitting the sauce when she died? He became an alcoholic, okay? There were mornings when I had to go out on the streets and find him and bring him home. It got to the point where he didn't bring food home anymore. I had to feed us."

I fumed and let out a hideous laugh at the same time. The whole thing blew my mind. I hadn't spoken about such personal matters with a woman, ever! Holly Queens was pushing my buttons, and in a weird kind of way, it was a sweet release.

"I'm bitter and I have a right to be."

"Mmm, mmm, mmm." She shook her head with a slight smile, her mouth sealed. "Have you ever put yourself in your dad's shoes? It sounds like he loved your mom. Can you imagine how he felt, losing her?"

"He had a child to look after, okay?" I knew in the deepest part of me that I should consider what Holly had just said, but I had never let myself get to that place. "Just because he lost my mom, that didn't give him the right to screw my life up! I needed a father. After Mom died, I never had one—still don't, as far as I'm concerned."

Holly looked down and shook her head, scolding me with her silence.

"Okay, another subject." I leaned back and clasped my hands behind my head. "What about you? You don't plan to stay in Las Vegas forever, do you?

She crossed her arms and rubbed her biceps.

"You cold?" I asked.

"Kind of."

"I can kick off the AC." I did so, then went to the hall closet and brought back a gray hooded sweatshirt. "Here you go."

"Thanks." She put it on, zipped it, and pushed up the sleeves, looking even cuter than before. "This is home for me. You saw my house. I've worked hard at it. I love it. My neighbors are great. That whole cul-de-sac has been rejuvenated; those are some of the city's original houses. Plus, my job is rewarding. And my church is here. I'm not supposed to go anywhere."

It pleased me that Holly had been able to continue the conversation after the negative stuff about my old man. I knew I had my share of baggage, which I wasn't ready to face yet. And it gave me great hope in my heart to know Holly refused to judge me or put up a wall.

"Sounds like you know what you want," I said. "That's good."

"It's not so much what *I* want. Believe me." She measured an inch between her thumb and pointer finger. "I've come this close to taking off in the middle of the night to get away from Kenny. But God hasn't let me. There's a purpose for me here in Las Vegas. Chester and the homeless community are a big part of it."

Every time I almost forgot about the beloved Chester, he arose, like some cryptic ghost—the infamous angel on my shoulder. But I didn't want to get onto that topic for fear Holly would bust me and I'd be forced to wake up from that intimate dream.

"You like your work."

"It's more than that." She faced me, her jean-clad legs curled beneath her, and one arm draped over the back of the couch. "My mom struggled with depression all her life, so it's in the genes. I battle it. But Chester's helped me get my eyes off myself. Life's about other people. It's about giving ourselves away. That's when you find real joy."

"The meaning of life, huh?"

"It is! Why do you think when you do something nice for someone, you feel so good?" She shook my arm in jest. "You have done
something nice for someone, haven't you?"

We roared.

"I'm serious." She threw her hair back. "Chester's on a mission.
He's contagious."

There it was. There *he* was. Chester Holte. The lie between us.

"His whole gig is about reaching people who are far from God.
That's what our church is about. That's what Ellery's about. It's what
I want to be about. You know what I'm saying?"

It was too much for me. Too much light. Too much purity. Too
much God. I was guilty, for crying out loud. I'd searched Chester's
dead body! I wanted his money. And yet, there I was, flirting with his
biggest fan, a woman who loved the God I chose to snub.

"You mind if I smoke?" I stood and didn't hear a response as I
headed for the kitchen.

Never mind!

I found a lighter and a scrunched-up pack of Vantages in the junk
drawer, fired one up, and quickly played out one potential scenario in
my mind.

*I could lay everything out for her, the whole truth. Tell her I made a
really bad mistake in searching Chester, and that I needed her to forgive
me, to love me unconditionally, like she'd just described.*

She'd go to Mars.

She'd go straight to the cops.

And I'd go to prison.

Her cup bumped down on the counter. "Thanks for the tea."
She stood within several feet of me. "I think I'd better try to get some
sleep."

"I'll make my bed up for you." I took a long drag on the fresh cigarette, exhaled away from Holly, and dowsed it under running water. The smoke tasted bitter and foreign. "I'm trying to quit these coffin nails. Actually down to two or three a day."

"That's good." She smiled.

I felt like an idiot for saying anything. What was I trying to do, justify myself?

"You think they've arrested him yet?" she asked.

I tossed the cigarette in the trash. The wall clock in the kitchen read 7:40 a.m.

"Don't know. You want me to call Fitzgerald?"

"No. He said he'd call."

"We can always try him in a little while if we don't hear from him."

"By the way," she said, "I left my cell phone at the clinic."

"We can get it for you after we get some sleep, okay?"

I headed upstairs, changed the sheets and pillow cases, and called Holly when the bed was ready. As I closed the curtains, she took off the sweatshirt I'd loaned her, kicked her shoes off, and slid beneath the covers.

"Can I get you anything?" I stood at the edge of the bed. "Need more ibuprofen?"

"I'm good."

"I'll be right downstairs. If you need anything, just call."

"Okay."

"Everything's gonna be fine."

"Thanks. I'm grateful for your help."

"Oh, wait a minute." I headed for a large chest that had been my mother's, hit my knees, pulled out the bottom drawer, and searched. "Aha."

Returning to the bed with my mom's Bible, I was struck by the immense smile that beamed from beneath her battered eyes and forehead.

"How sweet of you to remember." She wrapped her bruised arms around its worn, black leather cover. "Now I can rest."

It had been over forty hours since I'd had anything more than a cat nap, but it didn't feel as if sleep was coming then either. The living room was drenched in morning sunlight, and Holly's scent still fragranced the couch where I tossed.

Maybe I could still get out of the mess I'd made. I could go to the cops, tell them I'd found Chester's body, but was scared and had bolted. No need to mention the bankbook or key.

That will never work...

If the thing ever came to trial, there would be a dozen witnesses testifying that I'd been nosing around hours after finding the body, from Holly, Ellery, the coroner, and Arthur to Truax, Reed, Murphy the night cop, and the people at the bank.

No, I had to turn myself in before the authorities came looking for me, before Chester's body surfaced and I had to tell *all.* Going voluntarily could mean the difference between a slap on the wrist—maybe a bit more—and big prison time.

Again, I was whisked back to the putrid-smelling penitentiary in Victoria. "They scream and cry all night long," my old man whispered through the silver speaker, behind the glass partition. "The things that go on in here, Son, I can't even begin to describe. I try not to make eye contact with the other inmates, but there are days when I've been broken..."

What was he doing precisely at that moment? It was almost 9 a.m. my time, which made it 11 a.m. his. Maybe he was in the prison library. He loved it in there, even had a part-time job shelving books. Or, perhaps he was in his cell reading the Word, as he called it.

"The Word." Such a big deal to Christians. I recalled my mom's thin, soft hand resting on her black Bible, minutes before she gave up the ghost. And then the way Holly clutched that very Bible in her arms.

My cell phone rang. I hurried toward its ring in the kitchen, so it wouldn't wake Holly.

"Our officers arrested Ken Van Dillon at his apartment forty minutes ago, Mr. Ambrose," said Tom Fitzgerald of the LVMPD. "He's being booked now."

"Ah, that's good news." I sighed. "What happens next?"

"Once he's fingerprinted and photographed, he'll be seen by a judge, who'll either set bail or not."

"He can get out on bail? That's insane."

"Whether he gets out or not will be based on his priors."

"There's gotta be a restraining order or something, if he gets out."

"I would think so, but I'm not the judge."

"When do you think he'll see a judge?"

"Within seventy-two hours."

"Do they do that on Sundays?"

"Seven days a week."

"Okay. Thanks for following up. It means a lot."

The bank would be open in twenty-four hours. If I could just hold off until then to go to the police. That would give me time to search the van where Chester kept his stuff and see if anything was left in the safe-deposit box.

But why? What do I think I'm going to find in the van? Money?

Clues, maybe, to help solve the thing.

Why do I have to go back to the box? Why can't I just leave it in the hands of the police?

I needed to see if everything was still there. That would help me figure out—

Face it, this is still all about the money! I was living two lives. Part of me wanted to confess what I'd done, get it out in the open, and possibly be able to pursue a relationship with Holly somewhere down the road. But part of me was still conniving. Who knew what might happen if the money and stocks were still in the box? I might just take it all and never be seen again.

Finding a piece of scrap paper in the kitchen, I penned Holly a note telling her Van Dillon was behind bars and that I had gone to follow up on more Chester leads nearby.

> Call me when you get up and I'll take you to get your cell phone and get you home. Food in fridge. Make yourself comfortable. —Hud

She was on her stomach, sleeping hard, when I set the note at the foot of the bed and took off for the Lucky Lady, a deserted casino north of town that Arthur Peabody also called "The Graveyard."

10

I spotted the abandoned GMC conversion van right away, just as Arthur had described it. Dark green. No tire on the front right side. Covered in dust, about a hundred yards off the north end of the Strip, behind the boarded up casino.

Driving slowly toward the van with dust swirling behind me, I passed more than a dozen junk cars and trucks, all blanketed with Nevada grit. After coming to a stop in front of the boxy van, I got out and examined my surroundings.

There was movement in several of the vehicles. Thirty feet away, the door to an old, blue Chevy Nova sat wide open with someone sleeping on the black vinyl seat beneath layers of open newspapers.

I had nothing to defend myself with and made up my mind to work quickly and hightail it. Approaching the van, I took a deep breath and tried to prepare myself mentally for what I might find inside.

Cupping my hands, I peered in the driver's window, but could only make out several blankets, a red umbrella, and a cup and bag from Burger King. Walking toward the back of the van, I was unable to see in the tinted black windows along the side. When I got to the back, I looked around one last time, got my guts up, and yanked the door open.

Whew.

No people.

Good.

The rear seats were gone. Blankets, clothing, and newspapers were strewn about on the floor. I crawled in, preparing for the stench, but it never came. Tennis shoes caught my eye first. White Converse, with holes just above the big toe in each.

Chester's.

I found myself marveling at them, as if they'd been worn by some dignitary. The bottoms were smooth and shiny, with virtually no tread. A white book of matches dropped from one of the shoes. "The Deuce, Las Vegas." Inside, scribbled in black ink were the words "Jonathan Seabold."

Beneath the back of the front passenger seat, I spotted a small flashlight, a harmonica, and a pair of gold, wire-rimmed reading glasses. The flashlight turned on, bright, and I didn't like that. It made Chester too real, too recently there. The glasses were old-fashioned, with large lenses. I looked through them, not really sure why, wondering if they were his, I guess.

A small, white bucket tucked in the corner contained a toothbrush, a tube of Ultrabrite, a bar of soap, a washcloth, and a stick of Brut deodorant. I picked up the bar of white soap and held it to my nose.

Yep.

That was the way he smelled the other morning.

This was his.

I dropped the soap into the bucket. Several towels were folded neatly between the front seats. I opened the one on top, found nothing, and folded it up, then did the same with the other.

That's when an off-white envelope dropped in front of me. It was addressed, in plain type, to Chester Holte, P.O. Box 26722, Las Vegas, NV. The return address in the upper left corner read Living Word Fellowship, Atlanta, GA.

Quickly, I gathered and lifted all the blankets, clothing, and papers to see if anything was underneath them. Something small slid along the floor toward the back doors. It was a Bible. Brown. Slightly larger than a deck of cards. Its pages were frayed, some torn and stained. At quick glance, I found no writing inside.

There were six blankets in all, including the two from the front seat. The glove compartment was empty. There was nothing above the sun visors. I'd covered it all. But something called me back to the off-white tennis shoes. Who was Jonathan Seabold? I reached in to retrieve the matches. I would take them with me.

That's when the inside of my wrist grazed the small, brass key that was tied to the shoelace and tucked inside the shoe.

Working quickly, I unlaced the Converse and snatched the key.

His post-office box?

I found the book of matches, rose up, and pushed them into my front pocket, along with the key and the letter.

There was a quick blur just outside the van.

One of the homeless people?

I examined the parking lot.

Uh-oh.

The same silver Golf station wagon I'd seen in my neighborhood. Black windows, no hubcaps—

CRACK!

I jerked around to see the side window smashed into a million pieces, yet still holding together, as if by some heavy-duty, transparent tape.

A figure in dark clothes shifted beyond the disfigured glass puzzle. *Poof.*

A muffled crack sent the entire tinted window dropping into oblivion.

I rolled to the back and bashed the door open with both feet.

"Where do you think you're going?" A large black man smashed me in the chest with his brown work boot, sending me sprawling backward to the floor of the van.

"Huh?"

He banged open the other rear door and hoisted a boot up onto the bumper, running a gloved fist up the shaft of his black Louisville Slugger. Two others—one stocky Hispanic and one wiry Indian-looking dude—appeared at the back of the van with the big man.

Who are these guys?

I was flat out, still catching my breath from the blow—and shock.

"I was just lookin' around." I held up my hands in surrender, breathing hard, my mind tracking for a better answer.

"Why here?" The big man cracked my leg with the bat.

I cradled my knee, unable to think fast enough for an answer. Nothing came.

"Say somethin'!" the stocky one hissed.

"I'm just trying to find something." I began to sit up on my elbows, but Big Man gritted his white teeth and drilled the center of my chest with the bat, laying me flat again. "This van was a friend of mine's!" I gasped. "He's gone now, but he wanted me to come back and look for something."

"What?" yelled the Indian.

It flashed in my mind like an answer to prayer. "His Bible." I thrust my head toward the small book near his boot. "He wants me to send it to him, that's all. Believe me, I'm just doing a friend a favor, otherwise you wouldn't find me out here." I feigned a chuckle. "This is no man's land."

"Hurt him, Rio," the big man snarled.

Heat gushed through my system. "I haven't done anything wrong!"

Like a cat, the Indian was in the van, my hair in his fist, my neck locked in the crease of his arm, my windpipe closing.

Big Man smashed the inside of one of the doors with the bat. "You're in bad trouble." He dropped his boot, turned his back, walked ten feet, stuck his gloved hands on his fat waist, and scanned the red mountains beyond. "Shouldn'ta gone messin' in other people's business."

What do these thugs have to do with Chester?

The stocky Hispanic joined Big Man, their backs to me, and they began to wander away, as if this was the way they always did it—leaving the crazy Indian to finish off their prey.

Indian's arm ratcheted tighter, like a vise closing one jerk at a time around my neck. I felt my eyes roll and saw slides of black. White stars swirled in my brain, and I knew I had to make a move or I would choke to death.

Directing every ounce of life left in me to my legs, I shoved off the floor, ramming backward, and kept ramming until the Indian crashed against the seat and wall. His grip went loose, but I kept driving my head and shoulders into his rib cage, pinning him in the corner. Driving. Drilling. Trying to force the wind out of his skinny frame.

The instant he let the muffled groan slip through his lips, I made my move, spinning to my knees—*bam, bam.* Two rights to the middle of his face. His head bobbled, and blood spilled from his smashed nose. His mouth opened wide.

He's gonna yell!

Boom.

My right elbow snapped his head to the left and sent him slumping, silent.

The two others were out of sight from the rear of the van. Out of breath, I squeezed up to the driver's seat. There they were, standing at the Golf, one on each side, talking over the tiny car with their doors open. My Mustang was forty feet to the left.

If I run for it, one of them will catch me, then I'll have to take on both of them.

I have my cell. I can call the cops, but they'll find out what I did to Chester; they may even think I killed him. But at least I'd live...

Big Man and the Hispanic continued gesturing back and forth over the top of the car. Did they think the Indian was killing me or just working me over? Whichever it was, it was nothing new for them.

Hold on. Keep cool. Maybe they'll get in the car. That would give me a better chance to make it to the Mustang.

Maybe I should just wait here. They'll wonder what's wrong. They'll come...

I need a weapon.

Diving back to the Indian who was out cold—whose disfigured nose was certainly broken, and whose black T-shirt was soaking in blood—I ripped at his baggy pants, jabbing my hands into his pockets, wishing I'd never done the same to Chester Holte.

From the Indian's front left pocket I pulled a heavy black knife. I pushed the silver button on the side, and a five-inch, serrated blade sprung open, nearly slicing the palm of my right hand before clattering to the floor of the van.

What have I gotten into?

I snatched the knife from the floor and crept to the driver's seat. Could I actually stab one of those guys?

It'll be murder. You'll be in ten times deeper than you are now.

With the knife in one hand, I dug into my pocket for my cell phone with the other.

I'm calling the cops.

That's when Big Man threw his hands into the air, huffed, and folded into the driver's seat of the Golf while his sidekick slammed the passenger door and hurried around the back of the car, kicking up dirt as he headed straight for me.

Which door will he go to?

Back.

Both rear doors were wide open, so I couldn't bash him with one of those.

Have to get him inside.

Tossing the knife to the floor of the van, I grabbed the top blanket from the pile I'd seen earlier, shook it out, and covered the Indian's body. Snatching the next blanket, I lay down next to him and covered myself, hoping none of me was showing.

"What in the world's takin' so long, amigo?" the Hispanic's rapid-fire voice approached the back doors of the van.

I'd not been able to get the knife, but felt it, beneath my back.

"Blackjack is about to blow a gasket." The sidekick had arrived at the back doors. "Rio?"

There was no hesitation, as I was afraid there might be. Instead, the van bounced slightly as he jumped in. He mumbled something in irritated Spanish, but I was determined to stay frozen until he was well within my knockout zone.

"Ay, yai, yai."

He'd uncovered the Indian.

My blanket moved slightly at the floor near my head, and swoosh, there he was, black eyes big as quarters, silver gun in fist. I snapped his head back with a hard, compact left, scrapped to my knees, and hammered him with a full right. He dropped. My wrist cracked and throbbed. Shoving him to the left, I snatched his gun and crawled to the driver's seat. Big Man was still in the Golf, yakking on his cell, one boot on the ground, door wide open.

Dashing back to the Hispanic, I patted his pockets for more weapons but found none. Finding the open knife on the floor, I closed it and dropped it into my pocket. Pressing the button on the side of the gun, the magazine—lined with bullets—dropped into my palm. I slammed it back into the handle of the weapon, racked a live round into the chamber, and scurried back up front to watch for Big Man.

"Uhhh." The Indian moved.

Great.

The Hispanic guy's foot wiggled back and forth.

They're not gonna stay out long.

I dug the car keys out of my pocket. I'd hold them in my left hand, the gun in my right, and make a run for my car.

The Hispanic guy grunted.

That was my final cue.

Crawling between the two thugs, I moved to the back of the van. The Hispanic guy's head rolled sideways, his eyes opened and closed.

I took a deep breath. *Here goes.*

Like the Sundance Kid, I emerged from the van sprinting with my new gun at arm's length, pointing directly at the oversized man in the front seat of the Golf. The shock in his large, white eyes and gap-

ing mouth lasted only seconds before his cell phone clattered from the
car to the dust, and he was grunting his way out of the little car,
Louisville Slugger in hand.

Thank God he doesn't have a gun.

I was almost to the Mustang when I realized he would follow me.
Stopping in the dirt and taking aim at the Golf's front left tire, I fired.
A cloud of dirt arose near the tire as Big Man retreated behind the car.

I took aim again.

Bam, bam, bam.

On the third shot, the car shook. The tire went flat.

Big Man slammed the back door and arose with something that
glimmered in the sun. I didn't wait around to see what it was.

Pop, pop, pop, pop.

A line of dust sprayed up between me and the Mustang.

Machine gun!

I got to the door of the car, jerked the handle, and ripped it
open—

Pop, pop, pop, pop, pop, pop.

Metal clanged, and the glass in the passenger side mirror exploded.

I dove into the car, scrunched over, bobbled the keys, found the
right one, jammed it in the hole, and cranked it hard. Big Man was
jogging toward me like a soldier, both hands on the shiny gun at his
stomach.

Pop, pop, pop, pop.

Feeling the vibration of bullets pelting the car, I stomped the
clutch, jammed it in gear, and punched the gas. Lurching forward,
then swaying sideways, the Mustang finally found traction, shrugged,
straightened, and catapulted forward, my door slamming shut, and
my new enemy shrinking away in the rearview mirror.

11

The money no longer mattered, and I tried to convince myself that neither did Holly Queens. My life, future, and freedom were on the line. I was not about to play games with a bunch of deranged thugs. Nor was I going to prison.

I flicked the hot butt of my cigarette out the window, pulled in the driveway, bumped the Mustang into the garage, hurried out, and assessed the damage. A half dozen bullet holes riddled the back of the car, and I was thankful the gas tank hadn't exploded.

Entering the house, I found Holly nestled in a chair by the window in the living room, reading my mom's Bible.

"Hey there." She folded up the book and met me in the kitchen. "I saved some breakfast for you."

Her black hair wet and shiny, she removed the lid from a pan of scrambled eggs.

"You found the shower?" I asked.

"Yeah, I hope you don't mind."

"No. Your face looks a little better."

"Thanks. I iced my eyes down for a little while." She opened a cupboard. "Where do you keep the plates?"

"Holly." I closed it. "We need to talk."

I led her into the living room.

"About Ken?"

We plunked down on the same couch where we'd sat hours ago.

"No."

"Chester?"

"Yeah." I peered into her innocent eyes. "I've been lying to you."

She squinted and her head tilted, but she said nothing.

"On the police scanner at work early Saturday morning, I heard a call saying police had received an anonymous tip about an injured person at the Civic Center North bus stop."

Her head jutted forward, her brown eyes boring into me.

"I went. It was Chester... He was dead."

"What?" She shot to her feet. "That can't be. How do you know? You don't even know him."

"He had a bankbook. It was the only thing on him. And a key, to a safe-deposit box. I found the box later that morning. There were newspaper clippings. I recognized his picture—"

"Why did you tell me he was missing if you found his body?"

I took a deep breath, hunched over, my forearms on my knees, and heard myself sigh. "He *is* missing. Later that morning, I called the *R-J*, the police, and the coroner. No one's seen the body, except me."

"What did the police say? Why did you lie to me?"

"I haven't told the police. They were on the way to the crime scene when I left that morning. They were within a mile. I didn't think I was doing any real harm, but now I know I was. I'm sorry. I—"

"What do you mean you're sorry?" she screamed in my face. "Are you telling me you stole things off Chester's dead body and left before the police got there?"

"The bankbook said he had almost six hundred ninety grand in the bank. I guess I wanted to be the first one with the story. To me, he was just a homeless guy. I didn't realize what kind of person he was—"

"You wanted the money!"

"Maybe I did!" I stood and threw my arms up. "I'm sorry. I don't know if I wanted the money, the story, or what. But I want to make it right. That's why I'm telling you."

"You sat there and lied to me at Maxine's. You lied to me here, in the night." She stomped toward the side door. "You're sick!"

I ran and blocked the door. "Please, Holly, hear me out."

"Get out of the way!" She shoved me. I put my hands out, gently trying to keep her there.

"Holly, I just went to a van this morning. Chester stayed there sometimes."

She crossed her arms hard, her whole body rigid, her mouth locked shut, and her blazing eyes fixed on the door.

"I found some things of Chester's." I reached into my pockets for the key and matchbook. "But while I was in the van, three guys attacked me."

"Who?"

"They looked like part of a gang. Remember I told you I got robbed?"

She just stared at me.

"I saw a car pulling away that day; it's the same one these guys were driving today. I think they wanted to kill me."

"Why are you telling me this?"

"I'm trying to explain—"

"Explain to the police! If you don't, I will." She marched to the door leading to the garage, stopped, and put her hands on her head, as if to stop the spinning. "Please call me a cab."

"Holly, please." I eased into the kitchen. "Let me tell you the rest."

"There's more?"

"Whoever robbed my house yesterday took the things I brought home from Chester's safe-deposit box."

"Why? Who...that gang?"

I nodded. "Maybe they knew Chester had money. Did *you* know that?"

"No. Maybe. I don't know." She buried her head in her arms on the counter. "It doesn't surprise me. He was an angel. Nothing would surprise me about Chester."

I took a step toward her, and she straightened up like a frightened animal backed into a corner. "How did he die?"

"There was a wound up here." I rested my hand on my upper chest. "It was either a gunshot or a knife. I swear to you, Holly, the police were on the way. I didn't mean for it to turn out like this. I'm sorry I lied to you."

"Are you sure he was dead? Maybe some of his friends helped him."

"He was dead, Holly."

"Why? Why would anyone kill such a sweet man? Where is he? He deserves a proper funeral."

She bent over on the counter again, hiding herself in her bruised arms and crying bitterly.

I didn't dare touch her. "I'm going to the police—tomorrow."

Her shoulders shook with the sobs.

"I found some things in the van." I approached her, but stopped two feet away. "I'm gonna check them out. Go to the safe-deposit box one more time when the bank opens tomorrow. The more information I can give the police, the better."

With her back to me, she rose slightly, ripped a piece of paper towel off the roll, and wiped her face.

"You should go *now*." She sniffed. "Quit fooling around with it."

"All right, I'll go now, if you'll forgive me."

She faced me, the bruises beneath her eyes glistening, her lower lip quivering. "I need time." Her head dropped into her hand and the sobbing came again.

I took my chances, resting my hand on her shoulder. "Can I get you anything?"

She shook her head. "I need to get home."

"I'll take you. We can go by the clinic and get your phone, if you want."

She started for the door to the garage.

Will she forgive me? Can our friendship ever be what it was before this?

Christians were supposed to forgive.

My old man had wanted me to forgive him, for letting Mom die, for practically abandoning me.

But I would not forgive. And I wouldn't blame Holly if she didn't forgive me.

Life *stunk*.

I needed to get this thing behind me and get out of Las Vegas. Begin again, somewhere else. If anything had been starting between Holly and me in the past twenty-four hours, it was kaput.

"I'll go with you," she mumbled.

"What?"

"I need to find out who killed Chester; I don't care what it takes. If you take me to my place, let me change, I'll go with you to check the leads."

I stopped before opening her door and peered down at her. "Are you sure?"

With a quick, solemn nod, she shrugged yes. "If you don't go to the police first thing tomorrow, I am."

"Okay. Thank you, Holly. I know you don't have any reason to trust me—"

"Let's just do what we have to do."

As I drove toward First Street in Old Downtown, telling myself I didn't need another smoke, Holly read me the somewhat crumpled, off-white letter addressed to Chester that I'd found in the van behind the Lucky Lady. It was typewritten, from a man named Banyon Scribe, senior pastor, Living Word Fellowship, Atlanta, Georgia, and dated two months earlier.

Dear Chester,

I gave this letter to your son, Andrew, who promised he would get it to you. I pray it reaches you quickly and finds you in good health.

Several of the elders and I recently traveled to Las Vegas to try to find you. We scoured the city, but to no avail. Our hope was to restore you into the fold. The elders and I continue to pray for you, as if you were still one of us.

Your last words accusing me of "pride and self-righteousness" did not hurt. What did hurt was your judgment of my motives and my heart. You are a precious brother to me, Chester, but your bitter, critical spirit made itself known the last time you addressed the elders, accusing me of manipulating church growth, not listening to godly counsel.

However, I can say with confidence, as Paul did in

1 Corinthians 4:3–4, "But with me it is a very small thing that I should be judged of you...he that judgeth me is the Lord."

I believe you are on your own now, Chester, and that you are ignoring my counsel and that of the elders. Like the prodigal son, you are on the run from God.

You got very angry with me when I said I believe Satan is at work in this situation, and that I have very little respect concerning your relationship with God. But I know any of us can be deceived, including you.

I believe God is both saddened and infuriated by your decision to step away from this fellowship, and to renege on the $1.5 million commitment you made toward the construction of our new worship center. As you must realize by now, you have left us in the lurch, to say the least, as the new building sits like a white elephant for the entire Atlanta community to see—one-third completed.

Despite all that has happened, our arms are open wide to you, and our hearts are ready to forgive. You need us, Chester. You need the fellowship and sound biblical teaching. And we need your zeal for the Lord.

You will always be welcome here.

As the father of the prodigal son did, I watch for you from afar each Sunday. And I pray that God will have mercy on you until, as the prodigal son did, you return home to the path God has for you here with us—your family.

Until we meet again, may you work out your faith with fear and trembling.

Your shepherd,

Banyon Scribe

Senior Pastor

"Can you believe that?" Holly waved the letter and let it crumple in her lap. "It sounds like some kind of cult. He told me about this."

"About what?"

"Chester was very successful. High up in the Atlanta business community. He had *everything*. They lived in a huge mansion in Buckhead."

"Then his wife died."

"How do you know?"

"There were articles about it in his box."

"When Candice died, he lost it. Had a breakdown. Told me the doctors wanted to check him into a mental facility."

"And?"

"He went to church instead."

I nodded toward the letter. "That church?"

"Yeah." She slapped the letter against her thigh. "He sold the mansion and moved out to the suburbs so he could be near it. Was there every time the doors opened. Problem was, it was like a bubble. Once you 'entered in,' it was next to impossible to leave."

"Why's that?"

"It's a long story."

"We've got time."

"The pastor, Scribe, taught the Bible, verse by verse. And Chester grew like crazy. But the problem was, the people ended up almost worshiping Scribe. That's what happened to Chester. He was mesmerized by the guy."

"Brainwashed or something?"

"He told me Scribe knew the Bible so well. Quoted it verbatim. So admirable. But he would challenge the people to live up to the commandments, and to live like he did, as if he was on some spiritual pedestal. All very subtly legalistic."

"Isn't that what you're supposed to do, obey the Ten Commandments?"

She sighed and shook her head. "No one can obey the Ten Commandments. They're designed to show us what sinners we are. Once we realize that, we understand we need help beyond ourselves. That's where Jesus comes in."

"So, what was this dude doing?" I smirked. "Trying to build his own kingdom?"

"In a way, *yeah*. It's not funny. " Holly turned and stared out the passenger window as we flew along I-15. "It messed Chester up. That church became his life. He worked his tail off there. Became like a right-hand man to Scribe."

"Then what?"

"They asked him to lead a Bible study at his house, and as he dug into the Word, the lights started coming on. He realized that since he'd become a Christian, he'd become judgmental, as if he'd done something to save himself. He went to Scribe and told him that was the flavor throughout the church. Confronted him about it. Told him the sermons were heavy and condescending, and that he sensed pride coming from the pulpit."

"That went over well."

"It took guts. He told the guy the church was a bubble, that they'd become so comfortable among themselves that they'd forgotten how to relate to anyone outside their safe little world. Scribe wouldn't have any of it. Didn't even pray about it. Said Chester was wrong. Even implied he was from Satan.' "

"Those preachers are all alike."

"No they're not. Have you been to church lately?"

"I see 'em on TV with their fancy furniture and expensive suits."

"That's TV. Ellery Graham's not like that. He teaches the Bible, and he wants us to have a relationship with Christ and to love like Jesus did. The people in our church are contagious. They go out into the city and invite everybody. The place is filled with all kinds of people and all kinds of pasts. I know addicts and prostitutes at our church."

"You mean *former* addicts and prostitutes."

"Most. But some are still searching. We love them and help them meet up with God. That's what Chester was all about. He was the most Spirit-filled man I ever met."

I regretted not having known Chester and wondered how he would have treated me. What would he have said about my negative attitude toward my old man? Would he have minded when I smoked? Would he have forgiven me for searching him?

Holly's words brought me back to real time.

"Scribe's church is like an entity unto itself. If you go there, you're in. One of the righteous ones. They love one another like family, Chester said. But if you ever leave—"

"Excommunicated?"

"Just about."

"So he left."

"Yep. He said God led him to Las Vegas. His whole purpose was to help people find Christ. I thought he'd gone broke." She waved the letter again. "He never told me about the pledge."

"The pastor wants him back."

"Wants his money."

Silence rose up between us, and I felt guilty that my negativism had somehow seeped over to Holly.

"I shouldn't say that," she said. "I don't even know Scribe. Bottom line is, Chester realized he was too far inside that church. Out of touch with reality. The church, the pastor, the people, all the works—

they were his relationship with God, which turned out to be no relationship at all."

Makes sense.

"He loved this one poem." Her head dropped back against the headrest. She closed her eyes, and a lone tear trickled down the side of her face. " 'I Stand By the Door.' "

"Do you remember any of it?"

She breathed in deeply, opened her eyes, and stared off into the distance. " 'You can go in too deeply and forget the people outside the door.' " She seemed a million miles away, her shoulders back, almost as if she were reciting the work for a poetry club. " 'But, as for me, I'll take my accustomed place, near enough to God to hear Him and know He's there, but not far from men as to not hear them and remember that they are there too. Where? Outside the door. Thousands of them, millions of them. But more important for me, one of them, two of them, ten of them, whose hands I am intended to put on the latch.' "

12

itting in Holly's living room, waiting for her to change, trying to figure out—above the hum of the hair dryer—who was after me and if they would strike again, I realized I was attracted to Holly Queens. In the same breath, I noted that I had two big-league strikes against me in her book: one, I'd strung her along on a terribly selfish, hurtful lie, and two, I wasn't a Christian.

I was still trying to convince myself to forget about any emotional involvement with Holly when she sauntered out of her bedroom wearing torn Levi's, black tennis shoes, and a white and pink, three-quarter sleeve baseball shirt with the number nine on back.

"What's the plan?" She shook her hair back.

"How's the…?" I pointed to my own forehead.

She reached up and felt above her eyes. "Swelling's down. Now, if I could just get rid of these circles." She put on a fake smile and locked her fists and arms out front in a boxer pose. "I look like a prizefighter—one of your victims!"

I chuckled. "You look pretty to me."

I thought you decided to drop that?

She gently set her shoulders back and bobbed her head. "Thank you."

Perhaps she has forgiven me. Either that, or she is an excellent actress.

"I printed out all the post offices near Chester's van. There's a bunch." I retrieved the pages from her printer. "We'll save time if we wait till tomorrow and call them when they're open, rather than driving all over creation. They should be able to tell us what their box numbers are, don't you think?"

"I guess. What now then?"

"I called the coroner again. Still no Chester."

"Maybe he's alive, Hud. I'm serious. Did you take his pulse?"

"No, I didn't take his pulse, Holly. I've seen dead people before. I could tell by the wound and his...body. He was gone. Trust me."

Chester's soapy smell drifted back to me, and his sun-drenched skin, the rip in his overcoat, the puddle of blood. For his sake and mine, I wished I could have changed how I'd handled it.

Holly shrugged and headed for the kitchen. "You want coffee? I don't have Dr Pepper."

I laughed. "Ah. Now a Dr Pepper sounds good. How 'bout we go get some lunch, on me?"

"I made you eggs and you didn't touch them. You need some protein." She returned to the living room. "Do you think Ken's seen a judge yet?"

I looked at my watch. "That'd be pretty quick, but it's possible. You want me to call Fitzgerald?"

She ambled over to me. "I guess not."

"I can."

"He doesn't have a past record, as far as I know."

She was pale, and I noticed several freckles on her nose and cheeks that I hadn't seen before, as she stared past me.

"Holly, there'll be a restraining order, *if* he gets out."

"Uh-huh." She crossed her arms and turned away. "Can a restraining order stop a murder?"

"Holly." I stood and approached her. "It's gonna be okay."

"You say that…"

"You can stay at my place, if he gets out."

"I can't live my life at your place!"

"Look, let's just wait and see what happens. He may not even make bail."

My shallow words fell short of the sure comfort I desperately wanted to deliver, but I had nothing more to offer. I, too, was uneasy, even troubled, by the thought of Ken Van Dillon and his sick jealousy.

"He's got a rich uncle somewhere in the hills of Montana." She walked to the front window and gazed out, toward the shady front porch and bright cul-de-sac beyond. "He can get the money."

I pictured Holly in her white jacket with her clipboard, going about her duties at the clinic, and Van Dillon slipping in through the back door as he had the night before. How easy it would be. The thought of him torturing her again incensed me and ate at my stomach.

"Well, they better put him away," I spoke to her back. "What he did's a felony."

"There've been times worse than this."

The house was quiet. That same clock ticking.

I wanted her to talk. To get it out. To heal.

"I tried to call the police."

Her head dropped and she began to weep.

I went to her. She must've heard my footsteps—

"Don't touch me!" She lunged, bumping against the window, one hand covering her heart. "Please. Stay back." Her other hand was out to the side, as if she was balancing on a beam. She grunted, forcing herself to take short, loud breaths.

"Get back," she breathed.

This was bad. I'd not seen this. It had never dawned on me, until that moment, how deeply scarred Holly was from the past.

I stepped away, back to where I'd been. "I'm here," I whispered. "It's okay." My heart knocked, and I could almost taste the venomous hatred building in my mouth toward Ken Van Dillon. "No one's going to hurt you anymore."

I had no idea what to expect next.

Crossing both arms over her chest, Holly rocked. Back and forth, back and forth, back and forth.

Minutes later, the rocking slowed until it was almost unnoticeable.

"I'm sorry." She turned to me, her face red, her mascara smudged beneath one eye. "I need to be praying instead of fretting."

"It's okay."

"That must have freaked you out. It's ridiculous really. I act like…like I'm actually in charge of my own safety. I'm not. God is."

I could only muster a nod.

The whole topic of God was where we were planets apart.

"I need a few minutes." She headed for the bedroom and pointed an arm toward the computer. "Is there stuff you can do?"

"Sure. No problem. Take your time." I stepped toward her.

"Don't worry. I'm okay. Sometimes the memories just…overcome me."

"I understand."

"Why don't you figure out what we're doing next."

I pulled the matchbook from my pocket, half wanting to fetch a smoke from my car and collapse in one of the rockers on the front porch.

"The first thing I'm going to do is call this club and see if anyone knows who this Jonathan Seabold is. If I can track him down, we'll pay him a visit."

13

I told the *R-J* reporter, Hudson Ambrose, to meet me at the casino where I work as a pit boss, two blocks from the 135-story needle in the sky—the Stratosphere—one of Las Vegas's most recognized landmarks. He didn't tell me anybody would be with him.

But I didn't care.

"Mr. Seabold," the voice of Joyce Aloy, a casino administrator, approached my empty blackjack table from behind, "can you sign this for me?"

"Certainly." I scribbled my John Hancock and slid it back with a smile. "Have a good day, Joyce."

Since meeting Chester Holte, my life had become a house of open doors and windows. No more hiding or shame. Plastic-looking scars still disfigured portions of my face and neck, but I was whole for the first time in my life. Well, maybe for the first time since just before I tumbled from my father's grasping arms as a boy, somehow finding my way beneath the whirling, unforgiving blades of his yellow Cub Cadet tractor.

The girl who accompanied Hudson to my table was quite attractive, but badly bruised beneath her eyes, which shifted from my face to my neck and down to her hands when we first met.

I asked what had happened to her. Twisting the pearl ring on her right hand, she whispered that her boyfriend had beaten her. "For the last time," Hudson added.

I could tell he liked her; it was plain, even from across the vast, blinking casino floor as they approached for the first time. It was the way he placed his hand at the small of her back and ushered her through the crowd of daydreaming, meandering tourists.

After the curiosity of my appearance dissolved from their faces and our small talk quieted, Hudson took a deep breath and told me Chester was dead.

I can still see Hudson's face, and Holly's, coming closer to mine, with cracks and creases and ridges exaggerated, and sympathy oozing from their pores. They spoke, but all I could hear were the ringing, computerized beeping sounds of the twelve hundred slot machines that seemed to converge around me in taunting harmony.

The table and floor spun, as if I'd just stepped off a carnival ride. Heat engulfed me.

Chester…

I had to get out. Needed air. Space.

God, no!

Holly's slender, white hand moved across the green felt table to cover mine.

And I ran.

Hudson loosened my tie and undid the top two buttons of my dress shirt where he and Holly found me, clinging to a hot black metal bench along Main Street.

"Chester and I came here." I gripped the warm, faded bench, denying the fact that those times were gone.

"How did you meet him?" Holly rested the pearl-fingered hand on my shoulder, and I took her and Hudson back in time...

It was past 3 a.m.

I'd won big at one particular craps table at Mandalay Bay, and craps wasn't even my game. The money didn't mean that much to me, but the validation meant the world.

I'd cashed out, was riding a wave of adrenaline, and didn't feel like going back to my empty condo, because that's where the loneliness inevitably set in. The feelings of ugliness and worthlessness.

Basking in the afterglow of my win, I dropped by the men's room to use the facilities and decide what to do next.

The rest room was empty, or so I thought.

I stood at a urinal, staring at the gold and black striped wallpaper a foot from my face.

They weren't laughing at me tonight. Their eyes sparkled with envy. Several of them called my name. Even Angie, the woman on the stick, seemed interested—

The rest room door squeaked open, but I didn't bother to turn around.

The onlookers smiled and nodded and pumped their fists. I was the center of attention. And I don't want to let that feeling slip away. Maybe I should go back for one more round—

Click-click.

Cold metal at the back of my neck.

"Raise both hands, straight up." The shaky, young voice came from below the back of my shoulder. "Don't turn around or I'll mess you up—bad."

Three quick, hard pats on my bottom and I felt my wallet shimmy in my rear pocket. But he couldn't get it out. He yanked again, but it wouldn't come.

"You get it!"

Slowly, I reached back and removed the wallet.

He must have swiped at it, because it knocked from my hands, hit the ground, and slid several feet.

"One sound or move and I blow your guts out."

The tear of Velcro came low, from the floor behind me.

He's in my wallet.

Instinctively, I turned. He was a white kid—I guessed seventeen—with pimples and a small amount of wild brown hair on his chin. He wore a black stocking cap, baggy blue coat, and black work boots. His face had been amid the crowd at my winning table.

His head and the black gun jerked up at the same time. "Turn your ugly mug around!"

I did, but almost instantly, he was on his feet, twisting the collar of my shirt from behind, breathing in my ear, talking through clenched teeth. "I told you not to look, Scarface. Now, I'm gonna have to do you."

He's stoned out of his mind.

His clawing fingers dug into the back of my neck as he mashed my head against the black and gold wallpaper. "They'll see you anyway," I pleaded, "there are cameras everywhere—"

Thunderously, one of the toilets behind me flushed. In unison, the punk's head and mine whipped toward a long row of gold stall doors. His grip loosened, but he didn't let go; I could feel him trembling and smelled his pungent body odor. We waited and watched.

A door near the middle clicked and swung open, and out mean-dered a scruffy, tan, red-haired man wearing a lightweight black over-coat. He stopped just outside the door, his worn face scrunched in dismay. "Excuse me."

The punk's gun arm was riveted on the man.

Hadn't he heard us? Why'd he come out?

The man lifted his arms and stared at the gun. "I'm sorry to inter-rupt." Somewhat shaken, the scruffy-looking fellow made his way around the punk with the gun, over to the long row of lavish sinks and marble countertops. There, he pushed up the sleeves of his over-coat and stuck his hands beneath the faucet.

"You're not goin' anywhere, homey," the punk hissed, shaking his gun at the scruffy man.

"Okay." The homeless man moved gingerly, pulling on the soap dispenser several times, lathering his hands slowly, rinsing the backs and fronts like a surgeon, and hesitantly eying us in the mirror. "You know, fellas, I don't believe anything happens by chance. No sir, I walked right into the middle of this mess, and I know God has a per-fectly good reason for it—"

"Shut up, old man! You just made this harder than it had to be." The punk fidgeted and turned and fretted as if, at any given second, he would lift the weapon and end each of our lives.

Meanwhile, paper towels dispensed automatically above the scruffy man's dripping hands. He tore and dried the same way he'd lathered, slowly, as if everything was going to be fine. I tried to drink in the peace he exuded. In the mirror, I noticed scars on his ear and neck. It looked like the remnants of a bad burn. Although I hate to admit it, his imperfections made me feel better, like I wasn't alone in my quest for normalcy.

Gently wadding the wet paper towels, the scruffy man took

several easy steps along the marble counter and dropped them into a rectangle opening. "It appears, young man, that you want money, that you believe money will fill—"

"Cut it!" The punk again wrenched my collar and shook the gun at the guy. "You ain't been where I been, so shut your face! I mean it, or I'll blow you both straight to hell."

A heavy soberness came over the homeless man's face. It was not a look of fear, but of humble concern. "Son, you're right, I haven't walked in your shoes. Tell me what it's been like. What's gone wrong? I can try to help you—"

"Shut your mouth!" The punk bounced. "Just shut up. You understand? I'm tryin' to think..."

I attempted to make eye contact with the homeless man, to let him know the punk was crazy, freaked out on drugs, dangerous, but he proceeded to take both of our lives into his hands.

"Look, my name's Chester." The homeless guy raised both hands. "I have lots of money; that's what you want, right? Lemme show you, right here in my pocket, can I?" He lowered his hand and stuck his palm out by his left pocket.

"Do it—quick!" the punk snarled, shoving the gun within three feet of Chester's red face. "If you're messin' with me, you're dead, here and now."

"Be calm," Chester whispered, reaching in and pulling out a roll of bills in a quivering hand. "I'm willing to match what this gentleman had in his wallet. I'll even top it by a hundred dollars, if you let him keep his money."

The punk yanked me toward Chester. "Take his money and count it, Scarface."

He stuffed the clump of bills in my hand.

What's this bum doing with all this cash?

The moment was surreal. I felt fuzzy. There was nothing I could do but obey.

"Something good can come of this." Chester's blue eyes glistened. "Son, we're all like you, you know that? Each person is a vile, messed-up sinner destined for hell. Every one of us deserves God's wrath—"

"I can't take this!" The punk released me and pressed his hands to his temples. "Shut up, old man. Just shut up and let him count."

"Please, let me talk while he counts," Chester insisted. "There's nothing wrong with you! What you're doing here, now, it's a product of who you are and who I am. And you're on your way to hell for it. We're all on our way to hell. But we can be rescued!"

I stopped counting at $3,400 and looked up.

"Someone had the audacity and love to stretch out His hands and say, 'I'll take your nails. I'll take your sin and the punishment you deserve.'" Chester's weathered palms lifted toward the punk. "'I'll take it to the cross with me. And I'll plunge it straight into oblivion! Not only that, but I'll give you My character in place of the old you.' Son, you can have all that right now, tonight, if you believe."

What he said blew my mind. I needed what the bum described, and swore if I got out of that crucible alive, I'd live for God.

The punk bashed my shoulder, "Count!"

I continued where I'd left off, and silence seeped into the room.

"No one needs to be around," Chester said quietly. "Just give up. Surrender this way of life. Jesus said, 'Follow Me.' Do that, and you'll find what you're searching for, son."

The punk nudged me. "How much?"

"Wait," I blurted. "I'm not done. So far, over four grand."

Apparently, that was enough.

The punk plucked the bills from my fingers, ripped the ski cap from his head, and rubbed the sweat from his forehead with the arm of his coat. Hands shuddering, he stuffed Chester's money and my wallet into the hat.

"Get in there." He pointed the gun at one of the gold stall doors and shoved me toward it. "Both of you." He grabbed Chester's arm and dragged him toward me. "On your knees. Now! Heads to the floor. You dudes are in the wrong place at the wrong time."

According to my calculations, he had at least eight grand in his hat, and two live, coherent witnesses at his feet who could pick him out of a lineup faster than he could say "methamphetamines."

I was betting I had twelve seconds or less left to breathe.

Fitting; I'm about to die next to a toilet and a bum.

He buried the gun in the base of my skull with such force that I bit my bottom lip, tasting the blood, my mouth swirling with the flavors of nerves and fear and electricity and death.

I was so alone. And I was going to die that way.

"Son," Chester called, his face within inches of the tile floor, "what you're looking for is within your grasp."

The nose of the punk's gun left my neck, and I heard Chester grunt from its pressure. "Where'd you get all that money?"

"I'm a rich man," Chester moaned. "I once had a mansion, five cars, and a closet full of European suits."

Get out of here...

"What happened?" the punk screamed. "Hurry up!"

Thud.

Chester groaned from the punk's boot to his side.

"My wife died...in a plane crash. I started going to church, but I had no relationship with Christ. Then God led me here...to Las Vegas. It's no coincidence we've met."

With his ruddy face smashed against the tile, Chester's eyes pierced mine.

"Shhh," I mouthed, shaking my head, hoping he would shut up before the punk went completely postal. "That's enough."

Chester's eyes closed.

Thank goodness. Maybe he's giving up.

But his lips were moving. He was praying, I knew.

Then it was time. The nose of the cold gun found its way to the base of my skull. The punk would do it. He would kill. Execution style. It would all be over quickly.

Maybe it's for the best. I'll never again have to think about doing it myself.

"What is your name?" Chester's voice arose from the floor, calm and smooth, like water rolling over rocks. "I'd like to be praying for you."

Silence screamed in my ears. My heart bashed high in my rib cage and neck and head and wrists. The nose of the gun pressed hard against me.

I'm about to find out if hell is real.

"Sandy." The punk's gun left the back of my neck and he grunted.

He's standing.

"God be with you, Sandy." Chester spoke softly, with his eyes closed. "Thank you for letting us live."

You don't know that! What are you saying? Are you trying to push him over the edge?

The door of the stall crashed open. The punk's footsteps headed for the exit.

Can it be?

The rest room door whished open. The punk stopped there. I could hear his panicked breathing.

He's debating whether to come back and kill us.

Then he moaned, "I'm sorry," and his footsteps took off rapidly, fading with the sound of the closing door.

We never heard from Sandy again, but Chester often wondered aloud about him as we grew closer in the weeks and months ahead. The robbery and initial encounter with Chester would have had a life-altering impact on most people. I know I said it would on me. Certainly, I was intrigued by Chester's past and the new life he'd chosen to live in Las Vegas, but nothing outside myself ever stuck with me.

Ever since my childhood accident, I'd been completely self-absorbed. Everything was about me. My parents overcompensated for my scars, and our whole mission became centered on helping me live a normal life, which is precisely what made mine everything *but* normal.

Some six months after meeting Chester, my selfishness rose up to suffocate me. It was Christmas Day. My mother had passed away a year earlier, just eight months after my father had died of a brief bout with an aggressive form of lymphoma. I had the day off and was alone in my Las Vegas condo with the blinds closed, the miniature Christmas tree lit, and a fire going with the gas logs. As much as I tried to duplicate the warm spirit of the holidays at my boyhood home in Wisconsin, and find some semblance of joy and stability, some goodness in this world to which to cling, I was instead ravaged by the sheer cruelty of life and my fellowman, and the overpowering notion that I was inadequate. Even increasing my medication couldn't release me from the dark, dismal state of turmoil that consumed me. Despite Chester's friendship, which seemed to be the one constant that had kept me afloat, I'd given in to the menacing forces that wreaked havoc on my mind.

The city streets were thick with rain as I eased my Oldsmobile off I-15, barely onto the berm. Wearing an old, gray trench coat my father had given me, I yanked the hood release beneath the steering wheel and waited for a break in the traffic that blew past me, literally making the Oldsmobile wobble.

Torrents of rain ripped past, filling my eyeglasses with water, splattering off my balding head, and running down the back of my mangled neck as I stood over the steamy engine, pretending to make adjustments under the hood.

This was it.

As they'd been known to say, "Good-bye, cruel world." And I did mean cruel.

I peered around the propped-up hood at the dozens of oncoming cars, trucks, minivans, and SUVs—some creeping by with their flashers on, others catapulting toward me at the speed of sound, ignoring the slick conditions.

That's what I wanted. Something fast. A truck. A semi. A huge, bad, eighteen-wheeler in which the driver was putting the pedal to the metal like a bat out of hell.

I could see my breath.

Just think, in a moment, there will be no more breath.

I hadn't left a note, because I wanted it to look like an accident, like I touched a hot engine part, perhaps, and flew into the lane of oncoming traffic. Chester would know that wasn't what really happened.

Forgive me, friend, for giving up.

Through the steam from my lungs, I spotted it. Maybe a mile off. A big rig, barreling toward me, in my lane. No headlights. An enormous cloud of mist swirling behind him.

You can do this.

Staying concealed behind the hood of my Olds, I inched closer to the oncoming cars, the wind of which blew me backward.

The last car before the semi—a brown PT Cruiser—blitzed past me in a shroud of rain.

Good.

There were no more vehicles between me and the semi. I would have plenty of clearance to step out, directly into its path.

My mind clouded white with static. My heart thundered. As if in slow motion, I opened my coat and checked my chest to determine whether I could actually see my heart beating through my shirt. I could not.

The truck was several hundred yards away and approaching fast. It was time to go.

I reached up and ran my fingers over the smooth, wide scars on my face, then, with the same hand, touched the Oldsmobile's still-hot oil compartment, and flung myself backward into the northbound lane of I-15.

What sounded like a thousand tires let out a chorus of screeches. The stench of burnt rubber filled my nostrils. The only thing I could see was the enormous, shining silver grill of the semi, rattling with raindrops, three inches from my face. Behind it, the truck's pulsating engine idled deep and mean, as if it had just driven cross-country, giving off an odor like leaking radiator fluid and generating a wave of heat that made me feel as if I was melting, even in the Nevada downpour.

Standing next to the towering, rumbling semi—a very little man in front of a very big truck—it was as if I'd been in some kind of silent, protective vacuum for the past sixty seconds.

Looking up into the cab of the truck, I could see nothing but Las Vegas's gray and white skies reflecting off the wet windshield.

How could he have stopped in time? There's no way...

The nasty splash of a cold puddle doused my trousers and shoes. Vehicles screamed past in the adjacent lane, and those stacking up behind the truck waited with blinkers on and horns blowing, trying to get around the eighteen-wheeler.

I'd caused enough commotion for the day.

Taking a last glimpse up toward the cab of the semi but seeing only white glare, I headed toward my car to shut the hood and get out of there. That's when the passenger door of the truck bounced open, and a black umbrella popped out.

I banged the hood of the Oldsmobile closed and waited as the umbrella slowly made its way down from the cab, its owner blocked from view by his opened passenger door.

I supposed the driver was going to give me a good tongue-lashing. I just hoped he didn't want a fight. My legs were weak, and I thought I might throw up.

"I'm sorry about that," I yelled. "I touched something hot. It shocked me. I went backward, right into your lane."

The driver continued toward me, slowly, the umbrella slanted forward, covering his face. He wore pointy brown cowboy boots, faded jeans, and a black leather vest, and he held a foam cup in his left hand.

"Thank God you were able to stop." I chuckled nervously as he came to a halt within four feet of me and tilted the umbrella back.

"Thank God, indeed." The man's thin face was full of three or four days of gray beard stubble. His straight, brown hair was parted in the middle and pulled back in a ponytail. And his right cheek was packed with what I assumed was a large wad of chewing tobacco. "You okay?"

"I am." I looked down at the soaked ground, humiliated, and shook my head. "Forgive me...I...that was careless."

Cars honked, but the truck driver ignored them, spitting into the white cup that shook slightly in his large fingers. "I don't know how I stopped." He examined the long, black skid marks on the pavement, pivoted to where I had been standing, then glared at me. "You're one lucky son of a gun."

A white car pulled off the side of the highway, next to the truck, thirty feet from us. The passenger door opened. A man got out. Dark baggy pants, a flimsy black overcoat, old sneakers.

Chester.

"Listen, let me get this rig on down the road." The truck driver stuck out his hand.

I shook it. "I'm sorry...again."

He shook his head. "Just glad we had a happy ending." And he headed back to his truck.

Chester leaned into the white car, gave a wave to the driver, bent his shoulders back, and headed toward me. The car took off into the mist.

I raised my chin at him and got in my car, soaking wet, knowing he would get in too.

He plunked down next to me and slammed his door, but I couldn't look at him.

"This is a coincidence." I mustered a chuckle. "Who was that?" I motioned toward the car that had sped off.

"Just some guy I hitched a ride with," Chester said. "I saw your car and asked him to pull over."

"I don't know what's goin' on with this car," I lied.

"I've been praying for you, Jonathan. Praying we'd have another chance to meet. I didn't know it would happen like this."

"What do you mean, 'like this'?"

"Start it up, Jonathan. Turn on the heat. I know the car's working fine."

I finally looked into his piercing blue eyes, then started the car and flipped on the heat.

"I'm sorry, Chester. I couldn't...I just couldn't go on."

"Don't apologize to me." He shook his head. "It's God whose

heart's broken. I know He was weeping when you stepped out in front of that truck."

As Chester spoke, I couldn't take my eyes off his. We were locked on. I wanted to look away, change the subject, deny him and his God.

"How did he stop?" I blurted, looking over at the truck still blocking traffic. "I just wanted to go away quietly."

"You ever think about what that would have done to that man? How that would have affected his life? Hitting you? Killing you? Ever since we've known each other, Jonathan, you've never been able to get your eyes off yourself."

My head dropped. "You're right." I almost started crying. "I know you're right."

"I believe God's extending His hand to you, perhaps one last time." He patted my knee. "You know He's patient. He desires all to come to Him. But He will only take rejection so long."

An enormous, jagged fissure of lightning, from sky to ground, cracked like Las Vegas neon behind Chester, and I flinched with the thunder that rumbled seconds later.

"Then His outstretched arms retreat." Chester's hand dropped away. "His Spirit quits wooing, His back turns, the door shuts, and you find yourself facing eternity in the lake of fire. You think you have it bad now, but I assure you, if that truck had ended your life today, you would have found out what living hell was really like."

By the time I swallowed back the nausea that was erupting in my throat, Chester was out of the car.

"Where are you going? I'll drive you."

He leaned in at me and shook his head with his eyes closed.

"It can't be me any longer, Jonathan. I won't always be there. I'm only human. I can't keep propping you up. You need Christ, bud. You need to invite Him into your life."

The door closed. Chester waited, then dashed across the busy highway. Up and over the concrete median he went, stopping, waiting, then rushing across the other two lanes. Over the guardrail he hurried, and he was out of sight.

The rain came hard then, pelting the hood and roof and giving me chills.

I sat there for a long time that Christmas Day, two years ago. Considering Chester's words, his life, and his love. And for the first time, I attempted to celebrate the true meaning of Christmas, alone there in my Oldsmobile, crying tears of release, laughing at my scars, sitting next to the semi that should have sent me to hell.

14

I told you Chester was an angel," Holly said as we left our meeting with Jonathan Seabold, driving south toward Chester's post-office box, the whereabouts of which Jonathan had revealed to us.

"Pretty hard to believe." I looked at her from the driver's seat. "All that stuff about the truck."

I don't want to rain on Holly's parade, but the whole truck story sounds like one big exaggeration to me.

"Oh, come on, Hudson. At some point, you have to start believing something."

"What do you mean?"

"I mean, some people go through their entire lives dissing God, dissing His followers, dissing the things He's done: the miracles, the changed lives. I mean…do you have any convictions?"

My face flushed.

I have convictions, all right, but they don't line up with yours.

"Whoa, Holly, all I said was that story about the truck sounded like something out of a Stephen King novel."

"I know what you said."

I didn't know how much longer I could—or should—conceal the anger that had been brewing inside me for years. In fact, I hadn't ever done any real soul-searching about my feelings or hang-ups. Certain topics and beliefs and opinions were simply off-limits. But maybe Holly and I should have this discussion sooner rather than later.

"Look, don't get me started."

"Go ahead. I want to know what your problem is."

"Okay." I slapped my leg. "I question why God let my mom die when I was fifteen years old. I question why my old man didn't get help for her sooner. Those are two of my problems."

"Wait a minute—"

"And then He let my old man go to prison and left me alone!"

"Your dad made bad decisions."

"God could have stopped him. I needed a father!"

"Yeah, but look what happened. God used those trials to draw your dad to Him."

"Yeah, and now, all of a sudden, I'm supposed to believe he's some goody Christian. I'm supposed to forgive him. He just wants to ease his own selfish conscience."

"Boy, are you bitter."

"You're right I am."

"All I'm saying is, who can change a life like mine or your dad's or Chester's? I mean, really *change* it? No drug can do it. No human can do it—"

"I knew this lecture was coming." I glared at the road in front of me.

"At some point in your life, you need to forgive people, Hudson, and believe in them, and not be so negative about God."

"Look." I held up my hand for her to stop. "Thanks for the counseling session."

"Wait a minute. While we're on this, I just have to say this. Did you ever think that—through Chester, or Arthur, or your dad, or even me—that God may be trying to reach *you*? Hello?"

The last day has been so bizarre…maybe Someone is trying to get through to me. I balked at the idea.

"I believe in God," I said.

"Oh, you do…"

"That's right. I just have no regard for Him or what He's done to me."

I knew that comment would bring some fireworks, and once I'd said it, I felt guilty and almost apprehensive about doing so.

"Hudson, listen to yourself. You sound just like Jonathan, before he realized how selfish he was."

"Now I'm selfish." I reached in front of her, jerked open the glove compartment, found my cigarettes, and jabbed the car lighter.

"That's right, and now you're going to smoke so we'll all know it's time to have a big pity party for Hudson. Give me a break."

If she were a guy, I would have punched her. Instead, I stuffed a cigarette in the corner of my mouth and glared out the driver's window. Then I turned up the AC and stared straight ahead at the road.

"I'm sorry about that," she said.

"You said what you wanted to say, didn't you? Sorry or not."

"Yeah, I guess I did. You want to take me home?"

"Not until we know what's going on with your boyfriend."

"Don't call him my boyfriend." She crossed her arms and peered out her window. "You know I've been trapped." Her voice cracked and went up an octave. "That's mean."

"I'm sorry. That *was* mean. Please forgive me."

She nodded, choking back tears.

"You're a good girl, Holly. That was my bad. I'm sorry. Whoever can't get along with you has a real problem."

Her body convulsed as she laughed and cried at the same time, wiping the deluge of tears away.

"I like you a lot, Holly."

"I like you too." Still angled away from me, she got a Kleenex from her purse, rubbed her nose, and sniffed. "You just need some good theological counseling and psychotherapy sessions before we see much more of each other."

We both laughed.

And then the rest of the way to the post office I pondered her beauty and sensitivity, her faith, and what she'd said about Chester and my father—without ever lighting that cigarette.

By the time Holly and I climbed out of the Mustang at the post office that Jonathan had directed us to on South Decatur Boulevard, it was blistering hot—not a cloud in the blue sky. We found Chester's six-inch-by-six-inch box readily, and the key worked. Holly gathered its overflowing contents, and we sat on a bench inside the cool facility.

"He didn't check this box very often," she said. "Most of this stuff is pretty old."

"He had a regular income." I held up a dividend check for $1,837 from Home Depot and three envelopes from other large corporations.

"What did he do with the money?" Holly opened another.

"Like you said, he gave it away."

"Yeah, but I didn't know it was on this scale!"

"His bankbook had a bunch of cash withdrawals. Who knows?"

"Uh-oh. Here's another letter from Living Word Fellowship," Holly said.

"Look at this." I held up the face of a small, handwritten envelope. "Look who it's from."

"A. Holte. Atlanta."

"Andrew," I said. "Chester's son."

"Should we open it?"

"Holly, we have to. We're closer than anyone to finding out what's really going on. If the police put some Barney Fife on this case, none of us will ever know what happened."

She stared at the letter.

"Okay?" I asked.

"Okay."

I opened it, unfolded the small piece of off-white note paper, and began reading.

Dear Dad,

I know when you left Living Word Fellowship, you wanted to go quietly, not causing any discord within the church. And as I've told you before, everything has been fine. People have asked questions, quietly, among themselves, and there hasn't been any major upheaval—until a few weeks ago.

We had a churchwide meeting several Sunday nights ago. Near the end, during Q and A, the people began to get their courage up, one by one, and started asking pointed questions to Pastor Scribe and the elders about why you left so abruptly, why you withdrew your pledge, and why they weren't being told any more details. (Are you aware what a highly respected man you are, Dad? I hope I turn out like you.)

scribe told the people he was "completely confused" by your departure and said he had no idea
why you'd left. Can you believe that? Well, Dad, I
couldn't just sit there and listen to that. I told
you I was committed to staying at the church to
try to see this thing through, to be a catalyst for
change there. But when I heard scribe lying to
the people, not making public the concerns you'd
brought to light, I had to speak up.

As meekly as I could, I shared your concerns
about scribe, the leadership, the legalism, self-
righteousness, and works-based "religion." You talk
about fireworks. Half the people, including scribe
and the elders, wanted to stone me! The other
half were standing, clapping, and "amening" in
agreement.

The meeting went till 11:55 p.m., without any
solid resolution.

since then, scribe has only taught one sunday
morning. His topic? "Rebellion within the Church:
Wolves in sheep's Clothing." He's been absent the
other sunday or two.

Needless to say, I can't stay there, Dad. I've
tried. But the leadership's denial of your allega-
tions makes me see how truly hypocritical and
deceived these men are. Like you, I plan to continue
to pray for them and for God to intervene and
make things right.

I wish I could talk to you about this in person.
I want to get your opinion about what I should do

next, where I should go to church, etc. I've even
thought of paying you a visit. Would that be
okay? I could take some vacation time. I'd be fine
hanging out with you, whatever the living
arrangements! Write back and let me know what
you think.

 With love from your son,
 Andrew
 P.S. My landlord said my rent has been paid
for the next three months. Thanks, Dad. You
didn't have to do that. I am making a decent
living with the U.S. Postal Service. Just got anoth-
er fairly good raise recently. Love you. Andrew

"Wow." Holly took the letter and examined it. "This is five weeks old."

"Sounds like all's not well at Living Word Fellowship."

"Better open up that letter from them."

I slit it open, pulled out a lone, folded white piece of paper, and held it out for Holly and me both to read. But it wasn't a letter. There was no handwriting. Instead, it was a crooked photocopy of a pledge card filled out in the amount of $1.5 million to be paid over five years by Chester Holte, whose signature was in the bottom right-hand corner. Most glaring were the five bright red stamps that plastered the page, each one reading "PAST DUE."

It was late afternoon. Mentally and physically, Holly and I were running on empty. We rehashed everything over subs, chips, and beverages at Jimmy John's, where we sat at a high table as close as we could to the overhead AC vent.

Just before leaving the restaurant to pick up her cell phone at the clinic and try to get some sleep back at my place, Holly reached over and touched my wrist. "Would you mind checking on Ken again?"

I found Tom Fitzgerald's number at the LVMPD and dialed.

"Mr. Ambrose, I was just about to call you," Fitzgerald answered.

"What can you tell me, sir?"

"This news is going to disturb Miss Queens and you, I'm afraid."

"Oh?" My eyes met Holly's, and I winced.

"Mr. Van Dillon was released about an hour ago on $100,000 bond."

I closed my eyes and dropped my head. Holly squeezed my hand.

"There has been a restraining order placed on him," Fitzgerald said, "so he can have no contact with Miss Queens, he can have no access to weapons, and he can talk to no potential witnesses. He'll be expected back in court within thirty days for his plea."

"That's sick." I covered the phone and told Holly, whose hand muzzled her mouth. "How can you tell me this guy is out?"

"I'm sorry, Mr. Ambrose. From what I understand, he had no priors. Very clean record. Exemplary military service. He is being required to wear a GPS ankle bracelet. So, he is being monitored."

"By whom? How does it work?"

"He wears it everywhere. It's tracked by a global positioning satellite. So, if he goes anywhere other than home or work—or whatever parameters they've set for him—the monitoring office will know it, and authorities will be on him in half a shake. Those things can tell precisely where a person is, to within a few feet."

I glanced at Holly, stood, gave her a reassuring half smile, and walked to the window ten feet away. "I've read about people who've cut those things off," I said quietly. "What about that?"

"Very unlikely. I think only six to eight percent are removed."

"That's six to eight out of a hundred people on the loose!" I tried to contain myself. "This is nuts. This guy is a mental case. You saw what he did to her. And you're going to try to contain him with a plastic and rubber ankle bracelet?"

"They're comprised of metal too. Mr. Ambrose, I really think she's going to be fine. The instant one of these devices is tampered with, it sends a distress signal directly to the monitoring station."

"That's great, as long as the person supposedly monitoring it is doing his job."

"Look, Mr. Ambrose, I understand your frustration. I'd probably feel the same way if I were you. But I need to prepare you; this may not be the worst of it."

"What do you mean?" I turned around and saw Holly's pitiful eyes fixed on me, as if she were relying on me to save the day.

Fitzgerald continued. "A lot of these wife beaters and sexual offenders are doing negotiated pleas these days, where their attorneys negotiate guilty or no-contest pleas in return for lighter sentences than they'd normally get after trial."

I turned back to the window. "How light?"

"In some cases, no jail time. They're getting off simply by paying fines and doing community-service work, or, as in this case, maybe by taking anger-management classes. It saves the city money when they don't have to incarcerate these hooligans. All I'm saying, Mr. Ambrose, is that you and Miss Queens should fasten your seat belts. The ride could get bumpy."

15

he jagged line of dark, tattered homeless people standing outside the Las Vegas Rescue Mission was three blocks long and around the corner. Holly bounded up the steps of the Downtown Outreach Clinic and ducked inside in search of her cell phone as I sat in the cool Mustang across the street and wondered if Chester had ever waited in that line for chow.

How long had it been since any of them had sat in air conditioning as I was right then?

Amid the sea of sun-drenched bodies, I noticed Arthur Peabody's walking stick, then the yellow Georgia Tech sweatshirt swinging low behind him, its arms tied in a knot at his waist. He wore a gray T-shirt with a ring of sweat at the neck and baggy green cargo shorts. His skin was russet, his jaw protruding, and he had a bony nose that had to have been broken on more than one occasion. But most recognizable of all was the brown beret perched atop his matted, graying hair.

Holly came down the steps with a quick smile and a wave of her cell phone.

"That's Arthur Peabody in line over there, with the walking stick." I pointed as she plopped into her seat and shut the door. "Does he look familiar to you at all? He's been in the clinic."

"I don't think so, but I know the guy he's talking to."

"Which one?"

"Unbuttoned flannel shirt with cut-off sleeves. Sandals. Name's Weaver. Chronic asthma. He's always in and out of the clinic."

"Weaver. That's one of the guys Arthur mentioned. He may've been a friend of Chester's. You think it'd be okay if I go over there?"

She eyeballed the crowd, then gave me the once-over, from my beard to my flip-flops. "You'll fit in okay, but I'm going with you."

"No, you're not."

"Hud, I deal with these people every day." She opened her door and looked at me. "You're gonna need me. Come on."

It seemed everyone in the line stopped what they were doing, which wasn't much, and stared as we hurried along the smoldering sidewalk, crossed the street, and walked directly toward Arthur.

"Maybe this wasn't such a great idea," I whispered.

"Too late now."

"Arthur." I waved as we approached. "Hudson Ambrose. Remember me?"

He glared at me, did a double-take of Holly, then returned his gaze. "I remember."

Weaver nodded at Holly. "You're a nurse at DOC."

"And you're Mr. Weaver." She smiled. "How's your asthma?"

"Not bad." Weaver perked up at the mention of his name. "Boy, you got banged up. How'd that happen?"

Bodies closed in around us, and eyes began to devour Holly.

"It's a personal thing." Holly squirmed. "I'm okay now." She turned toward me, eyebrows raised, chin jutting out, and gave me one long, slow nod: my cue to hurry it up.

"Have you heard any more about Chester?" I blurted.

"I should be askin' you that!" Arthur said. "We thought we'da heard about your story in the paper by now. What's the holdup? Why ain't this thing bein' publicized?"

"This 'bout Chester?" A hairy, burly dude stepped in, and the temperature in my face got as hot as the sidewalk.

"Yeah." Arthur held up a hand to the man's chest and scanned the crowd. "This is the reporter from the *R-J* I told you about. Keep your cool, Jenkins, people."

"What the hay gives?" Jenkins's two huge paws slammed my chest, throwing me back two feet. "Ain't nothin' been done about Chester. Why?"

Another man, long blond hair and beard, snatched my collar and got in my face. "Nobody gives a flip. It's like he disappeared off the face the earth. Why ain't it been in the paper yet?"

Holly let out a scream, and just as I looked at her alarmed face, I was slammed to the pavement from behind, the palms of my hands digging into the concrete.

"Enough!" Arthur screamed. "Stop."

I rolled over, making sure Holly was okay, then clasped my burning hands. "Chester's body hasn't turned up with the police or the coroner," I yelled. "We've got some leads, but it's complicated." I got to my feet, seething, scanning the derelict faces for whoever had blindsided me. Then I homed in on Arthur. "I need to know what else you know since we talked! I'm going to the cops with all I know tomorrow."

Arthur reached up and squeezed my shoulder. "You can't go to the cops, Hudson."

"They're in on it," Jenkins insisted. "*You* need to break the story—"

"The cops will bury it!" said the blond guy. "What else do you know?"

"Tell me what *you* know," I scanned their blank faces, my heart thundering. "All of you."

Holly's arm slipped around my waist. It would be harder for them to attack me with her close. Smart girl.

"The name Needermire's all you gotta know." The blond's eyes burned into mine.

"He's on my list. What else?"

Arthur searched the crowd. "Where's Frazier?"

"Haven't seen him," Weaver replied.

"You need to talk to Ned Frazier," Arthur said. "He's one of us. He saw something that night."

"What?" Holly asked.

"Chester, at the bus stop with Needermire and another guy," Weaver said.

"A cop?" I asked.

"No," Arthur said. "Don't know who it was. Frazier can tell you more."

"Did they have weapons? Was the killing going down? Tell me what you know! I don't have a lot of time left to track down this Frazier guy."

"The third guy knew Chester. He and Needermire argued. That's all I know."

"Other dude was tall," came a voice from behind. I turned to face a pudgy man of about forty, solemn face, sagging features, wearing an oil-stained, sleeveless T-shirt. "Brown hair, cut short."

"How do you know?" I asked.

The pudgy guy pursed his lips and swung his head toward Arthur.

"You can believe him," Arthur said. "This is Jack Rabbit. He gets around. You know anything more, Jack?"

"Just that if something doesn't get done about Chester quick, there's a lot a people in this town who're gonna raise a whole lot of you-know-what."

My palms still burning, I fished an *R-J* business card out of my wallet and handed it to Arthur. "If you find out where I can find Frazier, or if you hear anything else, call me."

Arthur nodded. "I'm afraid if the police get aholda this we're never gonna know what happened to Chester. You get my drift? Needermire's bad news. They may try to cover it up."

"I hear you," I glanced at Holly. "We'll do our best."

Although the soft yellow sun was fading beyond the rocky Nevada mountains and the city's dazzling neon lights were beginning to perform, I shifted uncomfortably in the driver's seat where an undeniable urgency hemmed me in.

"I've got to do something, now." I maneuvered the Mustang toward my place, dodging cars one after another filled with out-of-state gawkers. "Maybe I could do a story on the whole thing, an exposé—"

"They'd never run it," Holly said. "They've got to be politically correct. They'd insist you go to the police first."

"Maybe I should go *now.*"

"What about the safe-deposit box?"

"Forget it," I barked. "I need to get this thing out in the open. It's a powder keg, and it's about to explode."

For the first time in a long time, I was coming unglued.

"What a stupid idiot I am."

I could still feel the bloody safe-deposit box key closed in my sticky palm. Chester's lifeless body was seared in my mind. *His blood was on my hands.*

Replaying the savagery of the gang at the abandoned van, a tide of nausea burned the base of my throat. I swallowed it back and kept driving, drumming my thumbs on the wheel, my mind ricocheting from one character to another in that surreal nightmare.

I could go to jail.

A sense of confusion literally shook me.

The ridge in my forehead felt an inch deep. My breathing was short and quick, and I had to force myself to fill my lungs with air, deeply, several times.

"You okay?" Holly sat up.

"Yeah," I sighed. "Just trying to figure out what to do. I'm in a blue funk."

"You're tired. You need sleep."

I'd gone into work Friday night and had barely slept since. Forty-eight hours with little more than a nap.

"I know." I looked at the purple half moons beneath her pretty eyes. "So do you. I'm sorry about all this." My voice trailed off. "You don't deserve this." I looked away, rubbing my blurring eyes with an unsteady hand.

Holly touched the crease of my arm. "What we need to do is get a good night's sleep."

Her hand on my arm was good. "You're right."

"Do you mind if I crash at your place, just for tonight?"

"I want you to."

"I'm just not sure how much I trust an ankle bracelet to stop Kenny."

"I'm with you on that. You can stay as many nights as you need to."

"One night will ease my mind."

"Sounds good."

"Once we're fresh in the morning, we can decide how you want to play this whole Chester thing. We really need to pray—for guidance."

"I want to go straight to the cops; to heck with Chester's box. I've gotta get this monkey off my back."

As gently as it had been placed there, Holly's hand withdrew from my arm.

Great. I'd ignored her comment about prayer, and the religion barrier reared its ugly head again. Or maybe I was just being paranoid.

"The key is finding the right person to confide in." I glossed over the potential snag. "We could go to Fitzgerald, but I don't think he's high enough up . I know another guy named Truax. He's got clout. I think he may be our best bet."

Holly remained silent, staring straight ahead at the busy road in front of us.

I hadn't been paranoid after all.

"You're mad because I ignored your comment about praying."

She crossed her leg and turned her whole upper body toward me. "God's important to me."

"I know that."

"I like you, Hud. That's why it's bugging me how you feel about Him."

"I like you too."

"But if you like me, God comes with the package." She leaned closer. "He's lives in me; He's part of me."

"So what are you saying? I mean, we still get along—"

"But this is a big deal. This is not like, I like musicals and you don't. Or I like Chinese food and you don't. This is the most important thing in my life. And for us to not have that in common…"

"I told you I believe."

"But do you really? You sound antagonistic. I think you just say you believe, and why you do that I have no clue."

"Maybe it's because I like you. Maybe it's because my mom believed. I don't know..."

I pushed harder on the gas, wanting to leave the whole frustrating topic behind.

"Okay, well, can we just clarify...do you believe in Jesus, or don't you?"

"Define 'believe.'"

"I don't know...to reverence Him. Embrace Him. A desire for Him to be active in your life."

"I believe something—or Someone—created everything..."

"Oh, come on, Hud! Be hot or be cold."

"What do you mean by that?"

"I guess I just mean, be for Him or against Him. But don't be lukewarm."

I felt as if I'd just been shot with a nail gun. The riveting clarity of her words pierced my soul to the seat and left me fuming, and— at the same time—speechless.

16

By the time we pulled into the garage, Holly and I were drained. Like sleepwalkers, we shuffled into the house in silence. I turned on a light, she squeezed my hand, whispered thanks and good night, and started upstairs toward the master bedroom. I grabbed my pillow, threw my shirt off, turned out the light, and dropped onto the couch in my shorts, sound asleep in record time—until the shrill ring of the telephone woke me.

Bolting upright in the pitch black living room, my heart banged high in my chest. I took several steps toward the kitchen and cracked my smallest toe on the coffee table. Suppressing a curse, I limped toward the glowing green numbers on the microwave, which read 4:38 a.m., and felt for the phone on the kitchen counter.

"Hello," I groaned.

No response. No name in the caller ID window.

"Hello?"

I heard movement on the other end of the line.

Finally, a male voice came low and tense. "I know she's there."

Assuming it was Ken Van Dillon, I chose to play it dumb.

"I think you have the wrong number."

"Don't give me that! You're in deep trouble, reporter. More trouble than you've ever known."

"Who is this?" I turned on the light.

"It's too late now. It's too late. I warned her. The damage has been done. It's all over."

"There's nothing going on between us," I insisted, as quietly as possible, "and you're breaking the law right now by calling here!"

I heard footsteps in the dark. Holly came to a stop at the entrance of the kitchen, her arm covering her squinting eyes, her pink and white baseball shirt hanging out over her jeans, and a pair of baggy white socks crumpled up at her ankles.

Covering the mouthpiece, I held the phone to Holly's ear. "Is this Van Dillon?" I whispered to her.

"It's too late to plead for mercy," he continued.

Holly nodded with a sickeningly white face, and I took the phone back and moved out of earshot.

"My mind is made up," he ranted. "I warned you to keep your distance. She knows. Holly knows what's coming. It's all over. I'm glad, really. I'm ready for it to be over. My military career's ruined anyway, thanks to you and her."

With my hand over the mouthpiece, I told Holly, "Call the police. Tell them he's threatening us. I think he's at a pay phone."

She turned and dashed.

"You know what happened to Chester Holte?"

I didn't know if it was a question, or if there was more coming—so I kept my mouth shut.

"Same thing's gonna happen to you, but worse."

"What do you know about Chester?" I boiled.

"He had the hots for her, just like you do. And you're gonna pay, just like he did."

Oh my gosh.

Van Dillon was tall, short brown hair, just like Jack Rabbit described. He was the third one at the bus stop with Chester and Needermire!

That's it.

"Why don't you tell me where you are right now, Van Dillon? I'll come right now, and we'll settle this thing once and for all—like men. I'll come to your house. The police won't even know. Come on, you loser. Let's do it!"

It was a line I hadn't ventured past in a long time. The temper my mother and father warned me about had arisen. My mind seared white, and a pressure-pounding anger ran so deep I thought I might flip the refrigerator.

"Believe me, I'd love that," he mumbled, "but that would not be smart of me."

"What's wrong, you coward? Afraid I may put up a little more fight than a woman? Come on, you dirty, spineless wimp! Let's see what you can do against a man. Maybe you'll try to bash my skull against the wall, like you did Holly's."

My pulse pounded in my ear.

With the phone glued to my aching ear, I stalked the perimeter of the kitchen, trying to regulate my breathing.

I thought he might've hung up.

Then he spoke one last time.

"I'll be coming for you. Both of you. When the time's right. And then we'll see about all your talk. Then we'll see what it's like to die— all three of us."

After several tense moments sprinting about the house in search of Holly, I found her in the dark garage, peering out the window at the street.

I put my hand on her shoulder from behind.

"Is he coming?" Her whole body shook.

"He made threats. That's all. Just threats. Did you get the police?"

"Yeah." She stared at the white streetlight.

"Are they on it?"

"They're getting with the monitoring service."

"They know where he is, Holly, exactly. This'll get him in deeper trouble. It'll help us prove our case. Don't worry. I'm here."

She turned around, her bruises blending in with the shadows, her eyes shining as she looked up at me. But she said nothing.

"I won't let him hurt you again. Never again."

My hands found hers. They were trembling. I lifted them between us and our fingers interlocked.

"I don't care if I die." She frowned and shook her head.

"You're not going to die, Holly. This thing is—"

"But I'd go to heaven, Hud." She gripped my fingers tight. "It's going to be so much better than here."

She made it sound so real.

Is my mother here?

For an instant, I could see Mom nodding at me, smiling. The background was white, stark white. It was raining, a soft rain. And she was laughing.

"I want you to go to heaven," Holly said. "Chester's there. And your mom…"

Holly had a glazed look on her face, and I was afraid she might've been slipping into some sort of breakdown mode.

"Holly." I squeezed her hands, "I need to ask you something."

Her mouth sealed shut, and she stared at me.

"Was Van Dillon jealous of Chester?"

"Why?" She winced. "What did he say?"

"I'll tell you in a minute. Just tell me if he was jealous of Chester."

"He's jealous of everybody."

"But Chester was homeless. He was older. I don't see how—"

"He was charming, Hud. He was strong and confident and happy, all the time. He didn't worry about anything. He was carefree. And he had a way of making everyone feel special. It was like magic. Whenever I had the chance to be with him, I wanted to. And Ken hated it."

"But it wasn't a romantic thing…"

"Of course not. Chester was like a father. But Ken had a fit whenever Chester and I saw each other. Chester always laughed it off. He knew just how to handle Ken."

"Van Dillon made it sound like he knows what happened to Chester, like he may've even had something to do with it."

Holly's eyes shifted to the window, the floor, the Mustang, and back to me. "The third guy at the bus stop. Remember what Jack Rabbit said? Tall?"

"With short brown hair. I know." I took her by the hand and led her into the house. "I need to get the police. It's time. Let's get dressed." I braced for the backlash from what I was about to say. "We'll get some breakfast, then maybe I can take you to your pastor's house while I head to police headquarters?"

"Are you nuts? I'm going with you!"

"I don't want you to be implicated if it gets ugly, Holly."

"I haven't done anything wrong. You just said Kenny may've had something to do with Chester."

I lowered my head into my hand and rubbed hard at my forehead, running my fingers over the deep crevice above my nose.

"I just think it would be safer if you stay out of the picture."

"They're gonna want to question me anyway, about Chester. And with all that's happening with Kenny, it only makes sense that I go with you."

I threw up my hands. "Have it your way. I just don't want to see you go down with me if I get in trouble."

"Don't worry about me, Ambrose. Remember, I'm the one who's been praying."

She shot me a smile and a wink and headed for the stairs.

I cracked a smile as Holly's statement and demeanor broke through my frustration.

As she padded away in those ragged white socks and that cute pink and white baseball shirt, I was charmed both by her personality and her beauty. But there was something more, something I would make sure she never knew.

I was intrigued by her shameless faith. It always seemed to be right there, on her sleeve, consistent and real. Perhaps most refreshing of all was the fact that there she was, with me, a sinner. Not afraid that my shortcomings would rub off on her or that my bad habits would corrupt her, but sure of herself. Or, I guess I should say, sure of her God.

"You are definitely the prettiest number nine I've ever seen," I called as she went up the steps.

She laughed and shook her head but didn't look back.

Just kept going.

Class all the way.

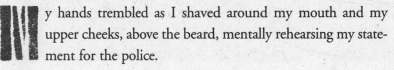

17

My hands trembled as I shaved around my mouth and my upper cheeks, above the beard, mentally rehearsing my statement for the police.

Ouch.

A cool sliver of pain burned at the top of my upper lip. Leaning closer to the mirror, I examined the growing dot of burgundy colored blood growing on my lip and was instantly transported back to the hot, sticky morning I'd found Chester.

How I wish I'd handled it differently.

I'd been greedy for money and a story. Now I had neither and was fighting to keep myself out of prison.

Idiot.

I looked myself in the eyes and shook my head in disgust.

How are you going to get out of this one?

Mixed with shaving cream, the blood from the small cut trickled over my lip and into my mouth. I spit the bitterness into the sink, wet my hand, and dabbed at the stinging cut with my middle finger.

If it weren't for this mess, you never would have met Holly.

After showering quickly, I threw on some cargo shorts, an army green Foreigner T-shirt, and sandals, and we took off for Holly's while it was still dark. Relieved to find her house undisturbed, she freshened up for the day, and by 6 a.m. we were standing at the front desk of the freezing LVMPD headquarters, ready to drop our bombshell about Chester Holte, Drake Needermire, and Ken Van Dillon.

When a young, dark-haired assistant sheriff named Barfield told us Nelson Truax wouldn't be reporting for duty until 7:30 a.m., we walked several blocks to the Cinnabon and grabbed a seat by the window. Holly drank coffee, and I had a Dr Pepper; we each put away one and a half cinnamon rolls and discussed our strategy. Holly even double-checked to make sure I had the keys to both Chester's safe-deposit box and his post-office box, which I did.

Assistant Sheriff Nelson Truax wore a neatly pressed, dark green LVMPD shirt with two small gold stars on the right and left tabs of the collar, a beige tie, and a star-shaped gold metal badge. His office was as neat as his appearance—nicely appointed, bright, clean desktop; two photos of the family; no clutter. But from the moment he ushered Holly and me into the vinyl chairs across from his big desk, I knew something wasn't right.

"So, we're going to talk about a missing person." Truax crossed his arms and worked a toothpick in his extra-wide mouth as he sat on the front edge of his desk. "Someone from the homeless community…"

"That's right." I nodded and began plodding my way into it, hoping what I was about to say would ring a bell with him. "What I discovered happened up at the Civic Center North bus stop."

"I see." He continued to probe with the toothpick, revealing a shiny, gold-capped tooth off to the side, on top. I was surprised he didn't seem to remember the phone call I'd made to him, inquiring about the bus stop incident. "And when did this happen?"

"Two days ago. Early Saturday morning."

Truax stopped with the toothpick and squinted at me. "And you're just now coming to the police?"

I squirmed. His words were so formal. We'd interacted kindly in the past. What was going on?

"I've had a lot of thinking to do since it happened," I said.

"Uh-huh…"

"Plus, a lot of new information has come to light."

"Okay, we'll get to that in a minute. What's the name of this missing person? Has a report been filed?"

"I don't know if anyone has filed a report." I glanced at Holly and back at him. "Chester Holte was his name: H-O-L-T-E."

"Wait a minute. 'Was'? What do you mean, 'was'?"

Everything came to a screeching halt, and I felt my chair wobble.

"That's right." I swallowed. "He's deceased."

Before the words were even out of my dry mouth, Truax was on his feet, walking around the desk with his back to us. I glanced at Holly, who closed her eyes and nodded slowly, signaling for me to stay cool, that everything would be okay.

I hoped she was praying.

Without another word, Truax stared at the dozens of buttons on his massive phone and jabbed one. "Kim? Is interrogation room B available?"

Holly covered my hand with hers.

"It is, sir."

I was weak and faint and tired and distant.

"Let me have it for a while, will you?"

In a room about the size of a closet, with a video camera rolling at eye level, I told Assistant Sheriff Truax every detail about the past forty-eight hours. By the time we were finished ninety minutes later, he knew all I did, from the call I'd heard on the police scanner in the *R-J* newsroom two days ago to the threatening telephone call I'd received from Ken Van Dillon earlier that morning.

Holly had not been allowed to sit in while I gave Truax my statement, but she anxiously joined me back in his office afterward where we stood, alone, waiting for Truax.

"Any news on Van Dillon?" I whispered.

"I haven't been able to get a thing. How did it go in there?"

I ran my fingers through my hair and sighed. "It feels good to have it off my chest."

She squeezed my bicep. "You did the right thing."

"He asked a ton of stuff," I said. "It was weird. Some of the things he asked…"

"What do you mean?"

"It was just spooky. I don't know. Maybe I just don't know the guy as well as I thought I did. He seemed cold."

"Well, hopefully he's good at what he does. That's what counts."

"You got that right."

Holly looked at the empty doorway, then back at me. "Are you in any trouble?"

"Not sure. Quite possibly. Like I said, he didn't have the best bedside manner. He was obviously peeved I'd searched Chester and left. And he was anxious to get his hands on the keys."

"Did you tell him about your house being robbed?"

"Oh, he had a cow. I thought he was going to—"

Truax breezed into the office without making eye contact. "Sit down." Tossing a manila folder on the shiny, wood desk, he made his way around it, stopped in front of his chair, crossed his arms, and exhaled loudly. "Houston, we have a problem."

My stomach rolled, and I felt my face flush. I wanted to look at Holly for solace but decided I'd look more innocent if I kept my eyes on Truax.

"What I *haven't* told you people yet is that I received a very interesting and somewhat disturbing telephone call in the predawn hours at my home this morning from one of this department's finest officer's, Sergeant Drake Needermire."

Truax's eyes bore into me.

Holly flinched.

My face lit on fire.

"Sergeant Needermire told me he received an anonymous phone call late last night, about a murder at the Civic Center North bus stop. Sound familiar, Ambrose? He wondered if he could come to my home or meet me in here this morning to fill me in on the details. Said he'd been up all night putting the pieces together."

The events of the past two days roared past me with vivid clarity. *This has to be a nightmare.*

I dug the fingernails of my right hand into the palm of my left. *No. It is really happening.*

"Sergeant Needermire came to my house." Truax stared at me with his big hands in the prayer position, pressed against his nose and mouth. "What he told me was that the anonymous caller told him a man from the homeless community, a well-respected man named Chester Holte, was missing. The caller told Needermire that *you* killed that homeless man, Ambrose, and hid his body somewhere in the desert."

"Excuse me, why didn't you tell us that when we got here?" Holly fired.

"Excuse *me,* Miss Queens," Truax leaned over the desk with a furrowed brow and pointed a fat finger at Holly. "I'll run this investigation, and I'll do it in a manner that gets to the bottom of this mess in the most time-efficient manner. For your information, my top priority this morning was to have your friend here brought in for questioning. When he showed up on my doorstop with a confession, I let him tell his story, naturally looking for differences in the two—and I found plenty."

"My story stands." I edged to the front of my chair. "Everything I told you is true. It's the way it all happened. Witnesses have told me Needermire was at the bus stop with Chester when he died. He's probably trying to cover for himself. He may've made that up, about the anonymous caller."

Truax chuckled. "You know, he told me you'd probably say that."

My eyes closed, and I tried to compose myself. "I told you, Needermire is no friend of the homeless—"

"Wait just a second." Truax smirked, moseyed around to the front of the desk, and sat there, with his hands clasped together. "Needermire told me he couldn't sleep last night. After he got that call, he started putting two and two together—"

"I'm telling you, sir, in all likelihood he's lying!"

Holly squirmed. "He and his henchmen beat and maimed dozens of people at the Owens Avenue sweep. Did you tell him?" She looked at me and I nodded. "That should tell you what kind of person Needermire is."

"What I know is this." Truax crossed his arms and threw his head back. "Sergeant Needermire tells me he came across a Mustang GT at the vacant van where Chester Holte used to stay. And he found you,

Ambrose, rummaging through that van, stealing things that would incriminate you."

"That's not true! I told you, I was looking for evidence about who killed Chester. Needermire wasn't even there—"

"Then how did he know you were there?"

"He was probably following me! He knows I'm getting to the bottom of Chester's death. He may've even hired those thugs to take me out of the picture."

"Oh, come on, Ambrose. This isn't the movies."

"Listen to me—"

"No, you listen to me. The fact remains that you yourself say you searched Chester's dead body, ran away with his bankbook and safe-deposit key, took things from that box, took things from his post-office box—"

"Yes, I made mistakes. I thought, because he was homeless, no one would know or care. I wanted to get the story, before the thing got buried in red tape—"

"You know…you know…" Truax's voice overpowered mine as he stood and wandered behind Holly and me, the leather on his gun belt squeaking. "What really bothers me about this is that Drake Needer-mire responded to the call at the Civic Center North bus stop Saturday morning, and as he reflected on that call during the night, he remembered seeing your Mustang leaving the scene of that supposed crime."

"What was he doing there?" Holly squealed. "Needermire again, everywhere Chester was—"

"Well, then, Miss Queens, do you want to explain to me why your friend here called this very office two days ago, asking me questions about what happens to the body of someone who's murdered within Las Vegas city limits?" He mimicked me. " 'Does it go to the hospital first, then the coroner?' "

Holly turned to me, and I looked directly into her eyes, shook my head, and hoped I wouldn't get sick from the helpless feeling brewing in my stomach.

Truax rambled on. "Do you know Gene Umberger, at the county coroner's office, is a friend of mine? Do you know I phoned him this morning and he said, Ambrose, you've been calling him a couple times a day, asking if Chester Holte's body has turned up? If I didn't know any better, I'd say you were having second thoughts about how well you disposed of the corpse."

"He was trying to find Chester!" Holly yelled. "Why would he have called you—the police—asking such questions, if he'd killed Chester and hid the body? He wouldn't call the coroner. He's not stupid. That's ludicrous. You need to open your eyes and call the cancer in your own department exactly what it is: cancer!"

"Don't you dare tell me what I need to do, Miss Queens." Truax stood directly in front of Holly's chair. "You two people think you can take the law into your own hands…"

But I was starting to boil as well. "Two days ago you told me to come to you if anything was up, and that's what I'm doing. You've got to believe me. Either Van Dillon or Needermire is responsible for Chester's death."

"We can get witnesses in here about the beatings at the Owens sweep," Holly blasted. "We will!"

"Van Dillon should be a prime suspect. At least one witness saw Needermire—and probably Van Dillon—with Chester at the bus stop before he died, before I got there," I said.

Holly added, "Needermire needs to be suspended while you sort all this out—"

"Okay!" Truax jammed his arm at us to stop. "That's enough!" He walked behind his desk and plunged into a big brown chair, which swiveled and rocked backward with the force of the big man. He turned the chair until we were facing the back of it and his slick, blond hair.

All I could hear was leather squeaking.

His chair tilted back.

Holly and I looked at each other. Her face was somber. I rolled my eyes in frustration. She mouthed the words, "It's okay, it's okay."

Truax grunted and swiveled around. His face was red. His dark eyes narrowed on Holly. "Miss Queens, do you consider yourself close enough to Chester Holte to fill out a formal missing-persons report?"

"Yes sir."

"That's step one. We're gonna go by the book on this thing. Next, I'm going to assign an investigator." He turned to me. "That individual will watch your videotaped statement, interview Needermire and Van Dillon, track leads and interview witnesses—including this Ned Frazier—and canvass the bus stop for evidence of the crime. He'll check bus schedules, video cameras at local businesses, all that."

I chimed in. "Don't forget Chester's safe-deposit box and—"

"And P.O. box." Truax stood and slapped his pants' pocket. "I know. You gave me the keys, remember?"

"What about Needermire and the beatings at Owens Avenue?" Holly dared ask. "He's got to be a suspect."

Truax yanked up his pants and took in an enormous breath. "The so-called beatings are a separate issue. But we'll be talking more in depth with Sergeant Needermire. Don't you worry." He headed for the door, leading us with an arm extended. "See Kim, on the right, as you leave, for that missing-persons report, and make it as detailed as possible. Witnesses' names, where they can be reached, et cetera."

As I was crossing in front of him to leave, Truax squeezed my arm, almost a pinch. I stopped within inches of his red face. "We're going to need to question you further. Much further." He patted my chest, at the base of my neck. "Make sure you don't go anywhere."

"You can question me all you want, but Van Dillon and Needermire are your boys. If you really want answers—and justice—put someone on their tail. Watch them. I'm serious. You'll get your man."

"Ambrose." Truax gritted his teeth, lowered his voice, and strong-armed me out the door. "As far as I'm concerned, you're a greedy, lying coward. What you did to that corpse is against the law. It's against every fiber of my being and what I stand for. And I got a feeling what you *really* did was much worse than that. I got a feeling what you *really* did was commit a homicide. If we had a body right now, I can promise you your hide would be behind bars with prime suspect written all over it."

Holly was already around the corner.

"You're judging me unfairly. I did not hurt anyone. I'm innocent! And if you try to frame me with this—"

"Then what, Ambrose? Huh?" He stepped closer and spoke through clenched teeth. "Get out of my office and stay out of my way, or I'll steamroll you."

18

t was 9:25 a.m. and must have been approaching one hundred degrees. Hud snapped his phone shut, groaned, and dropped next to me on the shaded bench outside the LVMPD.

"No Fitzgerald?" I asked.

"Huh-uh. I left him another message. Did you get off work?"

"Hud, I have to work. I'll feel safer at the clinic than I will at the house. There's always a ton of people around."

"I just want to make sure Van Dillon's not out running around where he's not supposed to be."

"We'll make sure before I go in," I said. "Besides, you've got other things to worry about."

Clasping his hands behind his neck, he arced backward and stretched. The hot breeze from the passing cars on Stewart Avenue blew his curly brown hair. His face and nose were long and distinct. He was enviably thin, yet extremely tough, and that made me feel safe around him. I enjoyed his company. He made me laugh easily and feel pretty. Often, I found myself silently, selfishly urging God to move in his life, thinking someday we might end up together. At the same time, I made myself swallow the cold truth that my desires weren't always God's. Hud might never be the man of God—the kindred spirit—I always thought I would marry. That was a disappointing reality.

Leaning forward with his elbows on his knees, he rubbed his forehead and stared at the sidewalk. "You know what I'm afraid of?"

"I could make a good guess."

"Two days ago I was worried about getting in trouble for searching Chester and leaving the scene—"

"Now you're worried about getting railroaded into murder charges."

He squinted up at me and nodded. "That's it."

I patted his back.

He turned away. "I suppose you're praying about all this."

I laughed. "As a matter of fact, I am. Do you think it'll do any good?"

"We'll see." He shot me a smile, stood, took several steps, and faced me. "I've got to find Chester's body."

"Aren't you afraid if you find it, the police will really think you killed him?"

"They already do! We need an autopsy. If a bullet killed him, that could free me; I don't even own a gun."

I nodded and forced a smile, but my stomach ached from the odds stacking up against Hud.

He came close and stood over me. "Why do you believe me?"

I shrugged. "I just trust you, that's all."

He eased onto the bench. "The problem is, Needermire and Van Dillon know I'm onto them. Whoever killed Chester is gonna make sure his body is never found."

Grudgingly, I agreed but said nothing.

"I've been thinking maybe I should follow Needermire. It's a long shot, but I'm running out of time. I need to turn up some leads." Hud's posture straightened. "Do you think I could use your pickup so he doesn't recognize my car?"

I wanted to say no. I couldn't fathom the thought of anything happening to Hud.

Why do I care so much?

My emotions surprised and frightened me.

"That's dangerous," I protested. "I mean, sure, you can use it, but I don't know what a great idea that is."

"You heard Truax. He's totally on Needermire's side."

"Arthur and his buddies were right, weren't they? About going to the police?"

"Humph." His head swung away.

"I'm afraid Truax is either going to bury the thing or try to hang you."

"The things I did look *so* bad."

It was true, soberingly true. He'd searched and robbed a dead, homeless man. The reality of it made me sick. He was the obvious murder suspect.

"There's got to be a way to prove I'm innocent."

"Go public with it." I threw my hands up. "Shoot, you could blow the whistle on the whole thing—Chester's murder, the bad sweep, police brutality…"

"Wait a minute." Hud grabbed my arm. "Wait a minute. Let me think…"

"I mean, you work for the city's biggest paper. This thing could go national overnight. You'd do what Needermire did, but on a bigger scale. You'd be the innocent one, crying foul—"

"You've got something." He shot to his feet, eyes zipping in all directions, one hand stroking his beard. "Let's think this through. I've got friends at the *R-J* who could do the story. Suzette or Reed. And I think the publisher would run it."

. "It would be crazy. I mean, we'd probably be talking national spotlight."

He dropped to the bench and buried his head in his hands. "I can't believe this is happening."

Selfishly, I took a fast assessment of my part in all this. Would my name come up? Would I be linked with Hud in a national news story? The facts could easily be misconstrued. It might look like I was sleeping with him, even helping him cover up Chester's murder.

"Hud." I leaned close to him. "Will you do me a favor? Please? I need you to do this one thing for me."

"I know what you're gonna say."

"Look at me."

He did.

"There's nowhere else to turn."

His eyes lowered, his head dropped, and he stared.

I rested my arm around his slumping shoulders. "Won't you pray with me?"

Hud stood, and my arm fell from his back. He paced ten feet and stopped with his back to me and his hands stuck to his waist.

"Are you just going to keep doing things your way?" I stood and folded my arms.

He turned around, mouth sealed tight, head tilting back toward the sky.

I can't force him.

"Maybe I should go home." I set my face toward the parking garage and took several steps. "Would you mind taking me?"

"Holly, wait. You need to understand—"

"I understand." I turned to face him. "Nothing more needs to be said. Really. I know you're processing a lot right now."

Hud dropped his head, shook it, jammed his hand in his pocket, pulled out the keys, and sauntered toward me.

But I couldn't hold it in.

"I just wanted to pray for you," I said, "for God to get you free of all this junk and to guide your steps. You need His wisdom now. Can't you see that?"

But he couldn't see it. Just couldn't.

His blindness ravaged my insides. I wanted to lash out, tell him he was too callous and bitter to ask for God's help. But that wasn't the way.

"I feel sorry for you, Hud." I didn't even mean to say those words; they just spilled over from the emotion swelling within me. Then I turned toward the car, urging myself not to cry.

"Holly, wait." He grabbed my arm.

"For what?" I shook free. "For you to do this on your own? To watch you call your own shots? It hasn't proven very effective."

The second I'd spoken, I regretted doing so and waited for the backlash.

"Fine." Hud huffed off ahead of me. "I knew your God wasn't big enough to let you love a pagan like me."

Silence shook my world as we pounded toward the car, ten feet apart, my heart breaking into smaller and smaller pieces each step of the way.

19

During the brisk drive back to Holly's place, I dragged hard on an overdue cigarette while she stared out her window at the bright landscape of dilapidated, one-story pawn shops, low-rent casinos, and chintzy wedding chapels.

Not a word was spoken.

When we rolled into her driveway, she was out of the car quickly.

"Good luck." She looked in at me. "Sorry about the turbulence back there."

Her door banged shut before I could figure out what to say or offer to walk her up.

To heck with it.

Backing out of the driveway and taking one last look at the cozy house, I had a feeling I wouldn't see Holly again for a long time. And it would be my fault.

My life stunk. I pitied myself for having lost my mom so young. And I cursed my old man for failing me, for being so weak, for being a drunken loser.

If it hadn't been for Truax's orders to remain in Las Vegas, I would have blown out of there. Where? Who knows. Seattle. Denver. Phoenix. Maybe even home, to the River Walk. *I could finally get to Mom's grave. Get it all cleaned up. Bring flowers...*

Ignoring the blasted yearning to call Fitzgerald again, to find out what on earth was going on with Ken Van Dillon, I swung back up to the *Review-Journal*, waved to Raphael, the parking attendant, found a parking spot, and hurried inside.

It was time to make some noise.

The *R-J* newsroom was buzzing with clacking keyboards, reporters on phones, people rushing with notes, small group discussions, and the adrenaline rush that inevitably comes with the pressure of a deadline. Reed nodded hello while cradling a black phone to his left ear and writing furiously on a yellow legal pad. He had a shorthand all his own.

Beth White was up at the city desk, pounding away at her PC with her gallon jug of 7-Eleven caffeine fuel at her side, all systems go. Suzette Graham's cubicle was empty, so I scanned the enormous room for her shiny blond hair and tall frame.

"What're you doing here, Ambrose?" came a female voice from behind. "I thought you worked the weekend?"

I turned around to see Suzette's gleaming smile. She wore a white, short-sleeve top with black pinstriped slacks. Her skin was golden brown from the summer sun, and I could see the evidence of bathing suit strap marks crisscrossing below the base of her neck.

"I did," I said. "I came in to find you actually."

"On your day off?"

"Yep. You got a minute?"

"Yeah." She looked at the silver watch on her thin wrist. "You want to go to the break room? I could use more coffee."

"I'll buy you a cup. Maybe we can take it back to your desk. I need to talk to you alone."

"Uh-oh."

We walked.

"What are you workin' on?" I asked.

"I'm slow today. Doing a piece on a stand-down at Cashman Center, but it doesn't happen till next week."

"What's a stand-down?"

"All the city's service providers set up booths, and the homeless come and find out about the different services available to them. There's a ton of great stuff they don't even know about. Food, shelter, clothes…"

Holly would like that.

"You're really into the whole homeless thing…"

"I am. It's been amazing. Some of the people are so sweet. They're just victims of circumstances. And so many are kids. But you wouldn't believe what goes on behind the scenes. There's so much politics involved."

I put a dollar bill in the coffee machine, and she pushed the black button. Then I got a can of Dr Pepper from another machine, popped the top, and we strolled back to her cubicle.

"I have to be careful about being biased." She looked around to make sure no one was listening. "My brother, Ellery, is the pastor of a church in Spring Valley where I go. We do a ton of outreach with the homeless."

"I know your brother."

Suzette's head pulled back. "Ellery?"

I nodded. "Just met him yesterday."

"Where?"

"It's a long story. That's part of what I want to talk to you about."

"Okay." She slowed. "This isn't about Ellery, is it? He's not in trouble or anything?"

"Oh, no no no. Nothing like that."

"Oh, good." Her stride picked up. "He's taken a lot of heat—I mean a lot—for having a church that reaches out to people the world considers worthless. I just wasn't sure what was up."

"Yeah, I read about his church."

"It's awesome. And Ellery's not the type to take any credit for anything. He's a humble guy."

"Are you two pretty close?"

"Like this." She held up crossed fingers. "Even though we're a year and a half apart and don't look anything alike, people have always called us the twins. They still do!"

She laughed.

We arrived at her cubicle. She knelt down and cleared a place for me in a black chair. I nudged it closer to hers and motioned for her to sit down. "Do you have a tape recorder?"

By noon Suzette and I were fried. On her digital recorder she'd captured my description of the entire Chester Holte saga, the brutal sweep at Owens Avenue, and my confrontation with Nelson Truax. She knew everything I did and every player involved.

"Hudson." Suzette shook her head and peered down at her notes. "I'm going to have to talk to Cheevers about this. He'll want to get the editorial board involved."

I threw my hands up, knowing she was right about our talented but paranoid editor, Donald Cheevers. "Whatever has to happen, has to happen. This thing is big. It's gonna be national. The question is, who's gonna break it first?"

"I should probably interview Truax myself, and Needermire—"

"Don't do that, Suzette, okay? Do me a favor. I'm coming to you with this scoop. Just run the initial story like I've told it. After that you can open it up."

"Cheevers is going to insist I talk to someone from the police. You know that. We've got to give them a chance to respond."

She was right. I'd done all I could. It was in her hands now, and the powers that be. "Okay. Do what you have to do, but I'm telling you, Suzette, a lot of fingers are pointing at Needermire. Keep that in mind if you talk to him. And Truax is one of these died-in-the-wool, law-enforcement-for-life rednecks who'll do anything to stop his office from getting a black eye."

Suzette's face was pink. She rolled her eyes, sighed, and turned several pages on her notepad.

"You're overwhelmed, aren't you?"

"Ye-ah," her voice broke as she gave me a "duh" look.

"If you're not up to it, I can take it to Reed. He can play the recording—"

"No. This is my beat. I want to do it." She hugged the pad to her chest. "It's just a lot to digest. I'll play the tape again, develop questions, and get busy. I may even just write the whole thing and give it to Cheevers when I'm done. We'll have a better chance of getting it printed that way."

"Now you're talking. Listen, do me a favor. When you find out if Truax has appointed an investigator, let me know. I also want to know what they found in Chester's safe-deposit box."

"I'll keep you posted."

I checked the familiar wall clock again. Holly would have been at the clinic more than an hour. *Maybe I'll drive by, make sure everything's okay.*

"When Cheevers gets my story, he's going to want to talk to you," Suzette said.

"Bring it on. You guys have my cell number. I'll do whatever it takes to get the story out. Who knows, someone who saw something may come forward. Finding Chester's body is going to help us nail whoever did this."

"And it'll get you off the hook."

I took a deep breath and exhaled. "Yeah."

"Do you have any photos of Chester?"

"Just what's online, and they're old."

My phone vibrated in my back pocket.

Holly.

"Excuse me." I'd always thought Suzette Graham was the hottest thing on two legs, but there I was, sitting three feet from her, and my mind kept rushing back to Holly. "Hello."

"Hello, I'm trying to reach a Hudson Ambrose, please."

Not Holly.

"This is Hudson."

"Mr. Ambrose, my name is Meg Ryder with the Citizens Medical Center in Victoria, Texas. I'm calling about a Mr. Glenn C. Ambrose. I believe he's your father?"

The sound around me faded.

I stood and walked.

He's hurt. Dad's hurt.

There was a quiet area in the rear of the newsroom. "Yes, he's my father."

He wanted my forgiveness more than anything.

I headed for a large window by the back stairwell.

"There's been an incident at the Texas State Penitentiary where your father was incarcerated..."

Was? I always assumed there would be more time, much more. He's still young.

There was an empty bench beneath the window. I hurried around it and stood in the corner, away from everyone, the sun beating down on me, bracing for the rest.

"I think you'd better get here as soon as possible."

20

From the phone in my cubicle at the *R-J*, I didn't divulge to Assistant Sheriff Nelson Truax that my father had been severely beaten while an inmate at the Texas State Penitentiary, only that he was in critical condition in Victoria. Hesitantly, Truax gave me permission to leave Nevada. But I was betting that within twenty-four hours—or however long it would take Suzette to put her story together—he'd wish he hadn't.

Before hitting my place to pack a bag, I swung past the Downtown Outreach Clinic. Holly's red pickup was there with its windows down and a silver sunscreen in the windshield. There was no sign of Van Dillon's car. Fitzgerald hadn't called back, so I assumed everything was cool on that front and that, if anything, Van Dillon was in more hot water than ever for threatening Holly while being under a restraining order.

After debating whether to go inside but deciding to let the waters calm between us more, I pulled the small notepad from my back pocket and jotted Holly a note. After two tries and two crumpled pieces of paper, I finally had it the way I wanted it.

> Dear Holly,
>
> I just found out that my dad is in serious condition at a hospital in Victoria. He was severely beaten by three inmates. I'm flying there now.
>
> Suzette Graham (R-J) has our whole story. Watch for it soon.
>
> No word from Fitzgerald, but I'll keep checking. You do the same. I'm certain Van Dillon is behind bars.
>
> I'm sorry about this morning. You are the brightest light that has ever dared enter my life. I hate to think that I would chase you away. That would be the greatest blunder of my life...although it may be for your best.
>
> I admire you, Holly. You are strong and wise and beautiful and faithful. And I know I would do well to be more like you.
>
> Yours truly,
> Hud

I folded the note and tucked it in the hot, black driver's seat of her truck, then took off for my house and an afternoon flight out of McCarran International Airport.

As my Continental Connection flight—a prop job carrying about twenty, mostly weary business travelers—touched down at flat, dry Victoria Regional Airport, I changed the time on my watch from 6:05 p.m. to 8:05 p.m. The quick drive southwest on Houston Highway got me to the parking deck at Citizens Medical Center in less than thirty minutes, not enough time to aptly prepare, mentally, for what I was about to encounter.

Beneath a jumble of tubes, IVs, tape, and gauze, my dad's swollen, purple and yellow face was almost unrecognizable. His poor head was wrapped tight with bandages, one eye was swollen shut, and he wore a cast on his right wrist. Vicky, a graying, middle-aged nurse in blue scrub pants and a bright flowered top, brought me up to date at my dad's bedside while he slept.

"Your father's been severely traumatized," she whispered. "He sustained serious injuries to the head, stomach, liver, and spleen. He lost several teeth, broke a wrist, and will probably lose that eye—if he pulls through."

If he pulls through...

"Has he been awake?" I mumbled. "I mean, will he come to and be in his right mind?"

"He's woken up several times. We thought he was hallucinating, but that's when he mentioned your name. So that was good. He's also mentioned a woman's name, repeatedly. Rita, I think it was."

"My mom."

"Ah."

"She passed away a long time ago."

"I'm sorry."

He's gonna die now too, before I have a chance to make things right. That'll be just like God.

"One thing, Mr. Ambrose, that the doctors are concerned about is that your father apparently had a series of heart attacks or TIAs during and/or following the incident at the penitentiary."

"What's a TIA?"

"Transient ischemic attack. Kind of a ministroke that lasts only a

few minutes. Whether those were brought on by the incident itself or
by a preexisting condition, we're not sure yet. But we're keeping a
close eye on him."

Three taps at the door.

"Come in," Vicky said.

The door opened and a tall, elderly black man wearing black
pants and a gray, button-down shirt quietly entered the room. His
hair was white at the temples; he wore black glasses; and his skin was
a dark brown, almost reddish, and noticeably shiny.

"You must be Hudson." He stuck out his hand and gripped mine
like a clamp.

"I am."

"I'm Victor Everson. I do a lot of visitation at the penitentiary.
Lead Bible studies. Counsel inmates." He nodded toward the old
man. "Your father and I are dear, dear friends."

He didn't look surprised at my dad's appearance.

"Have you been here already?" I asked.

"Oh yes." He chuckled. "I rode in the ambulance with him. I was
there when it happened."

"Really? What can you tell me?"

"Gentlemen, excuse me." Vicky stepped between us. "If you're
going to talk for a while, would you mind doing it outside? There's a
lounge just down the hall to the right. We need Mr. Ambrose to rest
quietly."

"No problem." Victor headed for the door. "We can go get us
some refreshments and talk a little bit. I'll come back to see Glenn in
a while."

Victor Everson seemed to know every inch of Citizens Medical
Center. I followed him the opposite direction Vicky had told us to go,
into a large kitchen where we each found a plastic container of cran-

berry juice in the fridge and several packs of graham crackers in marked drawers.

"Your dad is one fine gentleman." Victor peeled back the top of his drink, which looked to be the size of a shot glass in his large, worn, brown hands. "And he sure thinks a lot of you. I know that. He's proud of his reporter."

I opened my drink, threw the top in the trash, dabbed at the small spots that had flicked onto my shirt, and took a swig. "How did this happen?"

Victor shook his head and studied the floor. "He was talking to some inmates, five or six, during breaktime. I was with some other guys across the yard."

"This was outside?"

"Yeah. Have you seen the courtyard?"

"From a distance."

"Your dad was in the bleachers to the side of the basketball court."

"Okay, I know where you're talking about."

"Well, before I knew what was happening, your dad was lying on the floor of one of those metal bleacher boards, getting pummeled by two dudes."

"What happened to the others?"

"They'd scattered. But your dad didn't have a chance. These two nuts were amped up on some kind of crank. They had him down and dirty. Beating, kicking—"

"Why?" I seethed.

"A brother told me your dad was talking about the Lord again." Victor shook his head with a smile. "Just sharing, straightforward, friendly, like always—"

"Were these guys white, black, Hispanic?"

"White boys. Crazy. I mean, loony tunes. The guards in the tower fired shots, but by the time I got over there, Glenn was a mess." Victor shuddered and looked away. "I thought he might not make it."

"He still may not."

Victor waited and found my eyes. "No, he may not." He sipped his drink. "You two have some unsettled business to tend to."

What? How dare you.

"What do you mean?"

"He told me you were upset with him for not getting a doctor to tend to your mother's illness before she passed away. Also, that he wasn't there for you—"

"Man, that's none of your business. I'm sorry. I don't mean to be impolite, but that's a family matter."

"Hudson, your father and I read the Scriptures and pray together *every day.* We know each other inside out, upside down. Can you and I just come right out and be real for a few minutes?"

"Look, that stuff's between me and my dad."

"What are you afraid of?" He set his drink down and crossed his arms.

"Nothing, I just don't think—"

"Let me tell you something, young sir. There's a man lying in that room down the hall who is brimming over with love for you. Now I realize he didn't know how to show you that love, or may not have even had that love while you were growing up, but he's got it now. And more than anything in this world, he wants to share it with you. He wants your forgiveness. He wants one more chance to be a father to you."

Wanting to believe the stranger's words, I dropped my head, pinched the skin above my nose, and closed my eyes.

"Have you read his letters?" Victor asked.

I looked up at him. "No."

"Read them, Hudson," he pleaded. "When you do, you'll see—"

"I don't have them."

Victor's mouth froze open.

"I've thrown them all out."

He gawked at me, blinking back the rage behind his large, watery brown eyes. Without a word, he swept the drink off the counter, slammed it and his uneaten crackers into the overflowing trash can, turned his back, jammed the arm of the faucet in the stainless steel sink, and scrubbed his hands. Then he ripped a piece of paper towel, patted his hands, and faced me with a sigh.

"Okay, I'm not even gonna go there." He shook his head and searched the room. "Look, Hudson, all I can tell you is this. When my father died, we were on the outs, just like you and Glenn are. Now, he wasn't a great father. But I can tell you that still not one single day goes by that I don't wish I could go back in time and tell him I love him, thank him for being my dad." His head dropped, and his big hand covered his eyes.

"I understand," I mumbled.

"Do you?" His head shot up with anguish on his brow, and a large finger lifted toward my face. "Boy, your father's heaven-bound. He ain't got no worries about dying. He knows where he's going. But the one thing he wants more than anything is to make amends with you. Now, this is it," he raised his hands. "This may be the last dance. The question is, what are you gonna do about it?"

It was dusk. The end of a hot day. Staring out the window of the lounge down the hall from my old man's room, I decided that it was no longer light outside, but it wasn't dark yet either. Precisely how my insides felt. Like Holly had said, "Not hot, not cold." I contemplated the heartfelt words and emotions of Victor Everson. I thought of

Holly and Chester—what kind of people they were, what they would do if they were in my shoes. And I knew I had to make things right with my father.

I owe him that.

Before heading back to his room, I checked my voice mail. There was one new message, but it was time stamped earlier that afternoon. Between my flight and the hustle and bustle to get to the hospital, I'd missed it.

"Hudson, it's Suzette," the message played, "I'm working on the story from home. I contacted the police." Her words were choppy. She sounded almost short of breath. "Truax was furious you'd come to me. He said your story was totally contradictory to Needermire's and that he wanted to comment on it, but couldn't yet because he needed to get with their legal counsel."

Good!

"I'm almost done with the first draft, about ready to send it to Cheevers. Oh, one thing you should know, and this is a biggie: Truax put Jack Sloan in charge of Chester's investigation. I don't know if you know him, but he and Needermire are tight. Wait a minute, Hudson." She left the phone for a moment, then picked it back up. "Someone's at the door. I gotta go. If everything goes well, this baby should be in the morning edition. Talk to you soon."

I awoke in the turquoise vinyl chair in the corner of my dad's hospital room. It was dark and quiet, and Victor Everson was long gone. Slanting my watch toward the only light in the room, a dim fluorescent over the sink, I realized I'd slept almost six hours.

It was Tuesday. The story would be out soon. Just a few more hours.

Dad was in the same position, but his head had turned toward me. I stood and stretched, sore from sleeping in the chair. Pouring some diluted ice water into a plastic cup at the large tray by my dad's bed, I drank, and stared down. Even though his body was thin and badly discolored, he seemed at peace. He'd never been at peace before. I thought of what Victor had said, about the old man knowing his destination, being ready to go.

He will finally be with Mom. I could see the delight on their faces. Reunited.

But there's no proof.

None.

We all lived and died, and that was all we really knew. Those were the facts. No one had ventured beyond the unavoidable threshold of death and come back to tell about it, at least not with any substantial proof of afterlife.

There you go again, wanting proof.

Holly's words came back to me. *"Who can change a life like mine or your dad's or Chester's? Really change it? At some point in your life, you need to forgive people, Hudson, and believe in them, and not be so negative about God."*

"Hudson?" My dad's high, broken voice startled me.

"Dad?" I set the cup down and dropped to his side. His working eye was so bloodshot, I could barely make out his brown iris.

"Thanks for coming." He smiled and closed his eye at the same time.

"Can you see me?"

He nodded and smiled softly. "You need a haircut."

With wires and IV attached, his left forearm rose toward me. I took his warm, bony hand.

"Let me get the nurse."

"Wait." He squeezed. "Raise me."

Knowing better than to argue, I leaned over, examined the

switches on the inside arm of the bed, and pressed one. The mechanical sound fractured the silence. His head and slight shoulders lifted toward me. He winced.

"Sorry." I took my finger off the button.

"It's okay." He shook his head slightly and smiled. "Just a little while longer."

"Don't say that."

"We need to talk now—" He coughed, his whole body quaked, and I thought his ribs had broken.

"Listen, Dad." I squeezed his palm. "You and I are okay. Let's forget the past. It's time."

That bloody eye searched my face. He tried to speak, but nothing came.

"Our past is over. Mom was meant to go. And I know you were trying to provide for me when…things went bad."

Through the bruises and broken bones, behind the scars and rough edges, my father was crying, his feeble body trembling. "I waited too long to get help for your momma—"

It was true.

A bolt of rage reminded me of my bitterness. But I'd made up my mind. I would not be haunted by it the rest of my life.

"I forgive you," I whispered. "It's all behind us."

He jerked my hand to his chest, tears streaming down the sides of his face.

"Why?" he cried. "Why?"

I grabbed a Kleenex from a box at his bedside and wiped away the wetness. "I don't want any regrets."

He opened the one eye. "Son…"

I knew he was going to talk about God.

"Dad, I met a girl named Holly. She's a Christian."

His mouth closed, and he looked as if he'd fallen into a trance. Chills engulfed me.

"I like her. We argue some. She's way too good for me. And she's beautiful. She kind of reminds me of Mom."

With a crooked smile on his unshaven face, his body convulsed. Then it happened again.

"Dad, are you okay?"

He was still smiling, but at the same time appeared to be fighting off some kind of invisible jolts of electric shock. His eyes widened.

"I'm getting a doctor." I stood.

He clamped my hand with a surge of strength I didn't know he had left.

"Take that girl, Hudson. Cling to her." He coughed so hard that his upper body lifted off the bed. He groaned in pain and pulled me close, his whiskers scraping my cheek.

I pressed the red button on the inside arm of his bedrail.

"Follow her, Son. Never let her go."

His grip went limp.

A steady, loud beep filled the room. I pulled back. Red and green lights blinked on the equipment next to the bed. He looked asleep. And instantly I knew—life had left my father.

21

I had to get out of that hospital, breathe fresh air, drive. Something inside was calling me home. After the tedious process of signing paperwork and making arrangements about the transportation of my dad's body with a quiet, compassionate hospital administrator named Hershel, I took off in my silver Ford rental car for San Antonio.

The drive went fast, my mind swirling with childhood memories of my dad laughing it up with patrons at the Cat's Tail, and my mom hanging clean laundry to dry on the clothesline out back of our modest home, her soft hair blowing in the breeze. When the tears came, I concentrated on Holly, her joyful face and contagious laugh, but I couldn't dodge nagging thoughts of her troubled past with Ken Van Dillon. Regrets about what I'd done to Chester plagued me. And through it all, I had the distinct impression I was being urged by some unseen force to surrender my life to God. But that was something I didn't want to do, didn't know how to do, and was determined to move right on past like the road beneath my wheels.

Arriving at RiverMist Cemetery, I determined that not much, if anything, had changed since I'd last been there. The jets descending on San Antonio International Airport roared several hundred yards overhead, and the smell of jet fuel permeated the hot Texas air like an invisible net.

On my knees, I yanked the long shoots of Bermuda grass that had crept across portions of my mother's flat, rectangular tombstone. Brushing the grass from the raised, worn metal letters on the stone, I read the inscription: "Rita Lynn Ambrose, June 19, 1950 – August 13, 1987."

Only thirty-seven. Not much older than me.

I'd ignored the words below Mom's name but finally whispered them aloud: "Too Fine for This World."

The old man's words.

The dozen red roses I'd bought at Kroger were still cool and wet. I laid them just below Mom's tombstone. Sweeping my hand over the short, brittle grass next to her plot, I envisioned the fresh dirt that would be turned and the matching headstone that would be placed there for my dad in a few days.

What will I have them write on it? Something about being reunited with Mom?

What would he want?

I wished desperately that I'd saved his letters. The fact that I hadn't was just another guilty regret that I would force myself to block out. But that was becoming harder and harder to do as an overwhelming sense of remorse pressed in all around, threatening to suffocate me.

On my way to the River Walk downtown, I searched all the local AM radio stations for any trace of news about a homeless man's disappearance in Las Vegas, but came up with nothing. What I needed was Internet access so I could go to the *R-J* home page and see if Suzette's story had run.

Parking the Fusion outside an old billiards haunt called The Rack, a San Antonio landmark, I found the stairs I used to know so well and bounced downward, toward the River Walk.

Wait a minute.

Much of the stonework had changed. The trees were so much larger, and the landscaping had matured. Even many of the storefronts had undergone renovation. I stood for a moment near one of the gas lanterns that lined the river, trying to get my bearings.

There. Alfego's Deli. *Okay, now I'm getting it.*

As I walked south along the curvy river, beneath the large trees, I admired the many new establishments while relishing some old favorites, like Peter's Smoke Shop, the nightclub Silk, Aqua Terra Fine Dining, Anne's Gifts, Snyder's Ice Cream, and Cosmo's Pizzeria.

Momentarily, the tranquil river water, the smiling faces of tourists, and the familiar smell of coffee, pastries, and fresh-baked Italian bread freed my mind from its dungeon. I wanted Holly to see this place, to walk with me here, to let me show her my slice of heaven on earth.

A boy bumped into me from behind. I apologized after having come to a halt in the middle of the brick walkway, eying the old alley that led to Gordy's Gym. The boy's parents half smiled, half frowned, and hurried along as my gaze turned to the storefront that used to be the Cat's Tail.

The only thing I recognized was the orange neon Open sign in the upper left corner of the front window. Everything else had changed. Black spotlights pointed up at the words "New Era Grille," written in script above a fancy, maroon awning. The thick, rich wood that had given the Cat's Tail its dark, cool, log-cabin ambiance had been torn from the face of the building and replaced by large windows, which revealed a retro interior of sharp, odd-angled, stainless steel furniture, mod paintings, and a sleek glass bar situated where a row of tables used to be.

A computerized bell rang when I opened the door and walked inside. So much had changed. I could barely figure out where the old bar used to be. There were new walls. The booths had been torn out. The pool tables and jukebox were gone.

"Hi there. What can I get for you?" said a short, middle-aged man wearing pressed jeans, a pink polo shirt, and loafers with no socks.

"Hey. Yeah. My dad used to own this place. Are you the new owner?"

"Not quite," he said in a flamboyant tone. "The boss lady's away. Vacationing in Bali, of all places. There something I can help you with?" He raised his dark eyebrows, ran a hand across his neat, shiny hair, and slung a white towel over his shoulder.

"No. No. I grew up here, in this building. I just wanted to see it." I noticed an Apple iBook on the counter, behind the bar.

"Oh, I hear you. Have at it. Take a look around. All you want. You need something to drink while you hang out?"

"You got Dr Pepper?"

His eyebrows jumped. "Sorry. That we don't have."

It figures.

"That's okay. Listen, there is a way you may be able to help me." I ignored his anxious gaze. "Do you think I could get online for a minute and check something on the Web, real quick?"

"Go ahead." He nervously adjusted the screen on the laptop. "It's all yours. Stay on it as long as you like. Let me make sure there's nothing indecent on here."

"Thanks a lot." I tried to wave him off. "I'll just be a second."

"That's fine. Like I said, I'm just tidying up around here before the big lunch crowd."

His words faded as the home page for the Las Vegas *Review-Journal* unfolded. I got familiar with the track pad, clicked Nevada News, and searched the day's stories: Juvenile Delinquents Sentenced, Witnesses Testify Against Sebastian, Man Dragged to Death on Monorail, E's 'Entertainer' Rocks Casbar, Blazes Worst in Wildlife Refuge History.

Nothing about Chester.

I reread the top local headlines, then scrolled through the state and national news, with no luck. I even searched Suzette Graham's name and the last byline story it gave me for her was a day-old feature, something about the new vending kiosks popping up along the Strip.

The bartender had wiggled his way into the back. I surveyed the place. The smell of beer and smoke were long gone. It was as if I'd never been there before. I felt nothing of my dad's presence, as I assumed I would. And not one memory came back to me. It was all bright and new, as if the past had been completely whitewashed.

And now he's gone too. The actual man himself…gone.

"Thanks a lot," I yelled toward the back and started around the bar.

"Anytime." The bartender came bustling out and gave me a limp hand. "Are you in town for a while?"

"Just a day or two. I really appreciate the use of the computer."

"If you need it again while you're in town, drop on in."

"I just may do that." I nodded. "Thanks again."

The door chime sounded, and I turned right out of the New Era Grille, just wanting to wander, get my head together, figure out what to do next. There were people in businesses up and down the River Walk whom I normally would have been anxious to see, but I was in no mood for socializing and hoped no one would recognize me.

After buying a soft pretzel and large Dr Pepper at a tiny, bright nook called Shuvawn's, I set up shop with pad, pen, and cell phone on a bench near the river. My list of people to call grew quickly, and included Suzette Graham, the funeral home, the obituary person at the *Express-News,* and several relatives and friends who could help me pass the word about my dad's death and the pending funeral. I was surprised I hadn't heard from Holly after leaving the note about my father and decided to call her when I had a minute.

My head felt as if it rolled sideways, then swayed backward.

Whew.

I stared at a black wrought-iron clock post to stop the spinning.

A better diet would help.

But who was I kidding? Between Dad's death and the police investigation into Chester's disappearance, I was completely overwhelmed.

Keep busy. Just keep going.

I pushed through the blue funk and called information for the number of the Pendergrass Funeral Home, which I remembered from Mom's death, and began making a list of questions for them. Then my phone rang.

"Hudson, this is Ellery Graham, Suzette's brother."

"Hey, Ellery. What's going on?"

"I'm looking for Suzette. Have you heard from her? She mentioned you guys were working on a story together."

"Yeah." I thought a moment. "She left a message for me yesterday afternoon."

"But nothing since?"

"No, why?" My insides rumbled. "What's going on?"

"When I call her cell it says her phone isn't in service, which never happens. And she hasn't been home since...I'm not sure when. I went over this morning, because I was worried. Even went inside with my key, but she's not there. This just isn't like her. We're pretty tight. I usually know if she's going out of town or something."

"Yeah, she was just telling me yesterday how close you guys are." I replayed the call in my mind. "She was calling me from her place when she left the message yesterday."

"She was?"

"Yeah. She was working on the story from home. She called me and left a pretty detailed message. Then said she had to go because somebody was at the door."

Everything stopped cold.

Who had been at the door? Needermire?

Impossible. He didn't know about the story.

But Suzette had called Truax…

Nightmarish images of TV and newspaper stories flashed in my mind: "Reporter Missing," "Suzette Graham Kidnapped?" "Where Is This *R-J* Writer?"

Ellery's voice brought me back. "Did she say *who* was at the door?"

"No." I concentrated hard. "She didn't."

"Nothing sounded wrong?"

"No. I remember thinking she sounded a little uptight, but I just assumed it was because the story she was writing is such a big exclusive. It's about Chester. She was trying to get it done for today's paper."

"I know. She told me."

"Was her laptop there when you were at her place today?"

"No."

"What about her digital recorder?"

"I didn't see it," Ellery said.

"Hmm."

"What?"

"Do you know if the story ran today? I couldn't find it online."

"It didn't. I checked."

My world wanted to spin off its axis. Literally, I thought I might have some sort of meltdown. Mentally, I was drowning and just wanted to run, to drive, to escape, to leave all the problems in someone else's hands.

"My dad just died," I blurted, shoving my back to the passersby. "He got beat to death."

"Hudson, where are you?"

"San Antonio," I cried. "I've got to do the funeral, then I'll be back. I'll help…"

"It's okay. Calm down, guy. Calm down. Everything's going to be okay. We're going to get through this."

Ellery inquired about Dad's death, and I told him what I knew. After more probing questions I shared with him that my father and I had reconciled before he passed.

"That is so good, Hudson. What an accomplishment that was, to get things right with him before the end."

Amazingly, I'd turned Ellery's somewhat frantic inquiry about Suzette into a pity party for me.

"Back to Suzette." I took in a deep breath. "If anything happens to her, I'm afraid it's going to be my fault."

"Listen. You're under a ton of pressure right now, do you hear me? Your world has been rocked. Mine is *being* rocked. Let's be calm and work with each other, and help each other through this—"

"You need to know, there's a cop named Drake Needermire." I spelled it for him. "I'm very suspicious of this guy. If Suzette's…if you suspect any trouble, he may've had something to do with it."

The sickening silence that followed was finally overcome by Ellery's hesitant voice. "Is there any more you can tell me?"

"Not yet. Have you heard about the latest with Van Dillon?"

"Holly told me."

My countenance lifted.

"When did you talk to her, today?"

"Yes. She sounded fairly good. A little disappointed she hadn't heard from you. Does she know where you are? Has she heard about your father?"

"I left her a note…I'll be talking to her soon."

"I am sorry, Hud. Things are a bit overwhelming for all of us right now." His voice faded, as if he was trying to reassure himself. He mumbled something about Suzette that I couldn't understand. "I feel utterly helpless—"

"Me too," I admitted.

And the next thing I knew, Ellery was praying.

t had been a full day since Hud had driven me from police headquarters back to my little house on First Street, both of us in a huff. I spent that entire workday half expecting him to walk into the clinic with that dumb, crooked smile on his face, asking for forgiveness again. But it never happened. My heart ached for him.

What hurt even more was that he never even checked up on me that night. I still didn't know what had happened with Kenny, whether he'd been arrested for threatening me by phone and breaking his restraining order. I'd tried three more times to reach Tom Fitzgerald with the LVMPD, but he never called back. To say I didn't sleep well that night would be the understatement of the year.

As I slipped on my white lab coat in the back of the clinic Tuesday morning and mentally prepared to enter the waiting room full of hurting homeless people, my stomach burned from having eaten next to nothing since the cinnamon rolls Hudson and I had shared the morning before.

"Hey, Holly." White-haired Dr. Jim Jorgenson came back from the waiting room. "Wow, your eyes are looking a lot better today."

"Hey, Jim. Thanks."

"Listen, there's a guy looking for you out there. Says his name's Arthur Peabody. Insists he needs to tell you something earth-shattering."

I was gone before Jim finished speaking.

The small, rectangular waiting room was packed tight, with every seat around the perimeter taken by men and women of all ages, many sunburned, tough and tired looking, and quiet—except for an occasional violent cough or wet sneeze.

Along with several others, Arthur stood by the door. He wore his usual attire, twisting his wool beret in his pudgy hands and looking pale compared to the last time I'd seen him.

"Hello, Arthur," I said as I approached.

"Miss Holly." He perked up, wrung his hat even tighter, and stepped toward me. "Something terrible's happened." His words jolted the stale air, and all heads and open mouths turned toward us.

"Shhh." I held a finger to my lips. "Let's step outside real quick."

I led him out the door, down the wood ramp, and beyond the chain-link fence, onto the sidewalk at West Wilson Avenue. "What's happening, Arthur?"

"You remember we told you about Ned Frazier? One of our buddies who saw Needermire with Chester and the other mystery fella at the bus stop?"

"Yes." I nodded, trying to keep him calm. "I remember."

"He's dead, Miss Holly. He got dragged to death on the monorail sometime overnight. A horrible death. They found him at the end of the line, at Sahara Station, hangin' there by his feet."

"What?" I gasped, unable to process it.

"Yeah. It's sure true. Now, we wanna know what Hudson's gonna do about it."

"Arthur, we ended up going to the police."

"After I warned you not to?"

"You were right." I stared off. "Truax, one of the assistant sheriffs, seems to be taking sides with Needermire."

"I told you that would happen, doggone it."

"But Hudson was going to the *R-J* to tell his friends the whole thing. I don't know if he did or not. We had kind of an argument, and I haven't heard from him."

"Well, he better. We got to make this thing public. If we don't, I'm telling you, Needermire and the cops will find a way to bury it." He looked around nervously and put his beret on his head with both hands. "Shoot, listen, I gotta run, Miss Holly. I'll be seeing you around."

As Arthur stalked off down the hot, white sidewalk, I found myself frozen in my tracks, gripping the chain-link fence, wishing desperately that Hudson was there with me.

Why hasn't he called?

Maybe the Lord was protecting me. That's what I kept coming back to.

Wait a minute.

Kenny's car.

As fast as I thought I'd seen it, it was gone, behind some gray office buildings.

There are dozens of cars like that.

I rushed into the clinic, past the throng of waiting people, into the back where Dr. Jim was examining the badly ulcerated feet of a bony, dark brown–haired man with a matted beard and wild green eyes.

"Jim, I'm sorry to interrupt. I'm not quite with you yet." I wondered if the bony man was deaf, because his big eyes never left his feet. "I've got to make an important call. I'll be with you as soon as I can. Are you okay?"

"You take care of business." He glanced up and smiled. "We'll be here when you're ready."

"Thanks a million." I snuck down the narrow hall to the back where Hud had initially opened the door and entered my world. Finding my phone in my bag, I dialed his number. He answered on the first ring.

"Hey. It's me, Holly."

"Hey," Hud said. "I was going to call you once I got a break from all this stuff."

"What's 'all this stuff'? Have you gone to the paper yet?"

Pause.

"Yeah. I told you that in the note, didn't I?"

My head jerked sideways and I tried to think. *Note, note, note.*

"What note?"

"The note I left in your pickup at work yesterday."

"I didn't get any note." I racked my brain, trying to remember any pieces of paper in the truck, in the door handle, beneath the windshield wiper. "Where'd you leave it?"

"Tucked in the driver's seat."

I opened the back door of the clinic, bounded down the steps, and headed for my truck. An LVMPD squad car was parked three cars away from it, with a female officer inside. My windows were down. I opened the door.

"I never got it." I tucked my hand in the crack of the piping-hot seat. "Ouch. It's not here. What did it say? What's going on?"

"Oh my gosh." Hud sighed. "I've got a lot to tell you."

"Hud, Ned Frazier's dead. Arthur showed up at the clinic just now and told me Frazier was dragged to death on the monorail last night."

"What? Where are you right now?"

"Why?" I automatically searched the parking lot and streets for Kenny's car. The officer was watching me.

"Are you at the clinic?"

"Yes, Hud. You're scaring me! Is Kenny loose?"

"No. Don't you know? Haven't you talked to Fitzgerald?"

"He still hasn't gotten back to me. There's a cop car in the parking lot here. And I thought I might have seen Kenny's car."

"Get inside the clinic now, Holly!"

I took one last glance at the cop, then at the busy streets, and dashed back inside where the cool air of the clinic and the creepy circumstances sent shivers up and down my whole body.

"I'm sorry," he said. "I haven't had time to follow up with Fitzgerald. I don't know why he's not calling us back. I'm assuming everything's fine."

"Have you gone to the *R-J* with the story?"

He exhaled loudly. "After I dropped you off yesterday, I went. Suzette has the whole thing on tape. I thought it was going to be in today's paper, but it's not."

"I can't believe Ned Frazier's dead."

"Holly, Ellery called me a little while ago. He thinks Suzette may be missing."

"Missing! What? Why did he call you?"

"Suzette told him we were working on the story together. He thought I might know where she was. I told him she left a message on my phone yesterday afternoon, but in the middle of the message somebody knocked at the door and she had to go."

"Uh-oh." I felt my face flush.

"Ellery went to her place this morning. No sign of her. And her laptop and recorder aren't there. He's worried."

"I am too. My gosh, Hud, could this be Needermire?"

"Here's the thing. Suzette called Truax with our story—"

"What?"

"She had to. Our editor made her give Truax a chance to respond, but he couldn't; he didn't have legal counsel yet. But he could have told Needermire."

"I was thinking Ken might've taken the note from my truck, but it could've been Needermire."

There was only silence.

"Hud, I want you close. Where are you? Can you meet me?"

"Holly." He paused. "I'm in San Antonio."

"What? Truax will *kill* you. What are you doing there?"

"I got his permission to leave Las Vegas yesterday. My dad was in critical condition at a hospital in Victoria."

I stumbled over the word "was," but didn't dare go there.

"Oh, Hud, I'm so sorry. I knew I should have called you. How is he? What's wrong?"

It was silent. Dead silent.

"Hud? What is it?"

"He's dead, Holly."

My head spun. I wanted to be there, holding him.

"Some guys beat him in the rec yard."

"No. Oh no, Hud. I'm so sorry, sweetie. Oh, dear Lord, I'm sorry."

"I got to see him one last time." There was hope in his voice.

"You did? Was it okay?"

"Yeah. It was good." His voice broke. "I forgave him. We forgave each other."

"Oh, Hud, I bet he rejoiced."

"He did." He drew in a deep breath and spoke fast with his exhale. "He couldn't believe it. It was like a weight lifted off him. Me too."

I laughed and cried at the same time. "You poor thing. I didn't even know—"

"I told him about you."

Chills engulfed me, like electric static everywhere. "You did?"

"That you were a Christian."

Tears shot down my cheeks, and I mashed the phone against my ear.

"He told me to hang on to you."

I couldn't believe what I was hearing. Joy burst forth inside me, followed almost instantaneously by a tremor of panic about Ken Van Dillon and his unknown whereabouts.

What if Kenny finds out how I feel about Hud?

"I want you to hang on to me, Hudson Ambrose. Forever."

"Holly, I told you in the note I was sorry," Hud said. "I didn't mean to chase you away. I never want to do that. Never."

"We're okay, Hud. We're okay."

I put my phone in my bag and separated the dusty slats of the plastic blinds in the tiny back window of the clinic. Now there were two squad cars in the parking lot, along with a stocky officer who'd just rolled up on a police motorcycle.

What is going on?

Hopefully, just hunting down some shoplifters.

I went back to my purse, retrieved my phone, and found a piece of yellow scrap paper with Officer Tom Fitzgerald's phone number on it. Dialing the number, I rehearsed the stern message I would leave when I got his voice mail for the eightieth time.

reach you nonstop for—"

"I am sorry I haven't called you back, Miss Queens. And please
apologize to Mr. Ambrose for me. We've been having some problems
at this end." With each word, his voice became weaker and whinier,
and my stomach became queasier. "I was hoping to get this thing
resolved before calling you back and having you become worried or
anxious, but I haven't been able to do that."

"He's loose." I dashed to the back window, ripped the blinds up,
and scanned the parking lot for Kenny's car. "He's loose, and you were
going to tell me when?" I darted through the small hallway and eyed
each face in the waiting area, from one to the next.

"I was actually going to give it until close of business today, Miss
Queens. In these cases, usually within—"

"I slept in my home alone last night with him on the loose! This
is sickening, Fitzgerald. I honestly don't believe what I am hearing.
You saw what he did to me!"

"Miss Queens, please calm down."

"Once you've been terrorized by a monster like Ken Van Dillon,
then you can tell me to calm down, Officer!"

"Ma'am, we had a car staked out at your home on First Street all
night last night, just in case. And we will do the same tonight. Now,
if you are frightened to the point of—"

"Just tell me how he got away, please."

Fitzgerald sighed. "Not long after the call from Mr. Ambrose
Monday morning, stating that Mr. Van Dillon had called and threatened you, we checked with the monitoring service and found that he
was back at his residence. He may have been calling you from a pay
phone nearby."

"Were you going to arrest him? He broke the law!"

"We were, indeed. And we still are…"

I cannot BELIEVE this!

"That morning," Fitzgerald continued, "a car was dispatched to Mr. Van Dillon's residence. However, while it was en route, the monitoring service made us aware that Mr. Van Dillon's GPS ankle bracelet was being tampered with. The system sends an alarm—"

"Duh! I warned you about this!"

"Miss Queens, when this happens, these fugitives never get far."

"You don't know Ken Van Dillon! I told you that when I showed up at your office." I wanted to let him know my blood was going to be on his hands, but that wasn't up to me. I tried to get a grip. "Look, just tell me what you're doing about this and what I'm supposed to do until he's captured."

"Officers are scheduled to monitor you around the clock, non-stop, until Mr. Van Dillon is apprehended. You should see them at work, at home, and everywhere in between. If you don't, I'll give you my personal cell phone number. We've broadcast an all-points bulletin on Mr. Van Dillon. Our people have his photograph, his description, his car—"

"I saw him less than an hour ago, near the clinic, where I am now. At least, I saw a car that looked like his."

"Okay, I'll get that information out to the appropriate parties."

I didn't know what else to say.

"Miss Queens, I know this is not much comfort to you at the moment, but we've seen this before. People that get out of these GPS devices never make it far. Mr. Van Dillon will be no exception. He will be captured, and when he is, he'll be in extremely hot water. The state of Nevada has no tolerance for this kind of violation."

Again, I wanted to lash out at Fitzgerald, at the LVMPD, at the whole Nevada justice system. But I did not. Instead, I forced myself to take the bad with the good. For some reason, this was God's plan. He was my Caretaker, and I was determined to trust Him for my safety, not Officer Fitzgerald, not the LVMPD, not the people at the clinic, not even Hudson Ambrose—although I wished he'd hurry up and come home.

23

My editor at the Las Vegas *Review-Journal*, Donald Cheevers, had no idea where Suzette was, and although he'd given her the green light to write the Chester piece, he'd never received her first draft. I assured him long-distance from my hotel room two blocks from the River Walk that we were sitting on one powder keg of a news story and that we needed to get it to print fast.

"I can't run a story I don't have, Ambrose. Suzette told me she'd get it to me late yesterday, and I never heard from her. She was due in this morning, and she's not here. What can I say?"

"Look, Don, I know this is going to sound far-fetched, but there's a chance she may be the victim of foul play."

"Boy, you are really reaching out on a limb now."

"I'm afraid whoever's responsible for Chester's death may have abducted Suzette to keep the story out of the paper. And that homeless guy they found tied to the monorail last night—Ned Frazier—who killed him? I think we're dealing with a psychopath."

"Okay. What do you suggest we do? Just tell me that. This whole thing, so far, is based completely on hearsay—except your part—which totally incriminates you, if you ask me."

"Give the story to Reed. He and I can go over the whole thing by phone. He can pound it out in a few hours."

"No way. He's in the middle of the Sebastian murder trial."

"That thing's writing itself. He can hand it off for one day. Come on, Don, this thing is about to blow, and you know he's the best man for the job."

I scribbled on the hotel notepad, my heart racing through the silence.

"I'll have him call you."

"Good—"

"But listen to me, Hud. I'm going over this story with a fine-tooth comb before it runs, so don't get your hopes up. It may not see the light of day."

He hung up, and that was good enough for me.

Cheevers had a tough shell, but he was soft as silk underneath. He insisted I take the rest of the week off for my dad's funeral. But I felt completely frustrated and out of touch, sitting in that quiet Texas hotel room so far from all that was happening in Las Vegas.

I missed Holly's company, which reminded me that I needed to follow up with Fitzgerald to find out what had happened to Van Dillon.

My dad's obituary was due at the *Express-News* by that evening. Even though I had a heavy heart as I tapped it out on the computer in the small business office just off the hotel lobby, it also brought several smiles, chills, and tears. When all was said and done, overlooking some of the hard times, everything had worked out. I'd been the beneficiary of a loving home, mostly warm memories, an adventuresome childhood, and a mother and father who loved me, stayed together, and ultimately, shared their faith in God with me.

I pondered that for a long time, wondering if they could really be together at that moment, looking down on me from heaven, rooting me on to follow them through what my old man had called "the narrow gate."

No matter what I believed, the words I wrote in the obituary honored my father's memory. With one last glance and a spell check, I e-mailed it to the local paper. Next, I finished making most of the calls and plans for my dad's funeral, which would consist of a brief, closed-casket visitation at the Pendergrass Funeral Home, followed by a private graveside service at RiverMist Cemetery. Dad's prison buddy, Victor Everson, had agreed to deliver the eulogy.

After checking my e-mail one last time, I wandered by the indoor pool and exercise room. The place was like a morgue. The next few days leading up to the funeral were going to pass at an excruciatingly slow pace. *I will go crazy.* The thought crossed my mind to start writing the Chester story myself, even if Don claimed he wouldn't run it. In fact, standing at a vending machine, buying a Dr Pepper, that's what I decided to do if I didn't hear from Reed within another hour or two.

After grabbing a *USA Today* and exchanging pleasantries with a thin young man wearing a red tie and working the front desk, I flopped down on a couch in the lobby in front of a large color TV and got out my phone to call Fitzgerald. Whether I reached him or not, I was determined to get the skinny on Ken Van Dillon from someone within the LVMPD before I left that seat.

As I was scrolling through the contacts in my cell phone, video footage of the Strip in Las Vegas caught my eye on the large, flat-screen TV twelve feet away. The logo in the corner of the set read FOX News. I quickly crossed to the screen and turned up the volume.

The camera cut back to the studio and a model blonde at the

anchor desk. "Today in Las Vegas, KLAS-TV is reporting a news exclusive about the murder of a homeless man in that community who is said to have been a millionaire. You heard me right, a millionaire."

Eerily, the screen filled with footage of the Civic Center North bus stop and a First Federal Bank of Nevada bank. The anchor's voice continued.

"An unidentified member of the Las Vegas Metropolitan Police Department has informed Eyewitness News that a former Atlanta business mogul by the name of Chester Holte may have been murdered at a bus stop on the north section of Las Vegas Boulevard several days ago.

"Although Holte's body has not been recovered, the informant for the Las Vegas police says the department has talked with a veteran reporter for the Las Vegas *Review-Journal* by the name of Hudson Ambrose about potential evidence tampering at the crime scene before police arrived. Ambrose is the number-one person of interest in the case at this time, according to inside sources with the LVMPD."

The photograph from my driver's license popped onto the screen. *Thank God Mom and Dad are gone.*

"According to the Las Vegas police source, Holte is said to have been shot at close range during the wee hours of Saturday, August 12, then robbed of a bankbook and safe-deposit box key. The police source implied that Ambrose's fingerprints may have been found on items within a safe-deposit box belonging to Holte, which included thousands of dollars in cash, stock certificates, and jewelry. In addition…"

My face was on fire. I looked around at the empty lobby and the smiling kid at the front desk as if it were all a sick, surreal dream. I could feel my pulse pounding in my temple and thought I might black out as I watched the screen flash to footage of Las Vegas police headquarters.

"Fox News has confirmed that the reporter for the *Review-Journal,* Hudson Ambrose, was brought in for questioning by Las Vegas police several days ago, but was released after a lengthy interrogation. Sources at the newspaper say Ambrose has taken the week off, and Fox could not reach him for comment prior to air time."

Oh, come on. How hard did you try?

"In a new, but possibly related development overnight, another homeless man was killed near the Strip when he was dragged to death by the popular and sleek Las Vegas Monorail. The anonymous source for the Las Vegas police says Ambrose is a person of interest in this case as well…"

The phone in my hand vibrated, but it took me a moment to pull out of the funk.

"Yeah." I stared at the stock video footage of the Las Vegas Monorail on its maiden run.

"Hud, it's Reed. Have you heard?"

"Watching it now."

"You remember my friend, Lutz, over at KLAS?"

"Yeah," I stared at the screen.

"He called me and told me just before this came down. He says that cop, Needermire, is the whistle-blower. Everybody knows it. It's just not public yet."

"Did Cheevers tell you about Suzette? Has she turned up?"

"He told me, and no—no one knows where she is. Her brother, the pastor, is convinced something's wrong. He's arranging a search party for her and Chester. This thing is national."

"Did Cheevers give you the green light to write the story?

"That's why I'm calling."

"How bad is it, Reed, for me?"

"Dude, LVMPD has you on a stake, ready to light the match. I'm afraid city council's gonna side with them. It doesn't look good. The only positive thing is, they haven't found Chester's body yet. It would take some seriously incriminating evidence to put you behind bars."

Reed hadn't heard my side of the story, and I suspected even he might be suspicious of me. "I promise you, I'm innocent, man."

Momentary silence. "It's gonna be a tough fight, Hud. When the police claim you searched a dead body…"

"I'm gonna get to all that in a minute. While I think of it, after we're done you need to talk to Suzette's brother, the pastor, Ellery Graham."

"I already got a call in to him."

"Cool. Also, for future reference, track down a dude named Arthur Peabody. He's homeless. You can find him at the Rescue Mission, in line at mealtime. He'll give you more on Chester, the bad sweeps, the monorail death, and other stuff."

"Peabody. Got it."

"I'm glad you're on this, man."

"I'm sorry to hear about your dad," Reed said.

"Thanks. I don't know what to do. The funeral's not for two days. I feel like I should be back in Vegas."

"I wouldn't come back here yet; they'll fry you. Let me write your side of the story and see if we can get Cheevers to run it tomorrow. That way, all your explaining will be done by the time you get back from the funeral."

"Okay, let's do this thing. You got a recorder hooked up?"

"Hold on…yep."

"Let me just tell you what's happened since Saturday, then you ask whatever you want."

It was late by the time Reed and I hung up. The thin kid at the front desk was long gone, replaced by a plump but attractive black woman wearing a crisp white shirt, gray silk scarf, and radiant smile. I stretched, groaned, collected my empty Dr Pepper cans and pretzel bags, and stuffed them into a full trash can on my way to the elevators.

"Did you forget something, sir?" The woman pointed back to the small table where I'd been planted for the past several hours, next to a large picture window in the lobby.

"Thank you very much." I went back and retrieved the small pad on which I'd scribbled numerous reminders about what else I needed to tell Reed during breaks in our long conversation.

Riding up the elevator to my third-floor room, I let out a loud yawn, stretched on my tiptoes until I touched the metal grille below the ceiling lights, and massaged my aching neck. The story was in Reed's hands now, and I was confident he'd get it right, but I couldn't stop thinking about Suzette.

Where was she?

I checked my watch. It was almost 10:30 p.m. my time, which made it about 8:30 Las Vegas time.

Could she have gotten cold feet and bolted?

No. She wanted to write that story as much as I needed it to be written. *Her brother's a smart guy; he knows something's wrong...very wrong.*

Ugh.

Would her body turn up like Ned Frazier's?

It would be your fault. You lured her into doing the story.

No. She's a reporter, hungry just like me and all the others, chomping at the bit for the big story and the top byline. *Don't do that to yourself.*

As I'd done for Suzette, I gave Reed an arsenal of facts that would not be in the KLAS-TV story, including details about the robbery at my house; Needermire's violent homeless sweep at Owens Avenue; Ken Van Dillon's jealous rage and his implications about Chester's disappearance; and the gang that tried to rough me up at Chester's van, along with Needermire's knowledge of it.

The bell rang; I got off the elevator and examined my stringy hair, sagging eyelids, and wrinkled shirt in the full-length mirror that faced me. Turning left and heading down the long hall to my room, I vowed to get a long, hot shower.

That's when I heard the rapid-fire *ze-zing, ze-zing, ze-zing* of a camera's motor drive. A dark figure lowered his lens at the far end of the hall and ducked into a room, the door clicking shut quietly behind him.

Photographers. *For whom?*

I crept past my room another five doors to the end of the hall and observed where he'd entered: room 338. Although I couldn't see his shadow beneath the door, I could sense the stranger's presence within a few feet of me.

He's looking through the peephole.

I stuck my hands on my waist, glared at the hole, then walked to my room, realizing the mayhem was probably just beginning.

After chain- and bolt-locking the door, I flicked the light switch, which lit a lamp on the nightstand by the king-size bed and a crooked one in the far corner of the average-looking hotel room. Finding the remote, I turned on the TV, surfed to CNN, cranked the AC, and went to the bathroom, which I hadn't done for three Dr Peppers. Throwing some water on my face, I came back into the room, toweled off, and noticed the red light flashing on the hotel phone.

My heart somersaulted. Before I could process who might be calling on that phone, I picked up the beige receiver and pushed Play Messages.

There was a lengthy segment of silence.

"I see it's finally out." The male caller breathed slowly. "You musn't know who this is, I can't divulge that. But I know you're being framed." His voice was quiet and solemn; I guessed he was forty or fifty. "I'm going to try to help you, but I'm not sure I can." He paused and exhaled loudly. "What I have to say would exonerate you, but…I'm still processing all this. I'll talk to you again."

Click.

"End of messages."

That was it.

Whoa.

Ned Frazier was dead. Chester was dead. It wasn't Needermire or Van Dillon.

Who then?

Someone at the *R-J* or the Las Vegas police department?

How did he know I was in San Antonio?

My cell phone beeped. I checked it. One message from earlier, during the interview with Reed.

Could it be him?

I played it.

"Hud, it's Holly. I hope you're holding up okay. I don't know if you've heard, but Needermire went to a local TV station with the story and it's already aired at least once here. I've talked to Ellery. He's filed a missing-person's report with the police, and his church is organizing a search for Suzette and Chester, starting at dawn tomorrow. Hud, you must get your side of the story out." Her voice broke down. "They're making you look so bad," she cried. "Please, do something. I'm praying."

No mention of Van Dillon, so I crossed that off my worry list. But I couldn't forget the photographer down the hall. And I had the strangest feeling.

Crossing to the window, I turned out the light in the corner and spread the curtains about four inches. There was movement in the parking lot below. A man with a khaki vest closed the trunk of a black car and hoofed it inside, lugging two heavy equipment bags. Several rows closer, two men with shoulder bags and a tripod dashed inside from a red mid-size.

Either I was being paranoid, or the media was flooding my hotel.

24

I was nauseous, almost to the point of going back into the clinic rest room. At first, I assumed it was because I hadn't eaten much of anything since last seeing Hud the morning before.

Maybe it's the heat.

Although night had fallen, it was still pushing ninety degrees out back of the clinic where teams of us from Spring Valley Community Church cut out Missing posters of Suzette and Chester in preparation for the following day's search. Then it hit me cold. I'd been dishonest with Hud, and it was eating me up.

He would have wanted to know—would have *insisted* I tell him—that Kenny had hacksawed his way out of the GPS ankle bracelet and was on the loose. But Hud had so much on his mind, I couldn't bring myself to burden him with it.

You need to tell him before the day's over.

There must have been forty or fifty of us crowded around four fold-up tables in the steamy parking lot behind the clinic. Pastor

Ellery and his wife, Jenna, were there, along with dozens of familiar and unfamiliar faces from the church and camera crews from three TV stations. The crowd of well-doers—mostly wearing shorts, loose T-shirts, tank tops, hats, and bandanas—made me feel safe and upbeat, even though I found myself scanning the city streets for Kenny's car every time I looked up.

"Miss Holly?" The voice and hard tap on my shoulder came from behind.

I turned. "Arthur, how are you?"

"Doing okay, considering. I wanted to see if there was anything I could do to help you."

I introduced him to Ellery and Jenna, who put down what they were doing, offered Arthur a cold bottle of water from a cooler, and discussed his connection with Chester.

"I been tellin' a lotta people about tomorrow," Arthur said.

"That's excellent, Arthur," Jenna said. "We're going to need all the help we can get."

"I see the police are here." Arthur nodded to a black-and-white idling at the far end of the parking lot. "They're all over this thing. Afraid the truth is gonna come out, I suppose."

I explained to Arthur about Ken Van Dillon and told him it was Ken's escape that accounted for the police presence.

"Speaking of police, have you talked to Hudson?" Arthur asked.

The mention of his name hit me like a caffeine jolt. I not only missed him and mourned for him, but felt an inescapable sense of guilt over not having told him about Kenny's escape.

"I did earlier. Why?"

"I heard the cops searched his house today looking for more evidence against him."

"What? Where'd you hear that?"

"Cinderella Man told me. Said he heard they had a warrant. Went in when Hudson wasn't home. Don't know what they found."

"He's out of town! His father just died. I can't believe this."

Arthur shook his head.

"Holly." Ellery eyed me from above the glasses that had slipped down his nose with the sweat. "Have you heard all they've been saying about Hud?"

Before I could speak, Jenna stepped toward her husband. "Honey, Holly told you Hudson made mistakes—"

"But he had nothing to do with Chester's death." I looked around to make sure none of the TV reporters were within earshot. "I know that. You know that, Ellery. I've told you the details."

"I'm sorry." He whipped the glasses off, tossed them on the table, and nudged the perspiration from his forehead and face with the shoulder of his red Kentucky Fried Chicken T-shirt. "I'm out of it. Haven't had enough sleep. In a bad mood. Starting to get weird."

Arthur laughed and patted him hard on the back. "Well, it sure is refreshin' to see a pastor admit he's human, by golly. You're okay in my book, pastor, I'll tell ya that much."

We all chuckled, but Ellery's face remained ashen. He looked thin and pale and vulnerable, as I'd never seen him before.

"We all need rest." Jenna rubbed her hand up and down her husband's back.

After the posters were finished, a group of teenagers passed out candles, and we sat in a large circle in the parking lot, singing worship songs and praying quietly. Ellery said nothing publicly and denied requests for TV interviews. His eyes were closed most of the time, or he had his head down, between his knees.

By the time we shook hands, hugged, and wiped away the tears, the moon was bright against the black sky, and I was ready to get home. It would be a big day tomorrow. But I knew I needed to eat something, preferably healthy. So I stopped at one of my favorite places, packaged all the lettuce, veggies, and fixings I could into a foam container, and handed it to the elderly, sad-looking lady at the counter. She weighed it and charged me $3.49 for the feast of leaf lettuce, sprouts, carrots, blue cheese, eggs…yummy.

Back home, curled up in my favorite chair, sipping cold milk and devouring my salad, I was glued to the ten o'clock news, which led with the Chester story. This time, pictures of beautiful Suzette filled the screen, along with clips of our church family organizing maps, posters, and search routes for the next day's massive event.

Once again, Hudson's picture was featured, along with updated news about his father's death, the pending funeral in San Antonio, and footage of officers leaving his house with several bags of "evidence."

There was a noise in the kitchen. I set the salad on the ottoman and wandered in.

Icemaker.

Walking quietly to the front window, I realized I was almost tip-toeing.

Relax.

I peered at the squad car parked at the curb out front. The number on the back of the car was different from the one I'd seen at work. And this was a male officer. New shift.

My house phone rang. I went back to my chair and picked up.

"Holly, it's Hud."

"Hey there! How are you?"

"Okay, I guess. I think my hotel's filling up with reporters."

"I just watched the news, and it's big here. Have you seen the latest?" I held my breath.

"What do you mean?"

"Did you know the police searched your house?"

"When?"

"Today. I heard it first from Arthur and just saw it on the news."

"There's nothing there!"

"The TV story said they left with a couple of bags of evidence, whatever that means."

"They already have everything. I gave Truax the keys. Everything else was stolen. I'm not believing this. I'm gonna get framed for this thing!"

I buried my head in my hand, not knowing what to say. How was I ever going to tell him Kenny was loose?

"Reed called. He's done with the story," he said. "Now it's in Cheevers's hands. Tomorrow can't come fast enough."

I wanted to pray about it, about everything, but I was afraid to say so.

Lord, show me what to do, what to say.

"Hud, I'm praying for you, that God'll find favor on you—"

"Why would He, Holly?" His words cut hard. "I've never been loyal to Him."

"You forgave your dad. You let him be the happiest he'd probably ever been, right before he died."

"But I'm not like you. I'm not on God's team. I'm at odds with Him; I know that and so do you."

"But He's not the one making you at odds. You are. You're the one who hasn't joined His team. The invitation's there. He's waiting. He wants you in the family—"

"How would I get in if I wanted to? Just tell me that."

I laughed. "That is so you."

"Just answer me, will you? I'm not saying I want to be a Christian.

I just want to know the ground rules you people are expected to play by to get to heaven."

"Believe, Hud. You told me the other day you believe, but do you, really? If Jesus went to the cross for us, if that really happened, how should we live?"

What the silence meant was a complete mystery. But the adrenaline and exhilaration pounding in my chest told me, no matter how it came out, I'd done the right thing. If he laughed or seethed or bailed on me, it would be okay, because I'd been faithful to the One who mattered most. I'd testified. And the chips would fall where God declared.

"I just try to live a life of thanks to Him," I whispered. "A life of gratefulness. The minute you believe, His Spirit comes to live in you. You die and you let Him live. And He overflows."

He exhaled loudly into the phone. "I see that in you."

I said nothing.

"My dad's death, it's so bizarre, Holly. Nobody lives forever. We're all dying, really."

"I've thought about you so much. I'm so sorry."

"I don't even care about the guys who killed him."

"You don't?"

"No. It's weird. I have no vengeance toward them. All I want to do is make the most of each day. I forgot what it was like to lose someone so close. You know? Both your folks are gone. Do you remember what it's like?"

The words sent me back to my father's funeral. A thunderstorm. Muddy, dark, gloomy. My mother, planted in a folding chair underneath the funeral-home tent, staring into space next to the wet casket. A rent-a-pastor, whom none of us had ever seen before, doling out polite words and false hope. My mother was never the same after Daddy died.

"Are you there?" Hud asked.

"Yeah...I remember."

"I'm sorry, Holly."

"Don't apologize. I know what you mean. I know what you're going through. I'm just glad your parents are in heaven."

"Yours didn't believe?"

"No. I've tried to convince myself they did."

"Holly, not every Christian becomes a preacher or a missionary. Some believe quietly, in their own way. Look at Chester—"

"Chester gave it all. He laid down his life. He had nothing."

"What I meant was, maybe deep down your parents did believe and you just didn't know it."

"No, they didn't, Hud. I mean, it's a nice thought, but a spade's a spade."

"That just seems so harsh. How do you know people's—"

"It's just the truth, okay? The person who practices righteousness is righteous. The one who practices sin is of the devil."

The line was silent.

"You think that sounds judgmental, don't you?"

"Yeah, I do."

"Everybody wants to make the road to heaven so easy. But it's not easy. There's a cross to bear. If you decide to follow Christ, you make a stand. And there are going to be consequences. You're going to lose friends. People will think you're square. You're going to make enemies."

"But Chester didn't go around beating everyone over the head with a Bible. Neither do you. I don't understand what you're getting so hot about."

I had set down my food and was straight as a board on the edge of my chair. "Chester was a servant, Hud. He gave up all he had to help other people find God. I'm mad because so many people claim

they're Christians, yet those same people live just like the world, hyp-
notized by material things, and they're repackaging God to fit into
their selfish lives when the opposite should be happening. We should
be giving ourselves away, like Chester."

He sighed. "Okay, look—"

"I'm sorry. It just frustrates me how many of us say we're Christians, yet we never get out of our comfort zones to be Jesus to the
world. We're selfish, and we're ashamed of God."

"You're not selfish." He chuckled. "And you're certainly not
ashamed."

I laughed and closed the lid to my unfinished salad with trembling hands.

"You shouldn't change, Holly. You're alive. You're the most vibrant
person I know."

I picked up my glass and salad container and headed for the
kitchen. "Thanks. That's nice of you." I couldn't deny my feelings
for Hudson. He was smart and masculine, yet tender-hearted—
everything I'd prayed for in a man, except for one thing.

"Hey, you're not gonna believe what happened." As he described
the stranger's call to his room, I sponged my cup and some other dirty
dishes and bowls while asking questions, discussing who the caller
might be, and silently trying to figure out how I could gently break
the news that Kenny was loose.

However, as the conversation wound down, it seemed natural
and perhaps best to let the situation with Kenny rest until our next
talk. Then my intestines started knotting up, and he asked the deci-
sive question. "So, how did things end up with Van Dillon? I bet they
won't post bond till his trial now."

My stomach went hollow. I dropped the scrub brush and gripped
the counter, trying to steady things.

"Holly?"

"I…" The free hand that covered my heart shook uncontrollably. "Hud, wait a sec…"

I clacked the phone down and, with both hands crossed over my heart, made myself breathe in. And out. In. And out.

What was I afraid of?

"Holly? Is everything okay?"

I grabbed the phone, raced through the family room, and opened the front curtain. The police car was still there.

"Everything's fine." I caught my breath. "There was a problem with the ankle bracelet."

"What?"

"But the police are watching me around the clock, at work, here—"

"What do you mean, a problem?"

"He cut it off with a hacksaw, but it's okay, Hud. I'm—"

"When?"

"Not long after he called your house the other morning."

"Why didn't Fitzgerald tell us?" Hud yelled.

"He said they were trying to fix the problem before they got back to us."

"Are the police at your house right now?"

"Yes, Hud. They're wherever I am. Really. There's nothing to worry about. They were at the clinic all day. They'll be here all night. Fitzgerald assured me of that." I paced and found my way back into the kitchen.

"They know he's a nut case. Man, that burns me! I'm coming back."

"Not before the funeral, you're not."

"I can come back for the funeral."

"Hud, that's ridiculous. You'd be home for a day. Then you'd have to turn around and go back. It'd cost you a fortune." Even though I argued outwardly, my heart soared with a feeling of comfort and importance.

"I don't care. I don't trust those cops. They said *this* wouldn't happen, and it did."

We must have both been thinking, *What's next?*

I opened a kitchen drawer and examined the large knives.

"I'm gonna check flights," he said. "You keep your doors and windows locked. If those cops leave for one minute, you call 911, then Fitzgerald, then me."

"Hud, please don't do this." I pushed the drawer shut. "I'm fine! You're under enough stress. If you come back now, Truax may not let you go back for the funeral. You gotta think this through. You're not making sense."

Lights and shadows danced off the kitchen wall and disappeared.

I turned toward the sliding glass door leading to the patio out back. A flashlight? The cop, checking the back of the house?

"Let me go, Holly. I'm gonna make some calls. Okay?"

I was back at the front window. The cop was still there, in his car.

"Okay." I wanted to blurt out to Hud that I was scared, that I needed him. But he was so far away. It would do no good.

"Are you all right?"

I fought hard to rise above the fear and worry that raged like a flood just below the surface. "Yeah," I managed.

"Sit tight, little lady. I'm coming."

2 5

As I hung up the phone, my old man's words rushed back to me in high definition: "Take that girl, Hudson. Cling to her. Never let her go."

Everything was set for the funeral. Even if I couldn't be there, it would go on as planned; Victor would see to that.

The fastest, cheapest fare I could find to Sin City was on an America West flight that would depart San Antonio at 2:20 a.m. and arrive in Las Vegas at 1:20 a.m., with the time change. I booked it, threw my stuff in my garment bag, and hurried for the elevator without looking back.

When the doors opened on the lobby floor, I saw no one—until I turned the corner. Reporters and camera operators from what must have been a dozen media organizations had crammed into the lobby.

"There he is!" a childish male voice cried as the media people scrambled to their feet, fumbled for their cameras and recorders, and closed off the main exit.

"Mr. Ambrose, did you kill the homeless man in Las Vegas, Chester Holte?"

Microphones and recorders jabbed and bobbed around my face, and hot TV lights popped on throughout the lobby as reporters closed in around me. "Did you know him?" "Are you guilty?"

I continued toward the double doors, literally pushing my way through the sea of frenzied workers. "Make room, please!"

"Were you at the bus stop in Las Vegas the morning Chester died?" a young, dark-haired girl asked, sticking her recorder in front of my nose.

"I'm innocent." I looked at her while shoving forward. "I made some mistakes, but I never hurt anyone."

"Tell your side, Mr. Ambrose," a male voice yelled from behind.

I turned to meet the gray-haired man's brown eyes, which were underlined by large, gray bags. "There's gonna be a story in tomorrow's Las Vegas *Review-Journal*, by Reed O'Neil. I've talked to him. He has my side of this thing."

Finally, I made it to the doors, shoved the left one open, quickstepped through the vestibule, and broke free outside, a warm breeze rushing over me as I scanned the parking lot. Several stray reporters converged on me, but I dodged them and headed for the car, feeling the others overflowing from the hotel behind me.

As I ducked into the driver's seat, slammed the door, and hit the locks, yelling reporters converged on the car and strobe lights flashed— like a scene from a movie. I revved the engine, jerked the gearshift into reverse, and backed up at a medium clip that sent them scattering. "Hey!" they screamed. "Watch it! What do you think you're doing?"

They would have to move. I had a plane to catch.

Staring into blackness at thirty-one thousand feet, I gave in to the fact that the press would be waiting for me at McCarran International Airport in Las Vegas, even though it would be after one when we landed.

I eased my seat back and closed my eyes, hoping to catch a nap, but pain pierced my neck and back. *Stress.* My eyes opened. I couldn't believe the old man was gone. For more than thirty years I could talk to him whenever I wanted to; not anymore.

With a seat empty between me and a brunette in a pink baseball cap featuring sequined dice, I stretched my legs and realized what a precarious position I had put my publisher in by telling the media that my side of the story would be running in the morning's paper. *Big mouth.* If Cheevers decided not to run it, my credibility would be tainted even more.

I couldn't sit still.

The thought of jail was as real as my dad's death.

Everything seemed to be snowballing. Wanting a cigarette desperately, I wondered how much more pressure I could take. Up until that moment, I could have simply run away from life's problems, started over somewhere else. That had all changed. I was in the spotlight now. The law was watching. There was no more running.

But I will not go to jail.

I ached to talk to Holly, but cell phone use was restricted during the flight, and it was late her time anyway. I hoped she was asleep.

One patrol car at her curb. That would be *nothing* for a nut-case hunter like Van Dillon to tiptoe around. But blasting through the sky somewhere above New Mexico, I realized I had no control. *None.*

Holly would tell me to pray.

I closed my eyes and…smelled booze. The girl next to me dumped rum or whiskey from a small plastic flask into her Coke, then grinned at me and dropped the flask back into her big leather purse. Bangs covered one eye and large, white shells that looked like wind chimes dangled from her ears. She wore tight, dark jeans and red cowboy boots. I shot her a polite smile and looked back out the window.

"You a blackjack guy?" came her raspy voice.

I turned back to see her eying me as she sipped her drink. "Me?"

"Yes, you." She crunched an ice cube, giggled, and stirred the concoction with her finger, sucking the finger dry with a loud pucker.

"I don't bet much. But when I do, it is blackjack."

"I knew it." Her dark eyes widened, as did her grin.

"How 'bout you?"

"I like it all." She teased with her deep-set eyes.

This is all I need right now, more trouble.

"Where're you staying in Vegas?" She ran several of her French-manicured fingers along the rim of her plastic cup.

"I live there."

"Ooh," she purred. "Really? I'd *die* to live there. I love it. I mean, I totally cannot get enough."

"The glamour wears off."

"Oh." She lifted her armrest, leaned toward me, and pouted. "Don't be a party pooper."

Her sultry gaze and seductive smile were lazy and openly inviting. I'd tangled with her kind before. My eyes couldn't avoid the glaring cleavage she obviously meant to show off. Something dark caught my eye at the base of her neck. I leaned slightly so I could see. It was the hooked tail of a black scorpion.

My stomach went sour.

Her brazen eye followed mine, and she craned her neck to the side. "You like the tattoo?"

My face warmed deeply. I was aroused, yet strangely disgusted.

Part of me wanted to blot out Holly and the deaths of my father and Chester and all the pressure I was under, and flat out go after that babe. Forget everything else. Let the chips fall where they may.

But part of me saw danger.

Ruin.

"Actually," I managed, "I'm not crazy about tattoos."

My mouth felt as if it were packed with gravel. An eerie sense of discontentment trickled over me like warm rain. Sound faded and I vacuumed upward, as if watching the scene from above. The woman didn't seem to notice the sweat breaking out on my forehead or the blood draining from my face.

"Oh, come on." She pursed her lips and ran the back of her trembling hand along her cheek. "I have others you might like better."

Evil.

She was evil. And so was I. And I had had enough of evil.

I wanted to be clean, like Holly, like my parents, like Chester.

"Look." I ran my hand slowly across my wet forehead and through my hair to dry it. "I don't mean to be rude." My eyes blinked repeatedly, and I shook my head, trying to make things clear, trying to come back from the distance. "But I have a girlfriend in Las Vegas."

She shifted and grew rigid in her seat. "What do you think we're talking about?" Her eyes shrank and darkened and narrowed and pulsated. "You think I'm hitting on you?" She furrowed up like a cat about to pounce on its prey.

"Look, no offense, okay?" I stood, my head swirling ever so slightly. "Would you excuse me?"

"You are rude, you know that?"

"Just lemme out, please."

Her knees moved sideways. "Why don't you find another seat while you're up."

"Excuse me." Weakly, I plowed past her.

My head was as light as the altitude. Grasping the top of each seat I passed on my right and left, I made my way down the aisle, each step feeling like a moonwalk. With heads cocked in odd positions, propped on white pillows and resting above blue blankets, people snoozed in the dark. Others read by dim yellow beams of light. Still others simply stared at me as I staggered down the aisle and off into the night.

The lavatory on the left was taken, but the one on the right read "Vacant." I practically fell inside, locking the door, the lights flickering on. Clinging to the tiny sink, I peered into the smudged mirror. My hair was wet with perspiration. My eyes were sunk deep in their sockets, and there was no color in my skin.

What's going on?

I wanted that woman. Yet she repulsed me.

It's all the pressure…you're having a breakdown.

No. It wasn't that. That wasn't the truth.

I lifted my hand and touched the mirror.

God's trying to reach me.

The evil I saw in that woman, I saw in me. In my own way, I was just like her. We all were.

Whoa.

Turbulence bounced me against the wall.

The jet swayed and steadied.

I stared into the mirror.

"Are You here?"

The engines hummed and I waited, still as a statue.

Ba…boom.

The plane dropped and so did my stomach, like it does in a car rocketing over a hill.

Bling, bling.

The lights flashed and came back on, along with the seat-belt light.

The pilot's muffled voice blared indecipherably, but I figured he was telling people to return to their seats and buckle up for more turbulence.

My head dropped. "I just…I'm not ready." My hands rose to my temples, and my fingers raked through my thick hair, hard against my scalp.

A slight vibration met me where I stood, then the phone booth–sized cubicle shuddered like a rocket ship busting through the sound barrier. Beyond the narrow door, trays and cups clattered, and luggage rocked in overhead bins.

Bling, bling.

Again, the small fluorescent lights blinked, and the pilot's voice blared like a bad AM radio station, but I couldn't make out what he way saying.

Knock, knock.

"Excuse me," came a female voice from the other side of the door. "Please return to your seat. Captain's orders. Bumpy air ahead."

Her words jolted me back to reality. I yanked two paper towels from the dispenser and wiped the sweat from my face and forehead. Then, leaning close, I took one last look at my shaggy face in the mirror.

"Loser."

And headed back to my seat.

26

I never heard back from Hud before peeking out front at the ever-present police car, strolling back to my bedroom, and dropping into bed. *Will he really come back now before his dad's funeral?* Although I knew the back-and-forth travel would be a hassle, the thought exhilarated me, and a sense of warmth and security settled into my bones. But I feared for Hud's future. For *our* future?

There can be no future, unless he believes.

Once again, I vowed to keep that promise.

The slightest noises kept me awake. The icemaker gurgling again. The air conditioner fan kicking off. The ticking of the clock in the living room. I wasn't even close to sleeping, so I wandered into the bathroom and ran a drink of water. Looking at myself in the mirror by the glow of the green nightlight, the purple circles beneath my eyes appeared darker than they had. I set the cup down and flipped on the overhead. Nope. Actually, they were almost gone.

Shadows.

Virtually all of my bruises had disappeared. Now if the night-mares about Kenny would just go away.

Before leaving the bathroom, I turned out the light, went to the window, and separated the curtains. The low-watt bulb against the back of the house lit up the patio. Moths flitted around the light. The heat of the day lingered, and there was zero movement in the small backyard. I let the curtains close, walked to the living room, made sure the police car was still out front, and dropped into my chair.

The ticking clock on the wall said it was past eleven thirty.

Where could Suzette be?

I first met the radiant blonde at a Christian singles' club at her brother's church. She was sipping a mocha at the coffee bar, sur-rounded by laughing friends. She embraced me immediately and, after that, always asked about my work at the clinic and how I was doing; she only talked about herself when asked. I learned later she was a hard-nosed reporter for the *R-J.* Beauty and backbone.

Hud was convinced there was foul play in her disappearance. I flashed back to Needermire with his club and comrades the morning of the brutal sweep at Owens Avenue.

Does he have her?

I looked around the dimly lit room.

My problems were nothing compared to hers.

Something made me turn and examine the hole in the wall where Ken had slammed my head. I needed to fix it. My hand ran lightly over my forehead where the lump had been. It was gone now, but the memories were seared in the depths of me.

I relived the beating—and others. The sense of helplessness. The pain. And fear. The hair stood up on my arms, and my heart revved. Breathing suddenly became something I had to concentrate on, and I melted to the floor, leaning on the seat of the chair.

"Help me, Jesus." I buried my head in my arms. "I'm so scared. I know You don't want me to be, but I am. He wants to hurt me. I can't take any more. Protect me, please. Calm me. Give me Your peace—"

The words that were suddenly stamped into my soul were not audible, but they were spoken to me directly. I sensed them as clear as someone whispering in my ear.

Be still.

There was no question what to do. I froze.

Still.

Still.

Still.

Know I'm God.

I did not move.

My mind's eye panned snowcapped mountains, striking skies, and roaring seas.

I was so small, and He was so significant.

He was above me, around me, in me.

The Maker of all hemmed me in and washed me in serenity.

My fear fled like a startled intruder, and I laughed and cried, breathed deeply, and released everything to Him.

Out of curiosity, I took a seat at the glowing computer in the far corner of the living room, squinting at the various flights from San Antonio to Las Vegas that would arrive through the night.

Will Hud be on one?

Finding my way to the KLAS-TV Web site, I leaned within inches of the screen when I saw the red and white banner, "BREAKING NEWS," along with Hudson's photograph and a stark headline: "Odds Turning Against Ambrose: Vegas Reporter in Hot Water."

Clicking the "More>>" link, I closed my eyes and waited. The

story loaded within seconds. There were photos of Hud, Chester, and
Suzette. I took in the story, barely breathing.

> Items gathered from the home of Hudson Ambrose, near the
> Center Strip, have provided more incriminating evidence that
> may link the *Review-Journal* reporter to the missing-person case
> involving former Atlanta business mogul Chester Holte.
>   According to Assistant Sheriff Nelson Truax, of the Las
> Vegas Metropolitan Police Department, investigators found
> jewelry and other personal items belonging to Holte in the
> home of reporter Ambrose.

"What?" my voice shattered the silence within my quiet house.
"That's not right." I skimmed the remainder of the story, searching
for new information.

> Police would not confirm that Ambrose's fingerprints were found
> on the items, but did say that the reporter is a 'person of interest'
> in the disappearance of Holte.
>   Ambrose is reported to be in San Antonio, awaiting the
> burial of his father later this week. When he returns to Las
> Vegas, he is expected to be brought in for further questioning
> by the LVMPD.
>   In the meantime, the nine-thousand-member Spring Valley
> Community Church is mounting a massive, citywide search for
> Holte and *Review-Journal* reporter Suzette Graham, sister of
> Spring Valley Pastor Ellery Graham and a member of the bur-
> geoning congregation.
>   A spokesperson for the church says Suzette Graham has
> been missing for more than twenty-four hours, and family

members suspect foul play, saying they believe Ms. Graham's disappearance may be related to the Holte case. A missing-person's report has been filed with the LVMPD, and officials say they are looking into Ms. Graham's disappearance.

"There is no waiting period to report a missing person in Las Vegas, so we're on this thing," Truax said. "But it's important to remember that five to seven adults are reported missing in this city each day, and the vast majority of those are found or voluntarily return home within forty-eight to seventy-two hours. Of course, that's what we hope happens with Ms. Graham."

Another member of the Las Vegas homeless community, Ned Frazier, 48, was found dead after being dragged from a rope attached to the Las Vegas Monorail...

I dropped my head into my hands. *No mention of Needermire or Van Dillon.* All fingers pointed at Hud. It would be best if he *did* come in the middle of the night. Maybe then he wouldn't be so overwhelmed by the media.

I sighed, stood, and crossed to the front window. From the white glow of the computer screen inside the patrol car, I made out the officer on duty. Husky. Dark hair and mustache. *How does he stay awake?*

I thought about grabbing a carrot or cookie, or having a bite of my leftover salad, but I'd grown weary. Meandering back to my bedroom, I urged God to let Reed's story about Hud be in the morning paper.

Curling up beneath the cool covers, I flopped onto my stomach, hoping I would sleep this time.

Maybe I'll see Hud tomorrow.

My alarm was set for five thirty. I would get to search headquarters early.

Help us find Suzette, Lord, and Chester.

Hud will be grieving and under a ton of pressure.

Nothing you can do about it now.

I drifted.

Sleep came.

There was a noise, but I couldn't tell if it was real or not. It was far off.

I needed rest.

Too tired to get up...

The sweaty palm clamped hard over my nose and mouth, pinning my head to the pillow. My eyes felt as if they had lurched out of their sockets. The only things I could see in the blackness were Kenny's crazy eyes, large and wet, darting about.

"You're mine." His voice shook as bad as his hands. I could almost hear his heart thundering and the adrenaline driving through every inch of his wiry frame. His hand remained there, keeping me motionless.

I couldn't breathe and moaned to tell him so. He began pulling me up, both hands locked on my head.

"You're not gonna make a sound. I'm sitting you up. You're gonna get dressed. We're going out back."

I grabbed his hands, dug my fingernails in, and squealed—trying to tell him I couldn't breathe.

"Shut up." He jerked my head. "Do you hear me? Shut up!"

He moved his hand down, uncovering my nostrils. I sucked in a roomful of air through my nose, including the cheap, drugstore cologne that permeated my nightmares.

"Where's your boyfriend now?" He yanked me out of the bed, toward the dresser. "Get some clothes. Hurry up!"

I yanked a Dodgers T-shirt out of the second drawer.

"Get it on, over the pajamas."

I questioned him with a glance.

"Now!"

After the shirt, he forced me to put white painters pants on right over my boxers. "Hurry!" He squirmed, half yelling, half whispering. "What did you think? Did you think I was gonna share you? That'll *never* happen, Holly. Never again! We're gonna end this dance, once and for all."

I shook my head, tried to cry out, and squinted at him to have sympathy, but amazingly, it was almost an act. I did not feel panicked. Something inside, at the center of me, was keeping me balanced. The wheels in my mind were turning like the gears in a clock. I needed to find an out. Just one. An instant when I could scream to get the cop's attention or, better yet, to run.

"My career is ruined, you know that?" He yanked my hair. "If I stuck around here, you know what'd happen to me? Dishonorable discharge. Shame. No thanks. I'm goin' out with honor. And so are you. Say good-bye to your little house. You'll never see it again."

The sweat from his wrists rubbed cold against me as he forced me to step into a pair of sandals. He chuckled and gasped, still muzzling my mouth and bracing the back of my head as he dragged me through the hallway. Shattered glass reflected on the floor in the laundry room where he'd broken the small window to get in.

"We're leaving this world together, lady." He pawed frantically at the lock on the sliding glass door. "Do you understand? This is it. You'll never see this place again."

I couldn't go with him.

No!

I would rather die trying to get away.

He was probably parked in back of the plaza behind the house.

If I got in his car, that would be the end. He'd kill us both. Or drive us to Montana, brainwash me, and make me his slave.

"I can't see," he hissed. "Do this lock, quick!"

I could have unlocked it in my sleep, but he didn't know that. I moaned that it was too dark, but his hand covered my mouth.

"What?"

I gasped as his hand left my mouth. "I can't see it either," I lied.

He reached for his back pocket. *A flashlight? A gun?*

Something blared in my head.

Scream, Holly. Scream!

27

Sure enough, when I deplaned and trudged up the ramp into the dazzling terminal at McCarran International Airport, reporters and camera crews scrambled to meet me. And I'd decided to meet them head on.

Relishing the cool AC, I dropped my garment bag on the shiny floor by a large set of gleaming slot machines, stuck my sweaty hands on my waist, and waited. Beyond the panoramic, floor-to-ceiling windows, the entire expanse of the Las Vegas skyline was lit up like a mirage against the blackness. The brunette I'd initially sat by sauntered past with a furrowed brow, shooting an inquiring glance at all the chaos, then threw her chin in the air and blazed off.

Good riddance.

Converging like vultures, the reporters jockeyed for position, blurting out questions all at once. I recognized four or five from the Las Vegas media community, saying hello to those whose names I knew and nodding acknowledgment to others. Two colleagues from the *R-J* were front and center.

"Where's Reed?" I asked.

"Baby-sitting your story," said the lanky photographer.

"Will it run today?" I asked.

They both nodded and started to talk at the same time.

The reporter spoke loudest. "Last we heard, it was our top story."

I let out a sigh of relief.

"Guys." I held up my hands and gave it a second to get somewhat quiet. "I knew you'd be waiting for me. I know you've got jobs to do. I can relate." There was a smattering of laughter. "I just want to make a quick statement, and that's going to be it. So please don't pursue it after this, because I won't have any more to say right now."

"Are you going to confess to the murder of Chester Holte?" someone yelled.

Another butted in, "Are you friends with Suzette Graham? Do you know where she is?"

"You know." I gritted my teeth and shook my head. "It's guys like you who just asked those questions that give the media a black eye. I said I was going to make a statement." I pulled the small notepad out of my back pocket and flipped it open. "That statement is this: I've hurt no one. I had nothing to do with Chester Holte's disappearance, or anyone else's—"

"What about Ned Frazier?" someone shouted.

I shot an evil eye in that direction and kept going. "The *Review-Journal* has my full story. All the details. The article by Reed O'Neil should be in today's paper. After you've seen that, you'll know my side of it. I am completely innocent and will—"

"You said you made mistakes," barked a skinny reporter wearing jeans and a navy golf shirt with an NBC logo. "Tell us what mistakes. Have you broken the law?"

I raised my hands to calm them, and an electronic flash went off in my face. "What I've said is gonna have to do for now. I'm going home to get some rest. Thank you. Please leave me alone for now."

I bent down, hoisted the garment bag onto my shoulder, and searched for the path of least resistance toward ground transportation. A few more cheap-shot questions were fired as I left, but by the time I passed a large, glass-enclosed smokers' room, most of the reporters had dropped off. There were a few strays, however, who refused to take a hint.

A woman ran up behind me. "Where did you get the personal items and jewelry that belonged to Chester?"

What?

I was dazed by the blow but kept walking.

How did she know about that?

Another girl came up on my left. "If you weren't involved in Chester's disappearance, what were those things doing at your house?"

I didn't—

"Mr. Ambrose." A heavy-set brunette came up on my right. "Were you aware police found that evidence at your house late today?"

Keep walking.

"It's a simple question. Can you answer, please?"

I closed my eyes and felt the heat rush to my face.

Everything in me wanted to tell the hustling reporters I was being framed. But I kept moving faster, getting ahead, not wanting them to see the expression of shock that had etched itself onto my burning face.

Whoever had stolen Chester's things from my house had arranged for them to be planted back there as evidence against me.

Hurriedly, I passed below the enormous video screens and backlit signs that played endless gaming ads and steamy videos. My top priority was to get to my car and to Holly's place. *Make sure she's okay.* I didn't plan to go in, just drive by, make sure things were quiet and the cop was still there.

The Mustang had a coat of dust and grit on it, as usual when left outside in Las Vegas for more than a few hours. I started it up, got the AC blowing, and flipped on the wipers and fluid to clean the windshield.

There was one message on my cell phone, from an area code I didn't recognize. I played it.

"Mr. Ambrose. I'd hoped to speak to you, live." It was him again, the stranger. He spoke softly. I pressed the phone hard against my ear. "This thing is burdening me. I couldn't sleep. I can't concentrate on my work…"

The man paused at length, but I could hear movement.

"They're saying some incriminating evidence was found in your home—rings of Chester's, letters, newspaper clippings. Listen carefully. You need to pursue a Las Vegas police officer. I don't know his name, but he's average height, thin, strong, very tan. He has short, black hair; dark hair on his arms—"

Needermire?

"This is all I can give you for now. I know you're innocent." His voice broke with those words. He waited, then finished quickly. "I'll follow the story and try to give you tips as it plays out. I'm sorry I can't be of more help."

Click.

Who could it be? Another cop?

I glanced again at the area code where the call came from: 678. Not a Vegas number. I ran through every person I knew who was connected to Chester, and not one of them aligned with the man who was calling me.

He had details. He'd seen this dirty cop. He sounded like he knew Chester.

I dialed directory assistance. After two or three minutes of frustrating recordings, I got someone live who told me, for a charge of ninety-five cents, that the 678 area code was in Atlanta.

Chester's church.

I'd already crossed his son, Andrew, off my list of potential callers. *He's too young.* I'd also ruled out Chester's pastor, Banyon Scribe, who came across in his correspondence like a legalistic, money-hungry nut case; not the type who would be calling to help a stranger.

Atlanta had been Chester's home. The caller could be anyone.

How does he know so much?

Dropping the phone in the passenger seat, I gripped both sides of the steering wheel, lowered my head until it touched, took in an enormous breath, and blew out loud and long.

Need to keep going.

A jet roared overhead. I looked up and saw the white lights on its wings rising into the darkness.

My passenger door banged open. A man was in my car, sprawled across the seat with his back to me, ripping at the car keys.

Yelling instinctively, I bashed the center of his back with my elbow. He let out a groan but continued scrambling.

I pounded the side of his head with my fist, half expecting him to turn on me with a knife or gun.

The car shut off. The keys jingled. He had the keys.

I grabbed a fistful of his sandy hair and mashed his head against the dashboard. He grunted, but pushed hard against me to get out of the car. I clawed his navy, short-sleeved shirt and held on for dear life, hearing it tear as he continued to back out of the passenger's door.

"Let go!" He sounded more like a hurt sibling than a seasoned car thief.

I wasn't about to let go of his shirt.

"Drop the keys," I yelled, clinging to his upper body.

Somehow he got off a punch to my stomach, and another. My wind was gone. His shirt burned in my clenched fingers as he pulled away, pulled away, and...*rip*. The lightweight shirt tore, freeing him another foot, and allowing him to yank it free the rest of the way. He was gone.

I'd already figured out plan B, which was to get out my door ASAP and race him down but I couldn't breathe. Wheezing loudly, I fought for air, found my door handle and pulled, but could only lean against it as it cracked open six inches.

"Where's Chester Holte?" His voice was behind me now, outside my door.

"I don't know." I coughed. "Give me the keys."

"You tell me where he is."

"Who are you?"

"His son."

Pushing against the door, I lifted my feet out, bumping the door open the rest of the way.

"Don't try anything!" He stepped toward me.

"It looks like I killed your dad, but I didn't." I rested my elbows on my knees, took several more deep breaths, and stood up with a groan. "I'm being set up."

"By whom?"

The kid was about my height, trim and muscular, but innocent looking. His ear was bright red from where I'd hit him, and his eyes were green and wild.

"Either a Vegas cop named Needermire or a jealous freak named Van Dillon. I'm not sure yet."

"Why haven't you gone public with it?"

"I have. It'll be in today's paper." I leaned over, hands to my knees, feeling as if I'd been kicked in the groin. "Have you been calling me?"

"No."

With my keys in his hand, he snatched his shirt tail and wiped the glistening sweat from his forehead. "I just heard about the search tomorrow and got here as fast as I could. You just happened to get in when I did. I followed the commotion."

"I'm sorry about your dad," I said. "I just lost mine too."

He blinked several times but said nothing.

"Chester sounded like quite a man."

"Why'd you have his jewelry and things at your house?"

"Is your name Andrew?"

"Yeah, it is. Now answer my question."

"Did you rent a car? Where are you headed?"

"I don't know where I'm going. Just answer me! Why did you have my dad's belongings?"

"Look, Andrew, there's someplace I have to be. I'm driving into the city, and I'll be glad to give you a lift and tell you everything I know on the way—"

"Tell me now!"

My temperature spiked and my jaw jutted out. All I could think about was Holly.

"I've got to be somewhere, okay?" I stepped toward him. "You can either come with me and find out the whole story or read it in the paper in the morning. Your choice. But I've got to go right now."

The kid started to protest, but I pictured Holly, alone in her little house, with nothing but a lone squad car out front. "Give me the keys, Andrew." My heart knocked almost audibly in my chest. "Or you're gonna be sorry you followed me."

28

eading north, directly into one of the brightest spectacles I'd
ever seen (I'd never been to Vegas), something about Hudson
Ambrose made me want to believe he had nothing to do with
my father's death.

But I was far from there yet.

As he sped through the heart of the pulsating city toward Holly
Queens's house, he told me his story, from the moment he says he
heard a call about my dad's murder on the scanner in the *R-J* newsroom right up until now.

"If you didn't have anything to do with my dad's death, why'd you
search him? Just make that clear to me."

"Andrew, I told you, it was the dumbest mistake of my life. He
was obviously dead. He was obviously homeless…I was looking for
an ID or anything that would tell me more about him."

"Why didn't you just wait till the police got there?"

"They were taking forever. I knew the thing would get tied up in red tape. I just wanted to have his name for my story, knowing they probably wouldn't give it to me. Believe me, I'm not a thief."

"You're not? Then why—"

"Look, it's not like I went looking for riches on your dad. I mean, who would have expected to find what I did in his pocket—him being homeless and all?"

"Unless you had some previous contact with him and knew he had money."

"Which I didn't, but his killer may well have."

I stared out at the neon wonderland and the sidewalks packed with tourists shooting video footage and flash photos.

"When I found the bankbook and key, greed took over. I admit it. I messed up, big time. But I promise you, I did not hurt your father."

"In my book, if you're the type of guy who can rummage through the pockets of a dead homeless man, you're capable of just about anything."

Hudson's head bobbed as he peered out his driver's window. "I'm not gonna argue with you. You have every right to be ticked off at me. I'd be the same way if it had been my old man. I'm totally ashamed of what I did, especially knowing what kind of man your dad was."

"It shouldn't matter what kind of man he was. You don't do that to anybody!"

"I know." Hudson looked at me for several seconds. "Because he was homeless, I took liberties…" He turned back to the busy street in front of him. "I'm sorry. I regret what I did, more than you know."

He changed the subject by asking my plans for the next few days. I told him I planned to see the bus stop where my dad had died, and the van, and his other hangouts. Hudson said he would take me around during my stay, and even offered to let me crash at his place. Hesitantly, I accepted the offer, thinking that being close to him might lead me to some answers about Dad's death I otherwise wouldn't find.

"You going on the search in the morning?" Hudson asked.

"Absolutely."

"I know they're going to have a ton of people. Your dad had a whole bunch of friends."

"He thought a lot of his pastor, Ellery Graham, and the people at his church. I'm looking forward to meeting some of them."

"There's going to be a huge homeless turnout too."

"That's what I hear."

"Tell me about the church back in Atlanta, where your dad came from. You go there, don't you?"

Oh brother. I had my heart set on forgetting that for a few days.

"It hasn't been good; let's just put it that way." I peered out my window at all the hotels I'd only read about or seen on TV: Bellagio, Caesars Palace, the Flamingo.

"From the letters I read, it sounds like your dad and the pastor had some differences."

"To say the least." I chuckled, embarrassed by what Hudson might have read, afraid he would think we were some kind of fanatic cult. "Scribe's mad at my dad for not fulfilling a financial pledge he made for a new worship center."

"I heard about that." Hudson turned to me.

"The building's like an idol to Scribe. The thought of this megachurch with his name on it, that's what he lives for. It's become more important than God."

"What made your dad wake up to all this?" He stared at me for an answer.

"I don't really know. When Mom died, he clung to the church for help, for sanity really. His life became all about church works, church functions, and church people. Those things made him feel good. And church leaders patted him on the back for all he did—and gave. But over time God showed him there was a human race outside the doors of the church that needed God."

"And that's why he came to Las Vegas?"

"Ultimately, yeah," I said. "He did a lot of soul searching first."

I debated whether to go into it or not. I doubted Hudson Ambrose was even a Christian. But, on the other hand, maybe Hudson Ambrose was part of the reason I was there.

"It was like my dad learned the secret of life."

"And that is…?" Hudson glanced at me.

"Life's not about us or about pleasing man. It's about getting close to God and doing what He says."

"That's heavy."

"But it's where you find true contentment." I laughed. "Believe me, I'm not there." I dropped my head and forced back the memories. "Dad was the godliest man I ever knew."

"I wish I'd known him."

I could only nod.

"In a way, I did know him, I guess, because of all I've found out about him."

I could only smile and nod again.

Hudson kindly changed the subject. "I told you about the two calls I got from the stranger."

"The ones from Atlanta?"

"Yeah," Hudson said. "I toyed with the idea that Banyon Scribe could have been involved in what happened to your dad, but he wouldn't know any details about his death."

"I know he and some of the church leaders made a trip here awhile back to try to find Dad. But that was months ago."

Gently rubbing a deep crevice above his nose, Hudson stared glassy-eyed at the traffic-packed road in front of him. He explained that Holly Queens had been a dear friend of my dad's, and I could tell by the way his posture straightened and his eyes widened when he talked about her that Hudson had feelings for the girl. We were going to drive by her house to make sure she was okay. Apparently, her abusive boyfriend, who should have been behind bars, was on the loose; he might have even played a part in my father's death.

The car was quiet. We slowed and took an exit. Hudson maneuvered the Mustang across two busy lanes of traffic, over some tracks, and up to a stoplight in what seemed like an old part of town.

"You should know, your dad's life has impacted me." Hudson glanced at me, then looked back up at the red light. "His friends. The stories I've heard…I'd like to be more like him."

I nodded, clinging to his words, relishing the lifeblood in each one. "I know what you mean."

The light changed, the Mustang roared to life, and Hudson leaned forward and drummed the steering wheel. "Holly's place is right up here. Couple more blocks."

29

The second I pulled the Mustang onto First Street, we saw the cop car stationed directly in front of Holly's house.

"There he is," Andrew said.

"As promised."

I pulled down the short street and around the cul-de-sac, slowing just short of Holly's property, behind the police car. Her red pickup truck was in the driveway, and the house was dark inside. *Nice and quiet.* A dim light by the front door lit a small portion of the porch in yellow.

"I think the cop's asleep." Andrew nodded toward the black-and-white.

I eased the Mustang up next to the police car.

Sure enough, the cop's chin was glued to his chest.

"Las Vegas's finest." I pulled the parking brake, turned out the lights, and opened my door.

"Where're you going?"

"Wake him up." I unfolded from the car.

I walked around to the driver's side of the squad car. Andrew's window buzzed down. "You sure you want to do that?" he whispered.

"His job's to be watching this place, isn't it?"

The knuckles on my right fist were ten inches from knocking on the cop's window when a bloodcurdling scream echoed from the rear of the house and tore open the night.

Holly.

Dismissing the front door, I tore through the grass and pebbles on the left side of the house, hoping I wouldn't ram into an old mower or wheelbarrow in the blackness.

Wake the cop, Andrew.

Ducking at the last second before getting strung up on an empty clothesline, I saw light coming from the back of the house and sprinted toward it, almost losing my footing in the cinders as I rounded the corner.

Holly was sprawled out on her bottom on the concrete patio, a dim light shining down on her bloodied forehead.

"Holly!" I ran toward her.

"No, Hud. Look out!"

Crack.

My head.

Down.

Next to her.

She cried out and squeezed my arm.

Blue strobe lights lit the night sky, projecting a black shadow of the house into the trees.

A siren moaned to life, bleeping, then blaring.

"Get up!" Van Dillon's black handgun flashed as he stepped out of the dark house, his head swiveling right and left at the sound of the siren.

He yanked Holly to her feet by her hair and rammed the gun to my throat.

"Come on, you snake." He breathed hard but moved like a cougar. "We're going to my car."

I stood but wobbled. The ground spun.

He rammed the gun into my back. "Move!"

A portion of my head felt cold.

Blood.

I stopped myself from instinctively reaching up to touch it, thinking—almost knowing—he'd nonchalantly pull the trigger at my slightest movement.

Have to stall.

I opened my eyes wide and reached my hands out in front of me, as if feeling for something. "Wait, I...I can't see."

"Oh, my gosh!" Holly squealed. "Hudson?"

I looked in her general direction, above her, and shuffled toward her.

"He can't see!" Holly screamed, squeezing my face. "Leave him, Kenny, please! He'll just slow us down."

In a flash, Van Dillon locked Holly's bleeding forehead in the crook of his gun arm. With his free hand he snatched a knife from his pocket, flicked it open, and mashed the serrated blade against her throat.

Feigning blindness, I glanced at Holly and looked away, my eyes darting about, my arms outstretched.

Van Dillon pressed the blade into her white neck until she screamed and blood trickled to her chest. "Can you see me now, lover boy?"

"Stop!" I cried, cutting the act and swallowing the bile in my throat.

Holly's eyes bulged, and her mouth locked open in terror.

Van Dillon's face contorted, and the corners of his mouth curled down. Mechanically, he closed the knife with one hand, dropped it into his pocket, grabbed Holly by the hair, and pointed the gun at my face.

BAM.

The yellow flash blinded me, and the heat of the passing bullet melted the left side of my face and sent me reeling.

My head buzzed from the sound of the gunfire.

Holly sobbed, and her whole body shuddered.

The gun was pointed back at my face. Rage and hatred and gritting teeth filled Van Dillon's evil face.

I am going to die.

"Police!" a low voice boomed from the right side of the house. "Halt where you are! Drop the weapon!"

The nose of Van Dillon's gun whipped from me to the center of Holly's temple.

"I'll kill her!" He froze in his tracks, still facing me and the pathway leading away from the house. "I'm gonna die anyway. I'll shoot her. Then you kill me. It's the same thing I planned anyway."

"All right now," the cop yelled. "Everybody calm down. We're going to work though this." His voice came from behind a short, wide palm tree, and I could see the barrel of his gun coming around the side.

The sweat on Van Dillon's crew-cut scalp glistened as he caught his breath and continued to manhandle Holly.

"Let the girl go, Van Dillon," the cop called. "You don't want to hurt her."

"Nobody's gonna have her. You hear me?" He turned toward the cop, yanking terror-ridden Holly so she was directly between them. "She's mine. If you're smart, cop, you'll let us go."

"Let the man go then," the cop called. "You don't need him anymore."

The cop is stalling, waiting for backup.

"He's part of it!" Van Dillon cried in a high-pitched, maniacal tone. "He wants to be with her. That ain't gonna happen again. We're leavin' this dance together."

Before Van Dillon was done talking, the stocky cop bent low and bolted for cover behind a group of large rocks deep in the yard.

I jumped at the blast from Van Dillon's gun, which fired twice at the scampering officer.

"Don't do that!" Van Dillon yanked Holly in the direction of the officer. "I know what you're doing. Don't try to cut me off. I'll kill you, copper."

The officer was fifteen feet from the path Van Dillon apparently wanted to take, through some light brush, and into what I guessed would be another urban neighborhood or business area, where his car must have been parked.

"We three are walkin' out of here, and I advise you not to try to stop us."

With his gun to Holly's head, Van Dillon threw up a kick at me. "Go!"

Hesitantly, I started for the path, with him shoving a grunting Holly close behind me.

"I'll tell you what, Van Dillon," the officer spoke from behind the boulders with his big, boxy semiautomatic fixed on Kenny. "I'll let you go. But you've gotta leave those two with me. Go on. This is as good as it's gonna get for you."

"You don't understand." Van Dillon bumped me from behind, pushing me toward the path. "I don't care about my life. That's why you better be scared. My life's over. What we're down to now is, who am I gonna take with me? I'm not afraid to kill you."

The slight hum of a siren rose in the distance.

"Move!" He booted me.

The cop had nowhere else to go. He'd run out of cover toward the path, except for a few small trees. And Van Dillon was holding Holly so close, the officer had no shot at him. For a flash, as we worked our way down that path with the cop's weapon panning right along with us, I wondered whether I would go to heaven if Van Dillon dropped me cold with a bullet at close range. I was certain the answer was no.

"You stay put, cop."

"I can't do that, Van Dillon." The officer arose slightly from behind the rocks. "You're endangering the lives of innocent people."

The siren drew closer.

"Hurry up!" Van Dillon shoved me again.

We were through the clearing. It was dark, but I could make out a long, one-story building, the back of a plaza, perhaps. The officer was following us on foot, ducking from tree to tree as he came, putting his life on the line.

A small, dirty car with a flat tire was parked straight ahead. The only other vehicle in sight was a white Chevy mid-size, parked by a huge Dumpster. It was not the same car I'd seen Van Dillon in when he followed Holly and me to Maxine's. *Probably stolen.*

Once we hit the open air of the parking lot, Van Dillon began a panicky, jerky race for the car, dragging a whimpering Holly and ordering me to stay close. The siren was approaching. With each step, I became more aware of how quickly Van Dillon could shift the gun in my direction and blow me away.

Maybe I can tackle him when we're getting in the car.

The cop made a run for the vehicle with the flat tire.

This time I braced myself for Van Dillon's gunfire.

Boom.

Sparks flew off the trunk as the officer settled into position near the front fender.

A siren blared and groaned to a halt back at Holly's house, and the powerful, white beam of a searchlight panned the area to our far right.

"Down on your face!" Van Dillon shoved the gun in my direction, jerking Holly by the hair like a rag doll.

He's realizing he doesn't have time to get us both in the car.

I lowered myself to my knees.

"Lie down!"

I got flat with my hands above my head and my face against the cool pavement.

I'm going to die, execution style.

"No, Kenny!" Holly squealed as he tugged her toward me. "Don't...ahhh!"

His foot nudged me.

Holly sobbed uncontrollably.

It will be quick.

"Don't do it, Van Dillon!" the cop's voice boomed. "Leave him here."

But we all knew the other cops would be there with guns drawn within seconds. The talk was over. I shut my eyes tight, smelling his aftershave. Hearing his voice coming from three feet above the back of my head.

"You'll never have Holly Queens again—"

Boooooooom!

There was no pain.

I opened my eyes and slowly lifted my head.

Van Dillon had whipped around.

His gun was locked on the garbage Dumpster.

I would lurch for his wrist and smash the gun free if it was the last thing I did in this—

Boom.

Boom.

Boom.

Boom.

Van Dillon's riddled body crumpled to the ground.

Smoke wafted up from the wet holes in his torso.

Holly was frozen on her knees. Her whole body shuddering. Hands trembling at her mouth. Eyes filled with terror.

The police officer came toward us slowly, gun still drawn.

"Officer," came a voice from behind the Dumpster. "Don't shoot. I'm with these guys."

"Come out with your hands locked on top of your head." The cop braced his gun in front of him.

"I'm innocent." Andrew crept around the side of the Dumpster with his hands on his head.

"Who are you?" the cop demanded.

"Andrew Holte. I came with this man to check on Miss Queens." Dazed, Holly's head swiveled and she stared at Andrew.

The cop's arms dropped to his sides. "That was a good decoy." He nodded toward the Dumpster. "Slamming the lid of that thing."

"Thanks." Andrew approached Holly. "It was the least I could do for a dear friend of my father's."

30

Hud brought me a cup of hot tea and sat down gently next to me on the couch in my living room. Andrew sat quietly on my other side. The ticking clock read 3:42 a.m. The police had just left. I let my head drop back, sighed, and tried to force my stiff body to relax.

"You okay?" Hud asked.

"Uh-huh." I glanced at his welcome face and closed my eyes.

"It's all over now. No more looking over your shoulder."

I nodded, opened my eyes, and—not wanting to think about Ken Van Dillon—looked at Andrew.

"I can't believe how much you look like your father."

He smiled, resembling Chester even more. "You've been through a lot."

"So have you," I said and turned to Hud, "and so have you."

We sat there, all of us numb, I think.

Each of their heads dropped. They were grieving, and I didn't have an ounce of energy or incentive to console them. As I squeezed the handle of the teacup, it clattered uncontrollably against the saucer. Still, I tried to bring it to my lips, but the cup shook so violently that some of the tea sloshed hot onto my lap.

"I'll get something." Andrew headed for the kitchen.

"Here." Hud took the cup and saucer and put the cup to my lips. "Sip."

I did so, totally embarrassed.

"You need sleep."

But I felt like I'd drunk a whole pot of coffee. "I promised Ellery and Jenna I'd be at the clinic to pass out posters by six at the latest."

"Holly." Hud looked at the clock as Andrew returned with a wet rag. "You need to sleep as long as your body tells you to. The posters will get passed out. The search will go on without you."

"I want to be there!" My sudden burst of emotion surprised me. "I owe it to Chester."

Andrew patted the tea spots near my knees. "It's okay, Holly. I'll be there, and I'll make sure the posters get out. You come when you're ready."

"I don't want to miss it." I dropped my head in my hands and began to sob. "I'm so sorry."

My hands trembled. My entire body shivered. I lifted my head. They were watching me, looking at me as if I were a patient in a mental asylum.

"What?" I slapped Hud on the thigh. "You think I'm losing my mind or having a nervous breakdown or something?"

The men's eyes met, their faces somber.

I stood to walk. That's what I needed, to walk this off. I went to the kitchen, through the living room and back to my bedroom, then to the spare room, and did it all over again—and again.

The guys spoke in hushed tones.

I couldn't settle down. In and out I went, from room to room, thinking, hoping the walking would calm me down, bring me back to reality.

Was I going to need to go to some sort of mental facility? Is that what they were planning?

Give me peace, Jesus.

I continued walking, pacing, trying to catch up with the old me and get back inside, where I belonged. But I couldn't find normal—only frazzled.

"You came home for me, Hud." I stopped in the middle of the living room. "You shouldn't have. You should have stayed till the funeral."

"I wanted to come, Holly. I'm glad I did." He perked up to the edge of the couch.

"You guys should go." I stepped to the front window and peered out, still expecting Kenny to be coming for me. "I'll be okay." My words were hollow.

Hud quietly came to the window and rested a hand on my shoulder as I looked out. "I'm going to stay here, if it's okay with you. I offered to take Andrew to my place or to a hotel, but he doesn't want me to have to go anywhere else now. He'll crash too, if it's okay."

I stared into the dark, empty cul-de-sac. "You think I'm losing it."

"No. I think you're the bravest woman I know."

I couldn't help it. The tears came again. My nose ran, and I was sure I looked a mess, but I didn't care.

"Let's get you into bed."

Hud took my hands, turned me around, and walked me to the bedroom. "The couch rolls out." I expended the little energy I had left. "There are blankets—"

"We'll find them. Get those clothes off. Put on some fresh p.j.'s." He headed for the door. "I'll be back in a minute."

Like a robot, I did as he said and dropped in bed without brushing my teeth.

Maybe I'll sleep now. Hudson's here.

The light beyond my closed eyes went dark with the click of a lamp.

I bolted upright.

"It's okay." Hud's silhouette came toward me. "It's just me." He eased me back onto my pillow and sat softly on the side of the bed. "Kenny's gone. He'll never be coming back. You rest now. Things will be brighter in the morning."

"I'm worried about you," I whispered.

"I know. I'm scared too."

"If we can find Chester's body tomorrow, or Suzette…"

"Yeah." He sighed and tilted his head back, with his hand over his mouth. "An autopsy on Chester would help."

"It would clear you." I patted around until I found one of his hands and squeezed. There was a long pause. "Thanks again for coming."

"You're welcome," he whispered. "Can I tell you something?"

"Yes."

His handsome face came within six inches from mine. I searched his eyes.

"I think God may have led me to come back here tonight." He squeezed my hand and came even closer.

My soul stirred. "You think?"

He nodded. "I just knew to come. It was the weirdest feeling." He rested his head on my shoulder. "You're rubbing off on me, Holly Queens."

His words were like magic.

I latched on to him.

We fit together like cushions in a chair.
That was all I needed to hear.
Beautiful words. Glorious hope.
A golden moment we embraced together.
Then, sleep came.

I awoke to daylight and the sound of the TV on the other side of my bedroom door. The bedside clock read 7:20 a.m. My sleep had been brief, but deep.

Ugh. I'd missed the start of the search.

I pushed the memory of Kenny's bullet-ridden body out of my mind and headed for the bathroom to freshen up.

Once somewhat presentable, I crept into the living room. "Hey."

Hud held a cup of Dunkin' Donuts coffee and a copy of the *Review-Journal.* The local news was on.

"Did it run?"

"Good morning...yep." He stood, set his mug down, and handed me the paper. "The whole front page. How are you feeling? Did you sleep?"

"Like a rock."

I took in the entire front page of the newspaper.

Finally!

There was a large picture of a confident-looking Hud arriving at the airport , surrounded by microphones, cameras, and reporters. His editors must have held a spot for the photo right up to press time. The massive headline read:

AMBROSE: 'I'M INNOCENT!'
Reporter Admits Mistakes, Points Finger at Vegas PD

And there was more. Another story highlighted the day's citywide search party and even included a photograph of the missing-persons poster of Chester and Suzette. Set off in a light blue box in the bottom right corner was a story with the headline, "Police Involved in 'Dirty' Homeless Sweep?" Below it were mug shots of LVMPD officers Drake Needermire, Steven Loy, and Andy Sanchez.

"Whoa!" My face heated, I swallowed, and stared at Hud for a reaction.

"I know." He shook his head. "Wait till you read it."

"Bombs away, huh?"

He nodded. "No holds barred."

"Are you happy with it?"

"Reed nailed it." He shook his head. "Everything's in there… It's just scary. There's gonna be some serious fallout."

"I take it we haven't made any friends at the police department."

"No." He chuckled and stretched in what I thought was a nervous gesture. "They're gonna be furious."

"Can you believe Cheevers ran it?"

"I can't. I owe him big-time. I left him a voice mail."

"I want to read it." I curled up in my favorite chair. "Where's Andrew?"

"He took my car to the search." Hud headed for the kitchen. "I told him to hook up with Ellery. You want powdered, plain, or chocolate?"

"Powdered," I called. "Wow, you must've really found the faith since I last saw you…letting him take the Mustang."

"Very funny. Just cream, right?"

"Yep. There's nothing in here about Kenny, is there?"

"No. It happened too late. Tomorrow."

The spectrum of emotions I experienced while reading the stories, sipping my coffee, and getting powder all over everything ranged from exhilaration to downright fear.

"No turning back now, is there?" Hud clicked through the stations.

"Truax and Needermire are going to be livid."

"You got that right." He pointed at the TV. "All the local channels led with it this morning."

"You don't think Needermire would try anything, do you?"

"Like what?"

"Like hurting you?"

"It'd be stupid."

"Yeah, but if he would kidnap Suzette and kill Ned Frazier..."

"Believe me, Holly, the media is gonna be zeroed in on that creep. Now it's his turn."

I flicked the newspaper. "I can't believe this quote from Ellery."

"I know. He told it like it was. Read it to me again."

I found the text with my finger. " 'Police have ignored Chester's disappearance, either because he was homeless, because they had something to do with his death, or possibly a combination of the two. Now my sister is missing, and we believe at least one LVMPD officer may have had something to do with it.' "

We looked at each other and shook our heads in disbelief at the extraordinary story unfolding, not only before our eyes, but within our very lives.

"Well?" I said. "What next?"

"I want to run by my place, see what it looks like since they searched it."

"Reporters may be there."

"I know." He exhaled loudly. "I need to call an attorney."

We both knew Truax would be bringing Hud in for more questioning.

I'm not going to think about that.

"Will you go to the search with me?"

"I've been going back and forth on that." He turned off the TV, stared at the blank screen, and rubbed his forehead. "There'll be all kinds of media."

"Do you want to look for Chester and Suzette?"

"Of course I do, I'm just—"

"Then do it, Hud." I stood. "Don't change who you are. Be yourself. Don't you dare let them force you to stop living."

He dropped his head and laughed. Then he walked over and put his hands on my shoulders. "Can we take the pickup?"

"Now you're talking."

31

We easily dodged the reporters who straggled outside my place by zipping the red pickup right into the garage and closing the door behind us. Holly gasped when she saw what the police had done to the interior of my house. It looked like a Scud missile had hit it.

We walked the downstairs holding hands in a daze, shocked by the mess, and searching for anything out of the ordinary. When Holly said she was heading upstairs, I ducked back into the garage, which seemed undisturbed, and drilled the heavy bag with a barrage of punches until my arms ached so badly I couldn't hold them up.

"Hey," Holly's voice came strong from upstairs, "your attic steps are down."

I bounded up the steps, and my rage turned to panic as I climbed the pull-down stairs to the attic. "Uh-oh."

"What's wrong?" Holly was on the steps right behind me.

"See where this insulation is cleared away?"

"Yeah."

"I bet you any money that's where they'll say they found Chester's things."

"How do you know?"

"It looks like a good hiding place."

"You never came up here?"

"Only to change air filters in the furnace, but never messing around in the insulation. I mean, look at it! The stuff's a foot deep everywhere but in that spot. I guarantee you, somebody planted the rings and letters up here to make it look like I was hiding them."

Holly's silence confirmed my dread, and I knew from that moment that my freedom and future hinged on finding Chester's corpse.

She cleaned up the kitchen and living room, and I changed clothes and made several calls, including one to a local attorney. Then we headed for the Downtown Outreach Clinic, one of five satellite search stations situated throughout the city.

Andrew and Ellery were sweating it out side by side beneath the sweltering sun, leaning over maps, organizing routes, and talking to small groups about what areas of the city still needed to be searched. Jenna had taken charge of overseeing the distribution of posters, water bottles, free copies of the day's *R-J*, and sun visors that featured the logo and Web address for Spring Valley Community Church.

Had it not been for his scars, I wouldn't have recognized the pit boss Holly and I had met several days earlier, Jonathan Seabold, because he was dressed much more casually in denim shorts, a brown T-shirt, and one of those floppy green safari hats with the straps that tied beneath his chin. He and Arthur, who wore his same stifling Georgia Tech sweatshirt and brown beret, scurried like mice, following Jenna's orders to keep the coolers full and get more poster boxes and stacks of newspapers from the back of her SUV.

Jenna spotted Holly and me, waved, and hurried over. "I can't believe it—about Van Dillon."

We embraced. "It's over," I said. "Let's not talk about it now."

Jenna shifted gears without a beat. "Great article in the paper. That's what we needed." She nodded to a stack of *R-J*s on the table nearby. "We're passing them out free to everybody."

"Thank you." I gave her a thumbs-up. "You're doing a great job. It's going to pay off."

"I hope so." Jenna found her husband with her eyes.

Holly must have noticed. "How's Ellery holding up?"

Jenna turned quickly back to us. "This is hard." Her face scrunched and her shoulders caved in, as if she'd been holding out just long enough for us to arrive before she broke down. Holly put her arm around Jenna and pulled her close.

"He's always so strong." Jenna gasped and pinched the tears from her eyes. "He deals with people and trials and grief all the time, but this...Suzette...Oh, I can't even fathom—"

"Don't go there," Holly urged. "Just don't go there, Jenna."

I touched her shoulder. "This thing isn't over yet."

"The city's praying," Holly insisted. "Thousands of people are searching. Thousands!"

Glassy-eyed, Jenna looked back over at Ellery, who was leaning over a map with two other men. "He does so much for other people. His whole life's been like that." She shook her head, and her breathing jumped with the tears. "Don't let him see me like this." She turned her back to Ellery.

"Looks like he's just burying himself in busyness right now," Holly said. "It's probably good for him."

"Exactly right." Jenna gave a big nod and teary chuckle. "That's how he's coping."

A young man with tattoos and straight black hair down to the middle of his back approached Ellery, and the two men hugged. "He's helped a lot of people," I said, not really even meaning for it to come out.

"Oh." Jenna waved her hand. "He's the most grace-centered man I've ever known. He makes me feel so guilty." She wiped her eyes with her shirt sleeve. "There I am, judging people, condemning, blaming...you know, nasty criminals, people who cheat on their wives, people who spread gossip like poison in the church. But not Ellery." Her head went back and forth. "He's always so even. He says, 'Now, honey, you don't know what that person's been through.' He's so good about looking for the best in people and bringing it out."

Jenna took the sunglasses from atop her head, shook her curly blond hair, and slid on the glasses. "Oh, forgive me, you guys." She took in a deep breath and exhaled silently. "For some reason, when I saw you, Holly, I just let everything out. I knew you'd understand."

"That's what friends are for, right?" Holly said.

Moving through the crowd, we said our brief hellos to those we knew and immediately got caught up in the contagious spirit of the search, handing out posters, water bottles, and visors, and directing groups to Ellery and Andrew's table for search instructions.

As I began to work and sweat and get comfortable anonymously fitting into the system, I became intrigued by the masses of people pouring in to give of their time. Many single adults and homeless people wandered up, took what we had to offer, and headed off, wearing their new visors and staring at the posters.

"Are these people all from your church?" I asked Holly while collapsing empty boxes.

"A lot of them. It's a big church."

"They don't look like church people."

She chuckled. "What do you think they're supposed to look like, Dana Carvey, as the Church Lady?"

I laughed too.

There were minivans full of old folks; camp kids and counselors; parents with children and family pets; young singles groups; teams of men from Bible studies; ladies' hiking groups; Little League teams; and tattered-looking young people with tattoos and body piercings.

So unselfish.

Like Chester.

Distant laughter rose up less than a block away. The commotion came from a growing crowd situated between two large, local TV trucks and their towering antennas.

Do they know I'm here?

More laughter, then quiet. It looked like a political rally. The group had formed a large semicircle, and it appeared someone was speaking, either to the crowd or to reporters. A smattering of clapping broke out.

"What's up over there?" Holly put a hand on my shoulder, which was damp with perspiration.

"I don't know. Maybe I should split for a while. Stay clear."

"It looks like someone's being interviewed or something. See the TV cameras?"

Andrew and Ellery noticed too. So did the others. But we all kept working, everyone but Arthur.

"I don't like the looks of that." He nudged me.

"Why? You think they're coming over here next?"

"Somethin' doesn't feel right." He examined the large crowd.

"Well, I guess I'll just stay put—"

Two homeless men broke free from the crowd and sprinted toward us.

"Those are your friends, aren't they?" I said to Arthur.

"Weaver and Jenkins." He took several steps toward them.

They ran like two school kids who'd just witnessed an accident on the playground.

"Arthur!" Weaver came to a halt right in front of us. "It's Needermire."

"Needermire's here!" Jenkins arrived next. "He says he's going to help with the search."

What?

Ellery, Andrew, and Jenna closed in around us.

"He's makin' fun of Ambrose." Weaver nodded at me. "And the stories in today's paper."

As though looking through a long-range rifle scope, my eyes scanned the crowd and locked in on a man with a slender head, thin black hair, and a dark reddish tan, at the center of the brouhaha. He was wiry and muscular, with thick forearms and the toothy smile of a politician.

So that's Needermire.

"He's calling Hudson a liar and a serial killer." Jenkins swiped his stringy brown hair straight back over the top of his head.

"Yeah." Weaver panted. "He claims he's bein' set up, like a...what'd he say?"

"A scapegoat," Jenkins blurted.

"That's it. He's lyin', Arthur. Sayin' Hudson made it all up about the dirty sweep, just to get the attention off himself."

Holly grabbed my arm, but it was too late.

"Hud, don't!" she squealed as I shook loose.

"Hudson." Ellery trotted up beside me as I huffed toward the crowd. "You don't need any more attention. Let this go. This guy is gonna have his day."

"Cool off, Ambrose." Andrew rushed along at my other side. "The truth will come out."

But their efforts were futile.

One, two, three reporters busted loose from the pack of people and headed me off at the pass.

"Have you heard what Sergeant Needermire is saying?" one asked.

"What's your response, Mr. Ambrose?" Another fought to get in my face, but I burst past him.

"Excuse me." I dove into the crowd of bodies, parting the way with both arms, leaving Andrew and Ellery behind. "Excuse me."

As I worked my way toward Needermire, the loud noise from the crowd eerily reduced to shuffling feet, crowding bodies, and whispering clamor.

"Here he comes now," Needermire called.

Dozens of faces and eyes found me in the crowd, and the path to Needermire parted. I could see him from twenty feet. He wore khaki shorts and a pink and blue madras shirt, Ray-Ban Aviator sunglasses, and black sandals.

My path was blocked suddenly by two heavyset men with tree-trunk necks, then others closed me off as well.

"Stand down!" Needermire roared. "Let him come." He chuckled. "We'll have ourselves a little public court session right here."

The bruisers let go, and in another seven strides I was in his face.

"How dare you accuse me of the murder!" I shoved him in the center of his hard chest, with no resistance.

His smile disappeared.

"You're dirty, Needermire." I jammed my palm into his shoulder. "The truth's gonna come out about Chester."

"You're right." His face contorted into a bitter scowl. "And you'll do your time."

"What'd you do, hire those punks to get rid of me at Chester's van?"

Camera crews barged in.

"Let him have it, Needermire!" someone yelled.

Needermire glanced at the jovial crowd, released a tense chuckle, then threw several playful punches at me.

Laughter and smoke filled the air. People shoved and clamored like bettors at a cockfight.

"Arrest him, Needermire!" another man called.

"Come on." My fists were braced in front of me. "You're not in uniform. Let's go!"

Needermire held up his hands innocently. "Look at the rage in this man." His eyes swept the crowd. "He's a killer. And we're gonna prove his guilt by finding Chester Holte's body."

I took a wild swing at his face, but his head pulled back in a flash, my fist hitting only air, and the crowd erupted in loud, long *oohs* and *aahs*.

Needermire held up both hands like a sparring partner, backing up several steps, glancing at me and at the people. "What I really want to know is what you did with your colleague, the reporter. Is she alive?"

All common sense vanished.

My head was empty, except for the fury that blinded me.

Tackle him. Get his body.

My knees were bent, my legs locked apart, my hands rotating slightly in front of me, like a wrestler, sizing up my opponent.

Move slow, then dive!

Rowdy onlookers called for blood, and they would have it.

"Hud! Stop!" A female shouted from behind.

Holly.

"Babe, stop." She grabbed my arms and heaved me backward. "No more," she panted. "No more. Let's go."

"Ooh. Isn't that sweet." Needermire pursed his lips. "Momma's calling."

Suddenly the familiar faces of Cinderella Man and Jack Rabbit popped up around Needermire, like shadowy figures in an old black-and-white photograph.

Everything flipped to slow motion.

Cinderella Man's dark arm locked around Needermire's throat from behind. Needermire flailed and grabbed at the arm but couldn't shake it.

Thud.

An overpowering blow to the gut by Jack Rabbit.

"Oomph." Needermire folded like a lawn chair and dropped to the concrete. Smile gone.

With each of their backs to the groaning cop on the ground, Cinderella Man and a limping Jack Rabbit clenched their fists and faced off with the cantankerous crowd, then disappeared, like part of the scenery.

What've I done?

Reporters shouted angrily and shoved to get close to me, but Holly, Ellery, and Andrew screened my way to the red pickup. I dove in first, flanked by Holly in the driver's seat and Andrew riding shotgun. Holly gunned the little truck out of the parking lot, leaving Ellery to deal with the salivating crowd.

32

Hud and I sat on the edge of the love seat in my living room with sandwiches on TV trays, glued to the midday news. Live helicopter footage showed dozens of groups of people combing parking lots, patches of green, and vacant lots across the city, as well as lines of people—hundreds in each line—canvassing the vast, arid desert on the outskirts surrounding Las Vegas.

"If we don't find Chester and Suzette in the city and outlying areas, we'll take this search right into the mountains," Ellery told a tall, red-headed reporter, whose shiny hair blew across her pink-cheeked face in the breeze. "I know my sister is in danger. This is foul play. She's not the kind of person who would take off without a word. So, we're feeling a real urgency." His head dropped; he rubbed his forehead and looked up again. "Our church, the homeless community, and many Las Vegans have joined this effort—for that, we thank God."

The camera pulled back, revealing Arthur, standing opposite the reporter. "I know this is difficult for you"—she leaned close to Ellery, and the camera tightened again—"because Suzette Graham is your sister. Can you tell us, can you express what you're feeling as it relates to the battle that seems to be raging between the Las Vegas police and your friend, *R-J* reporter Hudson Ambrose?"

Ellery cleared his throat and took a deep breath. "Valerie, right now, I am frustrated. We want answers. We want to know why Drake Needermire is still on duty with the LVMPD. This officer has been implicated, not only in the murder of Chester Holte, but in my sister's disappearance, and in the death of another homeless man named Ned Frazier. Has Needermire even been questioned yet? We don't think so.

"He's been accused of brutally beating dozens of homeless people in a predawn sweep. We think Hudson Ambrose has been put through the wringer enough. Now it's time to put the interrogation lamp on the main suspect in this case: Drake Needermire. Our church and our homeless community aren't going to rest until justice is done here."

Chills flowed over my body like a current, and the hair on my arms zapped straight up. I glanced at Hud; his tired eyes met mine, and then they closed with his sigh.

"Speaking of the homeless community, we have with us a man who lives on the streets of Las Vegas." Valerie shifted toward Arthur, and the camera pulled back to include him. "Arthur Peabody is a friend of Chester Holte's. Mr. Peabody, what kind of person was Chester, and what are you feeling right now, with all the media frenzy swirling around this case?"

Arthur took his brown beret off and held it high at his chest, in both hands. His forehead glistened with sweat. "Chester was a godsend to me; not only to me, but to everyone I know—everyone who's homeless. You ask anybody 'round here. The man was an angel. He came to serve, not to be served." Arthur kneaded the hat in his dark fingers. "What was the other part of the question?"

"How do you feel right now about the case and all the media attention?"

"It ain't right." He shook his head. "It just ain't right. Hudson is a reporter who was curious about a murder. He made dumb mistakes; just plain stupid. But I'll guarantee ya, Chester was dead long before Hud ever saw him for the first time. I'm with the pastor here. We gonna raise Cain until the right man is charged for this, and the right man is a wicked son of a gun who calls himself a Las Vegas lawman. Now, that's about all I gotta say, young lady."

With pad and mike in hand, the reporter corralled Arthur as he began to stray right of the camera. "Mr. Peabody," she said, "what can you tell us about Chester Holte's wealth?"

"I don't know nothin' 'bout that." Arthur waved his hand and stuffed the beret back on his head. "I've heard this and that—that Chester was rich. Chester was a street person. He was one of us, you know? If he had money, well, he sure didn't give me none of it!" Arthur chuckled at himself, while Ellery and the reporter appeared relieved to do the same. "Now, I got work to do, so I'll be going." Arthur wandered off camera.

The reporter gasped at Arthur's sudden exit and buried her head in her notes, then stuck the microphone back in Ellery's face. "What can you tell us about Chester's wealth, if anything, Pastor Graham? After all, Chester did attend your church."

Ellery nodded. "Chester did attend our church, and he was, in my opinion, the ideal role model for our church family. I say that because Chester came to church to study God's Word and to become better equipped, but he didn't isolate himself within the church. What I mean by that is, he took the wisdom he learned in church to the streets and trenches of Las Vegas. He got involved; he gave to the church; but his main goal in life was to go into the world and lead others to God. He was most concerned about those who didn't have a relationship with Jesus. And as we learn more about Chester's life, through this story, I think God is going to use it to impact many lives."

The reporter shifted. "You say Chester 'gave' to the church. Do you mean monetarily?"

Ellery winced slightly and squeezed his nose. "I don't think I better answer that because there's an investigation going on. But I will say that he was extremely generous with both his time and resources."

"We understand, Pastor, that there was a scuffle between Drake Needermire and Hudson Ambrose out here this morning. What can you tell us about that?"

Shaky footage of the melee flickered onto the screen, but ended abruptly and was quickly replayed several times. "I can tell you Needermire came out here, right by one of our satellite search headquarters, and got a bunch of media around, and a bunch of people who had nothing better do to, and he began to malign Hudson Ambrose." Ellery shook his head. "What more can I tell you? Hudson overheard it. It enraged him. He's an innocent man—"

"Mr. Ambrose tried to start a fight, did he not, with Sergeant Needermire?"

"I'm afraid you or I would have done the same thing, if we heard someone talking that way about us. It was slanderous and malicious."

"What was Needermire saying?"

"As far as we're concerned it was all lies, and I don't want to comment any further on that."

"Sergeant Needermire actually took part in the search for Chester and Suzette late this morning, after the scuffle he had with Mr. Ambrose. What are your thoughts on that?"

The picture changed to footage of Needermire and a handful of civilians, along with four or five uniformed LVMPD officers, poking through underbrush with walking sticks in rocky, desert terrain.

"All I can tell you, Valerie, is that God knows what happened in this case, and He will bring justice, whether it's in this lifetime or the next. Whoever killed Chester and Ned Frazier, whoever abducted my sister, that person can rest assured that his sin will find him out." Ellery's lips quivered and he swiped at his eyes. "We just pray this thing will come to a close soon. We're praying that, somehow, our Suzette is safe."

The reporter shook her head and put a hand around his back. "Pastor, if Suzette is, by chance, watching this broadcast, what would you say to her right now?"

Ellery rolled his eyes and head at the same time, tears streaking down his cheeks. "We trust God, Suzie, with your life." He covered his mouth and cried but kept going. "You're His. We've given you over to Him. We're trusting Him to bring you home. But if He doesn't…we'll trust Him anyway."

Ellery's face contorted as he choked back the emotion that wanted to spill over. The camera tightened on the red-headed reporter, whose eyes watered and hand shook as she held the KVBC-3 microphone. "That's what I call blind faith." She lowered her head momentarily, then peered up at the camera, brow raised above sympathetic brown eyes. "This is Valerie Walsh, reporting live from the Downtown Outreach Clinic."

My eyes flooded.

Hud's face lowered into his hand. "Ellery's strong."

"He's a good man."

"It's all so sad," Hud moaned.

I inched closer.

"I don't understand why God would let this happen. I mean, Suzette and Chester were *good* people."

"I know." I wrapped an arm around him. "I don't understand either."

"But you still believe?"

"Yes, Hud. That's what faith is."

"But where's the love in this? Chester gave his whole life and look how he was rewarded—with a bullet."

"He gave his life, and now he's with God. He'll be with God forever. This life's a vapor. It's here and gone. Chester gave his life away joyfully. For him, to live was Christ, but to die was gain! He knew that."

Hud leaned back on the couch with his hands covering his face, grimacing as he ran his fingers through his hair.

"Chester lived for a greater purpose, Hud. He didn't care about rewards down here. See, that's the way *we* think—that if someone gets cancer or gets murdered, that it's not fair or that there's no love in that. But God thinks differently. He has a zillion things planned—good things, intricate things—that can come out of a person's trials or sickness or even death."

"It's just so hard to think like that." He sat up and leaned on his knees. "We treasure our lives. We love this world. No one wants to die."

"Chester was happy till the end, though, that's the thing. I never met anyone so full of life, so full of vigor. And all he did was give himself away."

I remembered him, playing his harmonica and laughing with the local children, calling each by name.

"Just think," Hud said, "any question he ever had has been answered now in heaven."

"That's right." I rested a hand on his back. "And ours will be too. Down here we see through a glass darkly, but later, face to face."

33

Dad's funeral was set for the following afternoon in San Antonio, and I desperately wanted to be there; but I dreaded calling Nelson Truax to ask permission to leave Las Vegas. Since we'd last talked, I'd publicly maligned Needermire and the entire Las Vegas police department, and I knew Truax would be furious. But I made the call anyway.

"We need to meet," Truax said in a dead monotone. "But not here. This place is crawling with reporters. You know where Bailey's is on Bonanza?"

"Yeah."

"Meet me there in an hour."

Holly couldn't sit still at her place and insisted I drop her back at the clinic on my way to meet Truax. There was no place to park near the clinic, so I squeezed the pickup into the first spot I could find—a tight one—and walked with her two blocks in the penetrating heat, greeting Ellery and Andrew, Jenna and Arthur, Jonathan and others who'd been there since dawn and showed it with their splotchy red faces and pink shoulders and arms.

"Hud, tell us again what Chester was wearing when you last saw him," Ellery said. "We got a radio call a few minutes ago from our west-side group. They've got teams out on 13-Mile Loop Drive."

"Red Rock Canyon?"

"Yeah." Ellery wiped the sweat from his face with the lower half of his shirt. "They found a small piece of fabric out there on some briers."

Red Rock Canyon was a vast national conservation area about fifteen miles west of the city. Charleston Boulevard took you right to it. I'd been there once before on a picnic with the *R-J* staff. It was dry, rocky, hot, desolate, and stunningly beautiful. There were red and white rock formations, bluffs, valleys, vistas, unusual trees and plants, and an array of wildlife, from snakes perched on rocks to wandering burros.

I envisioned Needermire out there in the blackness, with the headlights of his squad car pointing on the canyons, grunting and puffing as he hurried Chester's body to its final resting place in one of thousands of rock crevices or amid some thick underbrush.

A body wouldn't last long out there with all the wildlife.

I jotted down each piece of clothing I remembered him wearing that dismal morning, from his thin, black overcoat down to his black Converse high tops.

Andrew gave me the keys to the Mustang and told me where it was parked. I insisted he stay at my place while he was in town and explained that he would have the house to himself the following day or two—if Truax let me go home for my dad's funeral. Andrew took me up on the offer, we agreed to catch up later, and I took off for my meeting with Truax.

Bailey's was a bright, clattery restaurant serving greasy breakfasts, lunches, dinners—and free coffee to cops—24/7. The waitresses wore white, and people sat in small booths along the windows, which ran the entire length of the place.

The waitress who seated me was a short, peppy, graying woman in her fifties who wore black and silver "cat-style" glasses from yester-year. She promptly brought me a Dr Pepper over crushed ice, as well as a straw, silverware, napkins, and menus for two. Realizing I was faced away from the door, I changed to the opposite side of the booth, scanning the parking lot for Truax's black-and-white.

Suddenly the table jiggled, and there was a grunt and the sound of leather rubbing as Truax dropped into the cushioned seat opposite me. Once again, he was pressed and polished in dark green and beige, with shimmering stars and badge.

"You can't leave Las Vegas." His slick blond hair didn't move as he looked down, stuffed his napkin in his lap, and mechanically slid the fork to his left and the spoon and knife to his right.

"It's my father's funeral."

"You should've thought of that before you came back." His hard face burned red, and thick veins twisted like mole paths on his temples.

"Holly was in danger. You know what happened."

"Death has a way of following you, doesn't it, Ambrose?"

The same woman who had seated me popped between us and peered at Truax. "What to drink, hon?"

"Coffee. Black."

"Comin' right up." She hustled off.

"I promise you, I'll be back in two days; one if you want. I can leave tomorrow morning and be back tomorrow night."

"You're coming in for more questioning."

"When?"

"When I say! You can't leave. Period. Forget about it."

"You're holding a grudge because of the *R-J* story."

His mouth locked like a vise and he leaned over the table, his nostrils as big as a horse's. "You accused my people of murder, kidnapping, and cover-up. Do you have any idea what you've started?"

"Have you checked out my story?"

"Do you have any idea what this has done to our department, or how many *years* it's going to take to remove this blemish?"

"I repeat, have you checked out my—"

"*Stuff* your story! We've checked out the goods you *stole* from Chester Holte, that we found hidden in your attic, with your prints all over them."

"That was a setup! I never go in that attic. Needermire stole Chester's things from my house and planted them up there. I'm being framed. Can't you see that?"

"Right. The whole LVMPD's dirty. We're all crooks. You really think a jury's gonna fall for that?"

"You appointed Jack Sloan to the investigation knowing full well he and Needermire were close friends. Needermire got back in my house *before* your guys searched it. He planted that stuff in my attic."

Truax leaned back and forced a smile, his big forearms still on the table, his gold-capped upper tooth shining in the sunlight. "What you did is you picked on an innocent fella. You ended up robbing and killing him. And you thought no one would notice, because he was a nobody. But we did notice—"

"You're wrong—"

"And when you found out we had you," Truax's voice overpowered mine, and he leaned over the table, stuffing a fat finger in my face, "you started spreading lies, implicating innocent people, and accusing one of the nation's finest police departments of being corrupt. And for that, Ambrose, you're going to pay; I can promise you that."

The slight waitress paused next to the table, leaning back as if she wasn't listening, then ducking in with Truax's coffee. "Here you go."

He put on a plastic grin and nodded at her.

"If I'm guilty, where's the murder weapon?"

"We're working on that."

"I don't even own any guns!"

"Who said he was killed by a gun, besides you?"

Sitting face to face with the top authority in charge of Chester's homicide and knowing I was presumed guilty, my stomach churned and my entire body went weak. I thought of the Victoria prison where my old man had been incarcerated and the horror stories he'd told of life within the concrete asylum. Desperation seized me.

"How can you play dumb about what Needermire's done? You know he did that dirty sweep."

"He's been suspended for that, along with Loy and Sanchez. That's a small matter, but if it makes you feel better, it's under investigation."

"Since when?"

He glanced at his big, black Ironman watch. "A few minutes ago." He smirked and lowered his voice. "But between you and me, that's strictly to pacify the media. There was no foul play that morning. And if you tell the media I said that, I'll not only deny it, but I'll turn up the heat so high on you that you'll burn to a crisp."

My emotions were fighting their way up my throat, to my voice and eyes. "Have you questioned Needermire?"

"Normally, I'd say that's none of your business, but since you look like you're about to cry and run home to Momma, I can tell you I've interviewed him at length and his story checks out."

I dropped my head, shaking it back and forth. "I'm being framed."

"You'd be wise to get yourself some good legal counsel and start telling the truth. The sooner you do, the sooner you'll be able to work out some kind of plea-bargain. In the meantime, stay close by. I'm getting my ducks in a row. Then I'll want to question you in depth."

"My dad's funeral is one day. That's all I'm asking for."

"Look, Ambrose, if you want the truth, you're a threat to run."

"I give you my word, I won't run."

Leaning with his elbow on the table and one side of his face in the palm of his hand, Truax gave an achy smile and shook his head. "No no no no." He chuckled. "We've had way too many problems with your so-called *word*. You've done enough damage to my department. I'm not taking any more chances."

Bitter words of fiery rage banged the back of my front teeth. But if I let them go, I'd just dig myself a deeper grave. *Just leave.*

"Are we through here?" I asked, feeling my angry words melt into my cheeks.

"We are."

I stood and made for the door. "Thanks for the drink."

Revving the Mustang to life, I cranked the AC and scrounged in the glove compartment till I found an old pack of cigarettes. Smelling the foul tobacco, I squeezed the pack in my fist till my hand shook and slammed it to the floor.

Checking the parked cars beside me, I saw no one.

I lowered my eyes to the center of the steering wheel and breathed in a frantic whisper. "God, I don't understand why this is happening."

Raw, foreign emotions swirled and raged and threatened to spill over.

"I'll miss his funeral. Don't You want me there?"

Victor will be there.

"Prison. I could go to prison—for murder!"

Images of filthy jail cells and careless crew cuts, of pimps and gangs and battles to stay alive ravaged me.

"Help me, God." My voice trembled. "Please...help me."

I sensed a car move behind me and checked the rearview.

Truax.

His black-and-white glided past six or seven cars, stopped, waited for traffic, and turned right out of the exit, traveling east on Bonanza, directly in front of my car.

I stared at it, transfixed, until it was out of sight.

Within two seconds, my eyes shifted to another police car, identical, coming the opposite direction on Bonanza. My eyes locked in on it as it passed in front of me and headed west, into the bright sun.

Follow Needermire.

My mind was vacuumed utterly blank except for that notion.

Follow Needermire.

That was all I had.

It was what I would do.

By the time Hud showed up behind the clinic late that afternoon, giving me a quick hug as he did, our team of volunteers was sore, sunburned, and spent. But we pressed on, distributing posters, dispatching search parties, and trying to get as many sets of eyes as possible out into Las Vegas before sundown.

"Here." Hud rubbed a cold, wet bottle of water against the back of my arm. "Have you been drinking?"

His bleak expression told me he was somewhere else.

"I'm fine." I wiped my forehead and relished the cool as we moved beneath a large tent provided by a local restaurant. "Well, what happened with Truax?"

"He won't let me go."

His words sapped me of what felt like four pints of blood.

"I'm so sorry." I squeezed his arm. "I was afraid of that."

"I wouldn't change what I did, Holly." His clear eyes pierced mine. "I needed to be here for you. I'm glad I was."

I patted his hand. "Victor will be at the funeral."

"I know. I talked to him on the way over. It'll be fine. He said he'd take care of everything. And he's going to send me the eulogy he wrote."

I so wanted to tell Hud he would be able to go to his father's grave soon, but I stopped myself, not sure if I really believed it, not wanting to make any false promises.

"They're going to question you again, aren't they?"

He nodded. "They're putting together a case. It's gonna be tougher this time. I'm worried."

Hud told me Truax had interviewed Needermire and suspended him and the others accused of the dirty sweep, but that it was only a PR tactic.

"Truax is gonna be loyal to his people, come hell or high water. There's no doubt, I'm his fall guy. That's clear."

He was right. What could I say?

Give me words, Lord.

"We can't give up, Hud."

"Something's gotta happen. Something big."

Yeah, like a miracle.

"We've got to find Chester's body," I said. "That's the bottom line."

He looked around at the dozens of people at work on his behalf, then stepped close to me. "I'm gonna follow Needermire. It's time." Our eyes met, and I knew he was going to do it, no matter what I said.

"Hud, please—"

"Holly, there's nothing left to lose." His voice was just above a whisper. He scanned the tent to make sure no one was eavesdropping. "They could bring me in for questioning, arrest me, and I may never get out on bail. Truax said today he considered me a threat to leave town. This may be my last chance."

No. The relationship of my dreams was getting away from me, seeping through my fingers like sand. I had to do something.

"I'll go with you." I grabbed his hand, making him look at me.

"No you won't." He was dead calm. "I may ask Andrew."

I drew in a deep breath, sighed, and plunked down on a plastic folding chair. "You're gonna need my truck."

"Yep. You can use my car." He walked up behind me and squeezed my shoulders. "Thank you for understanding."

"Just remember, you're not dealing with Sam Civilian. Needermire's a cop. If you do anything stupid, he and the police will bury you. That'll be it."

"I don't know how things could get much worse than they already are."

"Believe me, they can. You need to be careful."

That wasn't the first time I began to wonder where Hud would be incarcerated if he had to go to prison. An Internet search I'd done while he was out of town showed several correctional facilities and one state prison near Las Vegas, but there were many others throughout Nevada.

"Hud, Holly!" Ellery blew into the tent with Andrew two feet behind. "One of our teams just found part of a black overcoat."

"No way!" Hud jumped two feet.

"It's torn and has some stains that may be blood."

Andrew's forehead was creased, and he wore a worried frown, standing there with Ellery; I knew for him the finding must have been bittersweet.

"What are you gonna do with it?" Hud practically grabbed Ellery. "Can I see it? You can't let the cops have it yet."

"Wait." Ellery raised a hand to Hud's chest. "There's more. The coat's been badly burned. Not much of it is left."

My heart thundered.

Did he burn Chester's body?

Is the coat all that's left?

I was short of breath. "Was there anything else?"

"Not yet," Andrew said. "Hopefully, soon."

"We're not gonna be able to keep a lid on it," Ellery said. "But we've got a professional photographer from the church shooting close-ups of it, just in case."

"That's a great idea." I nodded at Hud and Andrew.

"Can we see it?" Andrew eyed Ellery.

"Maybe, if you hurry." Ellery looked at his watch. "But we're going to have to turn it over to the LVMPD."

"No, Ellery—"

"Hud, we have to!" Ellery stomped. "We're not forensics experts. We can't tamper with evidence. Come on, you know better than that."

I rested a hand on Hud's back. "He's right, Hud."

Hud swung around and stuck his hands on his waist. "You're right. I'm sorry, Ellery."

"If you want to see it, you need to get out there *now*," Ellery said. "I'll radio out and ask them to stall, but there's a ton of civilians wandering around out there, cops, media… You need to hurry."

"What about the other fabric they found?" Hud handed the Mustang keys to me, and I gave him the keys to the pickup.

"It didn't match anything you described of Chester's."

"Okay." Hud took my hand and headed in the direction of my truck. "Come on, guys. Ellery, you want to come?"

"I can't. I need to be here." He looked at Andrew, then me. "You guys go. Hurry."

"Are you sure?" Andrew asked.

"Of course. Go. Can I count on you tomorrow early?"

"No doubt," Andrew said. "I'm all yours."

I peered out at Jenna, Jonathan, Arthur, and the other volunteers—still scurrying like ants.

"Tell everyone I'll be back first thing in the morning." I stood.

"Come on." Hud hurried us out from beneath the cool shade of the tent. "We'll come back for my car later."

The three of us weaved our way through the crowd.

"Beat the dark," Ellery called. "Let me know!"

I rode in the middle of the pickup, between Hud and Andrew. It was a quick jaunt to Charleston Boulevard. From there we went stop and go through city traffic and streetlights all the way out to the west side of the city. By the time we got on 13-Mile Loop Drive and started winding through Red Rock Canyon, the orange ball of sun was dropping behind the mountainous horizon.

"Keep your eyes peeled," Hud said, just as his phone rang.

I answered.

"Holly, it's Ellery. They're starting to find more! This could be it."

"What? What have they found?"

Hud and Andrew craned at me, all ears.

"Listen carefully," Ellery said. "Go about nine and a half miles out on Loop Road. Look for Cinderella Man or Jack Rabbit. They'll tell you where to go from there."

"What are we talking about?" I chose my words carefully with Andrew near. "Do we have...did they find Chester?"

"Put it on speaker." Hud took the phone and punched a button. "Ellery, we have you on speaker. What have you got?"

"Okay, we've got more remnants of clothing. It has been burned also. But they believe at least some of it matches your description..." His voice broke up.

"Are you there?" Hud spoke loudly, then waited a moment. "Do you read, Ellery?"

"I'm here."

"What else is there?"

"Guys, they've found some remains."

The cab of the pickup went silent, and Andrew turned toward the passenger window.

"I'm not sure," Ellery stammered. "You just need to hurry. The cops are gonna be all over that scene as soon as they find out."

We hung up, and I had a hunch Ellery hadn't told all because Andrew was with us. The little engine strained, and the truck picked up speed as we raced through the darkening desert.

Hud's phone beeped; I checked the screen and handed it to him. "You have a message. Area code 678."

He pressed several buttons and put it to his ear. "Shhh!" His hand went up. He listened, his eyes darting from Andrew back to me. "It's him!"

I leaned against him, and he turned the phone so we could both hear.

"It appears the heat is really turning up on you now." The man spoke in a calm, sterile voice, pronouncing each word with clarity. "Listen to me, somehow—and I don't know how—Needermire *knew* Chester was a wealthy man. Do you understand me? He was after Chester's *money.*"

The man paused at length.

"Look, my point is, you need to follow the money." He hesitated. "Oh my goodness, this is such a mess. I need to talk with you, *live.*" He let out an exhausted sigh. "Listen, Mr. Ambrose, Chester had a large sum of cash with him the night he was killed. Very large. Hundreds of thousands of dollars, in a bag. I don't know if you knew that or not. It hasn't been in the news; the bankbook has, the safe-deposit-box key has, but not the cash."

Hud squinted at me, and for a fleeting moment, I wondered if the relative stranger beside me might have taken the money.

Could I be that blind?

But the caller went on, making my paranoia flee. "I am 99.9 percent sure Needermire took that cash, and must still have it—somewhere. What I'm saying is, that would explain everything. If you could find that money, it would prove your innocence. Follow the money, Ambrose. And do it fast."

Click.

The unfamiliar one-way road, darkening landscape, and scores of weary searchers trudging back to their vehicles along 13-Mile Loop Drive forced me to keep my speed down as Holly, Andrew, and I anxiously closed in on what we hoped would be Chester's remains—and the evidence I needed to be exonerated of his homicide.

"There!" Holly pointed to several gleaming white lights in the distance, far off the left side of the road. I rolled the window down, slowed, and eased the truck into the rocks at the berm behind five or six other vehicles, including two LVMPD squad cars.

"This looks like it," I said.

"That's a long way." Holly grabbed a flashlight from her glove compartment.

Andrew was silent as he got out of the truck. I could only imagine what he must have been thinking: So *this* was the place Needermire had chosen to attempt to get away with murder, the murder of his beloved father. Way off the road. Far from civilization. Amid rocks, canyons, and quarries. In the blackness. With the animals.

I thought about trying to drive us out there, but the terrain was too rocky. The three of us walked close, often touching shoulders to make sure we were within reach. Holly and I held hands as we negotiated deep crevices, sharp underbrush, and large boulders. The feeling of her hand in mine was comforting and the beginning of something very special, which I feared was about to be taken from me.

Five people gathered around the first generator light we came to.

"Hello!" Andrew yelled as we approached.

One plump man from the group got up from a crouch and walked toward us with a distinct limp, the light casting a long shadow against a rock cavern behind him in the distance.

"Ambrose?" he called.

"Yeah, it's me." I stuck my hand out and shook his callused hand. "Good to see you, Jack. You remember Holly. And this is our friend, Andrew Holte, Chester's son. This is Jack Rabbit."

Jack nodded at Holly, then eyed Andrew with his drooping face. "Sorry about your dad."

"Thank you."

"Well." Jack turned and led us toward the light, dragging his right foot in the dust. "This is where the piece of Chester's coat was found. First thing that was discovered."

He grimaced as he bent down next to the tattered piece of black clothing, letting the light catch all of it. We knelt too, Andrew on his knees. The material was slightly larger than I'd envisioned, and more charred. But I still recognized it on the spot as Chester's. We didn't touch it but could see a gaping hole with ringed stains around it, as it hung precariously in the low branches of a spindly tree.

"A few cops are here, at the other areas." Jack's head bobbed. "They've radioed in. Pretty soon this place is gonna be crawling with law."

Andrew moved in close and took a deep whiff of the coat. I assumed the smell of smoke would have permeated the material, but almost instantly his face fell, his shoulders lurched, and he wept, ever so softly, at the realization that the coat before him had been his father's.

I rested a hand on his back. Holly did the same.

"As you can see"—Jack grunted, stood, and directed a pudgy hand toward the other lights—"we got three more areas under surveillance. I've been told the cops will tape it all off and keep watch for the night. Investigators will be here at sunup."

"Has someone gotten pictures of everything?" I asked.

"I have." A slight, young Asian-looking man stepped toward me. "My name's Joseph. Joseph Arco." We shook hands. "Pastor Graham asked me to come. I've got everything on film. Closeups. All angles."

"Of all these areas?" I waved my arm.

"Yes sir."

"That's great. Thank you," I said. "Jack, will you take us to the other areas?"

"That I will." He limped into the darkness.

"Don't you have a light?" Andrew said.

"Don't need one. You got one for yourselves, right?"

We walked in silence until we were about twenty yards from the next light. Jack Rabbit stopped and swiveled around. "I'm not sure the lady or Chester's son are gonna want to see this." The shadows made Jack's face look even more solemn than I'd remembered.

I guessed that was all the warning Jack was going to give us because after speaking, he did an about-face and dragged on toward the light. Holly and I glanced at each other and fell in tow.

My emotions were on purée. I wanted to find Chester's body so badly, to find a bullet wound, to get his corpse in for an autopsy, to prove it was Needermire's gun that killed him. At the same time, I didn't want Holly to see anything grotesque, and my heart broke for Andrew, who was trying desperately and courageously to find any semblance of his father.

As we drew near to the next bright light, Jack groaned, "Oh boy." He huffed and puffed as he limped onward. "I gotta warn ya." He spoke between gasping breaths. "This cop up here thinks he's Columbo."

As we hiked into the camp, Jack gave a cough to announce us to the ten people gathered there. Almost instantly, a uniformed officer with a medium build, large glasses, and unusually pale skin was at our sides. Jack glanced at him, looked at us, and rolled his eyes.

"You must be the family we were told would be coming out," the officer said. "We've been waiting for you."

I introduced Holly and Andrew, but purposefully didn't mention who I was, knowing most of the LVMPD were out to lynch me. Instead, Holly and I were "friends of the family." Several others from the search party approached and offered their greetings. Based on the prolonged eye contact that was made, my hunch was that at least one or two of them recognized me from the media coverage but were simply being gracious by not going there.

During the small talk, I did a quick visual sweep of the area, which was rocky, slightly sloped, and dotted with underbrush. Whatever it was we were about to see was most likely beneath a large piece of clear, thick plastic which covered a six-by-nine-foot patch of earth near the bright metal can light.

"Okay, everybody." The cop, whose name was Jablonski, addressed the whole group. "Let me have a few minutes with the family and close friends here, please."

Jack rolled his eyes again as the other volunteers turned and shuffled away from the light.

Jablonski lowered his voice. "What we're about to see here is several articles of clothing, possibly worn by the deceased, as well as a few actual, physical remains: definitely human remains."

I heard Andrew take in an audible breath, then the officer's words replayed in my head.

A few physical remains?

That threw me.

"I'm ready." Andrew stepped toward the plastic.

Ever since Chester's corpse had disappeared, I'd pictured it being found all in one piece, neat and clean, only one bullet hole, ready for an autopsy, just like I'd found it. But Ellery had mentioned "remains" and now Jablonski was using the term "few."

My stomach rumbled.

"I think I'll wait over here," Holly said, as she squeezed my hand. "Are you okay?" She stared up at me. "You don't look too great."

A few physical remains?

No, I was not okay.

What on earth were we talking about? The body couldn't have decomposed already.

I nodded at Holly. "I'll be okay," I said and ushered her off.

Inhaling deeply, I stepped toward the light where Jablonski stood next to Andrew. "I'm with you."

But my phone rang.

"Hold on." I practically ripped it out of my pocket, hoping it was the stranger from Atlanta. "Excuse me just one minute."

I turned my back and took the call, wandering away from the group.

"Hud, I need you down here, *now*," said my editor, Don Cheevers.

"Why? What's going on?"

His voice broke in and out, and I couldn't make out a word.

"I'm in the desert," I raised my voice. "Can you hear me?"

His affirmative response was barely audible.

"What's happening?" I called.

All I could decipher was, "Don't even…just get…quick…
you can."

"Okay. I'll be there ASAP. Tell me once more what it's about."

"It's a…guys…Wisconsin," his voice broke up. "Tourists…
video…*not good.*"

The line went dead.

Great.

Andrew and Jablonski waited for me, hands on their hips, shapes
silhouetted by the beaming light. I hurried over.

"Okay, gentlemen, here we go." Jablonski bent down, gingerly
grasped the plastic, stood, and swept the sheet away.

Flash.

I took one glimpse of the scene in front of me and spun around.

Andrew's body lurched as he dry heaved.

The cop turned around with us.

"I know," he said. "It's shocking at first."

I bent over, hands on knees, breathing deep, not wanting to look
at Holly, unable to get the charred, black Converse high top out of
my mind.

"The shoe matches the description we had, complete with holes
still visible above each big toe and bloodstains around the bottom." The
cop turned back around and knelt down by the findings. "The stains
left here in the dirt by the drag marks are blood. Obviously, scavengers
got to the body very soon after it was left. The next light you'll come to,
over there, is where we think the actual corpse was hidden—or left."

"You okay?" I put my arm around Andrew.

"I'll make it." He turned back around to the gory scene and so did I.

"What we have here, I believe, is a femur, a scaphoid, and remnants of the torso." He pointed to each like a science professor.

"Just bones?" Andrew mumbled. "Is this all there is?"

The dirt beneath the bones was stained brownish red, the same color as the drag marks.

"I'm afraid so," Jablonski said. "Even if scavengers hadn't gotten to the body, invertebrates alone could have reduced it to clean bones in less than two weeks."

The cop's coldness ticked me off, but I was so dazed, I just let him go, as did Andrew, who had dropped to his knees and was staring glassy-eyed at the scraps before him.

"A lot of people don't realize there are large carnivores out here. We're talking vultures, coons, coyotes, not to mention burying beetles, blow flies, flesh flies—"

"Okay!" I snapped. "We get it."

Andrew stood. "What's out there?" He motioned toward the remaining two lights.

"More of the same, I'm afraid." Jablonski rose. "We found where the body was initially left, among some heavy brush. But whoever did this knew the terrain, the climate, the predators; they knew the body wasn't going to last more than a few hours."

"Was the body burned?" Andrew asked.

"That's a good question," Jablonski said. "I'm not a CSI guy or an expert in forensic science, but it appears your father's body was stripped and that his clothes were kind of carelessly burned. There's evidence of that over there." He pointed to the next light, another hundred yards away.

I stood, sighed, and tried to swallow the fact that all that remained of Chester was bones, scattered who knew how far across the Nevada desert.

Looking at Andrew, I asked, "Do you mind if I ask about cause of death, the bullet?"

He looked down at the stark, brightly lit scene and shook his head.

"What's your thought on determining cause of death?"

"What do you mean?" Jablonski asked.

"I mean, if this man died of a gunshot wound, and was brought out here and left, do you think they'll be able to prove he died of a gunshot wound?"

Jablonski, who seemed to be enjoying the mind exercise, smiled, huffed, and stroked his jaw. "I'll tell you what, unless the bullet itself is found out here"—he raised both hands high and dropped them—"or they find a bone that was shattered or fractured by a bullet—I think it's gonna be next to impossible. Again, I'm not an expert. They may have ways—"

"What if a bullet went in right here?" I put my hand high on my chest, near the left shoulder. "If they find that part of his—"

"Look around here." Jablonski threw up an arm. "I don't care where the bullet may have gone in, it's not gonna be sitting here on the ground next to what's left of the shoulder blade."

Andrew walked away.

My phone rang.

Jablonski lowered his voice and finished his train of thought as I reached in my pocket. "These bones have been dragged all over this desert. Finding that bullet is gonna be like finding a penny out here."

"This is Hud." I covered my free ear.

"Where are you?" Cheevers blasted.

"Still at Red Rock Canyon. You need to get Reed and a photographer out here, posthaste."

"*You* need to get in *here* now! I've got breaking news on *your* case, and it's not good. Do you hear me? Get your tail in here!"

resolute Andrew insisted on staying at Red Rock to explore every square inch of desert that had the slightest hint of his father's remains. Hud, however, had had enough. Pale and bewildered, he led us to my pickup by flashlight, holding my hand and speaking not a word as we passed police officers and investigators, arriving one car after another and rushing past us with gloves, metal suitcases, lights, and tripods.

"What is it, Hud?" I broke the silence in the dark cab after Hud had driven us a mile or two along the black, desert road. "What happened back there?"

He watched the road. "There's nothing left of him. I'm not believing this."

"Hud, you're not a forensics expert, and neither is that Jablinksi guy."

"Jablonski. And he knew what he was talking about. They're never going to be able to prove how Chester died." He shook his head and hissed through clenched teeth. "That lead is shot. I'm gonna get framed for this thing, I can just *feel* it!" He banged the steering wheel.

Lord knew, I feared the same thing, and for a few miles there in the darkness, an oppressive spirit worked me over, urging me to doubt Hud and to view his circumstances as some rightful, revengeful sentence from an insensitive Judge.

But I knew better. I'd been the recipient of God's mercy. I was a walking infomercial for His patience and unconditional love. As we got back to reality, back to the lights of the bustling city, back to where I could see Hud's troubled face—I realized the Enemy was waging war against him. Instead of delivering a minisermon that would likely fall on deaf ears, I simply prayed silently, asking God to protect Hud and increase his faith. Hud was silent for the rest of the drive, and soon we arrived at the *Review-Journal* building.

Donald Cheevers, Hud's boss and the editor of the *R-J*, stood in his large, windowed office, arms crossed, papers in hand, talking to a short, trim young man with a blond cowlick who was scribbling furiously on a yellow legal pad.

"He usually doesn't work this late," Hud whispered and took a deep breath. "Something's definitely up."

Cheevers was lean, plain, and serious, with dark brown hair, a thick brown mustache, and a prominent Adam's apple. He wore khakis—wrinkled at the top of the thighs—a yellow dress shirt, a loosened blue and gold tie, and rectangular glasses with no frames, which reminded me of shop goggles.

When Cheevers caught a glimpse of Hud just beyond his large window, he froze and stared, then set his shoulders back and escorted the young man across the wood-paneled office, nodding several times, motioning with his hands, opening the door, and leading him out. "Just call me if you have questions."

The young man, still facing Cheevers, hesitated, knocking his pen against his jaw. But Cheevers nudged him along. "I'm sorry, Eric. I've got another appointment. Just give it your best shot. Call me later if you need to."

The young man's mouth hung open as he watched us enter Cheevers's office; I think he recognized Hud.

"What took you so long?" Cheevers grabbed a silver disk from the corner of his desk, ripped a yellow sticky note from it, and loaded it into a DVD player, which was set in a massive bookcase on the far wall. Grabbing one of many remotes from the cluttered shelf, Cheevers crossed back to his desk and took a seat on the corner where he'd retrieved the disk.

"Red Rock's a long way," Hud said. "We had to go forever on foot."

"I heard there's not much left."

"Not enough, I'm afraid."

"Shut the door, would you?"

Hud did so and walked back over to the middle of the room.

"I told you this was really hot." Cheevers unbuttoned his cuffs and rolled up his sleeves.

"Sorry, chief. We were in the middle of the Mojave. What can I say? Plus, we had a bad connection. I couldn't understand you."

"You must be Holly." He gave me a quick, obligatory smile.

"Holly." Hud stuck out a hand. "This is Donald Cheevers, my editor. Don, this is Holly Queens. Sorry about that."

"Good to meet you," I said. "Thanks so much for running Reed's story."

Cheevers's thin lips sealed; he crossed his arms and took in a deep breath with his whole upper body. "You're welcome." He exhaled loudly, and his eyes shifted to Hud. "We've got real problems."

Volcanic acid spit and bubbled in my aching stomach. Hud went ashen and said nothing.

"You want to sit down?" Cheevers asked.

"What's up?" Hud's voice cracked; he wrung his hands and stepped closer to the big desk.

My legs were weak. I dropped into the closest chair.

"This footage was shot by tourists from Madison, Wisconsin, while they were in town last weekend." Cheevers looked somberly at Hud, then me. "It's being distributed to all the major media and local law-enforcement agencies as we speak. That's why I was in such a hurry to get you back here. The clock's going to be ticking big-time now."

My insides were in shreds. I thought I might have to run out and find the rest room. Hud's hands were fixed to his waist, and he was stiff as a board.

"The guys who shot this were on a gambling junket. They filmed on and off the whole weekend, including when they were driving the Strip last Friday night, Saturday morning."

When Chester died.

"Since then, of course, they heard about the case, realized they were in town when Chester died, and went back and reviewed their footage." Cheevers hoisted the remote and jabbed several buttons. Of the four TVs in the bookcase, the one on the far right lit up, its blurry, shadowy picture freezing. "You'll see the time stamp. And you'll see the Civic Center North bus stop."

"What?" Hud gasped. "What are you saying?"

Cheevers shifted uneasily on the corner of the desk. "You're on here, Hud. With Chester. At the bus stop. It's not good. I'm warning you."

I wanted to grab Hud's hand and run. Get in the pickup and drive far away. Even fly someplace. Where no one would find us.

Cheevers hit Play, and the video opened to grainy, unrecogniz-able images with orange tint and a yellow time stamp reading 6:06 a.m. I finally took a breath. Seeing the low quality of the footage made me think Cheevers might have been taking the video too seriously.

"Turn it up," Hud said.

"They nixed the audio," Cheevers said. "Watch close."

Small houses passed outside an open car window... Two black men walking down the sidewalk... A woman leaving a convenience store with a carton of cigarettes...

"You can tell it's on the north side," Cheevers narrated, "away from all the glitz. These guys took in the whole city. They played a lot of the unknown casinos on the outskirts."

A pudgy man with black curly hair stuck his white face in front of the camera, then a waving hand. Once he was out of the way, the footage returned to the streets. A one-story casino...a run-down motel...a trailer park...a Laundromat...

"Here," Cheevers said. "Here it comes."

The bus stop was lit in bright white.

Chester was sitting, slumped.

A figure was bending over him.

Hud!

His hand was in Chester's front pocket, yanking.

Chester's head swung.

Oh, dear Father, no.

Vending machines whisked by...a chain-link fence...a brick wall...a neighborhood...and the screen went black.

No.

So brief, yet so damaging.

Hud's elbows were high in the air, his fingers raking hard and slow through his hair. He dropped down onto the end of a couch near the TV.

I could barely breathe.

Without a word, Cheevers played it again in slow motion.

Much worse.

As if a nuclear bomb had just hit a block away, desperation set in and we sat in silence, bracing for the fallout.

"It'll be on all the late news," Cheevers said evenly.

"Already?" Hud asked.

"Are you kidding me? It'll lead everywhere. This is *the* story right now—worldwide. And this just makes it more intriguing."

Hud buried his head in his hands. I moved over and sat by him, resting a hand on his back.

"This is exactly what Truax has been waiting for," Hud mumbled.

"I'm afraid you're right." Cheevers walked around his desk and plunked into a brown swivel chair. "I'm sorry, Hud. We're doing all we can."

"When people see this..." Hud shook his head in disgust.

"There's going to be a public outcry." Cheevers leaned on his desk. "No matter what you've said, they're going to see this and form judgments. Even the homeless community may turn on you. This isn't going to be good for you—or anyone associated with you."

"Wait a minute." Hud raised his head, stood, and stared at Cheevers. "I just realized what's coming—"

"I have absolutely no choice, Hud." Cheevers threw out his hands. "I've got to put you on leave of absence. The publisher wanted that *before* this DVD showed up. I held off. Now he's gonna be furious."

"How long?" Hud turned his back on Cheevers and crossed to the window, looking out toward the city desk.

"Indefinitely."

"With or without pay?"

"With…for as long as I can."

By the time we got to the long hallway leading to the *R-J* parking lot, Hud's phone was ringing.

He looked at the caller ID.

"Truax." He let it ring.

Once in the truck, he played the message on speaker.

"Hudson Ambrose," Truax blared. *"I need you at police headquarters tomorrow morning at 0800 hours—sharp. If, for any reason, you are not present, a warrant will be issued for your arrest."*

There was a long pause and a grunt. *"Oh, and by the way, pack your bags. You're gonna be staying a while."*

End of message.

No matter what words I contemplated speaking in the quiet of the pickup, I was certain nothing would penetrate Hud's shaken world. With his hands in the prayer position, covering his nose and mouth, he stared, wild-eyed, at the dashboard.

"Hud—"

"I'll be arrested, you know."

"No, we don't know that."

"Come on, Holly, *be real!*" His anger startled me and sent a wave of chills up my arms. "We've got next to no remains, we've got no weapon, we have my fingerprints on Chester's stuff, and we have me, on videotape, robbing the victim." Trembling fingers on both his hands dug into his forehead, rubbing, rubbing, rubbing.

"Stop, Hud." As rattled as he was, I ripped his hands from his face. "Stop!" I gripped his wrists with everything I had. "Please stop."

His head dropped back and thudded against the window. He pulled his hands away from me gently. I let them go, and he covered his face. "Why?" he moaned. "I wanted to make things right, and this is what I get?"

He pounded the ceiling with both fists.

The sudden rage and unsettling noise made me reel, and my gut reaction was to cower, thinking he might turn on me.

"I don't like it when you get like that." My words seemed to float and swirl into the turbulent air, and my hands were intertwined so tightly I thought I might cut off the circulation to my fingers.

"I'm sorry." He cranked the window, took in a deep breath, and locked his hands behind his head.

"I know it looks bad, but I'm not gonna stop believing. God has a plan. I think He brought us together." My words pierced the silence again, and strangely, it felt as if the Holy Spirit was holding back Hud's temper, keeping him open to God's promptings.

He glared out the top half of the windshield into a bright, yellowish light that hung from the side of the building.

"I still believe you," I whispered.

His hands fell to his lap at the same time his head dropped to his chest.

"Why are you sticking with me?" His voice was strained and distraught.

"Because"—I covered his strong hands with mine—"I love you."

With his eyebrows lifting like a drawbridge, he glanced at me, then looked down, his mouth curling into a frown, his eyes sealing shut, and his shoulders quaking. "That's the best thing that's come of this."

"There's more good to come." I leaned close and rubbed a tear from his face with the palm of my hand. "Press on, Hudson Ambrose," I squeezed the back of his neck. "You gotta press on."

"Pray for me." He drew in an enormous breath, leaned back, and wiped his wet face with his hands. "Just pray. 'Cause I got twelve hours to prove I'm innocent."

And I did.

37

olly sat close. We rode in silence, holding hands most of the way back to my car, periodically searching each other's eyes, pressing close in the darkness. I longed to abandon the pickup and hold her. The bond forming between us made my chest swell. Never had I experienced such elation. But those idyllic emotions turned bittersweet as I contemplated my predicament.

Finally, we parked the pickup. She scooted out my side after me, and I drew her close as we walked to the Mustang. A warm breeze blew our hair back, and her arm wrapped around my waist, a thumb hooking to the front pocket of my pants. I would have given anything not to leave that dream.

"Are you sure about this?" She looked up at me as we came to the Mustang.

"I could stay with you, like this, forever, Holly." I put my hands on her shoulders and turned her to face me. "But if I don't do this, there's not going to be a future."

She studied my eyes, then touched my cheek, as if to confirm the moment was real.

I stroked her cool, black hair.

"I'm scared," she whispered.

"So am I."

We embraced, and I cradled her head gently against my chest. She held me close, crossing her arms behind me.

"I hear your heart," she said.

"We're a good fit."

"I like you, Hudson Ambrose."

"Wait a minute." I chuckled. "A little while ago it was love."

She squeezed hard, let go, and giggled.

"Well?" I said. "Which is it?"

She pulled back and peered up at me, her hands resting on my waist.

"What's wrong?" I kidded. "Is this a case of short-term memory loss?"

But she just kept staring, searching me with those shining brown eyes.

Is she trying to see the future? Trying to figure out whether I'll go to prison? Be as devoted to God as she is?

"I'm thinking what a beautiful night it is and how I should be happy in the moment."

She was wise. That's what I admired about her. Nothing she said was fluff. Each word meant something.

"You're lovely, Holly. Inside and out."

She gave a half smile, but the glaze in her eyes told me her mind was getting ahead of her.

"What are you thinking about?" I asked.

She blinked, flashed the same half smile, then focused on my eyes.

"About you, about what's going to happen."

"Well." I nodded. "Like you always say, God's got to do something, right?"

She beamed. Our faces drew close. Her hands slid up to my chest. We kissed for the first time—a tender, sweet, unforgettable kiss. .

Our eyes danced and laughed and spoke of more passion, maybe, someday.

Her small hands patted my chest. "You'd better go." And she started to back away.

I clasped her wrists and kept here there. "Thank you, Holly, for sticking with me."

She nodded and started to leave. "I'm going to be praying."

I squeezed her wrists. "Thank you. Okay? You've shown me love. You've lived it. I've never known anyone like you."

I opened the door, and she curled into the driver's seat of my car with an apprehensive smile. We waved, and after I watched her rumble off I realized my hand was still in the air, almost coaxing her not to go and hoping that would not be our last good-bye.

Starting back to my place in Holly's pickup, a foreboding spirit seemed to seep into the cab like poisonous gas through the vents. My hope disintegrated like Chester's body. Fear rose like a rushing tide. Gold-toothed Truax was hellbent on hanging me, and he had the ammunition: the video, Needermire, the coroner, and an arsenal of evidence that put me at the crime scene.

I'm going to prison.

No more options remained.

Utter desperation forced me toward my house. I would change, load up, and find Needermire's house—which was almost as paralyzing as the thought of prison.

"God." I stared blankly at the congested road ahead. "I need You.

Will You intervene? Will You help me? I don't deserve it, I know. But I want to make things right with You. Amen."

I'm not saying the anxiety left me completely, but the rest of the drive was marked by an unfamiliar calmness that filled the cab and rode nicely, just above the tension and the sound of the tires rolling hard on the clean Las Vegas pavement. As I watched the colored fountains and the purple and green lines and curves of neon, the reflective hotels and the bright, digital scrolling messages promising mammoth jackpots, I took solace in Holly's God.

My dad's funeral was the next day in San Antonio. I would miss it, and I vowed to lay flowers on his grave—and my mother's—as soon as this debacle was over.

But when will that be? Tomorrow? One week? Twenty years from now?

By the time I swung the pickup into my garage, I had my game face on for the night. Working hastily, I tracked down Needermire's address in the phone book and found directions to his house on the Internet. Throwing on jeans, work boots, a Rangers cap, and a black, long-sleeve top, I collected everything I could think of that might come in handy: tools, a flashlight, video camera, binoculars, tape recorder, gloves, digital camera, a thick towel, and the only weapon I had, an old wood tire bat, twenty inches long with a five-inch cylinder of metal at one end.

Holly was driving the Mustang to Red Rock to pick up Andrew, who confirmed finding only more of the same remnants we'd seen earlier—burned clothes and deteriorating bones. We agreed he should crash at Holly's place for the night, and the two assured me they would be praying.

She's safe.

I had nothing to lose.

After locking the house, backing out in Holly's pickup, and watching the garage door go down, I pulled away wondering how long it would be until I would see my home again—if ever.

A block from my house, I spotted the silver Golf with black windows sitting at a stop sign. I drove right by it, my face blazing with the notion they were there to retaliate.

The little car pulled out behind me.

Great.

Zipping out of the neighborhood, I got the pickup humming down Buffalo Drive, made a left on Flamingo, and headed east toward the electric metropolis. The thugmobile was three cars behind me. Needermire's house was out past the Strip and the UNLV campus in Winchester.

The truck was low on gas and I couldn't afford to be stranded; I turned into an ARCO station on my side of the street, watching my rearview for the thugs. The Golf swung into an adjacent plaza several hundred yards away. I waited to see if anyone was going to get out, but there was no activity. As nonchalantly as possible, I filled my tank and went inside, plucking a twenty-ounce bottle of Dr Pepper from the cooler unit on my way to the cashier.

My phone vibrated while I stood in line behind a wiry black man and a large white woman whose unruly toddler squirmed in her arms like a ferret, trying to find freedom. I pulled the phone from my jeans, walked toward the greasy hot-dog machine, and felt a rush of exhilaration when I noticed the 678 area code in the display.

"This is Hudson Ambrose." My heart drummed.

Nothing.

"Hello?"

The toddler was red, spitting, and screaming at the counter, and the mother was dodging punches and trying to reason with him.

The silver Golf sat motionless outside.

"Mr. Ambrose, I assume you've received my phone messages," the voice in my ear was steady and close to monotone, just like the recordings.

"Yes, I have. I want to thank you for your help, whoever you are."

"I saw the video footage from the bus stop, just now, on CNN."

Fantastic.

Cheevers was right. The video was spreading like falling dominoes. "Yeah, and the Las Vegas police have called me in for questioning at eight tomorrow morning."

"The news said that too."

"Wonderful," I mumbled.

"Have you pursued Drake Needermire?"

"The police won't listen to me about Needermire! They're protecting their own. They've got an easy target in me. And now, this videotape—"

"I know you didn't kill Chester Holte."

"You keep saying that, but *how* do you know? Who are you?"

The silence screamed. I pressed the phone tight to my ear.

He finally spoke softly. "I was there."

A mixture of hope and panic flooded me. "What did you say?"

Loud and shrill, the toddler screamed, the veins in his neck purple and popping. I couldn't hear; I had to get out. Stepping on the rug that triggered the automatic doors, I made a beeline for the exit with my eyes on the waiting Golf the whole time.

"Sir!" The frizzy-haired, blond cashier cocked her head and a black eyebrow toward the Dr Pepper under my arm. "You planning on paying for that?"

I did a U-turn and took the first aisle to the motor oil, wiper fluid, and car products at the rear of the store. "I'm sorry. Did you say you were *there* the morning Chester died?"

"That's right."

"Did you see what happened?"

"I did. But I cannot, under *any* circumstances, come forward." His voice lost its evenness for the first time. "I'm trying to help you, but you must respect my anonymity."

"Did Needermire do it?"

"He killed Chester, yes."

Silence.

"Was he in uniform?"

"Yes. As I've told you before, he was after Chester's money, a great deal of money that was there at the bus stop at the time of the killing."

"Chester had no cash when I found him."

"That's because Needermire must have taken it right after he shot Chester."

"Shot Chester..." My gosh, this guy—this voice—can save my life!

"I thought you were there."

"I was there when Chester got shot. As soon as it happened, I ran. Needermire shot at me too."

"Why did Needermire kill him?"

There was an awkward quiet, and the man sucked in a deep breath. "Look, all you need to know is that Chester was shot at the bus stop. I left. Needermire took the money and ran. That's when you showed up. But Needermire must have come back after you left, to get Chester's body and clean up. Check his trunk for bloodstains. Find the cash he took. Find his gun. That should give you plenty to go on. I've got to go—"

"You have to come forward. The police aren't helping me! My

life's on the line. People have been hurt. I'll go to prison for this! Please."

"I know! Believe me," his voice cracked. "I've been to hell and back over this. Don't think I haven't thought it through. I'm not sleeping. But you're not going to convince me—"

"Please, sir, please. You're my only hope. I believe God sent you to help me. Please, just tell me, why can't you come forward? Let me try to help you. I'm a reporter. I can—"

"Wait a minute. Hold it. What do you mean, you believe God sent me?"

Uh-oh. I hit a nerve.

He's anti-God.

He'll hang up and never call again.

Maybe not. Maybe he's a Christian.

Tell the truth. Just tell the truth.

"For the first time in my life I asked God to help me." I threw it out there, knowing there was no return. "I grew up mad at God. He let my mom die at a young age. And I spent most of my life bitter at my old man…"

Where am I going? Idiot!

The caller was silent.

"Are you still there?" I glided around the corner toward the cheap white bread, because two oil-stained teenagers had begun a debate over motor oils in the auto aisle.

"I'm here. Finish what you were saying."

"I've always shaken my fist at God. But Chester helped me. His life. The lives of the people he touched. It's like their relationships with God forced me to come to terms with God myself. This is new for me. I asked Him to help me. I think He may be doing that through you."

"So, Chester played a part in leading you to God?

I actually laughed.

Who would have thought it?

"Yes, and the people whose lives he touched." Arthur and Jonathan and Ellery and Holly paraded through my thoughts, but I wasn't going to muddle things by going there. "I guess you could say, through his death, I learned the meaning of life."

The woman with the maniacal toddler had left the store, as had most of the other customers. It was quiet. The silver Golf remained where it was. I stood as still as a cutout cardboard end cap.

The man mumbled something I couldn't understand.

"Pardon me?"

"That's what he wanted." His high voice wavered.

"What's that? I can't hear you well."

"To put people's hands on the door to God."

That was the poem Holly shared with me.

The man whimpered, but he forged ahead. "Blind people with groping hands, starving beggars in cruel cities." He sounded like a Broadway performer, alone on stage, delivering his lines courageously before a teary-eyed audience. "One person, two, ten, thousands, millions—whose hands he was intended to put on the latch."

This guy knew Chester! He was floating into the past, going down memory lane. I needed to slip in stride with him, get him to keep going.

"How did you know Chester?"

He didn't hesitate. "I met him after his wife died. She passed away in a plane crash. He was burned badly, the side of his face and his hand. Besides his money, Candice was everything to him. He grew desperate. Suicidal."

"Where'd you meet?"

"He came to the church." Pause. "I'll never forget that day. I recognized him from the news stories. He sat way in the back."

The church in Atlanta!

"I know, now, my motives were impure," the man continued in a whisper, as if in a confessional opposite a priest. "I saw dollar signs. Sure, I saw a lost soul. He got baptized that day. But as quick as I lifted him out of the water, I saw the potential for gain. All I could think of was the expensive navy suit he wore and the polished leather belt and shoes. The fine jewelry. The dreams he could make come true for me."

Living Word Fellowship. The pastor...

"He was a worker. Anything we needed done at the church, he did it. He was always there." The man coughed violently, gasped, and went on. "I took advantage of him. I mean, he was a new believer. I should have been helping him build his relationship with Christ. But I used him, you understand? I let his walk with God be based on works for my selfish benefit."

Banyon Scribe!

"Then one day, he came into my office. His smile—he was always smiling—it was gone. He was more serious than that first day he showed up at the church. Said he wanted to talk. Again, I'll never forget it. It's seared in my mind. He wore overalls. He'd been building new shelves in the church library. He was almost finished."

How can I get this guy to come forward? To tell what he saw?

"But he came to me and said he was burned out." The man sighed. "Told me he'd been reading Ephesians, about how our works should stem from our thankfulness to God. I *said* I understood that, but I didn't. I said, 'That's what you're doing, Chester.' He said, 'No, it's not.' He said, 'I've been trying to please *you*.' Then, very politely, he accused me of being self-righteous and driven by vainglory. He said we were a proud church. High-minded. As if we'd done something to earn our salvation. He'd had enough."

"How'd you respond?"

"I denied everything. I hated his guts. I was convinced he was deceived and backslidden and a demon from the pit of hell." The man paused, then chuckled. "I was wrong."

"When did you find that out?"

The phone was quiet. Two young black men wearing short-sleeved baseball jerseys and denim shorts down to their ankles entered the store and headed for the snacks.

"Let me just finish this thought. It may help you." He exhaled loudly. "Chester had pledged a lot of money to our new building campaign, a lot of money. When he left, he withdrew his commitment. He left us completely in the lurch. But instead of asking why it was happening, and what *I* should be doing to change, I just hated him even more. Even to the point where I sought revenge."

"Is that what you were doing in Las Vegas?"

Pause.

"I've got to go."

"I know who you are," I said.

"Yes, but I need your word you won't tell. I've helped you. I'll help you more if I can. But if I come forward I'll be ruined."

"I don't know if I can give you my word. If I'm framed for Chester's murder—"

"I'll deny everything."

"Please... *Why* can't you come forward? From what you've told me, you've done nothing wrong."

"I can't say any more."

The arms of the black men were filled with munchies, and they checked out, one at a time. The Dr Pepper under my arm was getting warm.

I didn't know what else to say to Banyon Scribe.

He finally broke the silence. "I know you're in a bind. You must find the money Needermire stole from Chester. Or, tell Needermire you know the third man at the bus stop—without naming me. Say you've talked to me and will bring me forward to testify unless he turns himself in or turns his wrath elsewhere."

"Does he know who you are?"

"No."

"Will you call back?"

"I will," he said. "Promise me you won't divulge who I am."

I winced. "I don't know if I can do that."

"I'm trusting you."

Don't do that! "Look, Mr. Scribe, I need your help—"

Click.

He was gone.

I stared at my cell phone, then out the window.

The Golf was poised and waiting.

I have to lose those guys.

I exchanged the perspiring bottle of Dr Pepper for a cold one from the fridge at the back of the store, paid the blonde, got in the pickup, took a long swig, pulled into traffic, and headed for Winchester and the home of Drake Needermire.

38

Between the Golf behind me and the traffic in front of me, my nerves were rattled. Cars weaved, honked, and braked all the way across town until I got past 15, the Strip, and Paradise Road, and drew closer to Needermire's neighborhood; but somehow, the thugmobile stayed with me, three to five cars back the whole way.

This is not good.

A hundred different scenarios played out in my mind as I passed the low-rise delis, banks, strip plazas, and secondhand stores on the suburban east side of Las Vegas. If the Golf followed me all the way to Needermire's house, I'd be forced to keep driving; if I stopped, they would likely come after me or do something to the pickup, and my cover would be blown.

The presence of the thugmobile totally threw my concentration, and I was having a rocky time coming up with a definitive plan of action for when I got to Needermire's.

It all depends on whether he's home or not...

Before I could scheme any further, my headlights illuminated the street sign I'd been watching for: Sky Valley Drive. The Golf was about five cars back. Without hitting my blinker, I caught my breath and rocketed the pickup left in front of several fast-approaching cars into the middle-class neighborhood.

Gliding along the main road, I slowed to a snail's pace, waiting for the Golf and flipping down my visor to check the address I'd scribbled down for Needermire: 3600 Sky Valley Drive.

Where are they?

Not trusting the rearview mirror, I shifted around and looked out the back of the pickup, only to see an empty road behind me.

They missed the turn—after following me all the way across town?

It seemed too easy.

The empty, two-lane road in front of me was curvy and dotted with contemporary, single-story homes, set at various angles and neatly landscaped.

I goosed the pickup around the first big turn, almost positive I'd lost the Golf.

Minor miracle there.

The numbers were going up. He would be on my right...2200, 2600, 3000, 3600. I pulled to the side of the street and turned out my lights just shy of Needermire's property. It looked as if he was gone. The lot and house were pitch black except for a lone lamppost that lit the end of the short blacktop driveway. Wide, overgrown palm trees dotted the tiny front yard. The windowless, two-car garage door was closed.

I turned around again. No Golf.

Would those thugs go back to my house? Be waiting for me when I got home?

Leaning back, I filled my lungs with every last ounce of oxygen they would hold.

Protect me. Help me find what I need.

With one last, enormous exhale, I slipped on my brown leather gloves, grabbed the heavy duffel bag from the passenger seat, crept out of the pickup, and got my bearings. Golden lights glowed from the interior of the surrounding homes, but as far as I could tell, no one was watching. I pressed the door shut and hurried toward the house.

The double front doors were all wood, and there were only two high windows at the front of the house. No easy entrance there. I dashed through the gravel in the front yard, rounded the house and turned on my flashlight. Shrubs lined the side. I passed a large AC unit and a square window, and continued around back.

Hurry.

I jogged to the back of the house where there were two low windows, a concrete slab leading to a back door, and a large bay window. It was dark inside. If he had alarms, they'd sound if I pushed open any doors or windows. Instead, I needed to break the glass and go through the opening. I set the bag down on the concrete and dug out the towel and tire bat.

Not far beyond a wood fence out back, there were more homes. Another neighborhood. Quiet. Wrapping the thick towel around the metal end of the tire bat, I walked to one of the two low windows and, with my heart pounding like a jackhammer, hoisted the tire bat up like a plunger and jabbed the glass.

It didn't break.

I stood there, sighed, and stared at the window. Sweating. Beginning to panic. Wondering if I should turn back. Get out.

If you're going to break it, you've got to hit it hard.

It's going to be loud.

The video of me searching Chester lit up my frantic mind, and I smashed the window.

Shards of glass dropped to the windowsill and ground. With the towel still around the heavy end of the tire bat, I ran the club around the inside edge of the window, knocking off the large pieces of glass that remained.

You're committed. Go!

After brushing most of the glass from the windowsill, I snatched the duffel bag, hoisted my rear up on the ledge, and swung my legs into Needermire's house. The flashlight lit up a bedroom, probably the master. It was neat and smelled like cologne. I rushed around the full-size bed and pushed open a large, sliding closet door, my insides feeling like an alarm was going off.

There was a long column of neatly hung shirts, pants, and jackets within the closet, including a number of beige and green police uniforms. Shoes lined the bottom of the closet, which was about four feet deep. Across the top shelf were stacks of shirts, sweats, and various boxes.

One muffled knock made my head snap right.

What's that? A pet?

It had come from low, somewhere across the house. I could almost feel it in my feet. But the house had no basement. I'd looked as I decided where to enter…

It was nothing. Get going!

Reaching up, I ripped all the boxes off the shelf, holding several and letting the others tumble to the ground. Falling to my knees, I scrambled through what were mostly empty shoe boxes. One box held a gun-cleaning kit and various boxes of bullets. Another contained old birthday cards and letters. Several others held shoes.

Keep moving.

Shoving the boxes aside, I shined the flashlight under the bed.

Nothing.

With a quick on-and-off of the overhead light in the bathroom, I could see it was a dead end. Hoisting the duffel bag over my shoulder, I rambled into the hallway, half waiting for a motion detector to trip and sirens to sound. But they did not.

The small guest bathroom was polished—not a thing out of place. Its cupboards contained cleaning supplies and toilet paper. The spare bedroom was an office. It all looked too clean. The closet contained pads, pens, envelopes, and other generic office supplies. I was tempted to fire up his computer but decided that was a rabbit trail I didn't have time to hike.

As I raced through the neat family room and shined the flashlight around the organized kitchen, my heart plummeted. From the pantry, back to the entertainment center, to the hall closet, to the small laundry room, I dashed and searched.

There's nothing here!

Tension blared in my ears, and my head felt light.

The place was immaculate, as if he'd been waiting for a search party.

How long had I been in? Three minutes?

I ran to the front doors and peered out a small, oval window at eye level on my left. The street was dark.

No Golf. No Needermire.

Taking a small hall off the kitchen, I opened a door at the end and felt the heat of what I hoped was the garage. The room was black. I shined my light in.

The large, illuminated letters reading P O L I C E along the lower side of the black-and-white squad car lit up like cat's eyes in the dark.

My breath left me, and my head swung back toward the kitchen. For a chilling millisecond I thought Needermire was home.

No.

Calm down.

He would have been all over you by now.

Must have another car.

My yellowish light swept the garage, from an old workbench with a red tool chest, spray cans, and a big silver vise, to shelves full of tools, paint cans, scraps of wood, motor oil, gas cans, rags, and assorted junk. A practically new Sears push mower with a rear bagger sat on the floor next to a large brown garbage can, recycle bin, and shoe rack.

Then my flashlight fell to an industrial-looking machine in the corner that sparked something in my brain. With the duffel weighing heavy on my shoulder, I walked toward the machine, which resembled a car engine sitting on two tractor tires with a large rounded silver bar sticking up like a mower handle.

I shined the light on the words printed in red and black at the base of the unit. "Honda GX. 9.0 HP. Heavy Duty. Pressure Washer." My light fell to three large white bottles of bleach sitting next to the machine.

Zing.

Like a wheel with teeth, spinning at a hundred and twenty miles per hour, my mind dialed, slowed, clicked, and registered.

He used that to clean up the blood.

I set the duffel bag down, dropped to my knees, dug one hand in the bag and pointed the flashlight in with the other. Snatching the digital camera, I flicked it on, set the flashlight on the ground facing the pressure washer, framed the photo, and flashed. After three more shots, I dropped the camera into the bag, scrambled to my feet, and hurried to the back of the police car, which was a foot from the closed garage door.

Leaning over from the side of the car with my flashlight, the duffel bag clinking against the rear fender, I pressed the trunk button, but it was locked.

No!

Scurrying to the driver's door of the gleaming patrol car, I opened it, squinted as the dome light flickered on, and leaned in. Peering through the metal cage that separated the front seat from the back, I realized Needermire's car was as neat as his house. The worn, black leather interior was packed with a laptop computer on a swivel and a console filled with radios, microphones, and a cell phone—each angled toward the driver like the cockpit of a sophisticated aircraft.

Leaning over the equipment, I opened the glove compartment in search of a lever that would open the trunk. There were napkins from Wendy's, a tire gauge, a flashlight, toothpicks—

"Sorry, no trunk button in these things."

My head bashed the ceiling as I looked up at the passenger window, only to see the reflection of my own cap and curly hair hanging over my sweaty face.

I backed out of the driver's side to the sound of hideous laughter coming from the other side of the car, at the rear of the garage.

Reluctantly, I took two steps toward the trunk, lifted my flashlight, and pointed it toward the sickening voice.

"Boo!"

It was Needermire.

He sat relaxed in a black canvas chair just inside the doorway of a storage room. One leg was crossed over his knee, both hairy arms rested on the wooden arms of the chair, and he had a black, semiautomatic weapon angled directly at my face. He wore dark blue slacks and another colorful short-sleeve madras shirt.

"You like my pressure washer?" His laughter echoed in the blackness.

My heart banged at the base of my throat. "I came for evidence."

"You came," his voice thundered as he stood, "to *plant* evidence."

The bottom dropped out of my stomach, and I felt my legs weaken.

He's got a plan.

He snapped the overhead light on, and I squinted at his hard, brown face.

"You got me suspended," he hissed through gritted teeth. "Now you got the nerve to break into my home and plant evidence against me. Get in here!" He waved his gun from me to the door leading inside.

My chest felt completely hollow, and my organs seemed to have melted away entirely. The duffel bag felt like two hundred pounds on my shoulder as I rounded the front of the police car, wiping the sweat from my forehead and fearing his blows as I drew closer.

Tap...tap.

My head turned to the floor.

A noise like the other...

Needermire's eyes flared. "Hurry up!" He wrapped his gun hand behind my back and shoved me hard into the house.

The door to the garage slammed shut behind me, and the kitchen light went on. "You're as dirty as me, Ambrose." I was about to turn and face him when a searing pain shot through my lower back, and I crashed into a table and chairs, hitting the kitchen floor and bashing my lip.

"Give me the camera." He dropped to one knee, fished the digital out of my discarded bag, rose to his feet, and set it cracking on the counter. Then he bent over and pulled the tire bat out of the bag.

"What's this for?" Needermire whipped the bat at my legs but clipped the chair instead. "Get up!" He grunted, grabbing me by the back of the shirt collar, yanking me along the floor until I got to my feet, and shoved me through the living room. "Back to where you came in!"

I trembled, and my face blazed like a furnace.

Just get out alive.

"Put the boxes back up," he ordered as we entered the bedroom and he flipped on the light. "All but this one." He kicked one white shoebox with his big brown square-toed shoe, and it went spinning away from the others.

"Come on. Get the lead out."

He paced like an ogre, slapping the metal end of the tire bat in the palm of his free hand as I did what he'd commanded. When the last box was up on the shelf, I faced him.

"Put that box on the bed." He eyed the box on the floor.

I did.

"Give me your gloves."

He wedged the tire bat under his armpit, took the gloves from me, and pulled them onto his own hands. Not taking his eyes from me, he produced a clear plastic bag from his back pocket. Inside was a dark gray gun.

My face throbbed.

He's going to get away with this.

Before I knew it, the gun in the bag was in the air, on its way to me. Instinctively, I caught it, putting my prints all over the bag.

"Put it in the box, and back up there." He pointed the tire bat to the shelf in the closet.

"How can you possibly think you're going to get away with this?" I did as he said, took the box to the closet, and slid it onto the shelf.

"This is your gun. I know you used it to kill Chester—"

"No! It's your gun; the gun you used to kill that bum. It's stolen.

Its serial numbers are gone. And you're hiding it in my house in an attempt to frame me!"

Dropping to a small bench at the end of the bed, I almost threw up. I knew, I mean, knew, that was the end of me. He laughed. A sick laugh. And a surreal, ugly, dark heaviness settled over me.

"What'd you do with Suzette Graham?" I mumbled, halfway between awareness and unconsciousness.

"Don't know anyone by that name." The tire bat drilled into my side, and I squirmed. From the media frenzy that would follow, to the murder trial and prison—which I dreaded more than death—my future played out there in that room, and I became reckless.

"Where's the money?" I struggled to my feet, slumped, but facing him. "How much did he have on him?"

Needermire gritted his teeth, grabbed me at the collar with both fists, and shook. "You better shut up, boy. Or you'll end up like he did."

"Why didn't you take the bankbook and key when you robbed him?"

"Humph." He shoved me, letting go of my shirt. "Too complicated." He laughed. "Believe it or not, I don't like risk. Besides, cash will always be king, and old Chester had plenty of that."

"You thought no one was gonna care about a dead homeless guy." I chuckled weakly. "I thought the same thing. We both turned out to be wrong." Rage flooded his dark eyes like blood, and I set my face forward, almost begging for him to strike. "You had to go back and get the body and clean up. What a hack job—"

With an iron fist, he ripped the hair at the back of my head, pulling me backward until my hat fell off and I collapsed, right on top of the tire bat. With half my face in the carpet, I spoke again, not caring what he did to me. "I've talked to the witness."

His shadow seeped over me. He peered down, his hands locked in fists as big as mallets. "What'd you say?"

"Not the one you strapped to the monorail," I whispered. "The other one. Tall, brown hair. The one who's alive."

Lowering to one knee, he leaned over me, giving off a sick odor of perspiration and cologne. "Prove it."

I rolled my head back and looked smack-dab into his contorted face. "You were in uniform. You were after Chester's money. You stole thousands."

His jaw jutted out, and he wound my collar in his fist again. "Anyone could guess that after all that's been written, punk."

My heart stormed. "You took a shot at him, the tall guy, when he ran. Could I have guessed that?"

Needermire's eyes swelled like balloons being filled with helium.

"I know who he is." It was my turn to smile.

His head wrenched toward the broken window.

His grip went limp at my neck.

Uh-oh.

His eyes darted about as if he'd heard a frightening noise—or voices in his demented mind.

Then he froze. Like a stone pillar. Just froze.

For minutes.

He's changing his plan.

His head lowered and turned to me, his expression blank.

But the eyes. They were frighteningly cold, as if he'd already done whatever sinister thing he'd just determined he was going to do.

Ten thousand watts of electricity rushed into my lungs.

He's going to get rid of me.

39

How badly I wanted to waste that scared squirrel on my bedroom floor, that Hudson Ambrose *creep*. Desperately, I wanted to *snuff* him. He'd made what should have been a sweep-under-the-rug case a worldwide *spectacle*.

He'd forced me to hurt the others. His accusations got me suspended. He could have ruined me. I should've taken him to the lake, capped him, and sent him to his watery grave. But the world was watching. That was the problem. If he disappeared after breaking into my place, there'd be problems, there'd be evidence to deal with. The pickup truck. The duffel bag. The broken window. Too much to explain.

Too much risk.

I didn't like risk.

No no no.

Just keep your head.

Think it through.

The money's mine. It's safe. No one's ever going to find it. But if I blow this thing, I'll never cash in.

Ambrose will get his. Between the video of him at the bus stop—a total coup—and what he did here tonight, he'll spend the rest of his life in the can.

The one missing link is the witness—that skinny, stubborn meddler I tried to snuff that morning. If I could get his name, I could eliminate him. That would end this thing. No more complications. *No more risk.*

Lying on the floor by my bedroom, Ambrose was white as paper, even his lips had no color.

"You're scared, aren't you, reporter?" I said, still trying to figure out my next move. "Tell me the name of this witness."

Ambrose gulped. He might have been frightened, but he stared up at me with knowing eyes that seemed to plumb the depths of my hideous soul.

Just like Chester's eyes.

The eyes I never forget.

"I can't tell you." Ambrose closed his eyes, as if he was praying or bracing for my wrath.

I wanted to hurt him. *Oh, how I wanted to strangle him!* But I knew better. I knew I'd get carried away. The lashing I'd dole out would only lead to more questions. It would take away from the appearance of guilt on his behalf.

No.

This was one time I needed to restrain myself.

Cool it.

Think.

As I stared at Ambrose again for a good while, his eyes closed and it hit me like a flatbed truck. I heard myself snicker as I buried my head in my hand and relished the chill from the euphoria that swept over me.

"Your witness ain't coming forward." I dropped from my knee to the seat of my pants and hooted. "You can't get him to testify!"

Ambrose's dejected eyes followed me and confirmed I was right.

I flopped on my back and howled, tears streaking down my cheeks. "I should have known, the way that guy ran like a scared kangaroo." I shook my head and wiped the wetness away. "He's hiding something—"

Thud.

"Ohhhh." My legs and shoulders jumped off the ground involuntarily with the blow to my gut.

No wind.

I looked up. The tire bat was high above Ambrose's head. His face was sour. He swung the club like a lumberjack with an ax. I couldn't get my hands up in time.

Whack!

My body curled up.

I gasped.

The bat found my throat. He was on me, teeth clenched, rocking, forcing the choker down with both hands and all his weight. My hands got to the bat, just inside his locked hands, but his weight was too much. I couldn't breeeeeathe.

"You're gonna talk!" His curly hair draped over his face, covering everything but one wild eye and his drooling mouth.

While I was still sucking wind, he shifted like a cat, throwing his body over my head, wrenching the bat one turn, and forcing my hands off the weapon.

"Get up!" With both hands, he yanked the club deep into my throat, and I rose until I was sitting.

On his knees, breathing hard, he began crawling backward with my head locked tight to his chest by the choking bat, forcing me to shuffle on my bottom, along with him.

This guy is tough.

As we got to the hallway outside the bedroom, my breath was coming back and, with it, my fury.

"Ambrose, you're just giving me more—"

A grunt and the heave of the club wedging deeper into my Adam's apple, cutting off my speech and sending me into a quiet rage.

"You shut up," he seethed. "You're goin' to jail. Not me. Not me…"

Ambrose jerked the club again. It was severing my throat as he forced me to continue shimmying along the floor toward the kitchen. But I knew he couldn't keep it up. He was using every muscle in his body, every last ounce of energy, to keep me at bay. I just went along with him, building back my energy, getting ready for his slightest mistake.

40

I sat curled up in my favorite chair, trying to concentrate on the psalms open before me, but the ticks from the clock seemed five times as loud as normal. Over and over I replayed the kiss and good-bye with Hud. And I kept trying to convince myself that his going to Needermire's was a good idea.

My small house was still, but it wasn't like being alone. Andrew tapped quietly at the keyboard in front of the glowing computer in the far corner of the living room. He wore a black T-shirt and gray sweat shorts. With his reading glasses on, he reminded me very much of Chester.

"He should be calling soon," I said. "Don't you think?"

Andrew lowered his head and peered over his glasses. "I'm sure he'll call as soon as he can."

"I know. I just…I'm having a hard time waiting. Didn't you think we would have heard from him by now?"

He looked at his watch. "We'll hear soon, I bet." He smiled, pushed his chair back, and strolled toward me. "Hudson told me you spent some time…homeless." He surprised me.

"Oh, he covered that, did he?"

Andrew chuckled. "Yeah. Do you not like to talk about it?"

"No, I don't mind. That part of my life ended up changing me forever."

"How so?" He sat down.

"Well, for one, I got to meet your dad." I tilted my head and smiled. "And for another, it made me appreciate everything more—everything."

"What was it like?"

Where do I start?

"Well, for me, the hardest thing about being homeless wasn't finding food or clothes or a rest room—it was staying away from street predators."

"Really?" He scooted his chair closer.

"Oh yeah. Between the drug addicts and the mentally ill, being homeless in Vegas is almost like being in a huge outdoor jail."

"That's what I've heard," Andrew said. "Having Dad here, I did my research. Vegas supposedly tops the list for violence, drug addiction, suicide—"

"Not to mention dropouts and teen pregnancies."

"I read where it was voted meanest city in the country toward homeless people. Have you heard that?"

"It's true." I shook my head. "You've got to watch your back, even while you're sleeping. The main rule of the street your dad taught me: stay with a group. I got stalked a couple times." I giggled. "But ever since I was little, I've had this primal scream... Let's just say, it came in handy more than once."

"You and Dad were close, weren't you?"

My smile dissolved. "Yes, we were." Anguish squeezed my heart. I looked down. "I met Chester at a time when I felt ugly and completely alone. My husband had left me. My parents were long gone. Dad died of a massive heart attack and Mom of what? Depression? A broken heart? My brother was in the service overseas. There was nothing left for me…then your dad came along."

We talked for another twenty minutes, which I believe served as healing medicine for Andrew, who was hungry to find out as much as he could about his father's new life in Las Vegas. Andrew was holding up extremely well, especially after having canvassed all of the "find" areas at Red Rock Canyon and locating nothing larger or more significant than his father's femur.

"It's okay. I'm okay," he'd assured me when I picked him up in Hud's car. "The bones, the clothes, they just confirm he's not down here anymore. He's gone. But his spirit lives on."

When our conversation slowed, we turned on the news. I had warned Andrew about the new videotape of Hud with Chester at the bus stop. When it finally aired, he dropped to his knees with his mouth gaping open, right next to the TV, mesmerized by the last images captured of his father.

When I turned the TV off, the room fell silent. Did Andrew fully believe that Hud had nothing to do with his father's death? Would anyone?

I turned the pages of my worn Bible, looking for anything that would jump out at me, that would chase away the helplessness and give me hope. I landed in Proverbs where several lines of text had been circled in blue:

The curse of the LORD is on the house of the wicked,
But He blesses the dwelling of the righteous.

I moved my finger up to the verse before it:

For the devious are an abomination to the LORD;
But He is intimate with the upright.

My head dropped, and my spirit seemed to groan within me. Closing my eyes, I began to pray silently, but I needed more space and privacy.

I stood. "I'll be right out, Andrew."

"Okay." He examined me from above his glasses. "You okay?"

"Yeah, I just need a couple of minutes."

I walked back to my bedroom, closed the door, and dropped to my knees, leaning on the mattress.

"O Father," I exhaled deeply into the silence. Waiting. Focusing on the One above, whom I sensed was near and listening. "Hud needs you now. Please have favor on him. I pray You'll turn Needermire's corruption inward, on himself. Your Word says he's an abomination, that Your curse is on his house..."

Eyes closed, I lifted my head toward the heavens. "I know Hud's trying, Lord. He's getting closer. Please, keep drawing him. Show him You're real; show him You're alive."

41

Still choking me from behind, Ambrose nudged the duffel bag, then paused. Suddenly, his cocked left arm jammed into my throat, replacing the tire bat. He yanked my neck hard with the locked arm, and I gagged. The bat dropped to the floor, but he kicked it out of my reach.

He needed that free arm. *What for?* Panting, he dug through the duffel bag, his sweat dripping onto my head and shoulders. He stopped to examine something he'd pulled from the bag. I turned my head as much as I could, maybe two inches. It was a palm-sized tape recorder—a lot like the girl's.

Industrious.

It beeped, and he set it on the floor. Within seconds, he jerked my head up and slid the club back to my throat.

"Who killed Chester Holte?" He grunted as he heaved the bat into my cracking windpipe.

Everything went white. And hot. And there were spots.

I heaved, but nothing came up.

"Talk!" he screamed.

For the first time in my life, I thought I might die.

"I—" I tried to speak but didn't know if any words came out.

"What?" He cut the tension.

"I did it."

"With what?"

After three silent seconds, he pulled the club with all his might, and my trachea felt like it was thrashed for good.

I thought I was going to pass out.

"Stolen gun," my voice broke.

"Where'd you get it?" he growled, jerking the club again.

"Some punks I know."

"What'd you do with the body? Chester's?"

The club was digging into my neck. In a queer, sick way, Ambrose's grit and endurance fascinated me. At the same time, it made me want to squeeze his scrawny neck until his lights went out and ditch his meddlesome body—like the others.

I played his game and waited for my time. "Left him at Red Rock," I mumbled. "Burned his clothes. Knew the critters would get him."

"Who stole Chester's rings and stuff from my house?"

The club jerked tighter at my neck.

"Same punks I got the gun from."

"They drive a silver Golf?"

I grunted.

"Did they drive a silver Golf?" he screamed.

"Yeah!" I was about to explode. "They're the ones who told me you were on your way, jerk."

Ambrose grunted and shifted uncomfortably. The club loosened at my neck.

He's cramping.

With a pained voice, he spoke again. "What about Suzette Graham?"

I'd run out of nice. "What about her?"

He forced the club hard beneath my chin, but the strength he'd had earlier was waning. "Where is she?"

That, no one will ever know.

"She went for a swim."

"Where?"

"Lake Mead."

The bar tightened at my neck. "Explain!"

"I couldn't let her write that story—"

Beep.

Ambrose flinched.

My heart banged.

He's going to reach for the recorder.

The instant the tension released on the bat, I ripped my hands up to my neck, deflecting the arm that tried to come in and choke me.

"Ahhh!" I detonated, twisting that tired arm behind his back like a rag doll's and jamming it up almost to his neck.

He squealed like a baby as I rammed his face into the carpet.

But he had the nerve to reach for the recorder.

I stomped his hand and yanked his hair as hard as I could.

"How *dare* you confront me, you *punk!*"

I slapped his face hard and plowed a fist into his gut.

He went limp, dropping to the ground.

I snatched the recorder and grabbed his hair.

"Up!" Dragging him to my bedroom, I found cuffs on my dresser. "Hudson Ambrose, you're under *citizen's* arrest for breaking and entering and possession of an unregistered firearm." I snapped the cuffs onto his wrists. "Let's see what your friends at the *R-J* have to say now."

Ambrose dropped to his knees.

After slipping the tape recorder into my pocket and snatching his cap off the floor, I dragged and kicked him to the garage and forced him into the backseat of my squad car. He slumped down without a word.

"As much as I'd like to snuff you, I can't," I growled. "How I wish I could. But I need you too much."

As I floored it backward, out of the garage, I wanted to kill again. Ambrose deserved it more than any of the others. I could feel the satisfaction of it. *Could taste it.* But I knew that would finish me.

Keeping him alive was my ticket to the good life.

I punched Truax's number as I gunned the Ford out of my neighborhood. "I got a surprise for you."

"What's that?"

"I just caught Hudson Ambrose breaking into my house. He was planting a gun. I think it's the one he used to murder Chester Holte."

Truax was silent for thirty seconds. "You're pulling my chain, right?"

I laughed. "Huh-uh. I'm bringing him in now."

"I *knew* that weasel was dirty."

I snickered to myself.

"He's not getting bail either," Truax snarled. "I'm gonna see to that. Guy like that would hightail it in a New York minute. He's got nothing to lose anymore."

We hung up and I made one more call, to my contact at KLAS-TV. It took a while to track him down.

"Yeah?" he answered.

"Needermire here."

"Sergeant," the reporter sounded surprised. "What can I do for you?"

"Well." I chuckled. "You can get your cameras and crews, and everybody else you want to get, and have them come to police headquarters, pronto. I got some breaking news."

"What's up?"

"Hudson Ambrose just broke into my house. He was trying to plant a gun. I caught him. I think it's the weapon he used to kill the homeless man, Chester Holte. I made a citizen's arrest, and I'm bringing him in now. Be there or be square."

I hooked the phone into its cradle, cocked my head back, and laughed.

Adjusting the rearview mirror, I could barely find Ambrose slouched in the dark. But I finally made out the shadowy profile of his face staring out the passenger window, with the lights of Las Vegas reflecting in his watery eyes.

Too bad, worthless jerk.

I turned the mirror, examined my face, licked my fingers, slicked down the dark hair at my temples, and smiled the way I would in a few minutes, when I marched into headquarters with Chester Holte's killer.

splashed water on my face, patted it dry with a big terrycloth towel, and looked in the mirror. The bruises from Kenny were gone. I looked tired and skinny and strained.

Kenny's in hell.

I shook my head, and a wave of chills rolled over me.

It wasn't the first time I'd tried to figure out how eternal fire and outer darkness could coexist. Nor was it the first time I'd envisioned Kenny weeping in torment there.

I was glad he was gone.

Sweeping a brush through my hair, my heart grieved for Ellery and Jenna,. what they must be going through in those long, night hours when they couldn't be searching for Suzette.

Suzette.

Needermire's police uniform could have fooled her.

Could he be that sick? That demented?

Twisting the cap off my toothpaste, I froze and stared.

When's the last time Suzette brushed her teeth? Is she even alive?

If Needermire did kidnap her, he must've killed her. *There's no way he could take the risk of keeping her alive somewhere. And why would he—*

"Holly!"

Andrew's shout reverberated from my head to my toes and back again. I moved toward his voice, thinking how weird it was to have a stranger in my house, especially one who was yelling.

"Holly!" he called again just before I burst into the room from the fear and adrenaline propelling me.

He was on one knee in front of the TV.

"Hud's been arrested," he said sharply, turning up the volume, holding an index finger up to his lips, and watching the young African American reporter.

"Just when you thought this case couldn't get any more bizarre, it takes another extraordinary twist. That's what happened just about one hour ago when *R-J* reporter Hudson Ambrose was brought into custody at Las Vegas Metropolitan Police headquarters by none other than Sergeant Drake Needermire, the very man Ambrose has accused of murdering two homeless men, Chester Holte and Ned Frazier, and kidnapping *R-J* reporter Suzette Graham."

No...

The picture cut from the blue-suited reporter to earlier footage of a chaotic scene outside police headquarters, where bright lights cast shadows and cameras jiggled to capture a pompous-faced Needermire moving people out of the way with one hand and gripping Hud's arm with the other. In handcuffs, a black shirt, and baseball cap, Hud held his cuffed hands in front of his face and moved with the flow of the crowd.

My heart was on the floor.

"Police officials are telling us that Needermire—who was recently suspended from his duty with Las Vegas police because of the Chester Holte murder investigation—was alone at his home in Winchester earlier tonight when he heard a window break in his bedroom. Needermire caught Ambrose in the house, carrying a gun in a plastic bag. I must tell you that speculation is running rampant here at the station right now, with word spreading that Ambrose may have been attempting to plant the gun in Needermire's home. Some are saying it may be the murder weapon that was used to gun down Chester Holte. Ballistic reports will be done immediately…"

Unable to swallow or talk, I dropped to the floor by Andrew's side. He didn't move.

"Officials are telling us that Needermire and Ambrose wrestled in the home and that, at one point, Ambrose had the upper hand and was attempting to choke Needermire with a club he brought into the house. Along with the tourist videotape released earlier today of Ambrose searching what appears to be the corpse of Chester Holte at a north-end bus stop, this could be the one-two punch that knocks Hudson Ambrose out for good."

My hands came to my face which, unbeknownst to me, was soaked with tears. Andrew squeezed my shoulder, but said nothing.

Pictures of Suzette and Chester and Ned Frazier filled the screen. The victims.

This is so unfair, Lord!

The TV flashed to a live shot of the reporter standing outside police headquarters, with blue and red lights flashing and cars weaving in and out all around him.

"As you can see…excuse me, I almost got run down. As you can see, police, investigators, and scores of media are flooding the scene here at Las Vegas Police headquarters. I personally saw Assistant Sheriff Nelson Truax and lead investigator Jack Sloan arrive, just about when Needermire did, one hour ago. The feel you get here, if I can attempt to convey it, is one of high anticipation. What I mean by that is, although it's late, I believe the Las Vegas police feel they are right on the verge of making an arrest in the Chester Holte slaying, and I don't believe they're going to rest or go home until they have someone behind bars."

Bars. The one thing Hud said he could never endure.

"What's going to happen?" I stared at the screen.

"He'll probably be booked and interrogated."

"Tonight?"

"Oh yeah. This is serious."

"Will he get released on bail or something?"

Andrew leaned back and made sure I was looking into his eyes. It was like looking into Chester's. "Holly, I'm going to be honest with you. It doesn't look good." He shook his head. "They're not going to let him go for anything right now. He's the prime suspect."

"Don't say that!" I wailed. "What about Needermire? It's so obvious. Are we the only ones who see?"

Andrew squeezed my arms but again said nothing.

His silence entered my ears, went down my throat to the cavern in my midsection, and exploded, like the instant you learn some awful, unexpected, horrifying news that scrambles your insides like the drop of a roller coaster.

"You do believe he's innocent, don't you, Andrew?"

I searched his somber face and glazed eyes.

Vacant.

"Please, Andrew. Don't do this…"

His hands dropped away from my arms.

He turned back toward the television.

"Get out of here then!" I scurried to my feet, shooting a stiff arm and trembling finger toward the door. "Get your stuff! I'm going to the police station. I'll drive you where you want—"

"Holly, wait." He got to his feet and approached. "They're not going to let you see him."

"I don't care!" I spun around, went searching for my keys, then changed my mind and looked for the cell phone before realizing I needed to change out of my pajamas—

"Stop!" Andrew grabbed my arm. "Just stop. Look at me."

I yanked my arm from his grasp, huffed, and peered at him. "What?"

"I'm confused, okay? I don't know what to think."

"Well, I do. Hud's innocent. And I'm going to be there for him!" I rushed to the coffee table, shoving magazines onto the floor. No keys, only the TV remote.

They're Hud's keys. Remember? You're looking for Hud's keys.
Where's my truck?
At Needermire's? Towed to the police station?
My phone. Where did I put it?
Shoes. I need shoes. And my purse.
That's right, my gosh, I've got to change.
Hurry.

"He needs me," I muttered and paced and sweated and searched.

"Holly." Andrew's voice sounded far off, but he was there in the same room.

Hud's picture was on TV.

Then Needermire, leaning down into a reporter's microphone, laughing. I gritted my teeth, lifted the clicker, and zapped the channel. There he was again!

"I've got to go." Blindly, I headed for the door in my bare feet and pink pajamas with nothing more than the remote control in my hand.

Andrew slipped between me and the door, his hands in the air, as if coaxing a prowling tiger back into its cage.

"Just hold on, Holly. Hold on. Hold on."

He rested his hands softly atop my shoulders.

"Hold on," he whispered again.

My head dropped.

His breathing was heavy from trying to corral me.

"I'm sorry." I began to weep.

"I understand."

I fell against him there at the door, and he held me, supported me, just like his father would have.

"I'll go with you," he said. "You get dressed. We'll go together."

That made me cry even more.

43

It was 2:20 a.m. and so dark and still in the den of my suburban Atlanta home I could see and hear the glowing white ripples of static crackling across the TV screen as it flashed to black. I'd seen enough of the breaking news from Las Vegas.

Hudson Ambrose was finished.

Unless I intervene.

I was his ticket to freedom.

But with his freedom would come my imprisonment. And disgrace. And the humiliation of my family. And the condemnation of the church I pastored seven miles from the house where I sat, in the dark, in my familiar recliner, feeling as if the planet was crushing my chest.

I chewed the cuticles on my trembling hands.

What to do?

Sally, the devoted pastor's wife, was asleep upstairs. So were our three children—the PKs—Joseph, Leah, and Jacob. Bible names.

Huh.

Bible names.

I lowered my head, trying to shake off a lifetime of regrets. Mistakes. Pride. Greed. Lies.

What a father I'd turned out to be.

And what about your church?

I knew well what the Scripture said about teachers being held to a higher standard, that we would incur "a stricter judgment." I'd read it dozens of times since the morning Chester died. But once again, the thought haunted me as it had twenty-four hours a day during the past week. Indeed, I'd lived up to my name: Scribe.

Pharisee.

Legalistic. Self-righteous. Judgmental. *Greed-driven monster.*

Oh, enough with the self-pity.

You've got a decision to make.

For once in your life can you think of someone else?

No matter how hard I tried to justify keeping quiet about that morning, some remnant—some leftover residue of God deep within me—was crying out, was plaguing me. That's why I'd called Ambrose repeatedly. To try to help. The guilt was driving me mad.

But it was more than that.

Somehow, after all I'd done wrong, trying to build my own kingdom at the church, working to become famous, manipulating people to worship me—and succeeding—God had reduced me to nothing.

But that was right where He wanted me.

At the door.

And that was where Chester wanted me. Indeed, he turned out to be the conduit God used to put my hand on the latch.

Huh.

I had shown up in Las Vegas to rob Chester. Rob him blind. I justified it by reminding myself, by ingraining it in my mind day after day, for years, that he owed me $1.5 million. *He owed it to me!* He owed it to the congregation of Living Word Fellowship for their new worship center. And he owed it to God.

"You fool."

You've never known how to trust God. He's never been real to you.

Until now.

When you're broken and needy.

There's still a chance.

A flicker of hope down inside somewhere.

Thanks to Chester.

I shook my head, but still—still, still, still, still—was unable to get that terrible, murderous, shocking, merciful morning off the billboard of my brain. It was right there. Vivid and unrelenting.

After several hours of maneuvering the white Budget rental car in and out of Las Vegas's most well-known homeless districts, I spotted Chester sitting by himself in the baking sun on a curb along Owens Avenue. His skin was dark. His face was filled with joy and blond beard stubble. And he was playing the harmonica.

I pulled up next to him, put the passenger window down, and leaned toward him. "Hey, stranger."

He casually looked up and thrust a gritty hand above his eyes to block the sun. Without a word, he stood, came to the window, leaned down, and peered in.

"It's me." I chuckled. "Your pastor, Banyon."

"I know who it is." He nodded. "I'm just trying to figure out what you're doing here."

"Well, get in and I'll tell you. It's nice and cool in here."

He did so, not bothering to put on his seat belt as I drove away. "You're a long way from Atlanta." Chester looked straight ahead. "What brings you here, Pastor?"

"Are you hungry? How about a burger or a steak?"

Chester looked over at me. "You know I've never been one for beating around the bush, Banyon. What's going on? Are you here to rescue me? To bring me back into the fold?" He chuckled. "I thought I might never see you again."

I pulled the car into a small strip plaza and parked in front of a tiny used bookstore and a Mexican restaurant with tinted windows. Shifting into park, I looked at him. "I'm here to collect your pledge for the new worship center."

He howled so loud and hard his head bounced off the headrest.

"It's not a joke." I wiped my mouth and glared at him. "I want you to withdraw the maximum amount of cash you can today. I'll meet you at the Civic Center North bus station, north of the Strip, tonight at 2 a.m. You bring the money. I'll come back for more later."

Chester's laughter dissipated. With his mouth hanging open, he stared at me with those piercing blue eyes for a long time, then flung his door open, got out, and began to walk.

I leaned toward him, using the line I'd rehearsed so many times. "I'm going to have to hurt Andrew if you don't do this."

He stopped cold. For almost a minute, just stood there with his back to me.

My heart ticked hard and fast.

Slowly, he turned around and walked toward me, wedging himself between the open door and the car. He dropped his head, and I watched his stomach move in and out with each contemplative breath. He eased back into the passenger seat, shut the door, and dropped his head back against the headrest.

"Think about what you just said. Think clearly," he said. "Listen to your words. Listen to the desperation. Hurt Andrew? You're in a snare, Pastor. A trap. Satan's got you. It's all deception. Can't you see?"

"No! You think about what *you've* done, you ingrate! You came to me a babbling, blundering, crying widower. You didn't know which end was up. You were a complete, frazzled mental case. And I helped you. Our church helped you. We got you on your feet and brought joy back into your life."

"That's what's wrong with you, *Pastor*. You think *you're* responsible for transforming people's lives. But it's not you! It's not the church! It's God. God does it all. It's Him alone. We're nothing without Him. I can't believe you're the pastor of a church of how many hundred people? And you don't grasp that foundational—"

"Shut up!" I shook him by his thin, tattered black coat, spitting as I addressed him. "Just shut up and listen to me, you bum! You're going to pay God every last cent you owe Him. The program starts today. Consider this your first installment. Do what I say and your boy lives."

Chester was strong. Even though I was tall, I knew he could put my lights out at any given moment. But the reason I'd picked him, the reason I was there in his city, in that car with him, was because I knew Chester's heart. He was so unlike the world, so unlike the flesh. I knew he'd turn the other cheek. I knew Scripture coursed through his veins and that he would say, as Paul did, "Why not be wronged? Why not be defrauded?"

And I was right.

He sighed, looked out the window, examined the blue sky and the people walking past, then peered down at his hard, brown hands and rubbed them together. He looked at me and gave a quick smile. It was there and it was gone, and I had to turn away.

"Tonight," I declared. "Two a.m. Civic Center North. Bring the cash."

He opened the door and I faced him.

"You need God, Pastor. The real God, *Jesus.*"

His words blasted forth with such utter authority and compassion that I couldn't bear to hold his gaze. His words were like knives, carving their way into my heart. His speech was like a flood, coming at me in torrents of living water and fire and fury and love. "You need a relationship with Him, not *religion*."

I was blinded and breathless, and two seconds from weeping and having a meltdown. But the root of all evil—my secret love—stepped between us like a shadow, whispered my name like a lusty mistress, and repeated the promises that had propelled me to that place.

"Go!" I forced myself to look at him. "Do what I told you."

Chester got out of the car, leaned down, and looked back in. "What can I do to help you?"

"Do what I say!" My hands shook as I put the car in reverse. "Keep your promise. Pay the money you pledged."

I goosed the car backward, then hit the brakes, causing the passenger door to slam shut. He stood there, his squinting gaze entrancing me. I stared back, feeling the tension between us, yet much more than that, feeling the danger and rage and thunder and heat of an all-out war exploding in the spiritual realm all around me.

Chester was good and I was bad. He was pure and I was polluted. He was righteous and I was evil.

But the money cried out. The bigger building called. And the praise of the people—the popularity—shouted above all the other noise. And I stepped on the gas and went through with my plan.

Arriving at Civic Center North at 1:50 a.m., I waited a few minutes in the rental car, then got out and walked into the open-air pavilion at the deserted bus stop. The people driving along Las Vegas Boulevard were oblivious to the station at that time of morning.

I reached down and shook the door of the newspaper machine.

"I've been waiting for you, Pastor."

I flinched at the sound of Chester's voice, which came from behind, around the corner by the vending machines. He stepped into the yellowish light with his hands in the pockets of his baggy navy pants, and a bulky, blue and black vinyl bag tucked under his arm.

"How much did you get?" I shivered and stared at the bag.

"You're a mess, Banyon, you know that?" He walked toward me. "Why don't we go have a cup of coffee? Talk this over."

"How much did you get?" I demanded, stepping toward him.

He sighed. "Four hundred and twenty-five thousand." We both stopped in front of a row of concrete blocks. "Do you really think God's gonna honor this? Bless it?"

"Shut up!" I held my arms out. "Give it here."

Chester produced the bag readily, as if he were handing over a sack of tomatoes he'd grown and was giving to a neighbor.

I set the bag, which was heavier than I'd anticipated, on one of the concrete blocks, unzipped it, and peeked in at the dozens of stacks of bills, each bound with its own brown paper band.

Glory.

My heart swelled.

I lost my breath for a moment.

Get out of here!

"Okay." I gasped, trying to hide the smile as I fought to zip the bag shut, then found its black canvas handles and looked up at Chester.

But he wasn't alone.

Five feet behind him, in the shadow, in the silence, stood a cop with a gun in his hand, pointed at me.

It's a setup. He set you up!

"Wait a minute." I kept one hand on the handle of the bag and held the other up, my eyes darting from the cop to Chester and back. "I didn't do anything wrong. This was *owed* to me."

Following my eyes, Chester turned around and met the gaze of the Las Vegas police officer, who wore leather gloves and dark glasses.

"Move over by him." The cop wagged his gun at Chester, who turned and walked toward me.

"You're not in on this?" I squinted at Chester.

He shook his head.

We both faced the mystery cop, who looked wiry and bony and mean as an eel. He wore no ID. Another gun remained in his holster.

"Look," I said, "this is a personal matter, Officer. We've done nothing—"

"Cut it!" The cop raised the gun toward my face. "Toss the bag over here."

Chester looked at the cop, then me, but said nothing.

"Wait a minute!" I backed up a step. "Are you arresting us or what? We don't have any weapons; nothing here is stolen."

The cop's shoulders straightened, he inhaled greatly, reached down, and clinked the slide back on top of the gun, sending a live round into the chamber. Then he let the gun rest at his side.

"You're not gonna shoot us." I squirmed. "This is none of your business. I mean, you haven't read us our rights. What's goin' on? Tell us why you're here, what we've done wrong?"

Chester nudged me. "You should really shut your mouth," he whispered, "before this guy loses his cool."

The cop took one step closer. His skin was burnt orange. His forearms were wrapped in black hair. He lifted the gun, closed one eye, peered through the rear site, and pointed the weapon toward my heart.

"I don't know who you are or what you're doing here," the cop hissed, "but I'm gonna give you one last chance to toss that bag over here. If you don't, you die. It's just been that kind of day."

I felt my mouth drop open and my cheeks burn red. I looked at Chester. His head tilted, and he squinted at me, as if to say, "Why are you even contemplating this?"

But I'd come too far and waited too long. The money was in my hands, and I wasn't going to let it go without a fight. Besides, I knew the cop was bluffing. He was a typical badge-wearing steroid-head on a power kick, and I wasn't going to fall for it.

"Five…"

Oh, my gosh, the cop's starting a countdown.

No way!

He's not for real.

"Four…"

I swallowed hard and wrapped the handle of the bag tight around my fist.

No stranger is about to foil my plan!

"Give him the money," Chester pleaded, with tears forming in his bright eyes. "It's only money—"

"I won't! He's not going to shoot. This is *my* money!" I stuck my chin out at the cop. "He owes it to me. This is none of your business!"

"Three…"

Chester's face contorted and his eyes closed, forcing a flood of tears to overflow and streak down his weathered cheeks.

"Chester"—I grabbed his arm—"what is it?"

He knows something I don't.

"Two…"

"I don't care!" I hoisted the bag in the air. "This is *my* money. If you want it, you come get it."

"I will," the cop said evenly, "after I kill you."

Chester glanced at me wide-eyed, looked down the barrel of the gun…

"One."

…and stepped into the path of its bullet.

Bam.

The gun flashed and jumped.

Everything froze in a cloud of smoke.

My ears rang. Gunpowder permeated my senses.

Chester began to drop.

I grabbed him, clinging to his loose coat, guiding him down to the concrete box.

Dark, gurgling blood gushed from the wound.

I reeled backward. Couldn't breathe. Was afraid to look up. Bracing for another shot from the psycho's gun.

Chester squeezed my arm and pulled me by the collar to his face. "Lose your life," he groaned, "then you'll find it."

He coughed violently.

"Chester—"

"Go now," he whispered.

I let go.

He slumped.

I untwisted the handle of the money bag from my wrist, slid it toward the cop, and ran desperate and wild, covering my head, trying to become invisible.

Bam.

A shot blew past me.

I tore around a corner, feet barely touching the ground, past a man cowering in the shadows.

Gone.

I was gone.

But never the same.

The grandfather clock chimed in the foyer, bringing me back to reality. It was 2:30 a.m.

"I've got to do something."

It's the middle of the night.

I slid to my knees.

"God," I whispered. "For once in my life, I need to do what *You* want."

The figures of my wife and children faded in and out of the darkness, as did the artist's renderings of the new worship center and the shiny new pulpit I'd chosen. And the people. *My people.* The men of the church, who proudly hailed me as the best Bible teacher in the South. And the women, who looked at me, at times, perhaps, with a slight, suggestive sparkle in their eyes.

"You're sick."

Chester's life blazed across the room, every stage I'd known him. From the morning he'd shown up at the church after Candice perished, with his disheveled hair and wrinkled brown suit, until the afternoon he told me off, turned his back, and in denim overalls, made his way to Las Vegas and a life of surrender.

News photos of Hudson Ambrose, Suzette Graham, and Ned Frazier replayed themselves over and over again. And Needermire. That morning. His stone cold face. The echo of the gun blast. Chester's slumping body. The smell of gunpowder and death.

"I could try to serve You like Chester did."

It would mean prison. The marriage might not endure. And the children, what would it do to them? And the church...

"Lose your life, then you'll find it."

Chester's words swirled around the room as if they'd just blown in through an open window with a fall breeze.

An uncanny sense of hope filled my lungs and suspended my fears.

Everything's going to be okay. Not because I'm going to do the right thing, but because I'm going to do it for the right reason. For Him.

I felt around for my shoes, lifted myself to the edge of the chair, slipped them on, and sat there momentarily, planning my next move.

To the desk I went, feeling for the lamp switch, clicking it on, and sliding into the chair. On a crisp sheet of beige stationery, I wrote to Sally and the children, pouring out my renewed love for them, warning them about what they would see and hear as my story came to light with the new day.

Sealing the letter in an envelope, I set it upright on the island in the kitchen where Sally and I always left notes for each other. I picked up the cell phone and car keys and stood quietly, remorsefully, in the dim kitchen, taking one last inventory of the five chairs around the table, the children's colorful artwork, the basketball and paper airplane on the floor near the cats' bowls, and the note of Scripture in Sally's handwriting on the fridge: "The Son of Man did not come to be served, but to serve, and to give His life a ransom for many."

Sally did that. So did Chester.

I sighed and read it again.

It's what I'm being called to do.

I backed the car out of the garage with the lights off and scooted out of the neighborhood toward the interstate. At that time of morning, the six southbound lanes of I-85 were wide open, with only a car here and a pickup there, far from the Indy-like speedway it would resemble closer to 6 a.m.

As I rehearsed different lines, pieced my confession together, and tried to prepare myself mentally for the fallout from what I was about to do, the exits—Sugarloaf, Beaver Ruin, Pleasantdale—flew past in twenty minutes. Soon, I was rocketing beneath the architectural wonder known as Spaghetti Junction, and heading south toward downtown Atlanta.

The next ten to fifteen minutes were a sorrowful blur of what my "ministry" had been: a self-seeking quest to glorify *me*.

Exiting at International Boulevard, I came surprisingly close to swinging the car into Centennial Olympic Park, taking a walk, and giving my plan a second thought. But I knew if I stopped then, I would halt God's momentum and probably never help Hudson Ambrose or the people I was supposed to impact with the remainder of my life. So I kept driving. Centennial Park Drive to Marietta Street. Past the World Congress Center and the Georgia Dome. To the parking deck at CNN Center.

Where news happened, 24/7.

And was about to happen—right then.

I knew my way around the towers because several men from the church worked down there; we'd met for lunch in the sprawling food court. However, it was a different place at that time of night. Each noise—the loud elevator, the clank of the doors opening, my footsteps clicking across the shiny silver floor—echoed throughout the massive atrium.

"Excuse me." A large Atlanta police officer standing by a gated Wendy's startled me. "Can I help you?"

"No, thank you." I kept moving at a quick clip. "I know my way."

"Where you headed?"

"CNN studio."

"You work there?"

"No." I shook my head and kept moving, frustrated at the thought of having to stop and explain myself.

He yelled something else, about them not letting me in. But I hurried on. Down a long straightaway. Around another corner.

There.

Across the vast concourse, the glass-enclosed CNN studio was lit up like an electric oasis.

Marching past fountains and lounge chairs, I'd given up rehearsing what I was going to say and resorted to taking deep breaths as I made a beeline for the tall, round, blue desk just outside the studio.

From thirty feet away, a big-haired blond woman, sixty or so, stared at me from her tall perch behind the high counter.

"Hey there." I forced a smile and took in a deep breath, as if I was about to audition for a show.

She nodded in slow motion and blinked at the same speed. "Morning." Some kind of glamour magazine was open on the desk in front of her.

"I have an exclusive news story for you…for CNN."

My insides were empty.

She stared at me with almost black eyes, her yellowish skin wrinkling severely at the brow. "Employees only, at this hour." Her breath smelled like cigarettes. "Sorry about that."

"I understand." I held up a calming hand and nodded toward the studio. "If you'll just call back there—"

"It's a skeleton crew, sir. I'm sorry." Her head lowered toward the magazine; she licked her fingers and flipped a page.

"Okay, please hear me out, ma'am." I leaned on the counter. "Are you familiar with the recent Las Vegas murders?"

She looked up. "The homeless people? And the reporter?"

"Exactly."

"'Course I've seen it. Who hasn't?"

I looked around at the vacant concourse. "I'm a witness," I whispered. "I'm coming forward for the first time right now. I want you guys to be the first with the story."

She deflated. "Sir—"

"Ma'am." My heart thundered. "If you make me go to a local station, WSB or somewhere else, the president of CNN is *not* going to be happy when he hears I was here, standing at his front door, with the exclusive piece of the puzzle that's going to blow the lid off the Las Vegas murders, and *you* turned me away."

With a hand on my chest, I forced myself to calm down and lower my voice. "Now, I suggest you get on that phone right now, before I take my story down the street and you find yourself out of a job."

Her hands let go of the magazine. She glared at me. Thirty or forty seconds must have passed. My whole body trembled. Without looking, she reached for the phone and lifted the receiver to her ear. Looking down, her eyes scanned the numbers. She jabbed a button and her black eyes flashed up at me.

"Regina, I'm sorry to bother you. It's Tilly. There's a man out here. Name's..." Her eyes opened wide and her head dropped toward me.

"Banyon Scribe."

"Name's Banyon Scribe. He claims he's a witness to those Las Vegas murders."

She paused, her eyes darting from me to her magazine and back to me.

"I know, but he *insists* he was there. He says if we don't hear his story, he's going to WSB right now. He also says the president of CNN is going to be furious when he hears we had the story and let it go."

She turned back toward the wall of TV screens behind the windows of the studio, beyond the CNN logo etched in the glass. "Yes." She swiveled back toward me on the stool. "Thank you. Sorry to bother you."

She jammed the phone down and glared at me.

"Regina Meek is coming out to see you. She's the overnight anchor. This better be good."

My eyes closed, my head dropped, and my shoulders slumped over the counter as ten thousand pounds of guilt floated up into the rafters of the enormous atrium.

44

L ater that morning, after Banyon Scribe confessed to the world that he'd attempted to rob Chester and had watched Drake Needermire intervene and gun Chester down, I was released from the LVMPD jail amid a sea of frenzied reporters. Don Cheevers picked me up in his little Toyota and somehow got us out of there. He ordered me to get lost for two weeks or longer—however long it would take for the media mushroom cloud to settle.

I did so gladly.

And guess where I went?

That's right, San Antonio.

And take a stab who went with me?

Right again, the gorgeous Holly Queens.

Even though fall was just a few weeks off, San Antonio didn't know it. The sun was high and bright, and the heat penetrated deep, like a microwave, as Holly and I wandered down the sandy path, hand in hand, from the rental car toward my parents' graves at River-Mist Cemetery.

Her cell phone rang.

She squeezed my hand, let go, and checked the phone.

"It's Ellery, finally. Let me take this." She held up an index finger and headed toward a nearby bench. "Wait right there. Don't go without me. Promise?"

I nodded and realized I was smiling enormously.

She wore flimsy white leather sandals, cutoff jeans, and a loose white top with spaghetti straps, like something out of the sixties. Her legs were not tan, but her thighs curved appealingly from beneath the white fringe of her cutoffs, her calves were strong and sculpted, and her toenails were painted the color of orange M&M's.

We'd met Victor Everson for lunch the day before. My old man's funeral had been perfect, he'd said. A bit overcast and about a hundred people in attendance. *More than I'd anticipated.* I reached back and touched the copy of the eulogy he'd shared that day, which was folded up in my back pocket; I hadn't found the right opportunity to read it.

After lunch with Victor, Holly had decided we should visit the Alamo, then rent bikes. We glided forever through the city and along the curving, shimmering river where a thousand memories from my boyhood revisited me. Up on the main streets of the city, she insisted we stop to visit with an elderly homeless man named Samuel. He was sitting Indian-style on a busy street corner, panhandling. Holly knelt right down there with him, his countenance immediately brightening. She exuded the joy and spontaneity of a child, and I found myself learning from her every moment we were together.

"I could live here." She'd gazed down at the river from a stone bridge, the breeze teasing her soft hair.

"Oh, I'd move back here in a minute." I leaned over the railing and peered down at the dark water. "You wouldn't have to ask me twice."

"Okay." Her pretty lips curled into an alluring smile. "I'll remember that."

"I know I could get a job at the *Express-News*. You could find a clinic you like…"

"I thought you wanted to write novels."

"Someday."

"Why someday? Why not now?"

"I've been thinking about writing a book about Chester—the whole experience, his former life, the lives he touched…"

Her face went solemn and her eyes searched my face. "Are you serious?"

"Just letting the idea percolate right now. You like it?"

"Yes." She squinted at me with that same serious look. "Very much."

The thought of sharing the future with Holly was euphoric, as was the feeling I got that afternoon when she invited me to nap on the couch in her hotel room while she snoozed on the bed. After that, we freshened up in our own rooms and dined amid violinists making music beneath the stars at a romantic candlelit restaurant along the River Walk.

Hands down: I'd never met anyone as bright and beautiful as Holly Queens.

The headlines and stories I'd read that morning stirred me from my daydream. For the moment, I was a free man. And although charges against me were pending, the news media and Las Vegas homeless community were beginning to paint me more like a hero than a criminal. My attorney said I might get off with community-service work, which Holly was quick to point out, would do me good.

Funny girl.

"Well, that call couldn't have been much better." Holly trudged toward me, the sand seeping over her sandals and between her pretty toes.

"Tell me." I took her hand.

She kissed me quick on the lips and chuckled. "It's all good, Dr Pepper."

"Well, how's Suzette?"

"Incredible!" Holly beamed as we continued toward my parents' graves. "She ended up sleeping for, like, twenty hours after they found her, then got up and said she was starving. She's eating well. She's home—well, she's staying with Ellery and Jenna right now. She had a complete physical, and everything checked out fine."

"What about mentally?"

A jet roared low overhead, shaking the ground.

Holly covered her ears and let the plane pass. "Ellery said she's talking about the whole thing; it's not like she's in denial at all. It's all very real to her. She remembers Needermire abducting her and taking her to his house. She's facing it head-on, and Ellery says she's showing no signs of, you know, instability. She already wants to go back to work."

"Oh man, that's good." I reached my arm around Holly's shoulder. "Could he tell you anything about what went on in the basement?"

The online edition of the *Review-Journal* had described the underground hideaway at Needermire's house as a "nightmare chamber," accessed by crawling into a kitchen cabinet, opening a concealed trap door, and descending into a secret shaft. The "cryptic prison," as Reed O'Neil had described it, was ten by fifteen feet in size, had a toilet (no toilet paper), running water, and a small mattress that had been stolen from the holding tank of Las Vegas police headquarters, of all places.

"Suzette says she was alone most of the time, thank God. She could hear him upstairs when he was home, but he was gone a lot. She said he only went down there a couple of times and barely even touched her. He called her his 'insurance' and kind of just mumbled incoherently on his way in and out."

"That's unbelievable," I said, knowing full well what an attractive lady Suzette was.

"It's a miracle."

"What did he do when he went down there?"

"Got cash!" Holly took my hand in hers and swung them high. "That's the other big news. Suzette was able to tell the police where he hid the money he stole from Chester."

"You're kidding me. That's not even in the news yet."

"Nope." Holly shook her head like a proud kid with a secret. "He hid it in kind of a homemade wall safe. So, there's your scoop, Mr. Reporter."

"Needermire's dead meat."

"I saw on the news this morning that his lawyer was all ticked because he's not getting out on bond."

"That's insane. I don't think anybody realizes yet what a nut case that guy is, but they will once he goes to trial."

"What I don't get is why Needermire had Chester's things stolen from your house by that gang in the first place?"

"I think he wanted to cash in on what I'd found, but more important, get control of the evidence."

We walked in silence for a moment, nearing the graves.

With the ordeal almost behind us, I'd finally figured out who Chester Holte was: simply a guy who realized what Jesus had done for him and didn't just *act* like it, but *lived* like it.

"Ellery and Jenna are sure flying high right now." Holly kicked some sand.

"And well they should be."

"Ellery's taking the week off... Oh, and guess what?"

"What?"

"He's getting together with Banyon Scribe."

"What?"

"When Ellery heard Scribe's church had given him the boot, and that Scribe was being subpoenaed to Las Vegas, he called and invited him to come to the house when he gets to town. Ellery's helped restore a couple of fallen pastors before. Who knows, Banyon Scribe might end up at Spring Valley Community Church."

"Now, that's class on Ellery's part."

"You wouldn't expect any less from *our* pastor, would you?"

We laughed.

She's right though. I'd follow her anywhere—even to church. And not just to church, but all the way down to the very front pew, even up to the choir loft, if that's where she wanted to go.

I wrapped an arm around Holly, drew her close, and squeezed.

We came to the twin graves and stood there for a moment, staring down at them. Another jet thundered overhead. I knelt and pulled several shoots of grass that had crept over my mother's flat tombstone, then laid six yellow roses down and fingered the raised, metal letters.

RITA LYNN AMBROSE
JUNE 19, 1950   AUGUST 13, 1987
"TOO FINE FOR THIS WORLD"

The ground at my father's grave was a few inches higher than that of my mom's. I guess they figured it would settle with time. I crawled over to his headstone, also flat and rectangular. My knees sank slightly into the fresh sod.

Although no grass or debris covered my father's headstone, I swept over it several times with my hand, feeling the letters, letting my fingers linger there, remembering the new man I'd found in him those last few times we'd met. He'd found peace.

I chuckled.

Holly's warm hand touched the top of my shoulder as she stood behind me. "What's funny?"

I gazed down at the bright gray tombstone and shook my head. "After all those years, the old man found the door."

Holly squeezed my shoulder. "He would have loved your inscription. So would Chester."

I laid the remaining six roses beneath the headstone.

Yes, so would Chester...

GLENN CONRAD AMBROSE
FEBRUARY 2, 1948   AUGUST 15, 2007
"I HAVE ENTERED THROUGH THE DOOR AND FOUND PASTURE."

Dear Reader,

It has been a pleasure penning another suspense novel for each of you fiction lovers. I sincerely hope you enjoyed *Nobody* and that, if you haven't already, you'll go back and read my first two thrillers, *Dark Star: Confessions of a Rock Idol* and *Full Tilt*—a two-book series known as The Rock Star Chronicles. If you're interested in keeping up with my novels, appearances, contests, and blog—or would like to schedule a conference call with your blook club—go to crestonmapes.com. That'll do it.

Until the next story, share Jesus.

Your friend,
Creston Mapes
Galatians 2:20